Hy Brasil

MARGARET ELPHINSTONE is the author of
four previous novels: *The Incomer* (1987), *A
Sparrow's Flight* (1989), *Islanders* (1994) and
The Sea Road (2000). Her short stories have
been collected in *An Apple from a Tree* (1990)
and her poetry in *Outside Eden* (1991). She
lives in Glasgow and teaches in the Department of English Studies at Strathclyde University. Her sixth novel, *Voyageurs*, will also
be published by Canongate.

Hy Brasil

A NOVEL

Margaret Elphinstone

CANONGATE

First published in Great Britain in 2002 by
Canongate Books Ltd, 14 High Street,
Edinburgh EH1 1TE

This edition published in 2003

2

Copyright © Margaret Elphinstone, 2002
The moral right of the author has been asserted

Map on page vii by Jennifer Outhwaite

British Library Cataloguing-in-Publication Data
A catalogue record for this book is available
on request from the British Library

ISBN 1 84195 411 X

Typeset by Hewer Text, Edinburgh
Printed and bound in Germany by Bercker

www.meetatthegate.com

For Ruth and Ian

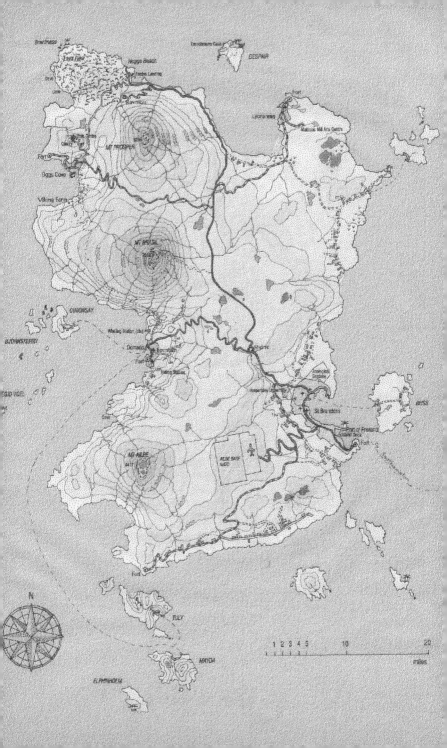

ONE

Sidony Redruth. Caliban's Fast Food Diner. May 8th, 1997.
Notes for *Undiscovered Islands* (working title).

I WOULD HATE to have to choose, but I think I'd rather have travelling than sex. This probably goes back to an early confusion about trespass. I was taught to say 'Forgive us our trespasses' but this never stopped me from climbing through the hole in the paling fence into the woods next to the churchyard, right under the notice which said that Trespassers Will Be Prosecuted. I thought that prosecuted was something to do with hell, but even so the risk, in relation to exploring new territory, was worth it to me.

When I came here a couple of my friends said that this place would be their idea of hell. So many people seem to associate hell with cool weather, but I learned in Sunday School that hell is hot. The mid-Atlantic is chilly and wet in winter, and often foggy the rest of the year. Winds of Force 5 and upwards are statistically normal. The temperature of the sea averages 53°F. There are good places to swim all the year round because of the hot springs. This afternoon I'll try the pool in St Brandons, which is outdoors and always warm, Olympic-sized with jacuzzis and natural hot tubs as well. Hell, if that's what sulphur, brimstone and a burning mountain amount to, has certain advantages. Another reason why early explorers thought this was either hell or the promised land is that the compass swings madly as soon as it comes within a thirty-mile radius of the place, which is either due to magic or mineral deposits, depending on your point of view. It also accounts for the inordinate length of time it took to get the islands fixed on the map.

I'm sitting in a café which could belong in any run-down fishing port between Maine and Aberdeen. The rain-streaked windows are fugged up on the inside; the stuffy dampness seems distilled from a brew of stewed tea and wet socks. It isn't quite twelve o'clock (2 p.m. at Greenwich) and a spotty boy in a striped apron is writing on the blackboard in green chalk:

dinner 12–2
deep fried fish (haddock, saithe or plaice) £4.10.6
steak mince £4.19.6
burgers £3.17.6
all served with chips and baked beans or mushy peas

Two fat raindrops wander slowly down the glass beside me. From where I sit I can read the neon notice that hangs in the window:

CALIBAN'S FAST FOOD DINER

This whole project began in a café. I want to say it was in Lyon's Corner House – that feels right – but the truth is that I was nowhere near Charing Cross, and I believe Lyon's Corner House only exists now in Golden Age detective stories. It was actually an anonymous café in Islington. It was raining then too, not in the fierce and salty way it's doing here, but in a thin London way, as if the weather was something the city couldn't quite be bothered with.

'A new list.' I was finding it hard to listen, as if none of this quite related to me. 'A series of travel books. Something that combines a guidebook – practical information and so forth – with a narrative. First-hand experience.'

This was my commissioning editor speaking. I'd never owned an editor of any kind before, and I was intimidated, and also mesmerised by the way she stirred her coffee round and round with the wrong end of a red biro.

I'm not sure about first-hand experience. Wherever I go I take myself with me, and that's the experience. This would seem to disqualify me from writing a good guidebook. I'd find it impossible even to describe this first twenty-four hours objectively. I could try, like this:

When we landed it was not quite daylight and not yet night. Through the plane window I saw grey, and as we landed there were streaks of raindrops. I couldn't tell if the grey was dark or fog. Below lay a strip of tarmac with a crack in it where grass had pushed through, and a flattened dandelion. A truck loomed up and vanished under our tail. I felt as though we would be here for ever; the steps would never come, the door would never open and we would sit here till we died. Meanwhile I read and re-read the one stamp in my passport as if I'd never seen it before in my life.

Kidd's Hotel is the main hotel in St Brandons. It's a depressing building, peeling stucco on the outside, and red plush wallpaper and acres of threadbare carpet on the inside, on which vast pieces of mahogany furniture float like jetsam from a Victorian steamship becalmed for ever in the doldrums. I seemed to be the only guest. My bedroom was grubby and smelt of damp. I managed to heave the broken sash window up a couple of inches and wedge it open with a roll of toilet paper. The smell of fog began to filter in. (And so is my own opinion, I notice, as I write.) I thought of having a bath but there was no plug, and when I tried to turn on the shower a vast cast-iron handle arrangement came off in my hand. This morning I ate a greasy breakfast in a huge dining room lined with spotted mirrors, so that the white empty tables receded into infinity like sheets of polar pack ice.

The receptionist accepted with phlegmatic resignation that I was checking out after only one night, and she let me leave my luggage in a cupboard full of dried-out tins of paint and the imposing prototype of all vacuum cleaners.

Outside it was the kind of thick fog which keeps trying to turn into rain, and soaks one through in a moment. I pulled my hood over my head, and walked slowly down the High Street. It's a narrow paved street which is supposed to be pedestrianised, but cars kept creeping out of the mist behind me, hooting mournfully. A foghorn chimed in from what must be the direction of the harbour. My eye was caught by a splash of colour in a window. I went to look. There'd been a wedding, in some faraway time and place where the sun still shone. A path wound across a hillside of terraced orchards where a fiddler walked ahead of the bride and groom. The bride was in white, the groom wore the traditional blue braided jacket I'd already seen on a couple of older men in St Brandons. The wedding party followed, over a pass and down to a small white church beside a sparkling sea. The bridal party stood in the church door smiling among a host of apple blossom. Then they were in a hall festooned with streamers, cutting a monumental cake, while little girls with flowers in their hair shoved their way in to get the first slices.

I read the sign over the door. KIRWAN: PHOTOGRAPHER. I wandered on, past a butcher and a stationer, and a massive flowering cherry tree dripping rain and pink blossom in a slippery mass on the wet paving stones. I wondered who'd planned to have it grow right in the middle of the street, the tree or the Town Council. Either way, I was glad to see that the one had been able to accommodate the other. Just beyond it there was a pleasing Georgian building with a big bow window. I peered into the dim interior. It was one of those curious shops you only get in small towns, which sell things like rolls of tweed, fishermen's socks and obsolete forms of underwear. There was a big woven bedspread in the window, woven in dark blues and sea greens, with a crescent island in the middle of it pierced by a lance, or possibly a sceptre. Or it might have been a ship with a bare mast, or a Celtic brooch with a pin, or even a cooking pot with a long thin spoon. Maybe it wasn't meant to be anything, but I loved the shape of it. I looked at the label. 'PENELOPE', it said, '£950'. I sighed. The reason I don't possess much is that everything I fall in love with is light years out of my price range. I must just have terribly good taste.

The tourist office was a little way further down. I went in and picked up a pile of leaflets and a street map of St Brandons. I looked over the cards offering bed and breakfast, but I didn't have the energy for phone calls just then. I was more interested in a flier that said:

ISHMAEL'S TOURS
WHALE WATCHING DESPAIR
ASCENTS PROSPER AILBE BRASIL
VOLCANO WEATHER PERMITTING
Phone Lyonsness 204

I wandered over to the counter where a young man wearing a label that said PETERKIN answered my questions. He was in no hurry. No one here is, as far as I can make out. He said yes, Ishmael was definitely the man if I wanted to get into the mountains; it would be dangerous to go by myself. Ishmael also had the best boat on the north side and if there were whales there he'd find them. What's more, if you didn't see any he'd give you your money back or take you again for free. Ishmael was a thoroughly decent chap, said Peterkin. I resisted the impulse to ask him to say that again. I daresay I'll soon get used to a vocabulary that makes me feel as if I've strayed into a black-and-white film. If I wanted to get out of St Brandons Peterkin recommended Lyonsness, and his aunt did the best bed and breakfasts there, if I didn't mind him saying so.

Peterkin asked me things about myself that I didn't really

want to tell him, but I think that's just the way they are here, as if curiosity were a virtue. I found myself listening to his accent more than to what he said. So far I've had no trouble understanding people. To me they sound half familiar, as if at some distant date they'd imported their voices from my own country, and half Irish – the whole mixture being heavily spiced with a trans-Atlantic twang. Already I've heard turns of phrase that make me understand why this is an etymologist's heaven. In fact, Peterkin assumed at first that I must be here to study the language. He said my own accent sounds to him like the way they speak at Lyonsness. Surely this place is too small to have regional dialects? When he said Dorrado was 'fair' it took me a moment to realise he meant beautiful, and not so-so. And he calls the open sea 'the deep', which sounds quite Biblical to me. He was talking about the failure of the fishing out in 'the deep'. He said even on the Grand Banks there are no cod left, and to the north there are always problems with Icelandic fishing limits as well. He thought the European Union was excellent for any nation that was not in it, but even so there were huge problems in this country, as I'd find out. Terrible unemployment, terrible changes. I should have come ten years ago.

'Ten years ago I was still at school.'

'Ten years ago my dad had his own fishing boat. He put five of us through college. Not me,' said Peterkin. 'I'm the last one. We can't afford college now. So here I am.'

'That's a shame.'

'To hell with it. There're no jobs anyway. It used to be the ones with any guts got out. But now there's nowhere to go. Not in all the world. So I stay. It's home, anyway.'

I didn't tell him what I was doing here. I felt bad about that, as he'd been so open with me. Another thing I learned at Sunday School was guilt. I feel it often, and I felt it now, almost the way I'd felt it back in that café in Islington where this whole adventure started.

*　　*　　*

At that stage I was overcome by the very idea of a commissioning editor. I expected her to be omniscient, though she turned out not to be, and I was terrified of being found out. I looked down at my hands, which were twisting themselves together in an anxious sort of way. I made them keep still, and decided that I'd have to tell her the truth.

'That piece I wrote . . .' I ventured.

'We loved it. Original and well written, and above all,' she beamed at me encouragingly, 'authentic. So much travel writing now has that second-hand feel. Pastiche. And so many places written to death, from Provence to Antarctica. Most people take the well trodden path. Now what we noticed about your piece was that freshness of approach, that genuine feel for the place, that willingness to go somewhere unusual and look at it differently when you got there.'

'Yes, but . . .'

'That's what Eileen said. She said it was appalling having to judge. You know there were twelve hundred entries? She said yours leapt out at her at once. A genuine account of a real adventure, just what they were looking for.'

'Yes, but it wasn't . . .'

'So as we were putting this new list together, she mentioned you. We'll need one or two names to start us off, but we want to get hold of some young writers. And some unusual places. Get off the map. That's what you can do for us. I mean, if you can get yourself to St Helena, South Georgia and Ascension Island, with no backing at all, you'll know just how to tackle this place.'

'Yes, only I didn't . . .'

'Now don't be diffident. You won the competition, didn't you? We know what we're looking for.'

'But . . .'

'You could do it in a summer. Couldn't you get leave for that long?'

'I'm not employed. It isn't that . . .'

'Well, then, isn't this just what you've been waiting for?'

Of course it was, but I was feeling awful. When I was young I thought my conscience was a little man who lived inside me who had an unpleasant barbed weapon, something between a trident and a toasting fork, with which he would prick me in the ribs from inside whenever I did anything untoward. I could feel him very plainly now. Of course she was right, I had not only waited for something like this but prayed for it, cast spells to create it, asked runes and the tarot and the stars to prophesy about it, looked up reference books in the library in pursuit of it, and written endless letters of application for it. My mother says you should take care what you ask for because you'll probably end up getting it.

'Listen,' I said desperately. 'Do you know what I did with the prize money?'

She was hardly listening. 'No.'

'I went to Venice. It was Christmas. I should have been with my family. My father's a vicar. Christmas is important. My brother's been ill. My mother has an underactive thyroid, and is always tired. They needed me. There's a lot to do – Midnight Mass and plum pudding and "Adeste Fideles" and the church wardens coming to drinks before dinner, and all sorts of things like that. I didn't go. I took a package tour to Venice. It rained all the time. On Christmas Day I splashed around St Mark's Square in my wellies, and then I stood on the quay and tried to remember that bit out of Browning where the Doges used to wed the sea with rings. I was happy, except for the guilt. But the point is – listen, please – that was the furthest south I'd ever been. Ever.'

I waited for her to understand.

'But you're giving me a splendid example of what we want. The unusual angle. The willingness to be self-sufficient, and to describe what you experience. This is exactly what we're after.'

'But what if it's not true?'

'You don't have an agent, of course. I'll take you through our standard contract back at the office. The advance is nominal, you must understand that, because your expenses will have to come out of it. But you're used to travelling on a budget.'

Conscience got in one last painful dig, and curled up in exhaustion. I had tried. If she utterly refused to hear that my whole prizewinning narrative was a fabrication from beginning to end, and that my principal means of travel had been inter-library loan (£1.30 per request) then that was her problem. I knew as much about Ascension Island as anybody by now, I reckoned, and I must have done something right because they'd given me a prize for it. I grew up with the sea and the rain, and now that I'd discovered that there is sea and rain in Venice just like there is in Cornwall, and, so my sources tell me, in the South Atlantic too, I supposed I could write about these things any-where, if pushed. I certainly would, if paid. I have very seldom been paid by anybody to do anything.

So here I am, in Caliban's Fast Food Diner, doing some-thing real, or so it seems to me. I push away my coffee mug and pick up my pen again:

This place is famous for its fog, and from that first glimpse I have seen nothing but fog. Fog all the way from the airport, fog in the streets of the town, fog outside my hotel window. Was it merely a literary coincidence that brought me, at the top end of the High Street, to the steps of the law courts? Neo-classical pillars rose into the fog. The oak door was shut. Government House hung beyond like a wraith while the mist swirled round it. At home a gale would blow away the fog, but here it just brings more of it. A volley of raindrops hit me in the face. They tasted of the sea. I decided I'd tackle Government later.

In front of Government House there was a huge bronze statue of what looked, through the foggy distance, like a sea monster with its young. I had to go right up to it to see it properly. It wasn't a monster; it was a horse, about three times life-size, and emerging improbably from its belly were four attenuated warriors in Homeric costume. The bronze was

rough-cast, and through my uneducated eyes the figures looked
starved and agonised. Perhaps they were unaccustomed to
Atlantic weather; they certainly weren't dressed for it. There
was a plaque set into the podium of the statue. It said:

αἶσα γὰρ ἦν ἀπολέσθαι, ἐπὴν πόλις ἀμφικαλύψῃ
δουράτεον μέγαν ἵππον, ὅθ᾽ ἥατο πάντες ἄριστοι
᾽Αργείων Τρώεσσι φόνον καὶ κῆρα φέροντες.

Th'unaltered law
Of Fate presaging; that Troy then should end,
When th'hostile horse, she should receive to friend;
For therein should the Grecian kings lie hid,
To bring the Fate and death, they after did.

Erected to commemorate the first founding of our
nation Hy Brasil. April 10th, 1958. In gratitude to
the four men who alone overcame the forces of
oppression and liberated our people:

Fernando Baskerville
Lemuel Hawkins
John Honeyman
James Hook

There be of them, that have left a name behind
them, that their praises might be reported.

I guessed from the salt wind blowing in my face that I was
facing straight down over the town to the harbour. If so the view
must be magnificent, but I was marooned in an island of small
visibility, alone with a bronze memorial and surrounded by the
wreathing mists. I'd had enough. A cobbled street led off the
hill, so I followed it, and wandered between terraces of stone
houses with fog-water dripping from their eaves. I smelt fish.

Then I was at the harbour, where fishing boats swayed queasily in greasy water. I still felt disorientated, as if I hadn't quite landed yet. From the quay only the lowest street of the town was visible: Water Street. There was a lighted window with a neon sign. Outside there were white plastic tables and chairs, all dripping wet, but suggesting that summer sometimes happened even here. When I pushed the door open, heat and the smell of chips and ground coffee met me.

The coffee is good. If it's good in a downmarket spot like this it'll be good everywhere. And look: I've started writing already. The fog slowly lifts from my brain, and at last I am arriving. I sit in the window with my back to the wall, so I can see both the fog outside, and the shrouded figures that drift past and vanish, and also the red tables inside, where no one sits but an old man reading *The Hesperides Times*. I can see the headline: 'New Patrol Boats at Ogg's Cove.' On each table there is salt and pepper, milk in a jug, sugar, and a red plastic tomato with ketchup in it. Behind the counter a girl sits on a high stool reading – I duck my head and peer through the glass shelves to see – *The Hesperides Times*. The back page is turned to me: 'Season Opens with Seven Wickets for Dorrado.' Is *The Hesperides Times* what everyone reads? Presently I shall buy a copy. Presently I shall begin.

TWO

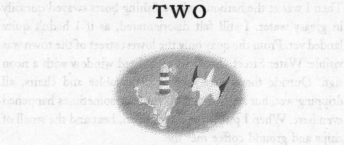

STANDING ON THE summit of Despair, a young man watched a pair of gannets sailing above the sea on black-tipped wings, their yellow heads outstretched. One dived, then the other, hitting the sea with white splashes, as if an invisible galleon were firing broadsides against the sheer north coast of the island. The sea was blue and sparkling gold, the sky today was the blue arch of heaven. A pale moon the size of a sixpence lingered like a belated ghost. Below it a half-submerged skerry marked the spine of lava that had made the lee of Despair a mariner's nightmare since the day the island was discovered. Down there, between the skerry and the cliff, lay the wreck of the *Cortes*, driven on to a lee shore by a following wind on Hallowmass Night, in the year of Our Lord 1611, on its way from Seville to Panama. The only survivors were the few who'd taken to the ship's boat, and come ashore on the white shell beach of Evanor, now lost forever under the lava desert of Brentness.

Looking south from the top of Despair he could see almost every island in the country dotted across the wrinkled sea. Despair itself was so steep that the green slope below him was out of sight right down to the edge of the white beach that faced the mainland. The backbone of Hy Brasil was a curving ridge with three volcanic cones for vertebrae: Mount Prosper, Mount Brasil, Mount Ailbe. Today the three peaks rose into air so clear that he could make out where the trees ended as far away as Ailbe. Close to, there was the thread of the waterfall this side of Prosper, and the whitewashed house across the sound at Ferdy's Landing, then further east the village street with the white church above it at Lyonsness. Between the two settlements, high up on the slopes of Prosper, hung the tall grey rectangle of Ravnscar with its battlemented roof. South of that, a gleam of metal on the slopes of Brasil was the road over the pass between St Brandons and Dorrado. Far beyond he could see the blue serrated edge of Mayda, eighty miles away.

The gannet colony had established itself along the edge of the cliff just below the summit. Gannets first bred here in 1991, and now there were forty nesting pairs. Between the nests the ground was already worn down to the rock, slippery with fish bones and guano. There had never been gannets before in Hy Brasil, and the hundred and twenty birds here had become a subject of much speculation among ornithologists. In Europe and Iceland gannet colonies had been growing for over a century; in Canada the rate of recovery after the slaughter of the nineteenth century had been much slower. But on either side of the Atlantic, gannets frequented the waters of the continental shelves, and no one had considered it a bird of the deep ocean. Yet here were gannets on Despair, as far from any land mass as an island in the Atlantic could possibly be. It was a mystery that the University of the Hesperides was willing to pay a small pittance to fathom; it was convenient for them that Jared was already on Despair, and they had taken kindly to his proposal.

He was pretty sure himself that the key to the mystery was mackerel. Later on, when the young gannets were hatched, he'd collect discards and send them back to the university, and they'd know for certain just what these birds were eating. The herring had been more or less fished out years ago, and now there were no cod either. But in the last year or two the number of mackerel around the shores of Hy Brasil had risen, maybe because the sea was warmer than it used to be, and the advantage of this for both people and gannets was that the fishing was well within coastal waters. The coastguard patrols were as stringent now as they'd been at the height of the Cod War. Even now Jared could see a patrol boat heading north-west on a parallel with the edge of the deep.

Jared watched the boat bumping into the tide-rip to the north of Despair, then he went down into the colony, just a few feet from the cliff edge. He came this way every morning, and the gannets ignored him; only once a yellow beak shot out from a nest and jabbed his boot as he passed. He'd sprayed the backs of the breeding birds with purple dye last week, and yesterday he'd finally got the last two, but none seemed disturbed by the experience now. He ticked off the nests in his notebook. The eggs had all hatched between ten and fourteen days ago. The plan was that Per Pedersen would come out sometime this week and help him get blood samples. Once that was done an answer might emerge as to whether these birds came from the eastern or western Atlantic seaboard.

He ticked off the nesting birds against his list, stuffed his notebook in his pocket, and set off back to the lighthouse. The Despair light had shone for a hundred and fifty years from the northernmost point of Hy Brasil. It was built five hundred feet above the sea, and its red-and-white tower was thirty feet high. The old foghorn was set on a thin promontory, flanked by cliffs on three sides, with a chain set into the rock to guide the lightkeepers across the foot-wide causeway on a bad night. The horn was abandoned now, and the light was entirely automatic. The houses were still there, three in a row, facing inwards across a windswept walled yard where the outlines of long-ago rows of earthed-up potatoes could still be seen under the grass and dockens. Until forty years ago there had been families here. They used to tether the children to keep them away from the cliffs, and the poultry were kept under wire mesh in the corner of the yard to stop them blowing away in bad weather. Then after the Revolution the families had been moved to Lyonsness, and the men came out here by themselves, in shifts.

Two of the houses were boarded up now. The third was his, courtesy of the Hy Brasil Commissioners of Lights. The front door opened straight into the kitchen. Jared left the door open to let the sun in, slid the kettle into the middle of the stove, and put his notebook away on the shelf with his reference books.

Breakfast was the major event of the morning, but today it was somewhat depleted. Time to go shopping again. After this he'd be out of bacon; the eggs had been finished since Tuesday, and he could barely recall the taste of a tomato. Jared stirred his porridge, cut slices from one of his own flat loaves, and chopped bits of yesterday's potato into the pan with the bacon. He measured three teaspoons of Cuban coffee into a jug and opened a new tin of milk with his Swiss army knife. Apples, he was thinking, oranges, bananas, tomatoes, mushrooms, milk, cheese. The farmer's market in St Brandons was on Tuesday, so it might be better to wait until then. Soap powder, eggs, a thing to clean the big saucepan with.

The table was already laid. He always put everything back as soon as he'd washed up: knife, fork, spoon, plate, mug, tomato sauce, salt, margarine. He added a paper and a green pen so he could write his list while he ate.

When everything was cooked he put the frying pan on the edge of the stove with its lid on, spooned his porridge into a pudding basin, added two tablespoons of brown sugar and half a tin of condensed milk, filled his mug with coffee and sat down. He ate slowly, and added items to his list between mouthfuls. Sugar, matches, tea. Compressed air, if Ishmael hadn't already seen to that. They used Ishmael's boat for the diving, and Ishmael always took the empty tanks home to Ferdy's Landing with him. The problem was that Ishmael had other things on his mind and wasn't always prompt about getting them refilled; he'd only take them when he was going into St Brandons anyway, and more than once they'd had to miss a day of perfect weather because of that. Jared added a note, borrow car? He looked up at the calendar on the wall opposite him. *Trink's Garage*, it said, *with the compliments of the Season*. Underneath was a picture of a blonde with improbably large breasts, and a tear-off calendar impaled on one of her stiletto heels. FRIDAY MAY 9th. The first eight days had been obliterated by green crosses. Jared frowned. Having the equipment ready was more important than the farmer's market. Better go in tomorrow. He scraped his bowl clean, and reached over for the frying pan.

He was thinking about treasure. 'Library' he wrote quickly. 'Check Faraday. Kidd?' He stared at the blonde. Her lips were parted alluringly, but he wasn't seeing her. 'Baskerville re *Cortes*'.

Money was a problem. He could live quite well, since his needs were minimal. The University of the Hesperides Department of Marine Sciences was paying him £30.10.6 a week for as long as the gannets were in residence. His monthly grocery and fuel bill was seldom more than £80, which left £40 or more for petrol and compressed air. The Commissioners for Lights let him run his electricity off their generator for nothing, wood for the stove came out of the sea, and he had more than enough clothes to cover him. Anything else had to come from his savings. The first thing he'd acquired when he came home was a fifteen-foot Boston whaler, which he'd bought cheap when Ishmael got his new model. It wasn't the boat he dreamed of: instead it was fibreglass, with a cathedral hull, no mast, and an ancient outboard motor, but it served his immediate purposes, and it was cheap to run. Even so he never seemed to have any money. Every single dive ate further into his savings, and there was nothing else left in Jared's life that he could reasonably give up.

He pushed his plate to the other end of the table, leaned back and reached for the rolled-up chart on the shelf behind him. He spread it open, weighed it down with the margarine tub on one side and the book of tide tables on the other, and pored over it for the umpteenth time.

It represented the whole of last summer's work. They'd followed the methods used on the *Santa Maria de la Rosa* in the Blasket Sound, as being the most similar site for which a detailed report was available. The *Santa Maria* had been in a hundred and ten feet of water, the *Cortes* was only ninety-two feet down, a small advantage, but one far outweighed by lack of resources. For surveying the *Cortes* they'd taken a jagged excrescence on the spur of submerged basalt running out from the foundations of the island as their base point, and the top of the layered lava outcrop at the head of the wreck site as the second fixed point. The main difficulty of the *Cortes* site was its uneven nature. On the other hand, if the ship had not found its resting place in a hollow of the lava beds that shelved out from Despair, its remains would have been swept away and scattered long ago, in the constant battering of the Atlantic against the basalt cliffs of Despair. But it had taken the best part of the season, with only two of them, to work out a constant level and fix the points on the grid. The University had provided the basic surveying equipment, and Ishmael had paid for the grid frame itself. The worrying part had been doing the grid points in the sand at the bottom of the hollow. Jared was all too aware that they lacked the necessary probing equipment, though they'd been as careful as they could not to disturb anything.

They didn't have a metal detector; in fact they had no electronic instruments at all. They'd not needed any for the initial identification of the site. Even thinking about that day now, Jared looked up from the chart and grinned at the framed print of Millais' *Boyhood of Raleigh* that hung on the opposite wall. That day when he and Ishmael had swum in to explore the eastern slope of the lava ridge behind the skerry, and shone their torches across the hidden hollow for the first time: that was when he'd seen the first gun barrel, lying black against the white sea floor like a carefully displayed exhibit under the spotlight of his torch. Jared reached for the shelf again and dragged out the file with the photographs, and opened it. No 1: 17-pounder full culverin. $5\frac{1}{4}$ inch bore. Length 31 inches calibre.

Since then they'd identified, beneath the encrustations of seaweed and barnacles, ten more bronze guns. Jared turned back to the chart. By plotting the position of the ordnance, they'd worked out the alignment of the *Cortes*. She was lying at an angle of 38° east of north. Right at the end of the season they'd also found an anchor, and part of the oak keel and scattered pieces of blackened wood from the hull. Once they'd been charted, he and Ishmael had salvaged various spikes and iron bolts, now in the Museum of Hy Brasil in St Brandons.

The good news was that when they'd gone back for the first time this spring, the permanent markers were all undamaged and in place. There was still no money, so a full-scale excavation was impossible, and serious salvage was out of the question. If they had a proper dive-boat, two more divers, lift bags, electronic surveying equipment . . . But they had managed to lay down a section of fixed grid over the sand in which the pieces of hull were half buried, and they'd begun to excavate the surface. Four dives so far this season, and they had two silver coins – two Spanish reals, Baskerville said – a nine-pound cannon ball, a bright-green earthenware pot broken into three neat segments, a pewter dish with the name *Cortes* engraved on it, as well as several congealed lumps of rust that must have been nails and bolts. In fact the stuff was just lying there, barely covered by sand, simply asking to be lifted. Hidden away in its lava-girded hollow, ninety-two feet down, and protected from the tide-rip that kept casual shipping well away from the wild coast of Despair, the *Cortes* was the kind of wreck one dreamed about.

But still there was no money. He and Ishmael had put in an application. He'd been waiting to hear something all winter, and now it was spring, perfect diving weather, and still silence. Jared suspected a scam. The word was out now, and although he had officially been granted exclusive rights of salvage he doubted if the coastguard patrols that regularly circumnavigated Despair would bother to enforce a licence so casually issued as this one had been. He knew the west coast of Despair better than anyone, even Per and Ishmael, the other two members of his team. Jared had discouraged unwanted investigators before, and he had ideas about how to warn people off. But so far no one had come, and there had been no letter from the Mayda Trust either.

Jared chewed the end of his pen. Then he wrote down quickly, 'Mayda Trust office?'

The other problem was that although Per was retired, Ishmael had a job. Last year they'd managed two dives a week if the weather and Ishmael's commitments combined to be favourable. Sometimes they hadn't been able to work for over a fortnight. It wasn't the sort of site you could work on every day; the boat had to work less than four hundred yards from the foot of the cliff, so if there were much sea nothing could be done. No one could have a better partner than Ishmael, either above or below water, but eventually Jared would have to bring in someone who could be on call whenever the sea was right. He tapped his teeth with the end of the green pen. Ideally it would be someone who was a trained marine archeologist, which Jared himself was not. Ideally, in fact, he knew exactly who he wanted. Jared was not a letter-writer, but he knew where to find the man he needed, and he knew that if the money were there, he'd come, even if it meant leaving the flesh-pots of Key West for the duration. But the money wasn't there. The site of the *Cortes* was littered with Spanish treasure beyond price, and Jared knew just what to do to get it, but still the money wasn't there.

He reached behind him and picked out one of the row of books on the top shelf. It fell open at a familiar page:

> This Indenture made the seventeenth of July 1585, in the seven and twentieth year of the reign of our sovereign lady Queen Elizabeth, between the right honourable Ambrose, Earl of Warwick, Master of her Majesty's Ordnance General, of the one part, and the right worshipful Sir Francis Drake, knight, on the other part . . .

He'd read all this a hundred times. These were English guns, and *Cortes* was a Spanish galleon, larger and more richly equipped, less seaworthy in every way. But it was a useful account. Jared had sketched the guns on site, and drawn them afterwards as well as he could, using Ishmael's photographs. But no real work could be done on them until they were raised. Raising a two-ton gun required the right equipment. That meant money, and he had no money.

Abruptly he shut the book, rolled up the chart and put both away on the shelf. Then he put the dirty dishes in a bowl and poured hot water from the kettle over them. The sun was pouring in through the open door. He sighed, stuck a battered green sunhat on his head, and went out.

The cliffs opposite Ferdy's Landing were barely a hundred feet high, but they formed a dramatic curve where the cries of kittiwakes echoed back and forth. Little waves broke over the rocks, and golden seaweed rose and fell in gentle undulations. There was little sign of activity; even the colony of cormorants on the farthest skerry stood like statues, outlined against a soft blue sea.

The jagged stacks at the south-west point of Despair formed as inhospitable a seacoast as it was possible to imagine. Ironically, they were barely two hundred yards from the pearl-coloured beach which made Despair, seen from Hy Brasil, look like a tropical paradise. Close to, the beach was not white but grey, grains of black lava mixed with pure shell sand. The Frenchmen, who had given the island its name as a token of their joyful thanks at their deliverance, had been driven, like the luckless *Cortes* a hundred years earlier, on to a lee shore, but somehow they'd managed to hit the shell strand, and every life had been saved, including that of the ship's goat. Nor did Hope deceive them; the story was that when they were delivered as prisoners to Richard Morgan the Pirate King, the French *capitaine* had suggested that he bargain for the lives of his whole company at piquet. So the *capitaine* and the Pirate King sat down to their cards in the Great Hall of Ravnscar, and played from eleven in the morning until the sun went down. The Frenchman won by the very last turn of the cards, and Morgan honoured his promise, and shipped the whole crew back to

Boulogne, where they arrived barely eight months after they first put out.

Since then the white beach had served as a cod-drying station for Portuguese, Irish, Icelandic and English fishermen successively. Only since the Second World War had the strand reverted to its pristine state, apart from the ubiquitous plastic jetsam. Otherwise, apart from the stone jetty built by the Commissioners of Lights at the end of the strand, it was as Brendan himself had found it, if it were true that the first landing had been, not at Ogg's Cove, as most people claimed, but on Despair.

Jared walked along the high-tide mark. He picked up scraps of wood as he went, and as soon as he had a bundle he dropped it at the top of the beach. He found a metal trawler float with a rope still attached, and chucked that up beyond the tide's reach too. There was nothing else today except seaweed and plastic bottles. He rounded the spit and Lyonsness came into sight across the sound. He was just turning for home when something white gleamed and caught his eye. He picked it up.

A sealed plastic packet. He felt the contents, and they gave under his fingers like sand. He knew at once what he was going to find, even before he opened his knife and slit the corner. He shook a little of the white powder into his palm. He'd seen it before. In London. In Rejkjavik. In Nuuk. In Aberdeen. And long before then, too. It wasn't his thing. He'd decided that years ago. He'd always needed his health and his wits about him for the things he wanted to do, but he'd never interfered with anyone else doing what they felt like. His attitude was that they hurt no one but themselves, and that was their own decision. Only lately that had been in another country. This was home. His hand shook a little, and he realised that he was shocked. That surprised him.

Jettisoned? He was thinking fast. He'd noticed various signs of activity since he came to live on Despair, but he'd done his best to ignore them. He hadn't wanted to know. There had always been unexplained money in Hy Brasil. In the twenties, during prohibition, the economy had boomed; Nantucket had been the main smuggling port, 2843 miles away. Before that, sugar, rum and tea from South America and the Caribbean had made their way into England from here without benefit of excisemen. These islands had lain at the centre of the triangular trade, and human beings had been bought and sold in the market place at St Brandons while governments preached abolition. Ironically, under the lawless reign of the Pirate Kings, the Africans who escaped into the hinterland of Hy Brasil did well. A country beyond the reach of law or constitution was for them, during the terrible years of the trade, an earthly equivalent to the Promised Land. For centuries the Privateers had also made their haven here, paid by one government to rob another, often bribed by several nations at once, literally holding the fortunes of Europe in their hands, but never officially. Nothing was written down; they were never acknowledged by any of the rich and powerful whom they held in place. So nothing changes, thought Jared, only what the gold is made of. Only the substance of the dream. He understood; he had dreams enough of his own.

What he was doing now was one: all his life he had intended to live on an uninhabited island. Ambition takes a myriad forms. He had an impressive CV. He could be diving for whatever survey company he chose, and be making his fortune. He could be teaching in the Marine Studies department of the University of the Hesperides, and have his own carpeted office on the third floor of the Cabot Building, with a fine view east over the harbour. Or he could be employed in any major maritime city in the western world. But he didn't like being indoors, was terrified of institutions, and had always got on best with informal employers, such as Francis Morgan who hired him to mow the lawn as soon as he turned fourteen, Ishmael Pereira, who had taken him on as part-time crew a year later, or Cally Simpson at Ogg's Cove, who used to pay him 3d per jar for collecting lugworms.

His island had always existed inside his head. He remembered waking from it when he was very small, and although it vanished as it always did, there were drifting shreds left behind that melted at his touch. One of those fleeing images contained the lighthouse, and another the cleft between the rocks where the boat crept in when the weather was calm enough. He had a picture in his mind of a surge of white water between black rocks, and the seaweed lifting and falling like a hairy submerged beast. Parts of the island must have been woven out of stories, but he had no recollection of anyone telling them. Other parts must have grown out of the shore at Ogg's Cove where he grew up, although that was so familiar that he only noticed what it was like when he went away, and understood for the first time what was familiar to him because it was no longer there.

He'd fallen for Despair on his first visit, twenty years before he came to live there. He'd been six years old; his father had taken him across the sound on a blue day of sun and breezes. They'd moored at the lighthouse jetty, walked up the steep green slope to the light, and had tea with Per Pedersen. He remembered best climbing up and up the red-painted spiral staircase inside the lighthouse, but he no longer had any recollection of reaching the top. They must have done so; Per must have shown him the light, but that part of the day was gone for ever.

There were forty-nine islands and skerries in Hy Brasil, of which seven had been inhabited. Jared used to argue with his friends about what constituted an island; his definition was that it must contain soil. If there were soil, it counted, even if it were less than a cupful. Thrift required less than that, and sea campion, and sea holly. Soil, he insisted, in pubs when everyone was discussing it, with soil there can be land-based life, and that makes an island. If you counted all the bare skerries that were never covered by the tide, there would be too many islands to count. But sometimes at night, when he was falling asleep, he did try to count. He always began at Ogg's Cove, sometimes turning north, sometimes south. North, he never stayed awake beyond Lyonsness, and south, he had seldom reached Dorrado. Insomnia had never been his problem.

Later he used to visit Despair as often as he could get hold of a boat. That was when the lighthouse was still manned. When Per and Romeo were on their shift he would be invited to stay, illicitly, for the night, and he'd be shown the light, still lit by paraffin then, with circles and circles of glass around it, magnifying the one small flame into a great ring of light that flashed out into the empty Atlantic night. Two short, two long, a pause, and then again. He used to lie in his sleeping bag on the kitchen floor while the light swept over him, and he would fall asleep to its rhythm. When Perce and Dan were on their shift he never got to stay at the lighthouse for more than a cup of tea; also, those two used to ask him awkward questions about why he wasn't at school.

The University of the Hesperides offered among its freshman courses Marine Biology, Atlantic Studies and Literature in English. Jared studied all of them desultorily for a few months, and then left Hy Brasil to seek a better fortune. He returned with a fund of stories which would have assured him a welcome in every pub on the island. Jared avoided all of them. He began to haunt the library archives instead, reading all he could find on the Pirate Kings, whose reign began at the end of the Portuguese supremacy in 1589 and ended with the capture of St Brandons by the British in 1812. He bought Ishmael's old Boston whaler, and began a survey of the shore between Ogg's Cove and Lyonsness. On every clear day Despair loomed over him across the sound, but it wasn't until the summer was more than half over that he paid attention to what the island was telling him.

As soon as he shifted his search to the shores of Despair he began to dream about the island every night, and woke each morning with a sense of loss so poignant that it hurt him like something real sticking into him just under his ribs. One hot night he was lying in his rented room above Caliban's Fast Food Diner in Water Street, naked except for a rucked up sheet that kept wrinkling itself sweatily around him, and he fell into a doze without precisely forgetting where he was. The light began to sweep over him rhythmically. Two slow, two long, and a pause. He accepted it drowsily, his eyes half closed, and then remembered that this was not where he thought he was, and he sat up suddenly. But it's all automated, he thought irrationally; no one lives on Despair now. Per had retired to Lyonsness, to a bungalow with a huge picture window looking over to the island. Romeo was dead. Perce was living with his married daughter just outside Dorrado, and Dan had gone back to sea and never been heard of since. The lighthouse had been empty for ten years.

Jared fell asleep again, and dreamed that the lighthouse was not real any more, but only a place he had read about in a book. He was sitting in a medieval library, somewhere in England, reading the title page, only the writing kept sliding away and he couldn't make out the words. Thousands of other readers were breathing quietly in the dark around him. He could not break the silence to ask. The book was heavy in his hands, and he knew that it was great and important. It held an authority that he dared not defy or question, certainly not in that dim library, but the conviction was growing in him, and he knew that there was something he must say.

He cleared his throat, and the echo whispered up and down the rows of tables, and every one of the readers heard it, and sighed impatiently. Jared put the book down with trembling hands, and spoke. 'I know it's good. I know it's important. But I have to speak.'

He felt their hostility breaking in on him like waves.

'It's wrong, though, about the island. The island wasn't like that at all.'

He woke in a sweat of terror, and the sheet was tight around his throat. The lights of Water Street illuminated the grubby window, and the lace curtains shone like frost. Jared got up and looked out.

Over the street lights the moon was up. The harbour shone like a sheet of Spanish gold. The fishing boats cast midnight shadows, and a small cat ambled along the pier past the fretted lobster pots. All that was left of the first dream was the image of a light flashing slowly, out into the Atlantic, telling every ship that passed that there was an island here, whether they knew it or not. Two short flashes – 'There . . . is' – and two long – 'an isl . . . and here'. 'There is . . . an island here.'

Two days later he and Ishmael found the barrel of a bronze cannon lying in a hollow of white sand.

So he knew something about dreams. He looked at the white powder in his hand, and for a fleeting moment considered what it might have to offer. The notion passed; he realised with extreme and final clarity that he did not want it. The only question that remained, what to do? For the law he felt all the repugnance natural to a young man who had once been the worst case of truanting Lyonsness Junior High had ever had to report. At present he had a personal grudge against the government, as well as the more general antipathy he usually felt towards it. Moreover, he had a filial duty of revenge towards the President, the implications of which he had avoided all his life. He knew exactly what it was like to risk his life in a small boat in order to defy authority of any kind. On the other hand, this was his island; he presided over one of the most unpolluted beaches left in the whole world. This thing intruded; it was a personal insult. He didn't want it here.

Ishmael. As soon as he thought of his partner his course of action was immediately quite clear. If he took the boat over tomorrow after he'd checked the gannets, maybe stayed the night at Ferdy's Landing, he could consult Ishmael, get rid of the packet, do his shopping, and come home. Jared poured the powder carefully back into its plastic envelope. He felt relieved. Ishmael would know what to do.

THREE

MARGARET ELPHINSTONE

Sidony Redruth. Hesperides Room, St Brandons' Public Library.

POSTCARDS

Art –   9/5/97

Today the fog cleared when I was standing on the tower of St Brendan's Cathedral, and for the first time I saw where I was. The thing I don't get when I read a map is the contour lines. I mean I read them in my head but I don't *see* the height until it's real. The islands rise straight out of the sea like dragon's teeth, and the mountains are isosceles triangles still capped with snow, just like we used to draw them. People are kind and talk to me. It's OK. Sid.

Dear Mum and Dad,   9/5/97

Today the fog cleared while I was in the Cathedral. Nice Romanesque architecture – most of it was built in the C15 by the Portuguese. It has a lantern tower over the transept a bit like Ely only smaller. Amazing mosaics – Jonah and the whale by the font and the calming of the storm in the chancel. Unusual. St Ailbe's chapel has a curragh hanging over the altar. I like that. Love, Sidony.

Dear Lance,   9/5/97

The answer's no. Finally and definitely no. As soon as the
plane took off I just felt like I was alive again. I'm sorry, but
I'd rather be lonely than stuck. It's not your fault. This place
is magic, like walking into a book. I want to see what
happens next. Love (really) from Sidony.

Notes for *Undiscovered Islands* (working title). May 9th

The archipelago of Hy Brasil first appears on a map in 1380, made
by the brothers Zeno. Experts doubt whether they actually
landed, in spite of the detailed and dramatic description of the
islands and their inhabitants (see below). It seems these guys were
a couple of chancers and no one was too sure what to make of their
admittedly fishy story. Whether they got there or not, the Zenos
were by no means the first discoverers. Scholars are still arguing
about whether Hy Brasil is in fact Hvitmannaland (see Eyrbyggia
saga). The archeological dig at Ogg's Cove seems to have produced incontrovertible evidence that the Vikings did get here
(write up), but no one's published a report yet, even though they
started digging back in 1972. Apparently archeological conclusions take that long and sometimes they don't happen at all.

I read over what I've written, and see that it's inadequate in every
way. Firstly, the style is wrong. Be informal, the guidelines say.
Does informal mean debased American gangster-style jargon?
Probably not. I put a wavy line under the beginning of sentence
three, signifying that the sense must stay but I need to find different
words. Secondly, the structure is wrong, back to front in fact. I
circle the bit about the Zenos and make an arrow putting it in after
the Vikings, who came first. That makes a hopeless beginning. No
one will have heard of Hvitmannaland, most people won't even try
to pronounce it. Thirdly, the content is wrong. The guidelines say
be informal but substantial. The readers want facts, but facts made
as digestible as possible. They need to trust you to be reliable and

accurate. Don't become involved in issues they've never heard of without explaining the context first. Fourthly, don't get controversial. Don't knock the government, the tourist office, the industrialists, the educationists, the entrepreneurs, the nationalists, the whalers or even the archeologists. Make a spicy stew without touching the salt and pepper. Start again.

I put down my pen, lean back in my chair, and look around the library.

I tried to resist starting here. Libraries these days induce in me an uneasy feeling of transgression, which is a shame, because all my life, until this happened, they have been places which made me happy. I like this one. The air smells erudite, and the oak chairs with green imitation leather seats are capacious enough to make me feel small and still full of wonder. The public library is downstairs. It is large and airy, full of varnished pine and municipal rubber plants.

Here in the Hesperides Room there is a long oak table with carving in Gothic letters round the edges, which I've not been able to decipher. I can't look at it all the way round because there are three people sitting at the table. A man in a brown mackintosh has a handwritten register open in front of him and is making cryptic notes in a red, spiral-bound notebook. I thought he was quite old until he looked up just now; I'd put him about mid-thirties. He has been looking at the same page for over an hour. Two girls in uniform – green gym tunics, green cardigans, green-and-black ties and white shirts – have maps and books spread out in front of them and are making notes sporadically in green jotters on which are printed crests identical to the ones on the green blazers that hang on the back of their chairs. Each time I pass behind them to get to the computer I glean another titbit of information. I have read the crest, *Ad Occidentem Navigemus*, and the name on the jotters, 'St Brandons' Academy'. I have looked at the open books. One has a reproduction of Gerard Mercator's map of the world (1587), the same one that I studied in Penzance library when I began my literary voyaging just over a year ago. The other book has rather dull drawings of what seem to be fortifications, of the British fort at Port o' Frisland, I think. I can just make out the date: 1812. And the spread map is one of the series I've bought myself, the 1:63,360 five-map series of the whole Hy Brasil archipelago. The one the girls are consulting is *Map 4, St Brandons*.

Sunlight glances across the polished table. I look up, startled. The air is bright with old dust. The stained glass panels at the top of the neo-Gothic windows are throwing a rainbow of sudden colours across the faded spines of the *Proceedings of the Hesperides Literary and Scientific Society Volumes I–LXVIII*: a blue-and-green spectrum from the sea and mountain, and a patch of red cast by the Saint's cloak. I look up at the original, and it sparkles now so that I can hardly see it. I'm not sure if it is his cloak after all; it might be the sail. In the glass panel he is standing right by the mast, and the artist has made him taller than the ship. Through the plain glass below I see the sky for the first time since I landed. It is the same blue as the cobalt that you get in medieval paintings, which they had to use sparingly because it was so rare and expensive. I thrust my pile of books together, grab my jacket, and make for the door. It clicks into place behind me and the sign that says, 'Hesperides Room. Key available from librarian only. By order. F. Baskerville', sways a little as I pass.

The street is transformed. Puddles gleam among the uneven stone flags, and now all at once there are people, wearing not raincoats but colours; red and green and blue. I can see their faces for the first time. My first thought is that this is a port, in fact it has never been anything but a port; that is all there is. Everyone has landed here: Irish, Moroccan, Scandinavian, Portuguese, Italian, English, Spanish, Scottish, African, French, American, Filipino, Vietnamese; so many people have landed and just a few stayed. Dorrado and St Brandons were famous for their brothels for four hundred years, and as I look at the passing people, representatives of a population of under forty thousand, I see the varying colours of their skin and hair and eyes, and I feel just for a moment that this sea-ridden outpost must be the centre of the world.

Suddenly everyone is walking in the High Street. I am reminded of Venice, because what I hear is the sound of footsteps, and the murmur of voices. The faint roar behind me might be traffic, but I choose just now to think that it's the sea. I stop outside the Frisland Bank to study the exchange rate; I'm going to have to cash another cheque before long. The sign reads:

To Buy 1 Hy Brasil pound

US 2.0000
GBR 1.2000
CAN 2.8356
POR 360.1200
DEN 13.4634
FR 11.8836
DET 3.5360
ICE 142.9138
SPN 297.7380
IRE 1.3569
JPN 257.3120

Damn. I thought this place was supposed to be going to the dogs, but its currency gets stronger every time I look at it, which isn't what I need at all. Just then someone speaks in my ear.

'They have excellent doughnuts at Finnegan's.'

It's the man in the raincoat, who was writing down all those mysterious numbers. He is now wearing a homburg hat like Humphrey Bogart's in *Casablanca*, which he lifts as I turn round. No one has ever raised their hat to me before. 'Finnegan's?' I say, for want of a better response.

'There's a coffee shop on the top floor. Better than Caliban's. Besides, you tried that yesterday.'

'How do you know that?'

'It's my business to know.' He's much taller than I am and

also good-looking in an austere, Spanish kind of way, like a Goya portrait. But his brown eyes look friendly. He holds out his hand. 'Colombo MacAdam,' he says. 'I work for *The Hesperides Times*. So you're writing a book about us?'

'I haven't told anybody that yet.'

'These things get around.' I see now that the mackintosh is not shabby after all, but on the contrary, very much part of the thirties effect. His hands are large and beautiful, and he wears an ornate signet ring on his little finger. 'May I take you for a coffee? And I seriously recommend Finnegan's doughnuts. They make their own blueberry jam. I might be able to assist you a little. One never knows.'

He takes care to walk on the side nearest the traffic. My grandmother told me how men used to do that. I glance sideways at him as he strides along. I like his hat. I want him to go on talking so I can savour his lilting accent, and the old fashioned phrases he uses.

Finnegan's is halfway up the High Street, just by the cherry tree. Now the sun's out the tree seems to glow from inside its pink cover like a candle in a paper lantern. That's why I hadn't seen Finnegan's: the shop sign is dark green and right behind the cherry blossom. When Colombo leads me inside I realise he's showing me a treasure.

The inside is much bigger than the outside. Colombo says this was once a chandler's warehouse stretching all the way from High Street to Water Street. Now it's a big open space with wooden staircases and half landings and odd corners stacked with books. The main part of the ground floor is all bookshop, with great sweeps of shelving stretched from white brick wall to white brick wall. It's hushed and warm the way that bookish places ought to be, and behind the dry book smell there's a whiff of tar, as if the ghosts of ropes and barrels and sailcloth have reached across time and settled like cats in the sunny window-shaped rectangles that cover the floor. Coffee smells waft down from somewhere under the rafters, but it's hard just to walk past all those books.

'Colombo! Hey, Colombo!'

I look round and there's a black man standing in the doorway, as tall as Colombo and twice as substantial, waving a newspaper at us. 'So what's this?' he's calling out. 'What does Tidesman know of Spanish gold?'

'Excuse me a minute,' mutters Colombo, and hurries over to him. They stand half-turned away, heads close together, talking in low voices.

I wander among the books, resisting an impulse to pinch myself, because if it's a dream I don't want to wake up just yet. I get to Languages, and walk among books in English, Portuguese, Gaelic, Catalan, Icelandic and French. I drift on between maps and bird books and Earth Sciences and Music and Cookery and Scuba Diving. I pass two World Wars and an alcove of Biography. I glance at Humour, ignore Sport, and meander towards Theology. My attention is arrested by a special display. A dozen copies of a fat, expensive-looking hardback are arranged tastefully on black drapery. There is a map, gorgeously printed in full colour, on the front cover. I know that map. I go closer. Yes, it's Ortelius, 1570.

'*Ubi insula est?*'

That's an odd title for a book, especially one that's clearly brand new. There's a lectern with a copy you can open and leaf through. I turn to page one, and I'm hooked.

It's a story. There was a man who wanted to know about early navigation. He went to the South Pacific, and travelled with islanders in a canoe, with no instruments of any kind, not even a watch or a pocket compass. They crossed the ocean for hundreds of miles. The sky was cloudy and they couldn't see the sun, and at night the moon was dark and the stars were obscured. They travelled for many days and then they made a perfect landfall on the little island they'd been heading for. The man couldn't understand this at all. 'How did you know the island was *there*?' he asked. The steersman seemed puzzled by the question. He replied, 'The island has always been there.'

Enraptured, I turn the page. But it's all a trick. The book isn't about navigation or islands at all. It's just a great turgid academic tome. As far as I can make out from the cover blurb it's an extended essay on the relative status of imagined and empirical realities. I open it in the middle and read a bit at random:

> It might be thought that fiction, unlike reality, is inextricably connected to an author, and that this partly explains its impoverished ontological status. This line of reasoning, however, is at the very least misleading. Fiction often does not involve its author, and when it does it is questionable whether this involvement demotes it to an inferior ontological status.
>
> The author of a work of fiction need not, and usually does not, exist in the fictional world of the work. Shakespeare is obviously not an inhabitant of Prospero's island, but neither need he exist at any time or place within the wider world of *The Tempest*. England may well be a place in the fictional world of *The Tempest* – the Mediterranean and the city of Milan certainly are – but *The Tempest*'s England may be one in which Shakespeare had never been born.
>
> Even if we allow that there is a sense in which the author creates much of the fictional world and many of its inhabitants, this does not mean that such creations are imaginary or ghost-like. Hamlet may be a creation of Shakespeare's, but, unlike the Ghost, he is very much alive: he plots, loves, and finally fights.
>
> Authors certainly do not know everything about their fictional worlds. Shakespeare did not know the gale force necessary to cause the shipwreck in *The Tempest* and could not have known that Hamlet had an Oedipus complex.

It's all getting horribly close to being back at university. Disappointed, I turn to the back flap. Academic works tend to be reticent about their authors, as if they're trying to pretend they don't really have any, but this one does have a discreet little note in white letters on the midnight-blue laminated cover.

> Brendan Hook was born in 1946 and educated at The University of the Hesperides, Hy Brasil, and Cambridge, England. He is now a professor in philosophy at Harvard University. He is married and has two sons and two daughters. His first book, *Images of Formlessness*, was published in 1989.

I turn back to Ortelius. Why do they give the most unreadable books the most beautiful covers? I'll never get a cover like that for my book. I'll be lucky if I get something like 'Fishing boats in the harbour at St Brandons' or 'Sunset at Dorrado'. I'll be lucky if I get anything.

'Doughnut?' says Colombo, and makes me jump.

He waits politely for me to precede him up the stairs.

He's right about the doughnuts, and full of information on other matters. I ply him with questions, trying not to do so with my mouth full. I can see he's impressed when I mention the exchange rate.

'You're quite right,' he says. 'I didn't know you were making a study of our economy.'

'I'm hardly doing that. But when a loaf of bread costs me twice as much as it does at home I can't help noticing. I thought with no fish left in the sea the country would be more or less bankrupt, especially as there hasn't really been much of a tourist industry.'

'Ah well, that's changing. But you're right, it does raise a question. In fact there was an article in the *Times* this week.' He delves into the pocket of his mackintosh, where it hangs over the back of his chair, and takes out a newspaper. 'Here, read this.' While he leafs through I read the back page which is facing me. It says:

Ogg's Cove have just beaten Lyonsness by three wickets. In this one-day game Lyonsness, batting first, were dismissed for a fighting 93. In reply, Ogg's Cove also struggled with Alton remaining not out and steering them home to a victory.

Colombo hands me the paper, folded back at page six. It seems to be a sort of editorial, with a rather fetching woodcut of a man in a cap with a pipe in his mouth by way of graphics. *Tidesman*, it says at the top. I swallow my last mouthful of doughnut and concentrate.

TIDESMAN ON OUR ECONOMIC FUTURE – WHAT PRICE NOW?

It's interesting that the schools' history curriculum in Hy Brasil stops sometime in the late 1960s. The last chapter in *The Jewel of the Atlantic*, published in 1976 and still used in primary schools throughout the country, is reprinted annually with little change bar the President's introductory remarks. It's entitled 'A Land of Promise', and it eulogises our freedom, our prosperity and our potential, and bases our good fortune on fertile soil, teeming seas and an indomitable will to succeed. Wishful thinking? Or wilful thinking?

In 1997, no citizen with open eyes can fail to recognise that the fertile soil provides a living only to the few who own it. A small, locally consumed cider industry, and a few cheeses for sale in St Brandons' delicatessens can hardly provide income for a nation. More and more of our food arrives pre-packaged from Spain and South Africa, Costa Rica and the USA. The sea is all but fished out by Portuguese trawlers and Icelandic long-liners. There are at least twenty local whitefish boats mothballed in St Brandons' harbour as I write. Tourism? The latest (third or fourth?) attempt to float plans for a new airport hotel has just fallen through.

Which leaves us with the will to succeed, the one assertion that does seem to hold water. Hy Brasil, despite its apparent deficit, is clearly doing very nicely. A new project has been announced in these pages almost every week this year: a branch library in Ogg's Cove, a swimming pool in Lyonsness, four new academic posts at the University . . .

Shrewd post-independence investment – to the tune of nearly twenty million last year – we're told, has proved to be Hy Brasil's bastion against a world in recession. The seven fat years were put to good use, and evidently all we have to do now is to thank a benign Providence for our President's timely prophetic dreams. And while the state provides for an ever-growing population of out-of-work fishermen and farmworkers, who's complaining? Big numbers go over most people's heads; who cares whether there are six or seven noughts on Hy Brasil's GDP?

But think about it: even at a 5% return, our country would have to have nearly half a billion pounds stashed away somewhere. That's nearly £15,000 for every Hy Brasil man, woman and child. It's about three times what all the real estate in the islands is worth at a liberal estimate. We can only hope the government knows what it's doing. Large sums need wise heads and steady hands. We don't want to hear in twelve months' time that First National or Citicorp has withdrawn credit facilities to a tiny mortgaged island state, or that they've suddenly decided to halve their rates to investors or – God forbid – that the President and his cronies have decamped to a Caribbean hideout – worth real money – which they but not we have known about all along.

'Who's Tidesman?' I ask.

Colombo shrugs. 'A journalist. Commentator. He's been on the books a long time.'

'How long?'

'He got his own column in 1876. Hasn't missed a week since.'

I glance at him suspiciously, then understand. 'Oh, you mean he's generic?'

'That's it. You'll find he's more or less proverbial here. He had a bit of a thin time after '58, but our President has a sense of proportion. Humour too, if you catch him at the right moment. And Baskerville was his man anyway, so it did no harm to have an obvious safety valve.'

'Baskerville?'

'Used to be Tidesman from – what would it be – '54, '55? for – oh, twenty years or more. It's OK to tell you that; it's an open secret now. But the current Tidesman is always anonymous.'

'So who is it now?'

'I said he – or she – is always anonymous. Anonymous, iconoclastic and informed. You could say it's the nearest to an opposition we've got.'

'It seems quite an outspoken article.'

'Ah well, we are living in a democracy. Would you like a refill?'

When he comes back with the brimming cups he seems to have reached some sort of conclusion. 'Speaking of which,' he goes on, so that I have to try to think what we *have* been speaking of, 'I'd like you to meet a friend of mine. You said you were thinking of staying up north next?'

'Yes. I have the number of Peterkin's aunt in Lyonsness.'

'Are you teetotal?'

'No.'

'Do you read your Bible?'

'I know it pretty well, but I can't say I read it much now.'

'Do you ever swear?'

'Yes.'

'You don't want to stay with Peterkin's aunt. I have a better idea. Listen to me.'

FOUR

THE COURTYARD FACED west, and in the late afternoon the sunshine poured into it like honey. Even the grim walls of the keep looked benign under the softening golden light. The white doves circling over the battlements shone bright as pearls against the sky. The castle enclosed the courtyard on three sides. The fourth wall of the courtyard was two feet high, a low parapet above a precipice. The courtyard was paved round the edges, like the floor of a cloister. In the middle of the grass quadrangle a gnarled thorn tree grew over a circular stone well, its twisted branches almost hiding the ancient stonework. A thin film of green had begun to creep over it. On the other side of the parapet the valley below was already hidden under a green mist of slowly budding trees. Beyond it the sea lay in shadow, a sombre hazy blue, like looking into a cave.

In the valley only two creatures were visible. One was a kestrel that hovered high over the trees, just level with the courtyard wall. The other was Lucy, who sat on the parapet writing in a yellow loose-leaf folder. The wings of the kestrel moved so fast it seemed to be motionless, and Lucy's hand travelled rapidly across the page, as if she never had to wait for a thought to come. She wrote in a spiky italic script, with purple ink, and even when she turned a page she never paused long enough for her ink to dry.

The kestrel plunged, and the trees closed over it. Lucy looked up, and pushed her short hair back, as if it were still long enough to have fallen over her eyes. She stared out to sea, blinking. There was another sound besides the waves beating on the lava shores of Brentness, which Lucy never heard anyway because they were simply part of life. A car was coming up the road behind the castle, its gears grinding on the steep corner below the old ice house. Whoever it was would reach the door in four and a half minutes. Lucy squinted up at the Spanish clock that one of her ancestors had intercepted on its way to Haiti in 1643 and had fixed to the tower just below the belfry, where three bells from a foundry in the ancient kingdom of Leinster hung in readiness to warn the island against eruption or invasion. Four thirty-two. Lucy frowned. She wasn't expecting anyone to tea, and all the ginger biscuits had been finished yesterday. She screwed the top back on her fountain pen, shut her folder, and went in to put the kettle on.

Three minutes later she was just putting two teabags into the Hester Bateman silver teapot that was used when there was more than one person for tea but fewer than four, when the door into the conservatory creaked open. She heard a familiar voice. Lucy smiled.

'I'm in the kitchen,' she called. 'I heard you on the corner. Whose car have you borrowed now?'

Jared climbed in through the small opening set in the left hand oak door. 'Don't you open the door any more? That hole isn't meant for people more than five feet high.'

'That's because in the seventeenth century they weren't. Those doors are supposed to be made out of timbers that came ashore from the *Cortes*. You should know.'

'At least they didn't have to bloody dive for them.'

'No one said you had to go diving off Despair either. You can't complain.'

'I wouldn't complain if someone would just come up with some *money*! They can afford to build another swimming pool and turn Maldun's Mill into an art gallery. If they want art, the bottom of the damn sea is littered with the stuff. But who cares about that?'

'Jed, be fair. We need swimming pools. People entirely surrounded by water should learn how to swim. It's logical.'

'But three?'

'Yes, three. One at Dorrado, one at St Brandons and now one at Lyonsness. Kids don't walk thirty miles every time they want a swimming lesson. We've got the hot springs: we should use them. The Portuguese did. The walls around the Lyonsness spring are fifteenth-century Portuguese, Baskerville says.'

'So? The stonework round the fountain at Dorrado is fourth-century Irish. That doesn't mean we're obliged to use the place as a jacuzzi for the next thousand years. So you like having an art gallery in Maldun's Mill? A hundred and one perspectives of Mount Brasil, with a skyful of dollars in the background?'

'Kirwan's photographs aren't like that.'

'Is Kirwan exhibiting there?'

'The first one-man show and the opening attraction. So there!'

'Wedged in between the café and the souvenir shop? I'm surprised they got Kirwan.'

'Kirwan wants to live, just like the rest of us. Most of us aren't betting everything on Spanish gold. Here, take this. Let's sit in the window.'

He took his tea and followed her. The kitchen was barrel-vaulted, built in the original storerooms below the main hall of the castle. The round German stove at the north end bore a strong resemblance to a steam engine, so that Jared always had an anachronistic sense of being in a railway station. He relished the impression all the more as they were 1388 miles from the nearest railway station to the east, which was Tralee, and 2383 from the west, which was Halifax, Nova Scotia. (The railways in Newfoundland and Cape Breton Island had ceased to function in the 1970s.) Perhaps this was why Jared had always liked the idea of steam trains, especially the huge saurian type that were built to cross continents, with memorable destinations printed on the windows: Paris, Geneva, Vienna, Athens, Berlin, Warsaw, St Petersburg, New York, San Francisco. In reality he hadn't seen a train at all until he was nineteen, and first boarded the British Rail boat train from Southampton to Waterloo.

Jared skirted a twenty-foot-long table, piled for half its length with maps, books, magazines, letters, a typewriter, a bowl of fruit and some models of plastic reptiles that had once come out of cornflakes packets, and followed Lucy to the window embrasure. In the twelve-foot thickness of the castle wall there was room for a round table with windowseats on each side, shelves with a few stray books, a toaster, a game of Cluedo, and a ginger cat.

'Hello, Ginger,' Jared said to the cat. 'Where's Simpkin?'

'God knows,' said Lucy. 'Killing something I expect. He's taken to leaving half a dead rabbit behind the sofa every night for me to find in the morning.'

'How touching.'

'I don't think it's intended as a present. There aren't any biscuits, but you could have toast. Dammit, that's the phone. Help yourself.'

Jared found a home-made loaf in the bread tin, and cut himself two large slabs. While they toasted he stirred his tea and listened to half a conversation.

'Hi-aye . . . Oh Colombo . . . Fine . . . Yes . . . sure, tell me . . .' A pause. 'A book about Hy Brasil? Why? Who is she? . . . Well, if they want a guidebook why don't they ask one of us? I suppose it's the full employment round here puts them off . . . No, no, fair enough . . . Here? Me? . . . Well, that's true . . . What's she like? . . .' A pause. 'OK, but will I like her? . . . What if I don't? . . . Sure, I could use the cash . . . OK, well . . . but . . . what? . . . Suppose we say in about a week? . . . No, that'll give me a chance, in case I want to get out of it . . . Fair enough . . . Yes, OK, bring her any time that week, and she can stay a week to start off with . . . Oh yes, well, I charged those Canadians twenty-five pounds fifteen

and six a night. That was last year. Do you think that's fair?
. . . OK, and if I like her and she stays longer I might make it
less . . . Oh, I think so. It only means one lot of sheets . . .
OK then, next week then . . . Yes, very nice, and so do I love
you . . . No, you know I won't. See you soon . . . Don't talk
about it . . . Bye.'

Lucy came back to the table looking slightly flushed.

'Poor Colombo,' said Jared.

'There's nothing poor about Colombo,' replied Lucy
tartly.

'Well, I wouldn't be in his shoes. Not that I have any shoes
of that sort at all just now,' Jared sighed.

'My heart bleeds. If you keep yourself immured on Despair
what do you expect? Ferryloads of avid blondes rowing in
formation across the sound?'

'Now there's a nice idea. Do I gather you're getting a
lodger?'

'A girl called Sidney – Sidony? – something like that. She's a
Brit. And she's writing a book about Hy Brasil.'

'Oh, Christ. I hate her already.'

'You won't hate her. Colombo says she's pretty. I should
have suggested she meet you. There's lots of things you could
tell her. Well, we can arrange that later, and then you needn't be
footloose any more.'

'Thanks. So she's staying here next week?'

'For a bit. She's at the hostel in St Brandons just now. I
expect it'll be fine. She can do Ogg's Cove and Lyonsness from
here.'

'*Do* them, eh? That'll be great.'

'Come on! From what Colombo says she's only a student, or
just graduated or something. Anyway, she's not the witch of
Endor or Colombo wouldn't want to help her. You're in a foul
mood, Jared.'

He was instantly repentant. 'I'm sorry. Read that. I picked it
up at the Post Office this morning. That's partly why. If she's

nice I think it's a good idea. I suppose you could do with the company.'

Lucy smoothed out the crumpled letter.

Dear Sir (she read)

Your application to the Mayda Trust has been carefully considered. It has been a record year for projects, which reflects the thriving state of artistic and conservationist endeavour in this country. The Committee has been impressed by the high standard of the projects brought to its attention. However, funding is necessarily limited, and our primary criterion had to be the potential benefit of each project to the community as a whole. We therefore regret to have to inform you . . .

'Oh Jed,' she said. 'But Spanish treasure isn't the only thing. It'll be there another year.'

'Want to bet? Chances are they'll sell the rights to some foreign company that's got all the gear and can pay anything they ask, before the year's out. I should never even have *told* them about it. It's out of the bag now.'

'Jed, I'm sure they won't.'

'And there's another thing. Why I'm here today: I found something yesterday. The more I think about it, I bet it all hangs together. Fuck the Mayda Trust. Has anyone ever seen their accounts?'

'Well yes, the auditors presumably. I expect it's Gunn and Selkirk. They do most of the public bodies. They do me, too, in fact. What about it?'

'I tell you, there's something behind all this. It's not just coincidence. And yesterday . . .'

'Behind all which? Get real, Jared. Who the hell wants to salvage the *Cortes* except you and possibly Ishmael Pereira? Who else do you think gives a damn? The bloody mafia?'

'Suppose you let me finish my sentence? Just because you think I'm paranoid . . .'

'I didn't say that. What I do think is that this Robinson Crusoe number isn't making any sense. Spending all your evenings out there brooding about conspiracies. It would do you a lot more good to have an active sex life. In the spring a young man's fancy ought to turn to thoughts of love. Have you thought of advertising?'

'Shut up, Lucy, and listen to me. You're not one to talk anyway. I'm trying to tell you something important. The reason I'm over here today is I found a packet of cocaine on the white strand yesterday morning. Seriously.'

Lucy stared at him. 'Cocaine?'

'Yes. On the high tide mark. In a waterproof plastic case. Jettisoned.'

'How did you know it was coke?'

'Well, it didn't exactly look like a pint of milk.'

'Thanks. But Jed . . . Surely no one's into that scene now? I mean, who would be? I don't know anyone. Do you?'

'Of course not. But they wouldn't tell me, would they? I don't use the stuff.'

Lucy turned her mug round and round in her hands. She looked perturbed. 'Oh Jed! I don't like it. Does it have to be someone local? Are you *sure* it was cocaine?'

'What else would it be? Nothing else comes through Hy Brasil now that I know of, except high-quality marijuana, and it certainly wasn't that. But you remember there was that bit in the *Times* about Customs patrols? They must have startled somebody. That's what you do if a search is imminent: jettison the cargo.'

'Why didn't they use lobster pots or something?'

'Maybe they did and one got dropped. Maybe they couldn't. How do I know? That was yesterday morning. I thought about what to do. You can see why I didn't want to get involved, can't you? But it bothered me, so today I came over to Ferdy's

Landing and showed it to Ishmael. He said I should have come at once. I'd never thought of it, Lucy, but Ishmael said, what if the peelers came over to Despair and found it on me? You think I'm paranoid. But Ishmael says I'm not careful enough; he thinks there's maybe folk out there don't want me on Despair, and I should watch out. I could get busted, and if they wanted to find stuff on me, well, that could be arranged.'

'Did he really say that?'

'Yes, and Ishmael doesn't dream up anything that isn't real.'

Lucy was frowning. 'No, he doesn't. Jed, I wonder . . . Do you see anything of Olly West these days?'

'No. I did when I first got back, because he never left me alone. He got this notion we could set up some partnership with a boat. Is it likely? I don't reckon that guy could row across the pond in Kings' Park. Then when I started diving with Ishmael, Olly was black affronted about it. I never promised him anything though; just stood about listening politely when I couldn't get away.'

'Well, when you first got back, according to Olly West, you were the best thing since sliced bread. Now: not, to put it mildly. Or so they tell me.'

'But Lucy, that's what he's always done: latched on to some unsuspecting chap, dreamt up some fantasy, and then slandered the fellow forever because it turns out the poor soul never knew a thing about it. I don't give a damn. Olly's harmless. No one listens to him.'

'I suppose not. But go on telling me. So what did you do?'

'Today? Oh, Ishmael drove me into St Brandons and we took the stuff straight to the peelers. And I tell you, I was damn glad he was with me. I didn't exactly get a vote of thanks. They made it fairly clear that my role was Prime Suspect. Lucy, do I *look* like a drug dealer?'

'No, m'dear, you don't. But does anyone? It would hardly be a recipe for success to look the part.'

He wasn't listening. 'They had me in there over an hour,

asking me questions. What the hell was I supposed to say? I kept on telling them, I found the damn thing on the beach. This morning, I said. Remember that if you get asked; I wouldn't put it past those guys to go round all my friends checking up on me. Ishmael said say this morning, not yesterday, so it looked like I'd leapt in the boat and come over right away. So I did. But even telling that much of a lie, I started feeling confused, and yes, maybe I am paranoid. I started wondering if they had a truth monitor beamed on me, things like that. It was this horrible little room without any windows. I hate not being able to see out.'

'Poor Jared. They did rattle you, didn't they?'

'I can't stand peelers. I used to think it was because I was young. When I was a kid they were after me all the time. You remember that time I got stopped for speeding? That was the first time I ever got into the Court section of the paper. Stopped for bloody speeding. I was on water skis at the time. Not even in the bloody boat. No wonder I left the country. But now I'm back it's no better. Worse in fact. If they framed me for smuggling coke I could go down for years. Years. Do you realise that?'

'Jed, stop, stop! No one's framed you for anything. OK, so the police gave you the third degree. Maybe they wonder what you're doing out there on Despair all by yourself. I suppose they have to eliminate you first.'

'According to our constitution they're not allowed to eliminate me, much as they might like to.'

'Not like that, idiot. All I'm saying is, I suppose I can see why Ishmael thinks you should be careful.'

'For Christ's sake! Lucy, you don't think I'm dealing drugs, do you?'

She was staring at him again, a sudden question in her eyes. Then she said, 'Of course I don't. But naturally I remember things. You must remember them too.'

'Lucy! What is this?' Jared stood up, knocking his mug over so it crashed to the floor. 'If you're trying to set me up too, I'm getting out of here!'

She caught him by the arm. 'No, Jed, of course I'm not! Stop! Of course I don't think you had anything to do with it! Jed, stop! I'm on your side. I would be anyway. Sit down! Listen to me!'

Reluctantly Jared sat down again and watched Lucy pick up the mug. 'I didn't break it, did I?'

'No, don't worry about it. Jed, I'm not accusing you of anything. But look at it this way. What do the police know about you? When you were at the Academy you were pretty wild. You weren't in school half the time. They know you've been working a boat out of Ogg's Cove more or less since you could walk. They know you know every inch of the coast between Dorrado and Lyonsness. You were busted for dope at the Hallowe'en dance in Lyonsness when you were in fifth year. Wasn't that when they put you on probation for a year? I was in New York myself but Penelope wrote and told me all about it. Remember? Then not long after that you were caught spraying "Free elections, free Hy Brasil" on the statue of Lord Clanroyden just outside Government House. Three people wrote to me about that, and Colombo sent me the cutting. And then they published your poem about the French Revolution being betrayed by – what was it – "a little man from a little island" – have I got that right?'

'Don't repeat it. I'm not proud of my early poems any more.'

'All right. But Jared, what I'm saying is, you may never have hurt a fly, metaphorically speaking, but in the legend you've created around yourself in Hy Brasil your record is as long as your arm.'

'Oh come on! I haven't even lived here since I was eighteen, until I came back at the beginning of last year. And what have I done since then?'

'Nothing. That's the trouble. Bought a boat and spent all your time mysteriously at sea, just when there's no fish. Gone to live in an empty lighthouse where you don't talk to anybody. OK, so you've kept a low profile. Too damn low, in my opinion.'

'Lucy, I swear to you I'm not involved in anything. I'd never touch the drug trade! What the hell do you think I was doing for eight years? It took me three years to get my degree, and the next five years I mostly spent in sub-zero Arctic waters. You can't do drugs at the same time as doing that. I've published four poems and two articles on marine salvage, all in proper upmarket journals. Would you like to see them? I've just not had time for a life of crime, so don't you think it! If you even suggested it to my friends away from here they'd think you were off your head! And I'm not eighteen any more either.'

'Unfortunately you still look it. And you know what it's like here. Your past is with you for ever. It's not like that when you're away. You know, and I know, and half the population of Hy Brasil knows that life can happen elsewhere and people can go away and change into whatever they like. But when you come home, you have to take the old story on again, even if it doesn't fit you any more. Yes, it's tough: you leave and become a successful whatever-it-is, and you think that's who you are, you've acquired something to be proud of, but the minute you get back here it means nothing, you're still the kid who stole the cookies, even if it happened forty years ago.'

'Jesus, it's worse than that! I hate it; I just feel like I'm not myself any more. The bloody peelers, for God's sake! It's like dreaming you're back in first year being given detentions, but then at least you wake up and find yourself grown up after all. But this is real.'

'So why did you come back?'

Jared looked out of the window. Over a low-lying mist the peak of Despair was just visible to the east, dark-blue against the dimming sky. 'I suppose I wanted to come home. It felt like time. And then Ishmael and I started diving, and we found the *Cortes*. I'd always suspected she was around there, but I had no way of diving before I went away. Didn't know how. No gear. And then last June Ishmael and I found her. That was some day! I'll never forget it. And then I thought, well, here's a project. I'm not an archeologist, but I can read, and Baskerville said he'd tell us what to do, take charge of the finds, write it up and stuff like that. Lucy, when all that was happening I thought we were made. I thought I'd found a way of coming home.

'And then I got the chance to be on Despair. I could live right above my wreck, so I could keep an eye on her. And also I wanted to see what it was like. I've been in lonely places but not on my own. I wanted to find out about that. I wanted to know what I was like when I was just myself, no one about and no one asking for anything.'

'And what is it like?'

Jared shrugged. 'It varies. Boring, sometimes. Melancholy. Exciting. I guess the place is beautiful. When you're alone you don't stop seeing that. Sometimes I talk out loud so as to hear a voice. I read a lot. I have a routine. Sometimes I think if I didn't find things to do I'd be afraid of myself. Other times there's nothing to do, and I'm totally at peace and afraid of nothing at all. Like I say, it varies.'

'But you can't stay there for ever, Jed.'

'Of course I can't stay there for ever! You're the fifth person who's told me that, and I can't think why anyone would need to point out anything so obvious. Are you going to live all alone in Ravnscar for ever? Does it make it wrong to be here if you're not?'

Lucy followed his gaze across the sea to Despair. 'The answer to the first is, I don't know, and to the second, I don't know. I'm not afraid of being on my own either, though my way is different.'

Jared looked at her. 'But you're afraid of the alternative.'

'If that's a question I'm not going to answer it.'

'It wasn't a question.'

Lucy said nothing, and presently he reached across and tentatively touched her hand. 'Sorry. I've been a rotten guest. Maybe I should go now.'

Lucy gave a little shudder, as if she were shaking something away. 'Are you going home tonight?'

'It's getting dark. I'll sleep at Ishmael's and cross first thing in the morning. Oh, before I go: could I borrow Monson's *Naval Tracts* again?'

'Help yourself. It's in the Great Hall – but you know where to find it. Make sure it doesn't get wet. But you could stay here if you like.'

'No, I can't. I've got to get Ishmael's car back to him. I'll come over next week as usual. I never did get my groceries today. The whole trip's been a bloody waste of time.'

'Oh Jed, do cheer up. Come over and meet the Brit when she's staying here. She might be the luscious blonde you're craving for, you never know. But Brits are supposed to be awful in bed; I can tell you a joke about that.'

'I don't want to hear your racist jokes. I've had three English girlfriends – at least, one was Welsh and one was Chinese – and I can tell you it's not even particularly true.'

'I knew your time abroad was educational and productive in every possible way. Goodnight Jared. I like seeing you even when you're horrible. Take care.' Lucy hesitated for a moment, and then reached up and lightly kissed his cheek. 'This place has to be home. We can't help that. I guess it'll turn out all right.'

FIVE

**Sidony Redruth. YWCA Hostel, Water St, St Brandons.
May 20th.**
Notes for *Undiscovered Islands* (working title).

'THEY PUT THE NATO base on Mount Ailbe,' said Colombo,
'because seismically it's supposed to be the most stable.'

'You mean anywhere else in Hy Brasil there might be an
earthquake any minute?'

'Anywhere in the world there might be an earthquake any
minute. Anywhere on the Mid-Atlantic Ridge you could call it a
strong possibility every minute. Mount Ailbe has been stable for
several thousand years. Mount Brasil and Mount Prosper, not.'

'I've read about the Mount Prosper eruption in 1783.'

'In Faraday? He's a good authority. You should look at his
Survey of the Ocean Floor. Did you find that?'

'No. That'll come under Oceanography. I'm still on History.'

Colombo swerved to avoid an exceptionally large pothole.
He was driving with one hand on the wheel, at six-o'clock, and
the other resting on the bottom of the open window. His right
forearm was much browner than his left, so obviously he made a
habit of it. This was the first time I'd seen him in jeans and a t-
shirt. He had a lean, rangy body: nice. I thought we were driving
a bit too fast.

'This isn't a very good road,' I remarked.

'It's good enough. The Brits have a mania for road-building: I noticed that when I was there. The object being to make everywhere look like Surbiton. At least that's what a Brit told me. I don't know what Surbiton's like, but it has a certain ring to it. I have an image of it inside my head.'

I stopped myself trying to justify Surbiton, where incidentally I've never been either, because this was not what I wanted to talk about. 'Before we go any further,' I said instead, 'please will you tell me about the Revolution?'

We'd reached the watershed. Suddenly the sea was directly south of us, a twinkling May-time blue dotted with islands. Foothills fell away to a rocky shore. Colombo pulled into the side with a crunch of gravel. 'It'll take a little while. Let's stop.'

I got out and gazed south. I knew the islands from the map, and pointed to a jagged crescent in the middle. 'Is that Mayda?'

'It is. That's Mayda, and that's Tuly. You can't see Elphinholm. Wherever you get to, it almost always turns out to be hidden behind something else.'

'A shy island?' I stretched out my bare arms. 'It's hot up here. It's actually *hot*.'

'Shall I tell you the story then?'

It was a good place for listening. Colombo sat on one rock, and I lay in eyebright-studded grass with my back against another, and gazed out over the Atlantic while he talked. The sea sparkled back at me, and when I half closed my eyes I kept seeing the shapes of islands that weren't really there.

'It begins during the War,' said Colombo, and paused for a long time. 'Let me think. I've heard so many stories all my life; let me think how to put them in order. I've never been asked to before, not by a foreigner. Certainly not by a Brit. It makes a difference.'

'Oh, don't let it do that.'

'I can't help it. I mean, I talk about the past – oh, a lot, we do it all the time – to other Brasils, and it's just history. Telling you, it feels a bit personal. Only it isn't really. I wasn't born till three years after '58 was over. You're even younger. It's just history.'

'Only it's your history and not mine, you mean?' I tried to sound disinterested, but I felt, quite irrationally, excluded. It occurred to me that if recounting a chapter of his country's history was for Colombo a personal act, his private life must just about count as classified information. It made me realise that, although this was our second fairly intense conversation, I knew absolutely nothing about him.

There was another pause before he answered me. 'Not exactly. No. I guess anybody's history is for anyone who wants it. That's OK. I respect your asking for it.'

I can't think why that made me blush, but it did.

'So,' said Colombo. 'In the Second World War, Hy Brasil, or rather, the British colony of Frisland, was in a critical strategic position. The garrisons moved straight in in '39: Brits, Canadians, Anzacs. This place was a supply base and static aircraft carrier for six years. You can hardly walk half a mile along our coasts without tripping over old gun emplacements.'

'I've looked at the ones round the harbour in St Brandons.'

'Yes. Baskerville wants those done up as a museum piece. I think we'd do better to clear away the lot and dump all that concrete in the sea. Anyway, no one's ever found the money to do either, so there's no point arguing. So. It's the end of the war, and things are changing fast in the North Atlantic. Independent Iceland: 1944. Faroe, semi-independence from Denmark: 1948. Newfoundland becomes a province of Canada: 1949. Hy Brasil has been a British colony since the Brits captured it in 1812. The Brits held on to it like grim death against France first and then the United States, and in 1816 the Treaty of Vienna gave it to them on a bit of paper. So now it's 1946, and Hy Brasil's been British for a hundred and forty years. A few folk have objected now and then: the revolution didn't quite happen in 1831, it was easily quashed in 1848, and two executions did the trick in 1871. But in 1946 things look serious. The Independence Party has a majority in the Assembly. Two shots are fired at Sandy Arbuthnot, the High Commissioner, as he leaves his Residence in an open Rolls, and for once the little colony of Frisland hits the headlines in London. Change begins to seem almost possible.

'Negotiations are under way. Students from the University of the Hesperides start a riot. A British soldier is wounded. The student ringleader, a Classics graduate born in Dorrado who is writing a thesis on the Persian Wars, is arrested. His name: James Hook. He's expelled from the university and remanded in custody. More riots. Hook is tried and released for lack of evidence.

'1947. Hook stands as candidate for the Independence Party in Dorrado, and is elected with an overwhelming majority. Things are moving fast. We set up an Iceland Commission, who come back from their research trip with a glowing report on the success of a new nation that has plenty of fish and less than a quarter of a million citizens. The issue is debated hotly in the Assembly. And we're winning, we're almost winning. There's a competition to produce a logo for a flag for a new country, the smallest nation in the world. It's won by a high school student called Penelope Hawkins. It's a motif taken from the rod and crescent, the only Pictish carved rock in Hy Brasil, the single proof we have that the Irish ever really came. But she's made it so it could be a diagram of a man standing on an island that turns out to be a whale. It's our history and our saint and our emblem of a possible future all in one. We resurrect an old name too, the one that Brendan gave us, so they say. Hy Brasil.

'And then comes the backlash. A dossier is published on Hook, the twenty-four-year-old white-headed boy of the Independence Party. So he's a member of the CP? So he's in secret communication with the Kremlin? Or is he? Who put this together? Suddenly there're reds everywhere. Lift the covers off the Independence Party and underneath it's crawling with them. It's a Communist plot. Or is it? Who said? Where did all this evidence come from?

'But it's in all the London papers, so it must be true. The story's out, and Hook's back in the town jail. But this time he doesn't hang about. One morning there he isn't. Where did he go? We know where he went first, because nine months later Penelope Hawkins turns up at St Bride's Maternity Hospital in St Brandons, a week after she wins the Fine Arts Scholarship endowed by the Pelea Fund, and what does she do? She gives birth to a nine-pound boy and registers him the next day as Brendan Hook. What's this got to do with national politics, you ask? I can only say, we're a small country, and small things matter here.

'So do large ones. This is 1948 and there's a very large matter looming, which is about to alter everything. It's NATO. Incidentally, there's a minor eruption of Mount Brasil the same year. That's by the by. Yes, NATO. Hook's out of the picture, tucked away in some Central American rainforest, and the Independents are riven with accusations and denials. Is this a plot? If so, whose? Consider this: November 1947: preliminary formation of the Atlantic command. There's a cold war settling over our sea. Only is it ours, or is it just someone else's battleground? If you get your pawns in the right position they can win the game for you. You don't hang around asking their permission. Pawn to king four. That's about the sum of it.'

'Pawn what? You've lost me.'

'Sorry. Put it this way.' Colombo was striding up and down in front of me, so his shadow kept falling across my face – light, dark, light, dark – flicking across my half-closed eyelids. 'The West must be defended. The maximum bombing range of the new nuclear B29 is one thousand seven hundred and seventeen miles. The Brits happen to own a few insignificant little islands, halfway between Europe and Fort Norfolk, Virginia. Very handy. Especially as Britain and the USA are secretly fighting it out as to who's going to get the lion's command of the North Atlantic. The Americans reckon they should run the whole show, and the Brits say – wait while I remember – that letting the Yanks just take over would be 'unacceptable to the United Kingdom'.

'So. During the war the Brits controlled the seas round us down to 42°, and south from there it was over to the Yanks. And of course in 1948 we have the Canadians wanting a say too. So the latest idea is to divide the ocean into three parts, like Gaul.

'The Brits don't have much going for them. They won the war, didn't they? So they're broke. It's Marshall versus Bevan and he who pays the piper calls the tune. Only the Brits have this one little pawn. A little pawn in the middle of the board, sitting right on the boundary of the proposed new carve up. Independence? You must be bloody joking. Communist infiltration? No chance! April 1949. The Treaty's signed. And the Independence Party of Hy Brasil collapses into ruin and oblivion. You can't blame anybody, of course. I mean, the world must be saved, even if it's sometimes tough on the little chaps.'

'Did everyone in Hy Brasil think like you do?'

'No one in Hy Brasil agrees about anything. We're an independent nation, every one of us. Have you had enough? Shall I go on?'

'Go on.'

'I'll skip nine years. Nine years during which the Brits and the Yanks argued endlessly about boundaries. Always trying to carve up the sea. Canute versus Moses. Which would you put your money on? They kept drawing new straight lines, and every time there were these little islands in the middle, always getting in the way. We were an occupied country, you know. A third of the population was NATO personnel. The airport you came into, that used to be NATO. It's the only place flat enough for a landing strip apart from the cricket pitches, which are sacrosanct, so we couldn't even have a civil air service. All flights courtesy of NATO. Same with St Brandons harbour. Somehow the fishing fleet managed to squeeze itself in around the edges. The only thing they didn't do was nuclear testing, because it might have been dangerous for the NATO guys. So there's something for the natives to be grateful for. Of course we were a prime Soviet target. Another plus. The bunker on Mount Ailbe was only for military personnel, so at least we could look forward to a quick ending. Better than a nuclear winter, I reckon.'

'But Colombo,' I couldn't help saying, 'it's too simple just to say it's the Brits. We'd have been blown to bits even before you were. You know where my parents met?'

He looked round at me as if he had forgotten who I was. 'Your parents? What about them?'

'They met on a CND march in Aldermaston in 1969.'

'Good,' said Colombo. 'I'm glad they met, or you wouldn't be here now.'

'Thank you. But what I'm trying to say to you is you can't just blame a whole nation. It's too simple.'

'History is always too simple. What do you expect?'

'That sounds like a very abridged edition of *War and Peace*.'

'Thank you. I have a great admiration for Tolstoy. Shall I go on?'

'Please.'

'No,' said Colombo, stopping suddenly and stretching himself, so that his t-shirt came away from his jeans and I could see the dark hairs on his stomach. 'I've got a better idea. I want you to meet my godmother. She can tell you more than I can. She lives in the hills just south of Dorrado. We can go there now.'

'OK.' I got up slowly and followed him back to the car.

We lurched through the potholes back to the paved road, where we took a hairpin bend at a 20° angle, and turned left. As we curved inland and began to rise, I recognised the place. Maybe I once dreamt it, maybe it was a touch of my own west country in this alien island, maybe I was infected for a moment by another consciousness, who knows what? But the curve of the road was familiar to me as the lines on the palm of my own hand. A potholed gravel road rising among birches and aspen trees. I hadn't expected so many trees would grow in Hy Brasil, but we were a couple of miles inland now. The valley was sheltered on three sides, narrowing as it rose. We took the next corner in second, and the wheels on my side ground on loose gravel. Now I could see right over the valley. Slopes curtained with trees fell and vanished into rolling cloud. St Brandons was lost in the mist to the east of us, and there was nothing left of the sea but the faint tang of salt blowing in the open window. The road curved again, with that same tantalising familiarity. I knew the fork in it; I even knew what the red-and-white sign would say before I could read it:

ROAD CLOSED: DIVERSION
ESTRADA IMPEDIDA: DESVIO

'Hell and damnation,' said Colombo. He braked abruptly and the car skidded to a halt, its nose almost touching the sign. One of the many wayside shrines in Hy Brasil stood just above the turning. Under the wooden eaves a blue-robed virgin clasped a fat Caucasian baby. There were fresh hyacinths at her feet. I read the notice again. ROAD CLOSED. DIVERSION. White letters on a red background. The metal was slightly rusted, the frame held down by a couple of soggy sandbags. As I watched, the letters pulsated gently but insistently. There was a hollow feeling behind my eyes, and suddenly I was too tired to think. I was here. I had my first scoop: a real native with a godmother, who also happened to be a journalist himself. But the sun had gone in suddenly, and we were inland, hemmed in by precipices. There were swarms of flies buzzing over puddles at the roadside, and scraps of cloud clinging to the treetops.

'Nonsense!' said Colombo, and jerked his poor old car into first again. 'Red tape and foolishness. Hold tight!'

We shot between the sign and the roadside. I looked from the passenger window on to the tree canopy forty feet below. When I opened my eyes again the trees were gone. The mist lay like a bleached eiderdown below us. The road ended in a pile of boulders, but no, we'd swung a hundred and sixty degrees and against my window I saw a basalt cliff. I'd just got used to that when we swung again, and there was the eiderdown much lower now. In between was the jaggedy road and steep green slopes strewn with boulders. When next I opened my eyes we were high on a ridge where silver pools gleamed under a pale coin of a sun. The weather had changed so fast I felt disorientated. I turned away, and looked north. Delicately outlined through the cloud I saw a mountain, symmetrical and steep, with a cone at the top of it as cool and harmonious as a Japanese brush painting.

'Mount Brasil.'

It looked like a picture postcard of itself. I hadn't bought any because I don't like sending people images of what I haven't seen yet. It was white from the waist up, and like Ariel it rode on the curl'd clouds, but not in flame or lightning, just cool and watercoloured, as if it weren't made of earth at all and didn't know what weather was. That was a deception too, I knew. 'It doesn't look active,' I remarked.

'Try walking on it.'

'Oh?'

'You feel the heat through your boots. Barefoot you'd burn. The springs are boiling. You can see the steam rising twenty miles away sometimes. If the wind were southerly you'd get the whiff of sulphur now. The last significant eruption was 1958.'

'The same year as the Revolution?'

'That's right. The bass note for our *coup d'état* was a subterranean harmonic tremor. Quite piquant, when you think about it. In fact '57 to '58 was an unstable year along the whole Atlantic Ridge. Same in the Azores. In September '57 there was such a big eruption they actually evacuated Dorrado, but it turned out OK. After three weeks the lava just stopped and everyone went home. Nothing was damaged, but the hot spring that fed the fountain in the market square had vanished, and they had to make a culvert from the Dorrado river. So it's cold water in the fountain now, which is a pity. I'm told on winter mornings it was quite a sight, steaming away in the middle of the village like a domesticated dragon. My sister says it's one of her earliest memories. In the Azores they weren't so lucky.'

'And Mount Brasil could still go up any time?'

Colombo shrugged. 'Or you could get run over by the 227 bus in St Brandons Square. The chances are about equal, within the year, say. We could bet if you like.'

'So when did it last erupt?' I couldn't take my eyes from that perfect cone. It looked like something out of Euclid.

'1981, '83, '87, '92, '96.'

'How come there's anything left then?'

'Oh, those were only little eruptions. Just big enough to get recorded. You'll have to go to the Pele Centre – the volcanic observatory down at Mount Prosper. The process is continuous really. Until we get to the big one.'

'And when's that?'

'That's serious gambling. Which is illegal here, didn't you know?'

'Seriously?'

'Quite seriously. So are prostitution, spirits and hard drugs. You can grow and use your own cannabis but it's illegal to buy or sell any, including the seeds. We have vineyards, of course, and our apple orchards produce the best cider in the world. But in 1982 two men were deported for operating a still. The tax on tobacco is two hundred per cent.'

I was still staring at the volcano. 'How far away can you see it from?'

'Two hundred miles in totally clear weather, that is to say, not usually. From the sea it sometimes floats on the clouds, the way it is now. Before it was charted, the early sailors thought it was a vision of heaven, the promised land of Ailbe. At least, they did when it looked like it does now. But when it was smoke and flame and ashes they said this place was the gateway to hell.'

'A bit of a paradox.'

'Not at all. The gate of hell lies at the foot of the throne of God; that's how Lucifer fell. You see, I know your English poets better than you do.'

'But one can climb it?'

'Don't go by yourself. It's tough. My friend Ishmael used to do tours occasionally. He might take you up sometime.'

The road dipped down from the pass as abruptly as it had gained it. The ridge coiled in a semicircle between us and Mount Brasil, green peaks rising out of the mist like fangs. There was something reptilian about it. I thought of the dinosaur's footprints they found on the coast of Dorset, which you can see in a glass case in the museum at Lyme. It occurred to me that no smoke rose out of the volcano, and that in my previous imaginings I had always seen it spurting out fumes like an autumn bonfire. The island was turning out different from the way I'd pictured it, and I had a disconcerting feeling that my project was not quite under my control.

'Penny for them?'

'Not worth a penny,' I said. 'They're all questions.'

'Ask away.'

'All right. How come there are two hundred and twenty-seven buses on an island roughly eighty miles by twenty?'

'Eh?' It took him a moment, then he laughed. 'Oh, that. We have one regular bus route, which circumnavigates St Brandons, goes ten miles down the coast one way, and three miles up the other until the road stops. It started running in 1935, and the first bus was shipped over from London, ex-LCC standard single-decker red bus stock. On the front it had written: *Crystal Palace Penge Beckenham Shortlands Bromley Market Bickley Chislehurst Stn Chislehurst War Memorial.* That particular bus came off the road in the sixties. Tommy Zakis lives in it now, just behind the old herring station at Port o' Frisland. But the number stuck. On this island 227 is the word for bus. Are you ready to go on?'

The road dog-legged over the edge of the ridge, and just before it plunged down there was another view that took my breath away, over the bite-shaped bay of Dorrado and the shining islands that lay to the west of Hy Brasil. I clung to the seatbelt to hold myself steady while I gazed and gazed. We were out of the mist and into spring sunshine again. I felt a prickling at my eyelids and my throat felt tight. I hadn't thought Hy Brasil would do this to me. I told myself it was just a place, and swallowed.

'Tell me about your godmother.'

'Penelope? She was my mother's best friend and a remarkable woman. She's the President's wife, officially, but she never does anything official. He visits her at weekends.'

'You mean *that* Penelope? She's your godmother?'

'And a very good one too. She and my parents were neighbours in Dorrado before I was born. My Papa was the Mayda ferryman. Things were a lot different then. Not much money about. After the Revolution she and Hook moved into the house we're going to now.'

'So you must know her son? Hasn't he just written a book?'

'Brendan? Of course I know him. When I was little he was my hero. He's a yachtsman, you know that? He used to take me sailing.'

'I thought he was a philosopher.'

'Nothing like sailing alone for philosophy. Think of Slocum. But Brendan's in America now.'

'So what happened after Hook left in '48?'

'To Penelope? Nothing. She brought up Brendan in Dorrado by herself for ten years. Everyone said Hook was gone for good, but she refused to believe it. My Mamma says she could have had any man she wanted, but she refused them all, and brought her boy up for ten years in the faith that his father would come home.' Colombo negotiated a hairpin bend with a casual twist of the wheel. 'She specialises in textiles,' he added, 'She used to do a lot of weaving.'

*　　*　　*

(I'm tired, it's very late, I've only two pages left in this notebook, and I'm not halfway through the day yet. It's no use doing sums like that or I'll start feeling like Tristram Shandy. Instead I'm going to skip on to part of the conversation we had at tea.)

Penelope said the best thing about the revolution is that no one had died for it. She said it was a hideous and misguided thing to die for one's native land. We talked about wars, and how Hy Brasil had always been a strategic outpost in someone else's war, but no battle had actually been fought on it.

'I suppose it's the same where I come from,' I said. 'We haven't had a war since 1685. The battle of Sedgemoor was the last pitched battle to be fought on English soil.'

They both looked at me. 'But you've had a civil war going on for the past thirty years!' burst out Colombo.

I felt so embarrassed, I almost said, 'I forgot', but decided that would sound too crass. I began, 'But that's on another . . .' then realised this sounded even worse, so I shut up.

No one else said anything either. I found Penelope oddly intimidating, in spite of her quiet brown eyes and soft voice. The other silly thing was that I'd forgotten she would be old. Colombo's story had been about a young woman, and now this elderly person with short white hair and skin like a winter apple disconcerted me. I began to blush, and the more I tried not to, the redder I got.

'My grandmother was from England,' said Penelope gently, as if that's what we'd been talking about. 'Have some more fruit cake. The thing I enjoyed most when I visited was the gardens. Hidcote, Blenheim, Sissinghurst. So lovely. I try to emulate Gertrude Jekyll, not that it's practical nowadays. I would like to show you my herbaceous border. You must come again in June or July. But I hope I'll see you before that.'

'Penny, I want you to tell her about '58.'

'Oh my dear, I'm not the one to ask. It's all so long ago.'

'But you've got the scrapbooks.'

'I only show photos of my grandchildren. Sidony's too young to be interested in those. You can show her anything in the library yourself if you want to.'

'She pretends to be octogenarian,' Colombo said, addressing me. 'It's all a front. Ignore it.'

'Nonsense,' said Penny. 'Very well, Sidony. I'm to tell you what happened here in 1958. It's quite simple. My husband, whom I'd not seen for ten years, although I'd received six unsigned postcards during his absence, knocked on my door in Dorrado one February night and asked me to supply food to an expeditionary force which he had just landed on Brentness. Have you seen Brentness?'

'No.'

'It's a lava field. What the Icelanders call "hraun". I was surprised to see Jim. The rumour was that he was dead, which I didn't believe, because I'd asked him to make sure I knew, if he died before we met again. Since I'd heard nothing, I was still expecting him, but not in the middle of a snowstorm. The fifties were austere times, and there wasn't a lot of food in Dorrado but we managed to scrounge what we needed. Jim had twelve men with him when he landed. We soon found more men. We'd been a NATO base for quite long enough.

'You can't beat NATO with their own weapons. It wasn't an army we needed, it was a plan. Jim was in his element. Just four men took the base on April 10th, and held it. Jack Honeyman was a plumber, you see, that was the key to the whole thing. I remember that white van of his, and the name on the side, *John Honeyman: Plumbing and Drainage Expert*. Partly luck, of course, but such a clever idea when you think about it. The others were there to back them up from outside, but their real weapon was the one NATO had forged itself. With his finger hovering over the button, so to speak, Jim had the White House, Westminster, and Geneva literally on a line. They talked. They didn't have much choice.'

'Tell her how they took the base, Penny.'

'Sweetheart, I wasn't there. There're two men left who could tell Sidony the whole story first-hand. They'd both be only too happy to do so. Why don't you bring her over one Saturday evening when Jim is here?'

'Could she do that? You're sure Jim wouldn't mind? I know he avoids foreign writers if he possibly can.'

'Sweetheart, let's be frank. Most foreign writers who come to Hy Brasil are not young, beautiful and female. I think he'd enjoy meeting her very much.'

It dawned on me they were talking about the President, and I felt overwhelmed. I knew this was a small and aggressively democratic country, but this was quite beyond my expectations. But Colombo was saying to me, 'That would be just what you want, wouldn't it, Sidony? Meet the man himself.' I managed to say thank you to Penelope as if hobnobbing with the head of a nation who was also a legendary hero of the left was quite a commonplace way for me to spend a Saturday night.

'I doubt if I'd be able to bring you,' Colombo was saying. 'I'm usually tied up on Saturdays. But that doesn't matter. Penny, won't you tell her your version now anyway?'

'My dear boy, what am I supposed to do? Burst into an aria? Sidony, m'dear,' she said, turning to me. 'It was a *sensible* revolution. Tactics, not reprisals. Four men took the base by surprise – Jim will tell you how they worked it. It was the mountain that gave them their chance. They say Ailbe is stable, but there's always movement under the surface. They had terrible trouble with the drains in there. The pipes kept breaking and then the lavatories would back up, too awful to contemplate. I'm so glad it's never happened to me. NATO were supposed to use their own personnel for everything, but no one in Hy Brasil knew more about dealing with sewage in a seismically sensitive area than Jack did, and I think those poor chaps in there must have been getting pretty desperate. Anyway, the upshot was that the four got in – Jim will so enjoy telling you how – and seized control of weapons that could have blown the whole world to atoms. They announced to the world, on radio and television – of course, that was quite a new factor in a revolution then – that all they wanted was to be an independent nation again. After the first shock the whole thing was done with great decorum. They appealed to the United Nations, and everything was arranged through a Treaty. They even agreed to keep a token NATO presence here, rent-free.

'Hy Brasil has no army and no defence policy. We remain a base for maritime patrol aircraft from the USA, and there're about two hundred NATO personnel, including families, still on the island. There's a USA admiral in charge. The base employs about fifty islanders, and that's better than a slap in the face with a wet fish, these days. We read all this propaganda about Hy Brasil being a nuclear-free country. It's extraordinary what people believe when they wish to. It's Jim's official line, of course. That, and up until '89, no truck with Moscow. Jim was always a realist. I was glad to have him back, of course, but one changes. One doesn't always realise until too late how much one has changed.'

Later, in the pub, Colombo explained to me that marital fidelity was not the President's strong point. I felt sorry for Penelope, but the place we were in cheered me up. The bar at the Red Herring is of polished oak, salvaged from His Majesty's ship of the line *The Irrepressible* which foundered on Tegid Voel at the mouth of Dorrado Bay in 1779. If the ship had got as far as the rebellious colonies which were its destination, it would probably not have changed anything in the long run. There were five survivors, including the Bo'sun, Hosea Honeyman. He never returned to his native Porlock; churchyards of all denominations in Dorrado, Lyonsness and Ogg's Cove contain his descendents, and his name still lives in the Electoral Roll, the Internal Revenue files, and the records of the Frisland Bank.

The present landlord, Ernest, inherited the Red Herring from his mother, and he likes talking about its history. He looks just the way a landlord ought to do. He wears a leather waist-coat, over which his beard flows down to the second tortoiseshell button. His white hair reaches to his massive shoulders. His shirtsleeves are rolled to the elbow, displaying muscular fore-arms tastefully tattooed with an anchor to port and a red rose to starboard. He was in the middle of explaining to me how he comes of a long line of Swiss pastors, and how his grandfather Ernest had been shipwrecked as a boy and grown up on a tropical island, when the door opened and a draught of cold air hit my back. The door shut with a bang.

'Oh God,' Colombo muttered, so only Ernest and I could hear him. 'It's Olly West.'

A tall man strode up to the bar. He wore wellingtons, a dirty waxed jacket and a hat with ear flaps. 'Evening Ernest, evening Colombo.' His voice was unexpectedly high. 'One Mars Bar please.' He laid half a crown on the counter.

'Two and sevenpence ha'penny,' said Ernest.

'No! And they seem to get smaller all the time.' Olly fished in his pocket and counted out three more coins. 'Quiet tonight?'

'Uh-huh.'

'It'll rain by seven. There's a depression moving up from the Azores. How nice to see you, Colombo. I know your mother misses you when you don't visit Dorrado for weeks at a time. I can only give you five minutes though. There's a meeting of the Mayda Trust tonight.'

'You're not on the Mayda Trust, are you?' asked Colombo, frowning. 'I thought you were one of its chief beneficiaries?'

'No, no. You're referring to the Pele Centre having received a grant. *I'm* not the Pele Centre. As a private individual I'm quite eligible to serve on the Committee. I was co-opted last month. They're using my expertise in fundraising; I can give them a great deal of advice from my experience setting up the Pele Centre. I'm working closely with Baskerville, of course. This year is the crucial period, with the forty-year celebrations coming up in 1998. We have to make some very important decisions. Tonight we're discussing grants for Arts projects. We need to have as many venues as possible next year. We expect up to twenty thousand visitors.'

'Please,' I interrupted, 'what's the Pele Centre? Is it an Arts project?'

I don't think Olly saw me; I don't suppose he's deliberately rude. 'I can help them on the administrative side,' he went on telling Colombo. 'It's a case of judging the projects on their merits. We have to think about achieving the correct balance. Anyway, I'm sorry to have to tear myself away. It would have been delightful to spend the evening with you. I must apologise.'

As soon as he'd shut the door behind him, Colombo burst out, 'What the hell's he doing on the Mayda Trust? It was supposed to be Ishmael. Ernest, you thought they'd appoint Ishmael, didn't you? That man wouldn't know a viable Arts project if it fell on his head. He got himself co-opted on to the Committee when we did the *In the Wake of Pytheas* exhibition. I don't know what he thought he was doing there; it turned out he hadn't even heard of Brendan's *Navigatio*. That man's never read a book in his life. And what's the betting his wretched volcano centre gets another whacking grant from the Mayda Trust next year?'

'I wouldn't worry,' said Ernest. 'I shouldn't think he and Baskerville will manage to work together for long.' He winked at Colombo. 'I thought Tidesman did a good piece on the Pele Centre, about that time Olly predicted a major eruption, had all the children sent home at dinner time, told the government to declare a state of emergency, and it turned out to be a small thunderstorm. I seem to remember Tidesman was quite gleeful in the way he covered that.'

Colombo didn't smile. 'But what I want to know is, why does the government still give him grants all the time, and acquiesce in him having a complete monopoly? It's not just immoral. It's downright dangerous. You know Olly had Allardyce working there? – Allardyce came back from Japan specially, gave up his job and everything – well Allardyce couldn't stay at the Pele Centre. He said West just dashes off to the beach all the time to build his breakwaters, and never delegates anything – never tells anyone what's going on. And there's Allardyce, who's worked everywhere from Mauna Loa to Myvatn, having to ask if he can have ten and sixpence out of the petty cash to buy a new stapler. That's what he resigned over. And all this low-tech monitoring – sure it's a good idea, but Olly cribbed all that from the Cascades Volcano Laboratory at Mount St Helen's. Does he acknowledge his sources? Does he hell! What I want to know is, how the hell did West get government funding in the first place?'

'Because he proposed the volcano observatory,' said Ernest. 'You know that. We needed a monitoring system, and he came up with the plans. No one else did. We've been over all this before. The young lady's glass is empty, Colombo.'

Colombo looked round at me and grinned suddenly. 'I'm sorry, I forgot about you. Will you have another, and then I'll take you back to town?'

SIX

A NEW FIFTEEN-FOOT Boston whaler lay to the west of Despair. The nesting season was at its height. There were puffins at the top of the cliffs, fulmars and kittiwakes lined the ledges, and right down at the sea's edge a rock full of black cormorants was washed by a gentle swell. Air and water were full of birds, their calls echoing to and fro between the rocks. Down in the boat, tossing about under the crowded lime-streaked cliffs, it was hard to make oneself heard, hard even to think.

It was the first really hot day, and Jared's wetsuit felt heavy and uncomfortable, in spite of the offshore breeze. He fastened his weight belt, and waited while Ishmael finished struggling into the bottom half of his suit. It was still early in the season, and the sea was as cold as it had been two months ago. It was more cramped than usual doing everything at sea with an extra person in the boat. If they were to do this job seriously there was no getting away from the fact that they had to have a proper divers' boat. Per was in the stern at the tiller, and today they'd brought along the photographer as well. Jared didn't really see the point of taking photos on the surface: all the interesting work was below, but he hadn't objected. Bringing Nesta Kirwan today might end up getting them the publicity they needed. It was worth the inconvenience of having her along, and she wasn't being at all demanding. She sat in the bows with her camera, small and self-contained, her equipment neatly stowed in a waterproof black bag. She'd taken several pictures on the way out from Ferdy's Landing but she hadn't asked anyone to do anything out of the ordinary. Jared had said rather ungraciously, when he'd called her from Ishmael's office, that they'd have no time to make any detours, or pose for her, or anything like that. He'd had an idea she was laughing at him then, at the other end of the line, but certainly since she'd joined them this morning she hadn't got in anyone's way at all. As it happened, in the end she'd got him to agree to all the detours she wanted, but he was scarcely aware of having been persuaded.

While they were getting ready she took several more pictures, and remarked that Jared and Ishmael complemented each other nicely. 'One black, one white, do you mean?' said Ishmael. 'Or one old, one young? Or are you just saying I look like a sensible man?'

'You don't look in the least old, and I'm sure Jared has his own kind of sense.'

'Forty this year,' said Ishmael. 'Maybe you'd do better to keep your film for the wee white fellow.'

'Huh,' said Jared.

Ishmael strapped on his belt and reached for his tank, and Jared heaved his own vest and tank over his head on to his back. As he was checking his regulator hoses a kittiwake with a fish screamed over him and suddenly his suit was spattered with fresh guano. Ishmael said something he didn't catch. Jared looked up, and grinned, and Kirwan clicked the shutter. 'Christ,' Jared said, buckling his vest, 'I feel like a bloody film star.' She laughed at him, and lowered her camera.

The tank was heavy on his back. He caught the line from the regulator on the top of the tank, and said to Kirwan just before he put in the mouthpiece, 'OK then? We'll be half an hour. Nothing else before we go?' She shook her head and smiled at him.

Jared slithered from the seat to the gunwale, awkward with the extra weight he was carrying. He strapped the finds bag to his belt, and put on his fins. Ishmael, on the port side, was doing the same. Jared spat in his mask, rubbed it round and washed it out in the sea behind him. He'd forgotten he was having his picture taken; his mind was already ninety-two feet down. Ishmael picked up his underwater camera from the bottom of the boat, and hung it carefully round his neck, under the regulator hoses. His movements were slower than Jared's, deliberate and careful. He inserted his mouthpiece and washed out his mask, and finally gave Jared a thumbs up sign: 'ready'. Jared thumbed back to him, held on his mask with one hand, and flipped neatly backwards over the side.

As soon as the sound of the splash had cleared he could hear the slow echo of the ocean moving rhythmically against the foundations of Despair. He kicked down out of the surface current and into still water. As he breathed in, he could hear his own breath like the sea itself inside his head, then the rich gurgling sound as he breathed out, and the bright shapes of the bubbles going up in a shoal in front of his mask. His suit pressed in on him as he dropped head down for the bottom. The water began to seep in, cold at first, crawling over his skin like little fingers. It was always chilly here from the upwelling under the cliff. The water grew dim. In front of his eyes it was dark green, framed by the black edge of the mask. Fishes flickered past like shadows, a shoal parting round him like water round a rock in the river, then flowing on. Jared switched on his torch and swam cautiously into the dark, while his eyes adjusted. The blackness ahead was the cliff, the hidden roots of the island of Despair. A jagged promontory ran westward then plunged into deep water. Jared turned and peered upwards into the filtered sea-green light.

The vague light up above turned into a shadow, turned into a moving shape, turned into Ishmael, swam right up, and signed to him.

OK?

OK.

Over the spine of the promontory that coiled away into the dark like a dragon's back. Over the black rock shapes that lumped themselves around the skerry hidden up above, down into a shadowed gorge that opened out into a hidden pocket of clear water. Below them was the hollow with the patch of shell sand at one end, intersected with steel grid posts. There were the green encrusted shapes of the cannon spilled among the rocks. And there right at the back of the hollow was the one square of grid in place around the sample excavation site. Jared had decided to start with an area that took both the edge of the shell sand, and part of one of the seaweed-covered lava fissures that led down into it. They swam down over it, the beams from two torches piercing the water a little way ahead. It was complex work to do under water, head down. To Jared it was a far more delicate art than excavation on land, which he'd tried when he was at college, and found clumsy. On land your whole body got in the way, messing up the site, and you had to scrape your way laboriously into the past. Here you could hover over the wreck like an industrious spirit, without even touching: a gentle fanning motion would shift the soft sand aside. But it was harder to concentrate, and time was limited.

Per took out his pipe and tobacco pouch and began to fill the pipe methodically, pressing the tobacco down in neat layers with his thumb. He turned his back to the breeze and cupped his hands around the lighter, more out of habit than necessity, for there was hardly a whiff of a wind. There was a short choppy swell, however, which sent occasional handfuls of spray over the seaward side of the boat. Per moved over to the dry side and sat on the gunwale. Nesta, who found it harder to ignore the uncomfortable tossing, took her mind off it by taking several close-up portraits of him. He pretended not to notice. Very high up in the northwest little streaks of cloud were forming; otherwise the sky was as blue as milkwort above the circling birds. The sea was strewn with feathers, and the smell of the birds wafted down to them from the shadowed cliffs. 'It's a day and a bit,' said Per.

'It certainly is,' said Kirwan. 'You've never gone down diving, Per?'

'Not me,' said Per. 'Not but what I wouldn't like to see the *Cortes* where she lies. I never learned to swim. Too late now.'

'It's never too late,' said Kirwan firmly as she screwed on a different filter. 'If the project goes ahead, though, you'll go on working with them?'

'Uh-huh,' said Per. 'He knows his stuff, young Jared. And Ishmael's a good man to work with. Always was.'

'You've worked with him before?'

'I crewed for him sometimes after Jared went away, before he got full time into this computer thing. And I helped him with the old house at Ferdy's Landing. You've not been in there since he did it up?'

'Only in the kitchen.'

'You should look around next time you're there. It's a pleasure to see now, all new timber and fresh paint, and clean inside as a scoured out washtub.'

'I can believe that.' Kirwan was unlikely to ask Ishmael for a tour of his house. She liked the Pereiras, but found their family life so thoroughly exemplary that she always went away feeling depressed. She said as much to Per, who disagreed. He told her that he and Ishmael had both been elders of the Lyonsness Presbyterian Congregation since 1985, and he'd never known Ishmael to be judgmental about anybody. Also, the house at Ferdy's Landing was the only place he, Per, would ever eat dinner away from his own home. The food was good but sometimes a bit fancy, he said, no doubt because Anna Pereira was the granddaughter of Greek immigrants who'd disembarked on impulse in Hy Brasil, on their way to Ellis Island back before the First World War. Apparently from their ship the resin-scented hills above Dorrado had reminded them of their own Sporades. But the three girls took after Ishmael. If you went down to Ferdy's landing any time when school was out you'd find them down by the shore, each with a cloud of wild hair, patched jeans and muddy boots, always with their hands dirty and some new project on hand. Ishmael's children were lucky, though, to belong to a family, in these degenerate days, which was all that a family should be.

'Thank God I never had children,' said Kirwan. 'I'm sure no one would have said that mine were lucky, in that case.'

The sand gleamed white in the torchlight, and as Jared fanned the water it shifted into new wave-like patterns. He suspected he was about a yard out of radius of the wreck itself, south-west of the wood from the hull. Maybe this way there'd be nothing more. He glanced at his watch. Ten minutes gone. He was almost up to the grid boundary. Just time to work right into the corner, confirm that it was off-site. Jared stirred the sand a little harder.

Something dark. A curved edge. Not iron. Not rusted. Experienced as he was, he almost held his breath, and had to remember not to. Very gently he washed the sand away. A regular curve began to emerge, like part of a circle. He touched it with his finger. Slippery-smooth: too smooth for stone, or clay. Fluted, like a shell. He fanned the water just enough to brush away the sand. A half-circle now, about three inches across. Black in this light, but that meant nothing. Smooth and flat on one side, fluted on the other, rising into a tight ring. A ring, then something more. A curved shape: a bowl, a cup maybe. It wasn't clay or pewter. Glass? The sand was very loose. Glass, if it had been flung overboard into deep water at first impact, could possibly have drifted down and sunk slowly into its soft bed, so much safer than ashore. Safe for nearly four hundred years. There was a whole outline now. It took on meaning. A glass bowl with straight sides, a wide circular rim, and a thick ring at the bottom, mounted on a fluted base. Unbroken, so far. Such things had happened: whole shiploads of ancient amphorae right through to bone china from the Titanic, the most fragile artefacts surviving whole when iron and bone had disintegrated and gone back to nothing. He fanned the sand away. The goblet lay, whole and lovely, just as it had fallen, untouched by time or tempest.

There was a touch on his shoulder, and he looked round. Jared couldn't see Ishmael's face, but he could read his reaction from his sudden stillness. Then Ishmael pointed to his camera. Jared wriggled back as far as he could go, out of the way, until his tanks bumped against rock. Ishmael swam forward, head down, until the lens was about a foot away from the find. A muted flash followed. Then another.

Move round. I'll take one from where you are.

Jared slipped over Ishmael's head, and looked down from above as Ishmael adjusted the focus. Another flash.

Ishmael put away his camera and tapped his watch. Five minutes.

I'm going to make a record. Then I can lift it.

Not much time.

OK.

Jared took his plastic notepad and a pencil from his belt, and an ordinary plastic ruler. He swam down and measured. Six and a quarter inches from one edge of the grid. Thirteen and a half from the other edge. He did a quick sketch, and tucked it away.

Be quick.

OK.

He looked down on it one more time, spotlighted by his torch. Untouched and perfect, caught out of time, untrammelled by the sea. A black shape on white sand. It would never look like that again. Very carefully he reached down with both hands, and lifted it.

He swam up slowly, the goblet in the finds bag. The sea turned greener and brighter, and gradually light surrounded him. Then everything was white and birds were screaming. The swell jumped at him, splashing water in his face. He held on to the goblet inside its bag, to stop it being bashed against his weight belt. Then he trod water and looked, and there was the boat fifteen yards away, with Ishmael in between. Jared spat out the mouthpiece and breathed deep, put in the snorkel, and swam back to the boat.

'Of course,' said Per, 'When you think about young Jared, he wasn't so lucky either.'

'I liked Josie Honeyman,' said Kirwan. 'She managed as well as anyone could. It must have been hell.'

'A boy needs a father, and Jed didn't have one, not when it mattered.' Per breathed out a cloud of tobacco. There was a scuffle in the water a few feet away: a drowning puffin fighting for its life against a black-back. If young Jared wanted to do something useful up at the lighthouse he'd be out shooting some of those things. Counting gannets for a living was maybe as much use as most things in this world. It seemed a harmless ploy for the lad while he sorted out whatever was on his mind. Seemingly he'd got his education while he was abroad, and to his credit he'd done all that work up in Arctic waters. Diving for your living north of 60° was no joke. And now he was daft about this salvage business. Per had been reluctant when Jared asked him to join them as boatman, but he was getting drawn into the thing. Like every other boy in Hy Brasil Per had once had his own secret dream of finding Kidd's treasure. Well, no one ever had, and it was fifty years since he'd even thought of it, but when Jed came round and talked him into this new venture, he'd had to admit to himself he'd felt a flicker of the old flame.

'It's a pretty dangerous job, though, isn't it?' said Nesta. 'Though not so bad as mountaineering, I suppose. But if you're not attacked by a shark you'll probably get the bends – isn't that it? – and if it were me I'd be nervous all the time about not being able to breathe.'

'I reckon they have more trouble with jellyfish than sharks, though Jed did tell me what you do if a shark does attack you. And the other thing is OK at this depth if they come up slowly. If there were any trouble the Coastguards have one of those decompression chambers down at Port o' Frisland. Ten years ago the nearest one would be fourteen hundred miles or so away, which is maybe a bit too far if you were in a hurry.'

'God,' said Nesta. 'It sounds awful. And the sea, to my eyes, does not look enticing.'

Per took a long puff on his pipe. 'We've been out here on days a good deal worse than this,' he said. 'But Jed's all right. He's careful, and if things look like going wrong he thinks clearly. You might not guess it, if you'd never worked with him. But you can trust him.'

'I remember he was pretty wild in his teens.'

'That's by with,' said Per shortly. 'He always wanted a boat. When he was a little lad his Pappa used to take him out, putting crab pots off Brentness. If there hadn't been that business with Jack . . . I didn't believe a word of it then, and still less do I believe it now. Even if I did, what's a British agent anyway? The old word was Loyalist. I can think of at least two houses where they still have a portrait of the Queen on the wall. Jack never cheated anyone in his life, and that's a fact.'

'If I remember rightly, Tidesman wrote an article at the time saying the very same thing.'

'Ah well, that was Baskerville. He'd defend Jack in public, of course. They were two of the four, after all. Well, I grant you Tidesman was pretty frank, but I'm not sure what that amounts to. I'd give something to know what hand Baskerville did have in Jack's disappearance. He's very thick with the President, after all. Always has been.'

'But Tidesman's never quit on freedom of speech. He called it . . . what was it now . . . "an unjust ostracism". Jared's father had been ostracised, Tidesman said. But you don't think he really meant it?'

'He might have added, "and the one who really suffers for it is the boy", though no one mentioned that at the time of course, nor ever has. The Honeymans were always Episcopalians, of course, but I doubt if Jack's boy has darkened the door of a church since he was twelve years old. And Jack's never been heard of since. It's tough on a lad; easier if his father were dead really. Less of a betrayal.'

'The Mayda Trust should have given Jed his money, no reason why not, surely? It seems to me all he ever talks about is salvage, and it would do the country good to find treasure right now. But having to do it like this, not having the proper gear, must be terribly frustrating. He needs it to be a proper job.'

'He had a damn good job, and seemingly he threw it away, but maybe he just wanted to come home.'

Voices always seemed so strange just after the dive. The sun touched Jared's cold hands and he spread them out to the warmth, palms upwards. He'd changed the top half of the wetsuit for a shirt, and the sun was warm on his neck, but his fingertips were still white. Braced against the tossing of the boat, he very carefully picked up the goblet again from the safe nest he had made for it with his seajacket, inside the finds box.

It wasn't black at all: it was a delicate green, dark at the base, and translucent in the bowl, like seawater. He ran his fingers over it. The stem widened out into a fluted base; the shape under his fingers was like overlapping petals. There were circular ridges under the bowl of the goblet. And on the side of the bowl, he saw for the first time, a rounded bump.

'It's got a crest on it! Moulded into the glass! Oh, look at that! Just look at that.'

Ishmael shifted over to sit beside him, and looked over his shoulder. 'Oh my!'

'It's a ship, see! It's a galleon. Three masts, look, and under full sail. I mean, that's obviously what it's meant to be. Isn't it? Pressed into the glass. It's amazing. The odd thing is . . . Kirwan, look at this!'

Kirwan smiled at him. If the photo she'd just taken came out right, it would be one of her best. She'd picked the right day to come. Not just because she'd caught the moment when the first real treasure, still wet from the sea, hit the light, but also because she was almost sure that at the same time she'd captured a moment of pure exultation in Jared's face, an expression of such joy that it could never have lasted for more than an instant, whatever created it. The treasure found. She laughed to herself. It sounded like the caption to a Victorian oil painting of rural life.

Ishmael was saying, 'Pass me the chart again.' Per handed a rolled-up chart forward. 'You know what this means? There's your find. We can't assume now there's nothing beyond this edge. I mean, we can't possibly extend our area now, but you do see that if this is only six inches from the edge of the site, we can't think of that as a definitive boundary.'

'God, no. You'd want to go at least six feet further back. Well into the lava fissure, in fact. Excavate all the cracks in the rock. Christ, if only we had some *money*. We can't stop now! Not possibly!'

Ishmael was packing his camera into its bag again. 'No,' he said, after a pause. 'We won't stop now.'

He looked up and met Jared's eyes. Jared reddened. 'I wasn't thinking that you . . .'

'No,' said Ishmael. 'We'll talk about it when we get home. But you're right, Jed, we don't want to stop now.'

'But . . .'

'When we get home,' said Ishmael.

Kirwan was staring politely out to sea, implying that her thoughts at least were far away. Per coughed, and tapped the ash out of his pipe into the water. Ishmael rolled up the chart of the wreck. Jared turned the goblet round and round in his hands, apparently deep in thought.

'I've seen it before,' he said suddenly. He looked up and saw them all looking at him. 'This goblet. It's the same one: same fluted base, same crest. I *recognise* it.'

'Maybe you dreamed it,' said Ishmael.

Jared took this quite seriously. 'That's what I thought at

first. Down there I thought it was just the – you know – just the inevitability of the thing. You see, I *knew* as I was uncovering it what it was, before I saw it whole. As if I'd dreamed it all already. But in the light – it's hard to explain – I recognise it. And when I saw the crest properly, I knew I'd seen it before. Not in a dream, but really.'

'It's not impossible,' said Ishmael mildly. 'There's plenty of things in Hy Brasil they say came ashore from the *Cortes*. They'd have needed more than one wine goblet, I imagine.'

'If everything that's said to be off the *Cortes* really had come from there,' remarked Kirwan, 'It would have to have been about the size of *QE2*.'

'That's right,' said Per. 'Plenty of old stuff about. You used to be up at Ravnscar a lot too, when you were a lad. The old man would have had stacks of antique glasses up there. No doubt but what it'll remind you of some of them.'

'No,' said Jared obstinately. 'It was one just like this. And you're right; it was supposed to have come ashore. You saying that reminded me. It was Nicky's. Nicky had it at Ferdy's Landing. He used it to keep matches in, on the mantelpiece. It wasn't just a bit like this one, it was the spit of it. It had the same crest on it: a galleon under sail. Nicky always said that was the *Cortes*.'

'Could well be,' said Ishmael. 'Why don't you find it? Take it up to the museum and let Baskerville look at them together.'

Jared stared at him. 'But I don't know where it is! I've not seen it since . . . since thirteen years ago. I don't know what they did with any of Nicky's things.'

'Presumably everything was left in the house,' said Kirwan. 'You didn't find any Spanish goblets when you moved into Ferdy's Landing, did you, Ishmael?'

'No.'

'So Nicky Hawkins had one like that?' said Per. 'Fancy that, now.'

'Might it still be lying about somewhere at Ferdy's Landing? Hidden away, maybe?' asked Kirwan.

All three men shook their heads. They'd all worked on the renovations at Ferdy's Landing. 'I gutted the place,' said Ishmael simply. 'Took it right back to the stone. All new timber. There couldn't have been a sixpence still there and us not find it. Anyway,' he was stowing the tanks in the rack on the gunwale, 'we should get a move on, if Kirwan wants to go into the caves still. It'll be calm enough round there, won't it, Per?'

'Short of a flat calm you'll hardly get a better day,' said Per. 'Another half hour and we'll get right into the Frenchman's Cave if that's what you want.'

'I do,' said Kirwan. 'I want to get those basalt columns with the afternoon sun. And you never know, after Jed's find on the beach the other day, we might find a stash of cocaine in there while we're at it.'

'No,' said Jared. 'Frenchman's Cave would be a daft place for smugglers. You can only get into it maybe a dozen days in the whole summer. And even if you could drop it off from the sea, who'd collect it from there? You need to sell drugs on as fast as possible, not stick them in a place they can't be got at for weeks.'

'You mean they'd pass their sell-by date? But surely they don't go off?'

'No, but in the smuggling trade you pay up front, strictly C O D. So that's all your capital tied up, or more likely a load of debt. You'd hardly want to leave it sitting in a tidal cave, would you?'

'I suppose it wouldn't gain much interest there,' admitted Kirwan. 'Sorry, Jed: I clearly haven't thought it all through properly.'

She was more than old enough to have been his mother, and every time Jared spoke to her he realised he was giving her something new to laugh at. But oddly enough he didn't resent it. It had never occurred to Jared before that Nesta Kirwan fell into the category of sexually desirable women. When he was a boy he used to meet her once a year when she came round to do the school photographs. He'd been vaguely aware of her as small for a grown-up, dark, and faintly exotic in an undefined way. She'd belonged in the same category as teachers, except that she never looked grim, and always smelled nice. She still smelled nice. It was unusual to smell expensive perfume when diving from an open boat off Despair. All day her presence had supplied a certain *frisson* which had been missing from Jared's life for over a year. He wondered, fantastically, whether she might want to extend her photographic research over another day, and whether he dared invite her to stay over on Despair tonight. He was almost sure he would not dare, but the idea opened up a train of improbable thought that was not at all unpleasant. He glanced at her as the boat got under way, and saw that she was regarding him with friendly amusement. He guessed that she knew what he was thinking, and realised that even if she did, he didn't care.

'Well, I haven't really thought about it either,' he said aloud. 'But after I found that packet, it did cross my mind that if there's a contact on this coast, it's most likely down Ogg's Cove way. The Lyonsness side is too overlooked. Once you're into the sound, Ishmael, for example, could watch every move you make from Ferdy's Landing.'

Ishmael looked round. 'You think I'm keeping a round the clock watch for passing smugglers? I have a job to do. Ferdy's Landing isn't going to bother them.' Kirwan passed round a box of sandwiches, and Ishmael took one without looking at it; he was watching the cliffs again. 'Jed, if anyone is smuggling off this coast, there's only one person who could possibly be in their way, and he's in this boat and he isn't me or Nesta or Per. Mind you, I don't think anything of the kind. The tide could have brought that packet from anywhere: Dorrado, Tuly, North America, God knows. Drugs are serious money, twenty-first century style. You're not about to find the answer in a sea cave.'

'No, but smuggling's still smuggling. OK; this is cocaine, not Spanish gold, but you still can't send it by e-mail. Someone still has to get their feet wet. Things still have to be packed in sacks, and someone still has to put them somewhere. And if they don't want to be noticed, and they come by sea, the possible places haven't changed that much since Kidd. That's a fact, Ishmael. You can't say it isn't.'

'Well,' said Per peaceably, 'We're not the coastguards so we don't need to worry about it. We should get moving if we're going into the caves. Kirwan can do her pictures, and maybe she'll give each of us a copy. I'd like that. I can look at it when I'm shorebound for good.'

'I can't imagine you ever will be, but you shall all have your copies,' Nesta promised. She turned away from them and towards the cliffs of Despair, into the wind.

SEVEN

Sidony Redruth: Ravnscar Castle. June 1st.
Notes for *Undiscovered Islands* (working title).

I LIKE LIVING with Lucy. I realised this yesterday as we sat on over the remains of breakfast drinking our coffee, to the soothing accompaniment of cooing doves, who were immersed in their springtime courtships outside the open window. The sun came in and caressed us through the romanesque embrasure that lit the table, and the warmth of it was bringing out new flowers on the cyclamen in the middle of the table. They hung exotically over the milk and marmalade. Somehow they reminded me of Lucy. Even their virginal white seemed appropriate, for Lucy has a nun-like aura about her, in spite of her sleepy sexiness, which may leave me cold, but I've seen fairly clearly the effect it has on Colombo. Possibly I'm a little envious. My sixth sense, in which, being a rational woman, I put little trust, tells me that Lucy's snowlike purity is deceptive. In fact the whole of life at Ravnscar has an element of illusion about it. I find I keep touching the walls as if to reassure myself of their stony substance. They're always hard and chilly under my fingers, even when I dream about them.

We have no difficulty in talking, Lucy and I. I think she's lonely. I would be, living just by myself in Ravnscar, but then I find it hard to judge other people's experience of loneliness, because I'm a twin and although Arthur and I are not at all alike there's always a bit of me that feels strange without him. I don't know if that's because we shared a childhood or an even more cramped space before that. I get the impression that Lucy has always been more or less alone. I see her as she was yesterday, sitting across from me at the round table in the window where we have breakfast, and I see . . . what? A woman a little older than me, early thirties maybe, with thick black hair that's rapidly growing out of the short style into which it's been cut. Her hair really is black, not dark brown, though when the sun catches it there are red lights in it. Her eyes are not black but very dark brown, dark enough to give you the impression you're looking into the depths, not just at the colour of someone's iris. Her skin against her white shirt looks tanned and sleek. She's already a little bit plump, but in a healthy sort of way, as if it's from olive oil rather than ice creams. She wears much tighter jeans than I do; I'd find them hot and uncomfortable but I've never seen Lucy look hot. I've yet to see her hurry over anything either. There's a lack of stress about this place which I like. I can feel myself slowing down in it.

Each meal takes about two hours. This is when I find out about Lucy. The rest of the time she simply potters. I can't make up my mind if she's the archetypal housewife or the ultimate museum curator. The place is packed with antiques, from fossils of ammonites through to Bell's prototype telephone, and more or less anything you could think of in between. I asked Lucy, who was drifting around the Great Hall absentmindedly wielding a duster, if the things were arranged in any order. She looked down at the Dresden shepherdess in her hands and thought for a while.

'Two orders,' she said at last. 'Aesthetic, and random.'

She's very ready to talk whenever I waylay her as she drifts about her domain, and she always gives me useful information about its history. She'd write a better guidebook than I ever will.

'The keep is fifteenth-century,' she told me, as we stood on the black-and-white diamond-tiled floor at the foot of the circular central stairway, 'from the Portuguese period. But the foundations are much older, and the passages underneath were used hundreds of years before that. They're natural.'

I'd been looking at the walls and wondering how well I would sleep if I kept an assortment of pikes, halbards, lochaber axes, scimitars, cutlasses, daggers, a two-handed claymore, muskets, duelling pistols, prototype revolvers, flintlock rifles and a small cannon arranged in tasteful geometrical patterns in my front hall, but the passages grabbed my attention. 'Caves, you mean? Natural ones?'

'Oh yes, they're lava tubes from a prehistoric eruption of Mount Prosper, apparently. One goes right through the side of the mountain and comes out above Ogg's Cove. In all the earthquakes and eruptions of Mount Prosper, Ravnscar has never been touched. It's safe because the rock is hollow underneath. There are caverns. Some you can get into, some not. And some not always.'

'Why not? Because of the tide?'

'No, not because of that. Nothing changes down there. The air temperature, for example, is always the same. No day and night. No seasons. It's nice when you go down in winter. Warm. Cool at this time of year, of course. You need a jumper.'

'But why only sometimes?'

As usual it took her a long time to answer. 'They were used, these places,' she said at last. 'Ravnscar has a long history.'

'And your family too? You've always been here?'

'Since the 1590s. Too long.'

I opened my mouth to ask why too long, and shut it again, for fear of being intrusive, till I thought of an easier question. 'What about all the furniture and stuff? Did your family collect all these things?'

'My grandfather was an antique dealer.'

'Oh,' I tried not to sound disappointed.

'And my great-grandfather was a pirate. Of a long line.'

'Wow! And now you look after all these treasures?'

'At the moment it's what I feel like doing. I sell things

sometimes. I worked for an antique dealer in New York. Making money's in my blood, remember.'

'Isn't it hard getting rid of stuff you've always had in the family?'

'I'm not sentimental. Didn't you inherit anything from your family you'd rather be rid of?'

'Not really. Guilt, I suppose, but that isn't quite the same. No one would want to buy it, anyway.'

'I thought you were writing a book?'

'What's that got to do with it?'

'Everything,' said Lucy. 'Your family imbues you with guilt: that's what families are for. What do you do? You make it into something tangible and sell it. Sometimes I think a castle full of junk is a soft option, but then I can't write.'

'Yes you do. I've seen you.'

'Ah, that's different, that's not for sale.'

'Private?'

'Very.'

I knew that. On my third day at Ravnscar I'd been sitting at the round table in the embrasure of the kitchen window writing a letter to my parents, and I'd noticed, in the pile of magazines and back numbers of *The Hesperides Times*, a yellow ring-binder entitled, in fine italic script, *Chemistry Notes*. It didn't sound enticing, but I casually flicked it open all the same, at a page closely handwritten in purple ink.

> . . . and other times I want to forget everything and just let myself love him back, but I know that would be the worst thing I could do to either of us. I know that I must never let myself . . .

I banged the file shut, and shoved it back under the newspapers. Not so much because I'm virtuous, as because if I read someone's private diary I could never face them again without feeling guiltily conscious of what I ought not to know. And supposing I read something horrible about myself? I hate complicated secrets.

I don't mind Lucy being so secret, because I know not to ask, and I know where I stand: on the outside. She is adept at wrapping herself in an inscrutable reserve. I just wouldn't know how to be so off-putting without lifting a finger. I was thinking about it while she explained to me about the corbelled ceilings in the tower, and how she'd sold the two original sixteenth-century chairs that stood against the wall opposite the great staircase.

'I'd never have managed without selling things from time to time,' she said. 'The chairs went about twelve years ago, when I was living in New York. I had to get away, you see. Things had happened here. I didn't have any cash; that's how it started. I was the sole heir of a castle full of priceless historical treasures and I didn't have fifty pounds in the bank. You know what happened to our land?'

'No.'

'Brentness. I'll take you there. Have you ever been into a lava field?'

'No. Not a new one, I mean.'

This one happened in 1783. That was the last great eruption of Mount Prosper, the same year as Hekla in Iceland. Before that we had the richest land in Hy Brasil, and the best cattle, stolen from Spanish ships going out to stock the new farms in South America and the Caribbean. Horses, too. You might wonder why you need good Arab bloodstock on an island this size, but my ancestors were proud of their horses. My father always used to say the horses in this country are far more intelligent than the people. All that land's gone now, under the lava. You can walk along the old channels. I'll take you there this afternoon.'

The lava field was the strangest place I'd ever been in my life. The melted rock had just hardened as it flowed, like a petrified tidal wave. It was sharp under my feet, even through the soles of my sandals, full of ridges and bubbles. There were winding paths through it like stream beds, following the curve of the rock. The very air seemed static and heavy, and our voices sounded flat as we walked in single file between the flows. Nothing grew except little bubbles of moss where rainwater had collected in the cracked lava, and various grey and golden lichens that had spent two centuries colonising this desert, but still only touched it with bright pockets here and there. I touched the bare rocks as we passed and grazed my palms. The whole place felt uncanny, out of the world. We scrambled out of the channel and stood on a solid waterfall, looking out to sea. There was nothing here to show that life had ever made it on to land at all.

'It's a bit scary, isn't it?' I said. 'Like time isn't real here.'

'A friend of mine who often used to come here wrote a book saying time isn't real anywhere. Not his own idea, of course. Einstein's. But Brendan used to sail a lot round Brentness, and I think maybe it was our mixture of geology and history that gave him the idea.'

'Brendan?'

'Brendan Hook. He grew up here but he teaches at Harvard now. It was him that talked me into going to America too. "Do it, Lucy," he said. "Get a life. That's what I had to do. You won't regret it." He was right. I haven't. If I hadn't gone then I'd have gone mad. Too many things had happened. It was like being caught in a web. If I hadn't got out I'd have been petrified too. He saved my life.'

I realised if I wasn't tactful she'd shut up like a clam. 'Was it very hard to get away?' I asked tentatively.

'Guilt,' said Lucy succinctly. 'I was the last one. Unbroken tradition, you know. That can be powerful stuff. You know Ravnscar has been lived in for fifteen centuries?'

'Fifteen *centuries*? You mean the Irish monks? But after that there was no one here, I thought, except for the Norsemen, and they didn't stay long, until the Portuguese discovered the islands in 1456. At least, that's what it says in the books.'

'You're thinking of the Ruysch map, aren't you? *Insula hic in*

Anno Domini 1456 fuit totaliter combusta. But you know Henry the Navigator didn't really do any navigating. He just collected a library of maps and sent other people off to do the real sailing.' Lucy jumped off the waterfall and led the way along another winding channel. 'Of course,' she went on, her voice muffled because she was ahead of me, so I had to strain to catch what she was saying, 'if the lava hadn't taken our land the revolution would have. No one can own more than forty acres in Hy Brasil now anyway. So in the end it made no difference.'

It occurred to me for the first time that the world must appear different if one is an aristocrat. I'd never met one before, at least, not consciously. I imagined the desert of Brentness as some kind of socialist utopia, neatly criss-crossed with flourishing smallholdings, ecologically run by a liberated peasantry. 'I would have thought it made quite a lot of difference.'

But Lucy was not to be drawn into that sort of discussion. She was a mine of information, but remained impervious to another point of view. She took me home and made me fresh scones for tea, because, she said, I was English and therefore needed to be fed on sweet things at four o'clock. I sat at the table and leafed through my notebook while I sipped Lapsang Souchong with lemon in it. 'I was reading about this spring festival in Dorrado,' I told her.

'You read too much. This was Baskerville's pamphlet, I take it? My father wrote a much better account. It's in a manuscript, upstairs. I'll show you when your fingers aren't so sticky. What did you read?'

'That there's a procession, and the King of the Year lies down in an open grave and everyone throws flowers in on top of him.'

'And then he gets out and takes a shower and they spend the rest of the night drinking. Here,' Lucy got up, and opened a drawer in a huge heavily carved bureau on the other side of the kitchen. She took out a floppy booklet with a photo on it and came back. 'You were asking about the caves,' she said. 'And only finding the way in sometimes. They weren't empty, you see.'

It took me a moment to get her reference. 'No?'

'Constant temperature, constant humidity. Ideal museum conditions. Someone knew what they were doing.' Lucy was leafing through the catalogue. 'And then, you see, I was the last one left. I told you I was trapped. Some career: bury myself on a mountainside all my life looking after stuff that's just been sitting there since the beginning of history. It gives people a buzz, certainly, the ones that know about it, but why should I have to encourage that? My mother was a good Catholic. She never approved of the Pirate Kings. So why should I help them out?'

'For God's sake, Lucy, explain! Who are the Pirate Kings?'

'Oh, you know,' she said impatiently. 'Funny handshakes. All that. You must have passed the Pirate Kings' Lodge in St Brandons. It's just down the alley from Kirwan's. With a skull and crossbones on the door.'

It was the first time I'd seen her in any state more turbulent than flat calm. 'I did notice that,' I said mildly. 'I thought it was a bit bizarre.'

'Well, there you go. Would you want those guys turning up for a party in your basement every Hallow'mass Eve? I bet you wouldn't. Well, nor did I.'

'Whatever for? Some kind of ritual?'

'Racist, sexist rubbish.' Lucy got up from the table, and strode up and down with unwonted energy, between me and the window so that her shadow kept falling across me as I sat at the long, carved table. 'So what do you think it was like for me, having all those Pirate Kings cavorting about in the cellar in fancy dress, getting up to God knows what? And that man Baskerville gives me the creeps. Remember I was all on my own by then. They even wanted me to have a ritual bath, in as hot water as I could stand. Because I was female, you understand. They never asked my father to do that.'

'But why? What was it all about?'

'You may well ask. Just another Great Mystery, ticking away

down our back stairs waiting for the End of Time. But has it changed anything? Has it saved the world? Has it hell! Look at the state we're in now. Granted, they never did get to use Hy Brasil for nuclear testing, but look at all the other things. Do you know there's bugs on our cabbages we've never had before because up to five years ago this climate was too cold for them? Do you know that if anyone does catch flounders any more off our coast as likely as not they've got two heads? Do you know that in calm weather we can smell the pollution from factories in Baltimore and New Jersey? This isn't an island any more, and that's a fact. Dreams don't save anything. I talked to Brendan about it thirteen years ago, when he was over visiting his parents. I was desperate. Too much had happened. "Brendan," I said, "I'm not a bloody legend. I've read a lot of books, seen films. I subscribe to magazines. I know what's out there. What do you think I should do?" I told you how he said, "Go for it." He sent me the application forms for university. He put me in touch with a guy in New York who sold my great-great-grandmother's diamonds. That paid for my first year.

'I asked him about the other things. Not the stuff in the house, the other place. I'd not mentioned it to anyone before. He didn't believe me at first. I mean, of course he knew the story, but no one thought it was real. So he came over, and we went down and had a look.'

'To the caves?'

'That's right. He'd heard, of course, but he was a rationalist at that time. It's interesting to observe a man who can't believe what he's seeing. Pathetic, in a way. But I respect Brendan. Anyway, afterwards we had a council of war. I didn't want to sell. I'm not superstitious, not in the slightest, but I didn't feel right about that. So Brendan said, "What about permanent loan? To a museum? It'll do more good than here, and you've not done anything irrevocable." I was so relieved. It was him that suggested the Metropolitan Museum of Art in New York. "They've got everything in there," he said. "Absolutely bloody everything. And money. It'll be safe there, and you'll be free of it." So that's what we did.'

'And what was it? The treasure, I mean? What was it?'

'Here.' She picked up the booklet again and tossed it to me.

'Metropolitan Museum of Art Bulletin,' I read, and a date almost ten years ago. The photograph on the front was of a golden chalice studded with jewels, apparently floating through the air against a pale grey background. I flipped through pages of lavish photographs and shiny text, which pleased me. So many pretty-looking pamphlets turn out to be disappointingly black and white inside. I found the chalice again. This time it had landed on a white cloth. There was a description opposite the photo:

> One of the finest examples of metalwork of the early Christian period, this solid gold Romano-British chalice is apparently unique. The simplicity of style and design suggests a much earlier date than the silver or bronze Celtic chalices of the eighth century (e.g. Trewhiddle, Cornwall, Hexham, Northumberland, Derrybaflan, Co. Tipperary), but there is no corresponding primitivism in craftsmanship. Indeed, it exhibits a sophisticated workmanship perhaps only rivalled in the eighth-century silver chalice found at Ardagh, Co. Limerick, in 1868.
>
> The Hy Brasil chalice is composed of two parallel bowls of beaten gold, one inverted against the other, joined by a decorated gold collar. Most of the external surface area is unadorned gold, which serves to emphasise the splendour of the nine jewelled panels which constitute the band just below the rim ...

I skipped over the description of the panels for the moment and turned the page. The next glossy picture was of an ornately decorated spearhead, set against a blue background like a summer sky. The paragraph underneath said:

The complete state of preservation of this lance from the late Celtic period must be regarded as little short of miraculous. No other example exists of a lancehead still attached to its wooden shaft. Carbon dating of the ash shaft suggests a replacement of the original wood in the twelfth century; the reason for the renewal of an archaic weapon at this date can only remain a matter of speculation. The extraordinary state of preservation of wood now seven hundred years old must be attributed to the perfect museum conditions of the underground chapel in Hy Brasil which housed these treasures for a prolonged period, until their removal to the museum. The ash has been treated at one time with linseed oil, and was originally, presumably, white in colour. The iron head of the lance is adorned with four decorated bands of chased gold. The weapon could hardly have been intended for use in battle, although chemical analysis revealed traces of carbon, possibly dried blood, at the tip of the lancehead; however, it seems likely that the weapon was specifically designed for ceremonial purposes.

There was more about the lance, but first I turned over the rest of the pages. Apparently there were thirteen treasures in all. There was a gold cauldron with a dent in one side. Next came a couple of magnificent golden candelabra, each holding ten candles, and a solid gold cross inlaid with rubies and emeralds. There was a thin gold crown, and a chessboard of ebony and ivory, and a decorated Celtic sword which had been mended about halfway along the blade. All the treasure together, even just printed on paper in a shiny brochure, was nothing short of dazzling. I looked at Lucy in bewilderment.

'Are you telling me that all these things were here at Ravnscar?'

'Read the Introduction.'

I turned to the beginning obediently.

THE ROMANO-BRITISH TREASURES
OF HY BRASIL

It is seldom that myth becomes tangible in quite so satisfac-
tory a form as in the Romano-Celtic treasures from Ravnscar
in the archipelago of Hy Brasil. The setting alone (Plates 1–
3), from which the treasures were removed this spring, might
seem to the imaginative like the embodiment of that arche-
type explored in detail by Emma Jung and Marie-Louise von
Franz, in their seminal study . . .

I skipped the psychoanalytical bit, and looked instead at an aerial
photograph of Ravnscar taken, I guessed, from somewhere just
above Ferdy's Landing. There was a picture next to it of the thorn
tree in the castle yard all covered with white blossom. I wish I'd seen
it like that; when I arrived the tree was green, although there were
still drifts of fallen petals across the lawn. While I looked at it I said
to Lucy, 'So you've seen them in the Museum where they are now?'

'Of course. They're all together in a case specially made for
them. It had to be thirteen feet long because of the lance.
They're at the end of the corridor to the left of the main
staircase, just before you get to Medieval Art. I'd imagined
them better displayed, actually, like in the middle of one of those
great halls. But even in that passage they look pretty good.
Smaller, somehow, than they did here, but they seem to be kind
of sharper-edged, because of the good lighting I suppose. I had
this weird feeling they'd got more real.'

'I suppose museums are rather authoritative places.'

'I like buying postcards though,' said Lucy.

'Where's this one taken, then? I can see the lance and the
chalice, and the candelabra, and the cross . . . Is it a chapel? It's
not the museum, certainly. Plate 3.'

She looked over my shoulder. 'Oh yes, that's the chapel here.
They took that just before they packed them all up.'

'But surely it isn't! You showed me the chapel, with all

those romanesque windows. This looks more like a cellar.'

'No, no.' Lucy got up. 'We have two chapels. St Joseph's chapel is underneath the other one. If you like I'll take you there now.'

She led me, not upstairs to the Portuguese chapel opposite the Great Hall, but down the back stairs from the kitchen. I'd been in the cellar before, because that's where the firewood is stored, as well as tools and fishing tackle. Apparently old Morgan had been a keen fisherman. Lucy led me past all that, and down into the wine cellar, where I'd only been once, when she'd sent me to fetch some burgundy. We crossed the wine cellar to another studded oak door at the back. There was a ledge inside with a torch and a skein of string. Lucy switched on the torch.

'If you ever go exploring down here,' she warned me, 'take the string to guide you. We don't need it now. We're only just going to the bottom of the stairs.'

I followed her down a flight of steps so worn in the middle I could barely keep my footing, even though she shone the torch backwards so I could see where to put my feet. At the bottom three oval passageways went off in different directions. Lucy turned left, and opened another door. I had to duck under the lintel. It was very quiet inside. A little flame burned overheard, refracted through red glass. I could tell we were in a small closed space, but there was nothing claustrophobic about it. Quite the contrary: the air smelt fresh and surprisingly sweet. There must be a conduit from somewhere. It smelt as if it came straight from the herb garden. I breathed in, and followed the beam of the torch as Lucy slowly swung it round.

We were in a corbelled cell, shaped like an old-fashioned beehive. It was oval, barely fifteen feet long, I would guess, and half that wide. There was a rectangular stone altar at one end. Once there had been a window above it, looking out to God knows what, but it was filled in now with stone. The floor was solid rock, cleanly swept. There wasn't a speck of dust anywhere. The place was quite empty.

Lucy shone the torch on to the stone wall over the altar. I could see the shape of a crucifix where the stone was paler. But there was no ornament now of any kind except for the little flame burning in the red glass. I could see now that it hung from a plain metal chain attached to the curved roof above. 'So you still keep something here?' I asked her.

'That, yes. The gold chain went, and the pyx with the ruby panels. But you can hang a light from any old chain really, and a bit of bread – it wouldn't make any difference if you kept it in a matchbox. Father Segato celebrates Mass upstairs in the Portuguese chapel on the first Sunday of every month, and he attends to this place too while he's here.'

'But the lamp doesn't burn for a whole month?'

'Of course not. I do the housekeeping bit.'

I looked round at the empty chapel, swept so clean and bare. I thought about those beautiful photographs in the *Bulletin* upstairs; or rather, I thought about the real objects that they represented, reposing now in the Metropolitan Museum of Art, New York. I felt bewildered, overwhelmed even, but above everything else desperately curious. Curiosity killed the cat, Arthur used to say when he was teasing me. My mother said it was bad manners to ask people personal questions. Also, I didn't want to make a fool of myself. I turned to Lucy, and almost opened my mouth to ask her if the fantastic idea that was floating through my mind could have any possible foundation in reality. But I didn't, and the moment passed.

She stood there a couple of minutes longer, almost as if she were waiting for something, holding the torch so that it shone the length of the chapel and lighted on the empty altar. Then she turned to me and gave a little shrug. 'Time to put the kettle on again, don't you think? I could do with another cup of tea.'

I don't suppose that was really what she was thinking, but I didn't say anything. She closed the door carefully after us, and led the way back upstairs.

EIGHT

THERE WAS A knock at the door.

Jared put his bowl down on the hearth. He stared at the door. There was no one else on the island. He'd been out until dusk. There had definitely been no one else on the island. He'd come back by the shell strand and the mooring place. You couldn't get ashore anywhere else. The only boat he'd seen was his own. She'd been tossing at the mooring, because the wind was southerly Force 5 and rising. It was raining hard. The tide would just be ebbing. It would have been the right moment to cross the sound. That is, if you could see in the dark and didn't mind not being able to go back.

There was a knock at the door.

Hardly anyone could have made it though, in the dark. Per? Ishmael? They wouldn't have knocked. Either of them would have walked straight in.

The light was on, and there was no curtain at the window. Anyone outside could see right in. Jared got up and stared at the black square of outer darkness. 'Come in.' He realised he wouldn't be heard outside. When he opened the door the wind snatched it out of his hand and blew it wide open. The fire behind him roared.

A tall figure with a feebly glowing torch in its hand detached itself from the dark, came in, and pulled its hat off.

'Colombo! What in God's name are you doing here?'

'Visiting, Jed, just visiting. Would you like to see my card?'

'You gave me one hell of a shock!'

'I'm sorry. I didn't mean to frighten you.'

'You didn't. I don't believe in things that go bump in the night. Man, you're wet through!'

'I'm sorry if I startled you, then. I suppose I'd never thought of myself in a supernatural light. Yes, it was a bit rough out there. Unpleasant, even.'

'Well, there's plenty of supper if you want. I've cooked enough for the next four days. And you'd better have a change of clothes.'

'Jed, do you *have* a change of clothes? I'm impressed. What's your supper then? It smells all right.'

'It's bean stew.'

'I daresay it has, but what is it now?' Colombo took off his sea jacket and hung it over the back of a chair. 'No, sorry, I don't mean to be ungrateful. Yes, please.'

Jared looked him over. 'You're not just wet. You're soaking.' He took hold of a fold of Colombo's jersey. 'Jesus, you've been in the sea. Haven't you?' He grabbed Colombo's hands unceremoniously and felt them. 'Quit making stupid jokes and get your things off. You're cold as a fish. Seriously, I know what I'm talking about. How long have you been out there in this state?'

'All right.' Colombo peeled off his dripping jersey. 'An hour or two, I think. I'm sorry. I don't mean to be facetious. To be honest, it's just fright.' He unbuckled his belt and let his jeans drop into the fast gathering pool of seawater round his feet. 'I did give myself a bit of a shock.' His teeth were beginning to chatter, and when he took his shirt off he was shivering violently.

'Here's a towel. Get by the fire. I'll get some clothes.'

Jared didn't ask anything more until Colombo was sitting in the chair by the stove with a bowl full of stew on his knees, and a mug of instant coffee on the hearth. He was wearing Jared's thick seaman's jersey, a pair of patched corduroys that reached about halfway down his calves, and two pairs of darned socks.

He looked a good deal less than his usual debonair self, but gradually he stopped shivering, and a little colour came back into his cheeks. 'Sorry,' he said again. 'I feel a fool. Better not tell the lads about this.'

'Too late. I'm already reckoning on the fortune I'll make selling the story to the *Times*.'

'"Man Falls In Sea: In Depth Probe By Sodden Hack": something like that, were you thinking of?'

'I'd like you to tell me what the sodden hack was probing into off Despair on a night like this.'

'Ah.' Colombo took a big spoonful of stew. He swallowed it and said, 'Now that's quite a long story.'

'Then you'd better start. I go to bed early.'

Colombo scraped the bowl out carefully. 'Jed, have you noticed any strange shipping off Despair recently? More activity than usual? Anything like that?'

'Coastguards,' replied Jared promptly. 'Sometimes I think they must be breeding out there. You know, spontaneous generation, like flies. One in the morning, ten in the afternoon. Well no, maybe not ten. But there's often a couple of them hovering about out just off the island. West to sou'west usually, but it varies. I guess I know what they're after.'

'You do? What?'

'No, Colombo, I'm not available for interview. Remember that was my supper you just ate. Suppose *you* tell *me*.'

Colombo picked up his coffee and warmed his hands on the mug. Jared waited patiently. 'OK,' said Colombo at last. 'There's talk. Even you must have noticed that. We're in a recession. Outside St Brandons more than half of us are unemployed. And the economy's booming. The Brasil pound's stronger than it's ever been. Something doesn't add up. Literally. I've tried talking to people, discreetly, you know. Either they know nothing or they're evasive. My own editor's warned me off. There's nothing in the paper. No comment.'

'Except Tidesman.'

'Tidesman's not exempt. He can't deal in plain speaking. You know that.'

'I don't see why not.'

'Because I need to get published. A point closer to the wind, and he'd be over. It's been close.'

'Does that worry him?'

'Yes,' said Colombo baldly. There was a pause. 'Did you think anything about those articles, Jared?'

'I told you, I'm not up for interview. You tell me.'

'OK. I talked to Ralph Gunn. You know he fishes out of Ogg's Cove. There've been trawlers lying off Brentness all this summer, he says.'

'So what's new?'

'What's new is there's no fish, so what are they doing out there? What's new is they lie offshore, on the edge of the deep, and don't come in sight of land till twilight. And what's newer than that, Jed, is that they come right inside our limits, just a mile or so off the Ness and they don't show any lights. Ralph said he damn near ran into one. It was misty, and he saw this bulk, just a patch of dark, you know, so he thought it was an island in the wrong place. I mean, he thought he'd lost his direction, but he hadn't.'

'Colombo, I've known Ralph all my life. I'd trust him with anything but the drink. And then I wouldn't. He has his days, you know that.'

'Of course I do. I go to the Crossed Bones in Ogg's Cove myself, which is more than you do these days. But Jed, I'll swear to you the man was stone-cold sober. And that isn't the end of it. I spoke to Ishmael. I've never seen Ishmael the worse for wear in my life.'

'You never will. What did Ishmael say?'

'Ishmael said he's seen lights at sea from Ferdy's Landing, a mile or two off, maybe. He said there was a port light out there three nights ago, moving south. It vanished in the middle of the open sea: clear night, at least a mile off Despair. It hadn't gone behind the island. And if the ship was turning – well, no other light came up, and if she'd put over to port just there she'd have been on Brentness next thing. Ishmael rang the coastguard, and they said there were whales out there. Phosphorescence.'

'Give us a break!'

'That's what Ishmael said. He didn't tell you about it?'

'I've not seen anyone at all for nearly a week.'

'Or anything?'

'Ah, that's different. But you go on telling me.'

'Was George Tinto still teaching senior history when you got to the Academy?'

'Yeah. I even used to come in for his lessons sometimes, which says something. I left school in '86. I think he retired the year after. Why?'

'You callow youth. Do you remember drawing a map of smuggling routes through Hy Brasil?'

'This is after the Pirates, you mean? Yes, I remember. Brandy and tobacco: 1795–1812. A red line from Central America, then from here to the channel coast. Then opium. A green line, round the Cape and up to here. Then a yellow line across to Nantucket for Prohibition. It's all coming back to me. And I remember that all the time the Brits had the forts manned at Lyonsness and Dorrado, we were using Nud's Hole and the Brentness caves for running illegal goods. The Brits kept patrols off Despair but they didn't have proper charts, not even then. The Brasils were just running rings round them.'

'And you say the government's keeping patrols out there now. And there's Ralph nearly crashing into things, and Ishmael seeing lights, and you – I know you've seen something, and in a minute you *will* tell me – and yet the coastguards have never picked up anything.'

'Not even a phosphorescent whale, so far. More coffee?' Jared got up and shifted the kettle to the middle of the stove. 'Well, I'll tell you what I've seen. More whales than I ever saw before. A real stirabout. There's something weird going on. And coastguards. But nary a smuggler. Shall I tell you why? There ain't none. That's what you think too, isn't it?'

'But you found cocaine on the beach.'

'I didn't say nothing was being smuggled. I just said there weren't any smugglers.'

'I wanted to handle that story. They wouldn't give it to me.'

'Did Ishmael tell you about the peelers?'

'He said they gave you a rough time.'

'Yes. And you still haven't told me how you ended up in the sea.'

'Simple. Ralph called me. I asked him to, if he saw anything new. He did. Lights, then – just like Ishmael said – nothing. A red light moving north-east towards Despair, then nothing at all. I took Baskerville's inflatable. I didn't say why, or where I was going. I launched it from Hogg's Beach.'

'Ishmael didn't see you?'

'There was no one outside when I drove past Ferdy's Landing. The kitchen light was on. I launched the inflatable and followed the coast up to the Ness. Nothing. Then I headed east, towards Despair. I didn't show any lights. There's a bit of a moon; I could see enough, and I had the Despair and Brentness lights to steer by. But I was out of sight of land and it was getting a bit rough. And then – hell, Jared, I saw it – just like Ralph said, a damn great blackness where there should have been none. I cut the throttle so she was just ticking over; I reckoned no one would hear that over the sea, and I went on slowly. Jed, I went right up to her. Right up under her bows, and next thing I knew, I was almost into her anchor chain. I knew then we must be near Despair; she couldn't anchor in the deep.'

'Half a mile, maybe. Not more.'

'I couldn't read her name. It was too dark. I could see it's a longish one. Two words. I started going round her, slowly. That didn't tell me much. Then I heard another engine, louder than mine. Low down, between me and the mainland. At which point our hero started to beat a retreat due south. It dawned on him as he put the tiller over that he'd been running before a southerly wind, and hadn't noticed that it was rising. He shipped enough water to make him pause for thought, and realised that he'd got himself far enough into the sound to have the tide-rip against him too. So he tried making west, back to where he thought Ferdy's Landing must be, a point or two south of the Brentness light, and the next thing he knew a damn great wave broke over his head. Submitting to *force majeure*, he turned east, and what does he see but a green light. Literally. Someone's showing a starboard light barely a hundred yards away. It vanishes and rises; the sea's pretty choppy by this time. But there's the Despair light right beyond it. Our hero grits his teeth, and heads for Despair full throttle, giving the port light as wide a berth as he dare. He passes it and looks back – and guess what – no port light – no light facing land at all. There isn't time to think about that. He needs to find the white strand. There's a lump of darkness which must be the island. Every time he turns a point south he ships half the sound. There's water round his ankles. He doesn't like it. He would fain die a dry death. But if he keeps due east he'll go bang into the cliffs. I don't mind telling you he's shit-scared. And suddenly there's a damn great shadow looming over him, and white water, and the inflatable tips fifty degrees, and he's reciting Hail Marys and trying to hang on to the tiller, and the whole damn ocean's washing over him and he thinks, well, that's it: Nearer my God to Thee. And then the inflatable's full of sea but floating in a bit of dead water, and there's rocks all round him. And miracle of miracles, he can see a dim white line and he realises it's the strand maybe thirty yards away just. What's more the engine's still running, I can't think why, and five minutes later I beach on the sand as soft as you please. I'm shaking so much I can barely pull the boat up and tip the water out of it, and I realise my hands are too numb to tie a knot so I just have to weight the ropes down with stones. I guess she'll be OK.

'So that's it. I wish I could say our hero climbed up the

anchor chain and brought all the miscreants in at gunpoint, with himself at the wheel sailing into St Brandons' harbour in the steely light of dawn. Unfortunately it didn't happen like that.'

'Jesus, man, you should be down on your knees thanking God for what did happen. You must be bloody mad.'

'The procedure you mention has not been omitted. You're a Protestant, aren't you, Jed?'

'I'm not anything.'

'Same difference. Is that kettle boiling? Thanks.'

'It seems to me,' remarked Jared, spooning coffee, 'that after all this you're not really any the wiser.'

'Don't rub it in.'

'OK, so they rendezvous at sea. Trawlers come in and meet – nobody. Strict government patrols fail to intercept – nobody. Nobody takes the stuff somewhere. Not Despair, that's for sure. I'd have noticed. Anyway, you'd only have to get the stuff off again. No public transport on Despair.'

'That's true of anywhere in the country.'

'Not true. You can get off the mainland.'

'Eh?'

'Straight to Europe. Could be plane, but security's tightish these days. But there's the ferry. You've landed at Southampton?'

'Never.'

'I have. The way those cars drive off, they could have more or less anything in them. They're not too bothered about Hy Brasil. As far as they know the only thing we've exported for two hundred years is people. That's how it's done, Colombo. Nobody takes it ashore on the west side somewhere. Nobody leaves it in some depot. Then nobody picks it up discreetly and takes it over to Europe on the ferry, and nobody puts the money in the bank here, and bob's your uncle, as long as nobody starts adding two and two together and realising that in this country that makes ten.'

'OK. So where does it come from? Which country?'

'Colombia. Maybe Peru. It comes through Panama. That trawler you saw will be on its way to Europe. But with a contact on shore here it's an ideal dropping-off point along the way. There used to be hardly any patrols. There's a lot more now, but I guess there's always a way through if you watch and time it carefully.'

'You think there's a contact here? Who? Where?'

'Must be, or they wouldn't be here. You're looking for a small boat. Could be very small if it's only carrying cocaine. Fifteen years ago there was a lot more dope, and the cocaine was bootlegged on the back of that, but even then the coke was taking over. Less bulk, lots more profit. You can just bag up cocaine in 50lb lots, and each one's worth a bloody fortune. Easy. One cargo could make you rich, just in that inflatable of Baskerville's. That's if you knew how to sell it on, of course. You have to lay out the capital first. That's the thing that really limits you.'

'You seem to know a fair bit about it.'

'I don't know anything, but naturally I've been thinking. You're still left with the question: who's the contact? I've thought about that too, and I can tell you there's no one it could possibly be who's working the right sort of boat out of Lyonsness or Ogg's Cove. I've gone through all of them, in my mind, and it just doesn't add up.'

'Couldn't they land the stuff from the trawler?'

'Lower a boat, you mean? No chance. What would they do with it? No, there has to be an offshore dealer – the chap who picks up the signal and goes out to the trawler, and buys direct from the smugglers. The point is – what's in it for the smugglers – is that he's the man who pays, up front. Cash. He's the one who brings the stuff ashore – there has to be a stash house somewhere – and he sells it on, in 1lb lots usually, to the small dealers. They might sell a bit here, but mostly it goes straight on to Europe, the way I told you. Once the system's up and running it's easy. But it all falls down, because there isn't the right man with the right boat. I tell you, Colombo, there just isn't.'

Colombo listened intently, frowning a little, his eyes on Jared's animated face. 'And this stash house? Where might that be?'

'God knows. But you're looking for an isolated spot, where a boat could come and go without being noticed too much. A dry place where the stuff can be stored. A place where one or two regular visitors won't attract attention. The shore dealers have to drop by and pick up the stuff, remember, so it has to be on a road. It's most likely someone's house.'

'That limits the possibilities somewhat.'

'That's what I'm telling you.' Jared stood up to put more wood on the fire. 'Fancy a trip round Brentness tomorrow?'

Colombo shuddered.

'It's OK. *I* can handle a boat. We'd better call on Ishmael too. He keeps an eye on things much more than he says he does. He'll have noticed your car at Hogg's Beach by then anyway.'

'With Baskerville's trailer on it. That's true. And I have to get the inflatable back.'

'Wind's supposed to die down tomorrow morning,' said Jared. 'We can get off by noon. We can tow Baskerville's rubber ring across with us. I have to do the gannets first. Right now I'm going to bed. I'd better find you something to sleep on first, I suppose.'

By morning, the wind had chased the last of the cloud away and almost blown itself out. The land was laid bare: Mount Prosper seemed to rise over them barely a stone's throw away, and as they crossed the sound the houses at Lyonsness, the tower of Ravnscar, and the ribbon of road winding up to the pass were etched as clear as the background in a Renaissance painting. As they rounded the headland the sea turned choppy, with little white-topped waves that slopped over the side as they met the breeze that was still coming in from the west. The lava ridges on Brentness basked and glinted in the sun like a comatose dragon. Anything could be hidden there among the fissures and hollows and crumpled rock. But in bad weather, as Jared pointed out, there were no possible landings, and even in a flat calm it was a risky business coming close in among the toothed edges of the lava. And in the lava field there was no road.

Colombo swept the horizon with binoculars for the tenth time. 'Well, they didn't hang about. Not very sporting to make off while I slept, after all I went through.'

'Maybe they'll send you a postcard from Boulogne. Well, do we go round to Ogg's Cove? There's nothing out here, unless it's a submarine. Jesus! . . . Colombo, look out!'

There was a queer sigh from landward, like a monster gently stirring in its sleep. A moment later the boat began to accelerate south-west towards the shores of Mount Brasil, as if the land itself were sucking them hungrily inward. The engine throbbed on ineffectually. A wall of water detached itself from the cliffs and sped backwards, obliterating the succession of white-topped wavelets. It was dark green, paler at the top, with curls of white foam along its crest. It came fast, much too fast to flee. Jared turned the bows right into it, and Colombo bit back a cry of protest. Green water towered thirty feet over them like an advancing precipice. They could feel themselves being sucked up into it. They were almost under it; they had to go under. Colombo shut his eyes for the impact. Instead he felt the boat tip backwards, much too far, then rise, and keep rising, like speeding up a lift shaft. He looked, and there was the crest still right above them, poised to break. Then it burst. Water crashed down, drenching them. The boat went down in a barrage of spray. But not under; they were still sliding, down and down and down. Colombo, blinded by a vicious sea that was trying to fling him out of the boat, grabbed on to the gunwales and hung on with all his strength. The boat bucked and tossed and tried to fling him out, but he held on. They were going over; they had to be going over. He clung with both hands to the port gunwale, ready to shove clear when she tipped. But it didn't happen. Suddenly the sea poured away so he could breathe. Through a blur of water he saw Mount Prosper reeling back into a clear sky and vanishing into the next wild wave. Then he was being pitched this way and that, with no pattern or reason to go by. All he could do was hold on.

'Colombo! Bale! There's a baler under the seat! Right under you!'

He scrabbled about in a foot of seawater and found a cut-off plastic milk carton at the end of a piece of string. He baled, as fast as he was able, still clinging to the gunwale with one hand, with lumps of water leaping into his face and trying to snatch the baler out of his hands. The whole sea seemed to be in the boat, and it wasn't getting less. But no more waves came over them. He was out of breath, clumsy from kneeling in the sea, and his arm ached. Jed was baling too, faster than he could. They were tossing so much it was hard to tell which way was up. Maybe the water was going down at last. Augustine and the angel. Colombo gasped for air and kept on baling.

'Good, good! Keep going!'

What the hell did Jed *think* he was doing? He kept going. Suddenly there wasn't so much water. The gunwales were out of the sea again, back where they should be. It was harder to get a full baler. Less water in the bottom. He kept on baling.

Jared wasn't baling any more. Out of the corner of his eye Colombo saw him pull on the starter cord of the silent outboard. Baskerville's dinghy had vanished. Colombo kept baling. Jared tried the starter again, and then again. All of a sudden the engine blasted out and the boat leapt forward, hurling Colombo down into the bottom. Jared turned down the throttle, and Colombo struggled to his hands and knees again, peered out and saw Brentness ahead of them. It was pitching violently to and fro. No, it wasn't. It hadn't moved; it was the boat that was being flung about like a plank in a whirlpool. But the whirlpool was vanishing too, down some diabolic plughole, leaving them lurching up and down on a strangely disturbed sea. Colombo looked up. The sun still beat down on them out of a calm blue sky.

'Jesus,' said Jared, dropping his baler into the boat. 'Jesus fucking Christ.'

Colombo let go cautiously with one hand, and crossed himself.

'Jesus, did you see that?'

'No,' said Colombo, 'but I certainly felt something. What happened?'

'We got through,' said Jared. 'I just cut the towrope and headed my boat straight into it. It was the only thing to do.'

'If I saw what I think I saw, there was a large wave going backwards, right on to us.'

'You saw it.' Jared spat into the sea. 'Earthquake. Well, something was on our side, that's for sure.' He looked at Colombo. 'You OK? You look a bit green.'

'Fine, thank you. But it'll be quite a relief to get to Tarshish.'

'Well, I'm not about to chuck you overboard. That wave came up a bit south of west. Off Mount Brasil, I should say, Dorrado way.'

'Dorrado? you don't think anything's happened in Dorrado?'

Jared looked at him. 'Of course, your family. No, it won't be Dorrado. It'll be this side of the mountain. Only under water, as like as not. Probably not a soul on land felt a thing. And a wave coming that way . . . no. Well, suppose we head for Ferdy's Landing? See what's happened?'

'Will Ishmael run to a stiff drink?'

'Coffee,' said Jared succinctly.

Ishmael was in his office. From a distance the building looked like it always had: a stone-built byre with a low-pitched roof just across the yard from the house. The only indication that anything might have changed were the big rooflights, and a satellite dish attached to the gable.

Walking in at the door was like walking out of Hy Brasil and into a cell in the great global honeycomb. You might be anywhere, not in the flesh but in words anyway. The inside of the office was wood-lined, windowless except for the two open north-facing skylights, which filled the place with the brightness of the summer sky. The walls were covered with tapestries, mostly from South America, and the floor between the two built-in desks was covered by a big Armenian rug. The desks were strewn with phones, a fax machine, printer, monitors and lap-top computers. At the far end of the room an ancient stereo system was belting out Palestrina, drowning out the sounds of the oyster catchers on the shore outside. Even so, it was hard to believe that Ishmael hadn't noticed anything local going on at all. When they went in he was talking against the music to someone on the phone who was apparently trying to sell new stocks on the Chicago market. Ishmael looked round at his visitors, noted their soaked state, and raised his brows. Jared and Colombo stood dripping on the doormat, and waited.

Ishmael put the phone down at last, and came outside with Jared as soon as they'd told him what had happened, but nothing looked different. The tide-rip in the sound was just as usual, and the peaks of Despair rose peacefully into the still sky.

'I think it's all right,' said Jared. 'I'd like to check as soon as possible.'

'Check?' asked Ishmael, following his gaze. 'Oh. The *Cortes*. The *Cortes* won't have been touched. Not by a wave going north by west from Mount Brasil. Think about it! Certainly not at ninety-two feet. Think, Jed! You know a lot better than I do.'

'You're right. But with disturbance in the area . . . I'd like to make sure.'

'If there's disturbance in the area I'm not about to do a dive just under a five-hundred-foot cliff. Not until we get an all clear,' said Ishmael firmly. 'Come on, Jed, don't be so single-minded. How about a bit of lateral thinking: like, is everyone still alive in Dorrado? Let's see if Colombo's got through to anybody.'

Colombo put the phone down just as they came in. 'It's OK,' he said. 'Only the sea went out in Dorrado. That was Maeve.

Not a tremor. But the sea went out.' He sat down heavily, shivering in his wet clothes. A moment later he reached for the phone again. 'Do you have the number for the Pele Centre?'

'It's 264. Go ahead. If you get West I'll have a word with him too.'

Half an hour later Colombo was still telephoning. Jared, by this time sketchily attired in a green towel, prowled around the office with a mug of hot coffee. The stereo, turned down low, had switched over to Monteverdi. While he listened to Colombo, Jared stared at the nearest computer screen. NASDAQ, it said at the top, and underneath was a section of an alphabetical list of company names followed by the latest quotes. The other computer screen displayed a company profile: a name followed by tables of figures lined up across the screen. Beside the keyboard someone had left a school exercise book open about half way through. The page was filled with careful writing, which said:

Meu nome é Raquel Pereira. Tenho doze anos. Tenho duas irmãs, três gatos e um porquinho da Índia. Um porquinho da Índia morreu. Moro em Ferdy's Landing. Não gosto da escola.

Colombo, resplendent in Ishmael's Royal Stuart tartan dressing gown, put the phone down, dialled the number of the *Times*, and began talking to his editor. The door opened and Ishmael came in. 'The dryer'll be another ten minutes,' he said to Jared in an undertone. 'Did he get Olly?'

'No,' whispered Jared, 'the Pele Centre's permanently engaged. So Colombo rang Hy Brasil Radio and gave them his story: accurate enough if you allow a twenty per cent variant for exaggeration. Seemingly they'd heard from the coastguards in Ogg's Cove and Dorrado but no eyewitnesses at sea, so they were thrilled to bits to get our man from the *Times*. Then he rang his brother-in-law, who'd seen it himself from Dorrado coastguard station, and also he'd spoken to Toby Ready at Ogg's Cove. Apparently at Dorrado the sea went right out and swept in again about six feet over the high tide line – thank God it was low tide – and at Ogg's Cove it vanished entirely, but Colombo couldn't get through to Ogg's Cove either. Now he's talking to his editor again.'

'The sea vanished?'

'That's right. No more sea. It just went right out and drained the bay. Of course their first thought was "tidal wave", and they just had time to turn on the siren, when it came back. It went right over the sea wall and washed out the houses along the harbour, and of course the dunes are flooded. But it's no worse than that. And you really truly never noticed anything?'

'I've just had another look. It's left a line of debris just below the high tide mark. Brentness must have sheltered us. I still can't believe I was in here and never knew a thing. I should have got windows in this place after all.'

'Well, I don't understand why you didn't. If I had this view I'd want to see out of every wall.'

'When I'm working I'm working,' said Ishmael. 'Besides, it would spoil the line of the building. But I can't believe I missed this.'

'Typing away right through Revelations,' agreed Jared. 'It sounds like a Beckett play. When Colombo's finished he'll be off to the west coast. I think I'll go with him. Do you want to come? Then we could tell you about this other business on the way.'

Ishmael frowned at his screen. 'I suppose I could. I'd like to talk to the coastguards in Ogg's Cove. If we take the four-by-four we can go over the back track. Save Colombo taking that tin can of his all the way back round the mountain. We could stop by the Pele Centre on the way. I need to talk to West. As far as I know the Emergency Service has no strategy for tidal waves or flooding. I never thought of it before, but they should have. And yes, I want to hear about this trawler. I'll come. Why not? I've missed it all so far.'

'You will? He'll fall on your neck.' Jared laid his hand over Colombo's to stop him dialling yet another number. 'Hear that, sleuth? Ishmael's going to drive us over the back road. Save you at least an hour, and we can drop in on Olly on the way. And you'll have dry clothes in ten minutes. Come on, Watson! The game's afoot!'

NINE

Sidony Redruth. Ravnscar Castle. June 5th.
Notes for *Undiscovered Islands* (working title).

IF YOU GO to the end of Harbour Street in Ogg's Cove, you get to a long concrete harbour wall, where on a calm day you can walk out to the small skerry which has the harbour light on it. I'd been sitting there for a while, watching the waves break lazily on the black beach that lies just south of the town, and now I was walking slowly back to the shore. On the seaward side the waves slapped against the wall; on the harbour side the water was flat and green, and I could see down to the little fishes scavenging below.

The coastguard station is on the promontory where the harbour wall meets the land. It's a timber-framed building, smartly painted in white picked out in red. Big double doors open on to the slipway where the Ogg's Cove lifeboat is pulled up. I walked round the building. There were two men standing outside the open doors, one small and weatherbeaten, with greying hair under a coastguard's cap. The other was the man I'd seen talking to Colombo in Finnegan's, the one who'd asked about Spanish gold. He was wearing faded jeans and a red checked shirt, but even so he looked like Lawrence Fishburn in the film of *Othello*, at the beginning when he's just going off in triumph to re-capture Cyprus. To my surprise he called me by name as I passed. I went over to them.

'Ishmael Pereira,' he said, and shook my hand. 'This is Tobias Ready, who runs this station. Toby, this is Sidony Redruth, who's staying up at Ravnscar. Colombo tells me you're writing a book?'

I could murder Colombo; I realise now I never asked him to be discreet, but he doesn't *look* like a gossip. It's too late to complain now. The good part, I have to admit, is that it makes it more possible to ask questions. In fact I ended up getting a tour of the station, and that was useful. It isn't very big. They're most proud of their two new twenty-eight-foot medium rescue boats with their twin 200 Merc engines. At least, that's what Mr Ready said they were, and certainly the boat on the slipway had engines that looked large and powerful out of all proportion to its size. They need to be, because the boats go at fifty knots, which is almost sixty miles an hour when you work it out. The boat looked fat like an inflatable, but you could tell it's actually very strongly built. It has a curved deck round a solid wheelhouse, and really not much else. It only needs a crew of two, which doesn't seem much when you imagine what a rescue at sea must be like. Mr Ready showed me the gear for getting a man out of the sea. On a warm spring day on land, I found it difficult to imagine.

The rest of the station was small-scale and friendly. Next to the new boat there were open lockers with each man's survival gear, and a pile of yellow drysuits on top. Each locker had its owner's name on it: J. Outhwaite, L. Hilton, I. Cavalcanti, C. A. Alton, A. Bardens, J. Williams, J. Button, J. Howell, P. Kinnear, N. Frodge, G. Fuller, J. Pauquette, T. Collins, R. Elphinstone, T. Ready. I read the last name twice, and wondered if he'd been teased much at school, and whether this had helped to build his character sufficiently to become a chief coastguard. As well as all the boat gear and life-saving equipment there was a table tennis table at the back, which made the whole outfit seem more homely. When we went through to the mess there were a couple of young men at one of the tables. Ishmael told me later that most of the crew are under twenty-five. Above the mess and the galley there's a big radio room, and Mr Ready's own office looking over the harbour. He has pictures on his walls of lifeboats crashing through tremendous seas, which personally I would find discouraging, but then I don't pretend to be either knowledgeable or brave.

While we were there Mr Ready was called to the radio office, so Ishmael and I stood chatting for a bit. He used to work part-time for the coastguards when he first moved from St Brandons to Ferdy's Landing. The station is primarily for search and rescue, but he said it has a law-enforcing function as well. I thought of an article I'd read in last week's *Times*, and I asked him if he meant smuggling. He laughed, and said it was more often cases of speeding and drunk driving, and not keeping to the wake restrictions in the harbour. Not very exciting, really, or so he said. But the training had been useful. For example, he'd been seconded to do a diving course, and he's done quite a bit of that since. It turns out he's been working on the Spanish shipwreck off the island of Despair. I wanted to ask him more about that, but then Mr Ready came back. I didn't want to outstay my welcome, so I thanked them both, and left.

It was getting hot. I wandered back to the beach, picking up my bag on the way from where I'd left it tucked under one of the spectacular tree ferns that grow along the west coast. I ran down the dunes, and walked through black sand that burned the soles of my bare feet, down to the sea's edge. I went right on in, and little waves broke and lapped my ankles, then fell back, leaving their curled outlines etched across damp sand. I waded to my knees, where wavelets splashed my shorts and soaked me. I didn't care. Three swans swam outside the pointed rocks that marked the entrance to the bay. I walked up and down just where the sea met the sand, in and out of the water as it came and went. When I turned south I had to pull my sunhat over my eyes against the light; when I turned north the heat beat through my cotton shirt like a weight I had to carry on my back.

I ran across to the rocks where I'd left my bag. There wasn't a soul about; the village was invisible behind the pine trees. It took me less than a minute to change, and then I was running back into the sea without stopping, right up to my bare middle. I stood there for a while, holding my tummy in as if that would help, so all my ribs stuck out like a skeleton until I couldn't bear hovering any more, and I dived headfirst. The water sang chilly in my ears. I surfaced in a sparkling shower of drops, and swam fast for the rocks. Suddenly the sea wasn't cold any more, just liquid and milky. The swans floated a few yards away. I came up to the rocks and seaweed brushed my skin. I sat in the sun, and saw my arms and legs winter-white against the golden weed. Then I plunged again and opened my eyes, and there was a waterscape of rock and weed and night-coloured sea over black sand. When I came up into the sun everything looked bleached. The smell of pine trees drifted over the water. I rolled over on my back and stared into a bottomless blue sky.

In the end I stayed in too long, because when I came out I was shivering. Someone else was walking along the tideline, a man. I looked once, then twice. My first impression had been correct. He was wearing nothing at all. I hesitated. I too had very little on. Nakedness is not an offence in Hy Brasil, but I had been here long enough to know that it was unusual in public places. But he was already waving to me, so I could hardly rush away.

'Hi-aye.'

I'd already discovered that this is what they say for hello in Hy Brasil, so I said hello back, and stopped.

It was Olly West. Last time we'd met he'd literally not noticed I was there. This time he was staring. He himself looked, as far as I could tell out of the corner of my eye, extremely fit, but in spite of his unclothed state there was an odd lack of physical presence about him. I could imagine he might have been the sort of boy one would avoid at school. 'The water's quite warm today,' he remarked. 'Sixty-seven degrees at the surface. It warms up when it comes in over hot sand.'

'Is that what it is? I thought it was quite pleasant.'

'It's warm for the time of year. This time last year it didn't go above sixty. There were upwellings from the deep.'

'But not this year?'

'No.'

That seemed to end the conversation. I was shivering, but I didn't quite like to turn my back on him and walk away. 'You've been swimming too?' I asked conversationally.

'I swim every day.'

'All year?'

'Yes. Let me show you the breakwaters.'

He led the way, and I followed nervously. I had vaguely noticed a couple of lines of stones jutting into the sea. I saw now that the sand was piled much higher on one side than the other. 'Eighteen years' work.'

'Is that right?'

'Yes, I came to Hy Brasil eighteen years ago. The tide flows round Brentness, you see, out of the sound, and sweeps the sand southward. You see where it's eroded the grazings away at the top of the beach?'

'Isn't that above the high tide line?'

'It is now. Eighteen years ago the spring tides used to flood the saltmarshes almost as far as the village. I observed the currents, you see, and decided on the two breakwaters. I build them by hand. Dry stone. They need constant maintenance, of course. All that sand's piled up since I started. There's a nice beach for the children now.'

'Do you work on it every day?'

'If I can.' His gaze swept the horizon. I opened my mouth to say goodbye, but he spoke first. 'Are you interested in volcanoes?'

'Yes, I mean, one can hardly help being interested when one's living next door to an active volcano, but I don't know much about it.'

'You should come up to the Pele Volcano Observatory. Let me give you my card.'

I wondered a little hysterically where he was going to produce it from, but then he said, 'You'll have to come back to my bicycle. Do you know that we receive half-a-dozen minor eruptions or earth tremors a year, sometimes as high as five on the Richter scale?'

'No, I didn't know that. I know Mount Brasil is an active volcano though.'

'You must come and have a tour of the Pele Centre. The activities of the Centre will obviously be one of the main features of your book. I've finished down here for the present. We can go up there now. You're fortunate that I'm able to spare the time this morning. It's barely forty minutes' walk up the mountain.'

'Listen,' I said, wondering if Colombo had been gossiping to this man as well, 'I really would like to come and have a look. Truly I would. But just now I'm getting very cold.'

'Do you want me to give you a rub down?'

'No! I mean no, thank you. I think I should get dressed.'

I'd thought the hint was fairly obvious, but he didn't move. 'You *are* the young English lady that's writing the book?'

I thought this made me sound positively Edwardian, which, with dripping hair and dressed in a wet bikini, I was far from feeling. I tried to sound like a character out of E.M. Forster who has been studying her Baedeker to good effect. 'Yes. I came to Ogg's Cove today to look at the dig. The Viking farm. I don't know if anyone's working on it just now.'

He smiled and held out his hand to me. 'Olly West,' he said. I put my clammy hand in his, and he shook it for a long time. 'There's not a lot to see, everything's still under turf, but the diggers'll be back next week. I can show you as much as there is to see now if you want.'

'Oh,' I said, trying to stop my teeth chattering. 'You work on the dig?'

'Oh, no. As I say, I'm a volcanologist.'

'Excuse me,' I said. 'I really have to put some clothes on.' I started up the beach, and Olly began to follow me. 'Please,' I said rather desperately. 'I'd rather get dressed on my own.'

'Oh, certainly, certainly. I'll wait for you here, and then we can get the card from my bicycle.'

He left the beach, but when I climbed up the dunes on to the path he was waiting on the path to the village. He'd put on a pair of jeans and some Biblical-looking sandals, and I saw as I came closer that he was flourishing a business card in my direction. 'Though, as I say, we could go straight up to the unit now. What are you doing this afternoon?'

'Lucy will expect me back before too long.'

'Oh yes, you're staying at Ravnscar. I can telephone Lucy and tell her you'll be late.'

'But . . .'

'No, no, it's no trouble at all. You don't mind walking uphill for a mile or two? I can't very well offer you a lift.' He mounted his bicycle and began to ride off along the road north. 'I'll telephone Lucy for you while I'm waiting for you to catch up,' he called as he disappeared ahead.

I spent about five minutes making up my mind whether to follow him or not. I'd heard about the Pele Centre, of course, and it occurred to me that if I offended this man now, I might never get another invitation. And I did need to find out about the volcano. I was here to do a job, and that meant carrying on regardless. I skirted the top of the beach, and began to climb the dusty track into the foothills of Mount Prosper.

On the outside the Pele Centre was an unassuming L-shaped one-storey building set into a flat terrace hollowed out of the mountainside. The inside was like walking into the inside of a spaceship, and, apart from the pointed ears, there was an unnerving resemblance between Olly West and Mr Spock.

'Come in, come in,' said Olly. 'Welcome to our humble abode.'

The humble abode was an airy office with windows all down one side looking over the sound to Despair, and an impressive array of computers on the work benches which lined three walls. The monitor nearest me was displaying a list of seismic magnitudes, at least, so Olly told me. Above every work station was a noticeboard overflowing with pinned-up graphs and tables of figures. The board nearest the door had posters, obviously done by primary school children, with messages like, EARTHQUAKES DON'T KILL: BUILDINGS DO; FIRE: THE REAL DANGER and DROP, COVER, HOLD, with a graphic illustration of a person under a table clinging on to one of the legs.

'Oh, yes,' said Olly, seeing the direction of my gaze. 'We had Lyonsness Elementary School up here doing a project. Earth shocks are often associated with volcanic activity. Most adults in this country will have experienced at least one minor quake. Education is a crucial factor in eliminating casualties.'

Someone with cropped orange hair and a heavy-metal t-shirt was working at one of the computers. He didn't look round when we came in, which in Hy Brasil struck me as unusual. The fourth wall was given over to filing cabinets and untidy bookshelves full of unbound journals. Above them was the whole of the one-inch map of Hy Brasil, all five sheets put together. It had yellow marker pins scattered across the mountainous areas. I made straight for it, as being, after the posters, the most comprehensible and attractive object in the room.

The young man at the computer turned round when I walked past him, and I recognised him at once, in spite of his changed hair. 'Peterkin,' I said, and after a moment I took the hand he held out to me. I still don't expect anyone younger than me to shake my hand. 'But weren't you working at the Tourist Office?'

'Finished there last week. This is more interesting, and I can live at home.' He winked at me, and added, 'Money's better too.'

'Well, that's good. I suppose tremors are more exciting than tourists really.'

'There aren't any tourists. And until someone puts on an excursion fare there won't be.'

'So you're waiting for the volcano to erupt instead?'

Peterkin touched wood, I noticed, but before he could speak again a hand was laid on my shoulder and I jumped. 'Let me show you round,' said Olly.

I don't know what it is about Olly West's style of delivery that makes everything he tries to describe increasingly obscure the more he goes on talking about it. Luckily, after the first five minutes, Peterkin got up and joined us, and from his *sotto voce* interpolations I did begin to make some kind of sense of the place.

Peterkin says that I need to go up Mount Brasil to see the monitoring stations for myself. They're around the crater and on ledges inside it. They put them in oil drums, he said, and seal them against the weather, and fix them on concrete bases so unless there's a really violent earth movement they remain stable. Inside each one there's a computer, powered by a solar panel, and connected to a radio transmitter. Peterkin showed me pinned-up printouts on his noticeboard of signal amplitude measurements which looked to me like an irregular heartbeat, which he explained to me were previous eruptions. He and Olly explained quite a lot about a possible eruption. Apparently Mount Brasil has a history of sending out very fluid lava flows. He showed me another map of Hy Brasil, a smaller scale black and white chart-like map, with contours both above and under water. The existing lava flows were marked in diagonal grey lines, and projected ones in grey spots.

'But that's the whole of Dorrado!' I said.

'That's right,' said Olly. 'You see it's the southern aspect of the mountain that's most unstable. We've monitored half a dozen tremors there this year already. What's more, they've been getting stronger and more frequent just in the last few weeks.

Nothing you'd notice, even if you were there, but there's definitely something going on underneath. But then it's been doing that since records began in 1858, and probably for a thousand years or so before that.'

'But Mount Prosper erupted only two hundred years ago,' I said. 'You've hardly drawn any projected lava there.'

'Mount Prosper's kind of quiet these days,' said Peterkin. 'Mind you, that could be partly because we haven't got the monitors up there, so we might not know.'

'That's not very comforting. Would they have time to get out of Dorrado, or would it be like Pompeii?'

'No, not like Pompeii,' said Peterkin. 'Like I say, we don't get that sort of chemistry. When it erupts – which it does in a minor way quite often – we get a gradual build-up of pressure inside the mountain. A lava lake starts to rise inside the crater. Then suddenly the pressure inside makes the surface crack open along a fissure. Then we have a line of lava fountains followed by a liquid flow like a slow river. Here, look, these are photos from just below the crater in 1989. See, quite pretty really, like fireworks. And you notice the sky is still almost blue. I was just a kid, but I can remember we could see the glow from Lyonsness for about a week. For us it was exciting, but I'd be nervous if I lived on the west side. In fact there is a plan, if it were flowing towards Dorrado, to try to divert the flow down the Dorrado river bed. It might or might not be possible. But what they'd do first is evacuate the place. The Emergency Services have a strategy ready for that.'

'You mean it's *expected*?'

'No, I mean it might happen, and it's as well to be ready.'

Olly West kept on talking through all this. He seemed unaware that Peterkin was with us at all. He pressed graphs and figures into my hand so by this time I was carrying quite a sheaf of printouts. It was very kind of him to bother.

'And this is my office.' Olly led me out of the main room through a chilly-looking kitchen area and into a small office at the other end. My first impression was of a huge screen across which the faint heartbeat of a catatonic patient was slowly pulsating, screeds of computer paper spilling over the floor like an unwound toilet roll, and shelves full of files and what looked like the leftover remnants of several jumble sales.

'I don't know how I'd behave in an eruption,' I told him. 'I'd be terrified, I know, but as long as I wasn't actually about to die I think I'd be very interested at the same time. But then the most interesting things often involve a certain amount of fear, don't you find?'

'No,' he said. 'But then I'm a man.'

'You don't mean nothing ever scares you?'

'No,' he said, with what I reckoned was a smirk. 'Why should it?'

This, coming from one who confronted the utter insignificance of humanity at every moment of every day of his working life, reduced me to unaccustomed silence, which Olly instantly misinterpreted. 'I'd be happy to take you on to the volcano,' he said. 'I can't spare the time this week; I'm afraid you'll have to wait until I've got a space in my diary. But then I'll certainly explain it all to you, and you needn't be frightened with me.'

'Thank you,' I said. 'I think I'd be more comfortable with someone who knew how to be afraid.'

He opened his mouth, and I knew, with a slightly sick feeling, that he was going to offer me the kind of reassurance you'd give to a pet poodle on its way to the vet's for a lethal injection, when suddenly the fax machine bleeped and churned into action.

'Ah,' said Olly. 'Excuse me one moment.'

Out of the window I could see where the slopes of Mount Prosper cascaded down to an azure sea. To the east the double peak of Despair rose out of rainbow-coloured vapour into clear blue air. It was impossible to imagine how the scene could ever be different, but when I looked to the left there were the fanged lava ridges of Brentness reaching almost to a whitewashed house which I knew from my map must be Ferdy's Landing. From here one could see where the lava stopped as a pencil-sharp line between green pasture and grey rock. Another hundred yards and Ferdy's Landing would have vanished forever in 1783. That, I knew from my research in the library, would have been a pity. According to F. Baskerville's *Architecture of Hy Brasil* parts of the house at Ferdy's Landing dated back to the early seventeenth century. It had originally been built as a fortified house, similar to the tower houses on the Scottish borders, by Nicholas Hawkins, one of the first of the Pirate Kings who had made Hy Brasil their secret base. The house had been rebuilt after a fire in 1688, and then remained relatively untouched, according to Baskerville, until modern times. At the time the book was written (1972) the building was in a state of neglect and disrepair, and the account ended with the recommendation that it merited careful restoration, as nearly as was possible, to its original state.

It was a beautiful day outside. I wondered if I should signal my thanks to Olly and creep away. He had his back to me, though, and was typing rapidly away at the keyboard with two fingers. I looked at the shelves, and took down a couple of glossy pamphlets from the US Geological Survey and looked at awe-inspiring photographs of eruptions in Washington and Hawaii. I found another coloured bulletin, all about the Western Wrangell mountains in Alaska. Now there's a place I'd like to go, maybe second on my list after Hawaii. I looked at all the pictures, put the pamphlets back, and surveyed the rest of the shelves. The journals of the USGS and the *Transactions of the American Geophysical Union* I was content to take as read. There were piles of computer printouts which couldn't be of much use to anyone, I thought, without some kind of filing system. Instead they were all mixed in with sundry trifles such as a miner's lamp, half a dozen glass fishing floats, a beach ball, some scraps of whitened driftwood, a car battery, an old green wine glass with a crack in it, a coil of climbers' rope and a school satchel. It was the first place in Hy Brasil, apart from Kidd's Hotel, where I'd seen dust. The air is so clear here that only serious accumulation produces any.

Olly had read his fax, typed and sent an answer, and now he picked up the phone, dialled a number, and began a one-sided discussion which, as far as I could make out, was about whether someone or other should be allowed to have money for some sort of salvage operation. Olly seemed to be arguing vehemently against the idea. I assumed he'd forgotten all about me, and I began to sidle towards the door. Suddenly he turned round and began gesticulating wildly, talking down the phone at the same time. I signalled back total non-comprehension, and made my escape to the other office.

Peterkin had his feet up on the table and was studying the cricket scores in the *Times*. He jumped up when the door opened, but when he saw it was only me he relaxed again.

'I think Olly's forgotten me,' I said. 'I need to go now, anyway. But thanks – it's a pity there're no tourists really. You'd deal with them very well.'

'Natural charm,' said Peterkin. 'Have a coffee. I'm due for a break.'

I hesitated. 'Can we sit outside?'

'Sure.'

We settled ourselves on a grassy bank littered with cigarette ends, which looked out over Ferdy's Landing and Despair. I could see a boat just crossing the entrance to the sound, and I said to Peterkin, 'Isn't that one of the new twenty-eight-foot medium rescue boats from Ogg's Cove coastguard station?'

The amazed respect in his eyes was balm to my soul. 'Yes,' he said, glancing from me to the boat and back again. 'They go up the west side of Despair, and sometimes all the way round the island, depending on the tide. It hardly seems necessary. Nothing ever happens round here. But it's a job. I wish I could get into the coastguards, but I'd never pass the medical.' I was too polite to ask why not, and he didn't say.

We looked across the water in silence for a bit. Then I asked, 'So no one lives on Despair now? It seems a pity.'

'No one till last year,' said Peterkin. 'Right now there's a guy out there monitoring gannets. We've got a brand new gannet colony in Hy Brasil. Did you know that?'

'Oh yes, come to think about it I did know about him. He's the one who found a packet of heroin on the beach about a fortnight ago? I read about it in the paper. I'd like to get to Despair. Do you think there's anyone who'd take me over there?'

'Cocaine, not heroin. Per Pedersen at Lyonsness goes over. Jed – the gannet guy – he'd take you, but it's hard to get hold of him.'

'I think Lucy knows him.'

'Oh yes, I'd heard you were staying up at Ravnscar. Now there's a place! Found any hidden treasure yet?'

'Is there any?'

'Of course. Ravnscar is heaving with treasure, everyone knows that. It's built over the chapel that St Brendan used when he came here. That's why it's an unlucky house. It was built on holy ground.'

'I should have thought that made it lucky.'

'Sacrilege,' said Peterkin with relish. 'At least, it was all right for the Portuguese, because they built a chapel there—'

'The chapel's still there.'

'—they built a chapel, and they kept the lamp burning and a . . . what do you call it? I don't know, we're Methodists – but they kept the bread already blessed or whatever it is . . .'

'Reserved sacrament.'

'Yes, that. They did all that, and the ghosts were satisfied. But when the Portuguese were gone, and the Pirate Kings took over Hy Brasil – this would have been in the sixteenth century, something like that – they say the original Morgan marched into Ravnscar, into the chapel with his helmet on and his spurs, and when the old monk, or the chaplain, or whoever it was, tried to defend the door Morgan cut him down with his broadsword.

And the pirates desecrated the altar and flung down the sanctuary lamp, and held their secret ceremonies before the crucifix. At least, I'm not sure if that was supposed to be there or in the original chapel, because like I say, Brendan's chapel is underneath the later building somewhere, so they say. So Brendan put a curse on Morgan and all his house, and said that though they might survive until the end of history they would never prosper long. And it's true, that's how it's been. In the eighteenth century the Morgans got rich and even respectable, I believe, but then the volcano went up and they lost all their best land.' Peterkin pointed dramatically at Brentness. 'See that? That was all vineyards and apple orchards until then. And so it went on, right up until now.'

'I don't see many signs of a curse now.'

Peterkin gave me a strange look. 'You don't? But surely you know . . .'

'Ah Peterkin! Sidony! Taking a break, I see. Sorry I was called away. An urgent message came through, and I had to deal with it at once.'

'That's fine,' I said, getting up. 'I was only waiting to say goodbye. And thank you very much for showing me round.'

'Come again, come again. Feel free to drop in whenever you like. And if you want a companion for your swimming expeditions, I'm down on the beach every day. The morning is the best time to find me.'

I caught Peterkin's eye, and realised that he was reading my thoughts. I blushed.

When I looked up from the first bend in the road the Pele Centre was already invisible in its snug hollow. Olly had gone, but Peterkin was still standing on the grassy bank, two empty mugs dangling from his left hand. The last glimpse I had before I turned the corner, was of him still waving to me. And then I was on my own again, with the rest of the day before me.

TEN

'ISHMAEL'S IN ST BRANDONS. He's gone to talk to the President.'

'What? About smuggling?'

'Smuggling?' exclaimed Anna Pereira. 'No, of course not. He wants a working group on his new employment project.'

'Oh, is this what he was saying about 800 numbers?'

'That's right. You see, these companies can have answering services anywhere in the world. Location doesn't make any difference, now that everything you want to know is stored out there in the ether anyway. And the big companies could be attracted here because people in Hy Brasil learn a high standard of literacy and politeness at school. Also they have an accent which other English speakers find attractive, and they're prepared to accept low wages. Ishmael says information technology is the only way forward for us, and if we can land contracts now that provide a lot of clerical employment it'll address the immediate problem, and there's no reason why more interesting projects won't follow.'

'I see: nice manners and low expectations,' said Jared. 'I suppose that's one way to go down in history.'

'Well, I didn't expect you to be realistic. Your coffee, Jared.' She put a small cup of espresso and a glass of water in front of him.

'Thank you.' Jared took a spoonful of sugar, and stirred it

in slowly. Whenever he was in the Pereira kitchen he found himself thinking with vague nostalgia about domestic life. At home in Ogg's Cove they'd had a white-scrubbed kitchen table just like this one, only half the size. His mother had had pots of plants on the windowsill too, only she used to breed African violets, not geraniums. There had been a drying rack over the stove too, just like the one that Anna had lowered now. He watched her sorting socks into pairs and rolling them together in little balls, and suddenly the memory of his mother was so near that he could hear her voice in his mind, a thing he'd hardly ever been able to do since the day she'd died. A familiar sensation of sorrow mixed with guilt rose chokingly inside his chest. He cleared his throat and said to Anna, 'I wish I hadn't missed him. I wanted to talk to him before I went to St Brandons.'

'Were you needing the car?'

'I borrowed Per's motorbike. My boat's at Lyonsness. No, there was just something I needed to tell him about.'

Anna took down Ishmael's blue workshirt, and began to fold it. 'Jed?'

'Yes?'

'We've talked about this smuggling business, you know, Ishmael and I. Has something else happened?'

'Well, sort of. Maybe.'

'OK, you don't have to tell me.' Anna pulled down a line of children's t-shirts, and sorted them rapidly as she talked. 'Only have you seen today's *Times* yet? Tidesman's written another piece that might interest you.'

'He has? Already? Where is it? Can I see?'

'Sure, the paper's over there on the rocking chair, under the cat.'

Jared carefully lifted an ancient cat without uncurling it, and slid the newspaper out from underneath it. He turned to the centre page, and read:

TIDESMAN: FREE ENTERPRISE OR A NEW VERSE TO AN OLD SONG?

There's no hiding the facts; not even a government can do that. The statistics speak for themselves: sixty per cent unemployment in rural areas. Outside St Brandons we have seven thousand adults registered for employment. Just over four thousand are in work, which leaves approximately three thousand unemployed. Nearly all those drawing government benefit are male; nearly all were fishermen. And they're just the tip of the iceberg. The adult population of employable age, outwith the capital, is close to eleven thousand. Granted not all want work, but how many, in this depressing climate, even bother to register?

Life on the dole is a new concept in Hy Brasil. We're an independent people. Traditionally we've survived by pursuing what might arguably be designated the second oldest profession. Piracy is one form of theft, smuggling another. It's pretty clear to most of us that there's as much revenue coming into Hy Brasil as there was in the heyday of the Pirate Kings. So who's bringing it? Where's it coming from?

Disregarding my iconic status and advanced years, it seemed incumbent upon me to undertake a little practical investigation . . .

Jared read to the end of the article, and looked up. 'He's right, you know. What did Ishmael say when he read this?'

Anna pulled up the empty drying rack. It wasn't until she was refilling the kettle that she said, 'Ishmael's being very cautious. But while I was trying to read that, he was talking about the drug trade. Apparently all the stuff that comes here is grown in South America, then exported to Europe. So it has to come in by sea. Anyone who could offer a halfway house, as it were, could make a fortune.'

'Precisely. So *is* anyone making a fortune around here? Apart from Ishmael?'

'Ishmael's about the only one around here doing a job that makes sense. There's got to be a way forward, Jed; all the more so if you're right, and we're filling our treasury out of the wickedest trade the Atlantic ever saw. One of the most wicked, I mean. Someone has to do something, and if they don't do it for good they'll do it for evil.'

'OK, so if it's not cocaine, it's Silicon Valley. Did I ever say I had any objection? It's this 800-number business that bothers me. Anyway, I hate the things. It's like if you phoned to find out what time the 227 gets to the harbour War Memorial, and you found yourself talking to some chap in Nebraska. If you're lucky enough to get a human being at all, that is, never mind a sexy accent.'

He was interrupted by scuffling sounds and shrill voices at the door, and he turned round, smiling.

'Jared! We didn't know you were here! You didn't come by boat!' The youngest Pereira flung herself upon him and climbed on his knee, wedging herself between his arms and the table. 'Jared! We might be getting some Rhode Island Reds. Rachel and Pappa are looking at some chickens on the way back from St. Brandons.'

'Jared, Eva found a glass fishing float on the beach. A pink one. Did you ever find a pink one?'

'Leave him alone and let him drink his coffee.'

'They're all right.' He couldn't say to Anna that he loved it that her children adored him, that their attentions were a delight at a time when no one else ever came close enough even to touch him. With Susanna's arm around his neck, half choking him, and Eva leaning on him and getting between him and the page he was trying to read, Jared was happy, but only half aware of it. He was trying to concentrate.

'Anna, you do agree? I've thought about everyone I know who seems to be making any money, and there really isn't anyone, apart from you lot. And you keep pretty quiet about it, apart from the holidays in Bali and a byre that's turned into something out of *Star Wars*.'

'I don't know if I agree or not. It's so far-fetched. But I read the paper, and I find that this year we've spent public money on a swimming pool, an art gallery, and a new wing for Ogg's Cove Elementary. For the first time we're supporting unemployed people on welfare; for the first time there *are* any unemployed. It doesn't seem to be bothering us much, does it? And who, apart from my husband, is doing the kind of work that brings the money in, that's what I'd like to know?'

'Our Pappa brings our money in,' said Susanna, dipping a wet finger into the sugar bowl.

'So does your Mamma,' said Jared, 'when she works at the hospital.'

'Speaking of which,' said Anna, 'This year we applied to get a radiology unit of our own, so we wouldn't have to send folk into St Brandons. And we got it. We got other things too, more or less everything on the list. Hardly anyone in Lyonsness is earning a decent wage any more, so where's it coming from?'

'Is this what Ishmael says too?'

'No, Jed, it's what I'm saying. And if I'm right, the last place you should be just now is on Despair.'

Susanna wriggled off his knee, and stood expectantly beside him. Jared smiled at her absently. 'What's that got to do with it? Can you tell me why ever not?'

'No,' said Anna. 'You must see that I can't.'

The children were determined to wait for him, obviously. 'Yes, I see. Well, I'll have to think about that. I must be off now.'

'You're going into St Brandons?'

'Yes, I'll hitch in from Lyonsness. It's my shopping day.'

'You won't do anything foolish, will you, Jed? Not without talking to Ishmi first?'

'No, I won't do anything foolish.'

*   *   *

Jared stood in the President's office in front of the President's vast knee-hole desk, behind which a big plate-glass window looked out on the most famous view in Hy Brasil, which had once adorned the front cover of *Time* magazine. Jared was conscious of his seaboots on the thick pile carpet, and that he was wearing the same jeans and sweater that he'd had on for the last week while he did his bird rounds on Despair. He was also painfully aware of himself as the same Jared who'd found the transition from Ogg's Cove Elementary to Lyonsness Junior High an agonising denial of everything that he'd ever understood himself to be. Deliberately he conjured up an image of his later self as he'd been in England, in Norway, in Iceland, everything he'd learned to become away from this ridiculous little country that happened to be his own. Thus he faced the President.

James Hook sat behind his desk, against the backdrop that had become a cliché in any televised discussion of the state of Hy Brasil. He leaned back in his chair, and regarded his latest petitioner with the saturnine look that had become so associated with his image it was hard to imagine now that it was not a deliberate part of the performance. He reserved it, however, for citizens like Jared. Where he met with no opposition or hostility, he became the jovial epitome of approachable government. The likeness to Charles II was an asset he still exploited for all it was worth. The current underground joke in Hy Brasil was that he was already apologising for taking such an unconscionable time a-dying. As he well might, some would add, seeing that only the life of the President stood between them and the democracy he'd sworn for ever to uphold.

Good form, however, had always been maintained. Good form demanded that the President be accessible to all who wished to speak to him. Good form disguised the electronic metal detector discreetly within the Georgian panelling of the door frame through which all visitors must pass. Good form placed his personal bodyguard six feet away in the ante-room with a Smith and Wesson 357 at the ready, watching every move in the President's office on screen. Good form arranged his alarm button under the desktop so that it was invisible to any suppliant on the far side of the desk. Good form revealed the great man himself: alone, unarmed and affable.

'So,' Hook was saying, 'Mr Honeyman. I heard that you were back in Hy Brasil. You did well abroad, so I was told. Won't you sit down?'

'Thank you.' Jared sat uneasily on the edge of an uncomfortably low chair. 'I want to talk to you about the Mayda Trust.'

'The Mayda Trust? An excellent institution. Have you visited our new Art Gallery at Maldun's Mill? I was there for the opening ceremony, and I have to say it's most impressive.'

'No,' said Jared, and took a deep breath. 'I applied to the Mayda Trust for a grant so that we could salvage the *Cortes*. Maybe you saw my application?'

Hook made a dismissive gesture. 'I may have glanced over it. I'm afraid I don't remember.'

Jared bit his lip, and remembered the part of himself that had gone away and made good. He told Hook about the project with the same quiet assurance that had got him everything he'd wanted when he was out of Hy Brasil. He convinced himself all over again. The President pressed his fingertips together, and listened with apparent attention.

'Yes, Mr Honeyman, I appreciate all this. However, you must see that it would be quite unconstitutional for me to dispute any decision reached by the committee of the Mayda Trust. All I can really suggest is that you re-apply next year. You do understand, of course, that in a time of recession we can't follow up every cultural project, however meritorious it may be within its own terms.'

'But this is the thing that concerns me,' said Jared. 'I see no signs of recession. There's more money in Hy Brasil now than I've ever known. If you travel around and see what's happening, you'd begin to assume that this is one of the richest countries in the world.'

'And so we were, Mr Honeyman, as you well know. We retain an infrastructure which has been very carefully built up through better days, and we draw upon investments that were made to insure our nation against such a reversal of fortune as has indeed occurred, and thank God, I say, that we have done so. Our wealth was built on the fishing industry, and as a maritime expert you should understand better than anybody why we're in serious trouble now. You can't blame the government for that.'

'I don't blame the government for that. But I'm not a fool, Mr Hook, and I can see with my own eyes that this government is not poor.' Under those imperturbable hazel eyes Jared was beginning to lose his temper. Careful, he thought, I have to be careful.

'So what are you trying to suggest?' The question flashed out at him so suddenly it took him by surprise.

'I'm suggesting to you,' said Jared, 'that you could very easily find the money for me to salvage the *Cortes*. I'm suggesting that the reason that I didn't get it has nothing to do with lack of funds. I'm suggesting that maybe this government would prefer to have no inhabitants on the island of Despair.'

'Young man,' said Hook. 'Either you're dangerously arrogant or a complete fool. Do you think it wise to try to blackmail a President in his own office?'

'It would be unwise anywhere, if that's what I was trying to do. Only I'm not.'

'So what did you come here for?'

It was the way the President leaned back so comfortably in his chair, accusing him of blackmail, for God's sake, and looked down on him through half shut eyes, that did the trick. Jared forgot everything he'd learned to be; he was just a boy from Ogg's Cove who wore old hand-me-downs and who hadn't got a father, alive or dead, and since that was all he was, Jared knew he could be no match for this. It had taken him years to learn to keep his temper, and with a look Hook stripped all that time away from him, and Jared flared up in a blaze of useless anger.

All he'd gained abroad now was the ability to speak his mind; it might have been much better if he had not.

'I came to say,' said Jared, red and furious, 'that if I were to find myself a citizen of a country that made its money out of destroying other people's lives, that was secretly engaged in a trade that made fortunes by working towards the ruin of other nations, that lied about its contacts and its revenue, that evaded any kind of enquiry and thought itself beyond accountability to anybody – if I ever found myself a citizen of a nation that behaved like that, I'd fight to expose it with everything I'd got! I wouldn't rest until I'd found out what was going on and made it public. I'd fight for the freedom to vote against it and bring it down. I couldn't live with myself if I did anything else! That isn't what I came to say, but it's what I think. And if you can't deny what's happening in Hy Brasil, if you can't give me proof that all our money is coming to us the way it should, all above-board and accountable to any citizen who wants to see the books, then I'll fight back until you admit what's going on and move heaven and earth to change it!'

There was a silence. The President didn't move, and gradually Jared realised with horror exactly what he'd just said and done.

'Mr Honeyman.' It was the coldest voice he'd ever heard. 'In my time, you may recall, I organised a revolution. Before you were born we created a free country and called it Hy Brasil. If I had been inclined to give way to the kind of display you have just exhibited to me, I think we would be a British colony today.' He looked Jared in the eyes. 'But you would rejoice at that, no doubt. As your father's son, you would presumably rejoice if that were so.'

Jared was up on his feet. 'My father was not a traitor!'

'Your father was a British agent. Your father was trusted by this government, and he sold the information he received to the British Secret Service.'

'I don't believe it!' But the trouble was, perhaps he did. Jack

Honeyman had never taken his eight-year-old son into his confidence. No one who knew the truth had ever told Jared anything about it. And his father *was* a traitor; Jared knew that all too well. He was a traitor because he'd left his family and never sent a message, never so much as a postcard. He'd gone out into the wide world beyond Hy Brasil and he'd never come back. So this time Jared didn't even have his own conviction to support him. 'He was not a traitor,' repeated Jared. 'It was only your word against his.'

'The Government's word. I'm sorry, Mr Honeyman. I can understand the episode is a distressing memory for you. You would do better to forget it. Forget you ever had a father, and this government will have the courtesy to do the same.'

'I bet it would! It was you that exiled him! He never had the chance to speak!'

'Mr Honeyman, I think you'd better go.' As the President spoke, the door magically opened, and a uniformed bodyguard appeared. 'Mr Hands, you may show this gentleman out.'

Bewildered and appalled at what he'd done, Jared turned to follow. At the door Hook softly called him back. 'Mr Honeyman!'

'Yes?'

'You accuse me of having Jack Honeyman exiled. I don't think you quite grasp the position.' Jared waited, mute. When Hook spoke again his voice was so quiet it was almost gentle. 'I could so much more easily have had him shot.'

'Open the Madeira, Jim. It's been that sort of day.'

'But you're all set for Friday?'

'It all came together just at the last minute. I shifted the lighthouses. They were a section, but now I've made them more of a theme. Interspersed. It's better. Like scraps of reason in the void.'

'Eh?'

'Drops of light, I mean, where there wasn't anything before.

A metaphor, maybe, for the beginnings of history and habitation. God, I'm tired. Am I talking nonsense?'

'Nesta Kirwan, you are as beautiful as the sun on Prosper at the dawn of a clear June day. You are the light of my life, a beacon in the terrible void of endless weekdays, and I adore you.'

'Even when I'm preparing an exhibition?'

'More than ever.'

'You know, it's not till I see them all there, on the wall, that I begin to understand what it is I've done. It's all fragments up until then. Bits of the elephant. But I've got it, Jim, it works. One sees the place. I didn't even know myself, that I could make it be like that. I'm sick to death of it. I shall put a padlock on the darkroom door and sit in the sun for the next month. I shall be a lizard on a rock.'

Nesta put down her glass with a thump, leaned back on the sofa and shut her eyes. Jim sat down cautiously at her feet, twirling his glass so that the Madeira caught bits of lamplight like silver fishes in a brown net. She poked at him with her foot, and he looked round at her.

The way she was lying was perfect, just as all her movements, all her poses, were perfect. It had always fascinated him, this extraordinary way in which she inhabited her body, as if she were more present than other people. Not more substantial; she was still as slight as she'd been at twenty; it was more the way she was as suggestively animal yet deceptively refined as a well-bred cat. He'd been watching her for thirty years, off and on, and still he was acutely aware of the actress in her, even though she'd never stood on a stage since the day she left drama school. She never seemed to age either; perhaps that was all part of it. Her brown hair was cropped short in a way that few other women in their forties could have got away with. No one could have looked less masculine. Her hands, folded on her chest, were brown and slender like a peasant Madonna's, and her lashes curled on her cheeks as innocently as a Murillo bambino. He wasn't sure, though he knew her better than anyone else in the world, if the effect she was having on him now was calculated to the last detail, or if the only images in her mind were the remembered imprints of her own photographs. Perhaps it made very little difference. He knew her work, perhaps better than he knew her, and was quite aware of the technique that lay behind the blazing simplicity of her compositions.

She was wearing the scarlet tracksuit she did her yoga in, and bare feet. That was Nesta. On Friday, at the opening, she would be the most elegant woman in Hy Brasil, in her own offbeat idiom. On Friday, he guessed, she would wear black, with amber and old silver, and some sort of floating scarf that always draped itself the right way, however she stood or sat or gesticulated, as she always did when the conversation began to excite her. On Friday it would excite her, because everyone would be talking about her work. He could never describe the details of what she wore, or the content of what she had said, but the way she looked, the way she spoke: he could have gone on forever about that, if he had been enough of a poet to find the words.

He was not a possessive man. When he gave her this apartment he gave himself no corresponding entitlement to ownership. He had only thought that the view was what she needed. On those mornings when he woke up in her bed and looked out over St Brandons and straight into the sunrise, and watched the light shine back into her austere white room and tinge everything with a flush of pink, he never reflected on his own generosity in bringing this about. He simply thought that this place was right for her. If it was mostly his money that had paid for the pale carpets, the three well-chosen items of Regency inlaid furniture, the white sofas with their dark green and maroon cushions, and the pre-Raphaelite painting of Hercules plucking the golden apples, it never occurred to him to count the cost. Nor did he worry about whether any other man might lie in the white bed with linen sheets when he was elsewhere. No one else would know quite what he knew. His most possessive thought was that Queen Anne Terrace was very handy for

Government House, less than five minutes' walk, and that was very convenient for him when he'd been working late.

'Jim?'

'Uh-huh?'

'Do you think my work is important? I mean, really important?'

'What's that supposed to mean? To you? To me? To Art with a capital A?'

'It isn't political.'

'What does that mean? Of course I think it's important.'

'Why? What you think is important is freedom and power and all that stuff.'

'You're always telling me what I think. Freedom and power? These days it's more a case of All That Stuff. The other was a long time ago. Nesta, am I getting old?'

' "And deeper than did ever plummet sound, I'll drown my book." Did you have a tiring day as well?'

'Not too bad. I had to deal with an enraged young man after lunch, and in the morning I had an interesting encounter with a crocodile.'

'Oh, of course, you said. You had to open the new reptile house at the zoo. Is it nice?'

'Charming. Though it crossed my mind halfway through that possibly it's unwise to encourage a collection of poisonous snakes in a seismically sensitive zone.'

'Oh?'

'They have a black mamba and two cobras who will no doubt reproduce, since male and female created he them. Certainly they seemed to be passionately intertwined. Are cobras passionate? Do they lay eggs? Natural history isn't my strong point, but in my opinion Brendan did this country a favour when he banished the serpent. I've never been partial to anything that crawls on its belly. Obviously I shouldn't have gone into politics.'

'I don't quite see where the earthquakes come in.'

'Just a thin pane of glass between us and them. If the earth moved, what then? I'd have been caught between a grinning crocodile and a posse of poisonous snakes. Given our seismic record, I'm not sure it's a wise project. Ishmael Pereira began it when he donated that damn stingray. I don't like zoos anyway.'

'But you smiled and smiled and cut the tape?'

'Just so.'

'I like Ishmael.'

'Oddly enough, he had an interview with me today as well. Now there's a man after my own heart. He actually seems to understand that the country needs to generate an income before it spends it.'

'You were cross with him last week because he wanted you to put more money into seismic monitoring after that tidal wave on the west coast.'

'That was no tidal wave. That was an excitable young reporter trying to get himself on to the front page.'

'Tidesman is thirty-six, m'dear, and past worrying about being on the front page. Nor is Ishmael an excitable young reporter. Nor are the Ogg's Cove coastguards, so far as I know.'

'Neither Ishmael nor the coastguards produced this week's piece of sensationalism. However, it won't happen again. I spoke to the senior editor this morning. Ishmael had to admit that this remarkable cosmological event passed quite unnoticed by him, and he was at Ferdy's Landing all the time. Now he does know something about the sea; I would accept him as a reliable witness.'

'Jed Honeyman was quoted as saying it must have been "quite a quake", and I should have thought he'd know if anyone does. I enjoyed that day I did the diving photographs with them. But they told me the *Cortes* project didn't get its funding after all?'

'Nothing to do with me. This is a democracy, remember. We have committees for all that sort of thing. All projects must be (1) banal, and (2) anodyne. If Ishmael wants to go diving he can afford to pay for it himself, and young Honeyman, who came in and ranted at me earlier today, can't expect a government subsidy in order to play Robinson Crusoe on Despair.'

'Jared came and ranted at you? I thought he was a delightful young man. I got a brilliant photograph of him. You'll see it in the exhibition.'

'Delightful? That freckled whelp? I've seen enough of young Honeyman this afternoon not to wish instantly to repeat the experience.'

'Well, he was charming to me. Are you sure you weren't horrible to him, Jim? Why did he come?'

'Angst, m'dear. Avoid young men; either they're exhausting or they're disappointing. Honeyman has ideals and is therefore exhausting. Look him up when he's forty. I'll be dead and he'll be just what you need by then I expect.'

Nesta screwed up her eyes and studied the lamp. Then she said, 'I don't see why you shouldn't live to be eighty-eight. Jared's older than you probably think. He was off the island quite a while, remember.'

'Christ, Nesta, do I want to be eighty-eight?'

In one graceful movement she was kneeling beside him on the sofa, his head cradled in her arms. 'Oh Jim, my love. You're not old. You won't ever be old. Not to me, whatever changes.'

'Liar.' He leaned his head against her breasts. 'Don't lie to me, my sweet. Just forget. Come here, come here. Yes, like that. I want to forget. Just for a little while, I want us to forget.'

ELEVEN

Sidony Redruth. Ravnscar Castle. June 12th.
Notes for *Undiscovered Islands* (working title).

THE PARLIAMENT OF the new independent state of Hy Brasil only met once, in October 1958. It held one major debate: whether the rule of the road should be altered from the British Left to the European Right. The argument was passionate, and lasted until three o'clock in the morning. One can see why. The symbolic significance of Left, so pertinent to the recent Revolution, warred in delegates' minds with the association of Left with an aggressive British insularity, seen now as a bloody-minded insistence on being different for its own sake. Driving on the Right, seen in that light, was concomitant with removing the statue of Nelson from the harbour entrance to the drying green behind Back Lane elementary school, or changing the names of Palmerston, Gladstone and Disraeli Streets – which formed a grid at right angles to Water Street and High Street – to Liberty, Egality and Fraternity Streets. (You can still see the old names etched into the stone buildings on street corners, just above the modern black-and-yellow road signs.) Driving on the Right was an assertion of a new and independent foreign policy, in which Hy Brasil would take its place among the relatively normal nations of the world.

But, the Left drivers argued, this reasoning was entirely spurious. The facts were these. (1) Hy Brasil is fifteen hundred sea miles from the nearest road outside its own boundaries, which, as it happens, is in County Kerry, in the Irish Republic, where they drive on the left, a small point which actually invalidated the whole Right argument. (2) Contrary to popular belief, it isn't the rest of the world (as opposed to the UK) which drives on the Right. In China, Japan, India, Australia, New Zealand and Africa, and in numerous islands scattered across the five oceans, they drive on the Left. Right, in fact, is not a symbol of global solidarity, but of Western dominance, and as such, argued the Leftists, it could hardly be read as a radical step into a post-colonial world. (3) The new State of Hy Brasil was born into debt, and faced a future dominated by interest rates. No one was about to buy a new, left-hand drive car. Even to dream of doing so was seen as a capitalist, and therefore an unpatriotic, fantasy. With every driver in the country on the wrong side of the vehicle, possibly for years to come, the accident rate would soar. Mass emigration already being a problem, the wilful subtraction of accident victims from the total population could only be regarded as a shockingly irresponsible waste of human resources. (4) Even if the government encouraged the purchase of new vehicles, this would tie up the slender freight resources of the country to an alarming degree. The cost of imported goods, and the difficulty of attracting freight shipping to such a small market, was already one of the new government's major problems, now that the UK subsidy was withdrawn. It would be more logical to forbid the import of vehicles than to encourage it by creating a false demand. (5) The entire public transport system of the nation, viz. the 227 bus, possessed right-hand drive. (6) Since all the roads in the country, with the exception of Water Street, were single track, the effect of the change would be negligible anyway, except when two vehicles met, at which point both drivers had to remember, preferably at the same time, on which side they were supposed to be. What would that be like on a Saturday night in Dorrado?

I'd heard all this from Colombo over a cup of coffee at

Caliban's, and I was thinking about it now as I drove cautiously out of St Brandons on the left hand side of the road. I was glad to be behind a wheel again. I felt free and powerful, in charge of my own destiny, and I realised I'd been missing this. I wasn't used to driving an ancient Land Rover, however, and getting from first to second, which one has to do all the time on these hills, was still a minor nightmare. So it was freedom and power with reservations. Lucy had offered to lend me the Land Rover for the day, which is something I would never have asked for. She was planting out young brassicas, so couldn't get away. She said to tell Colombo she'd see him at Kirwan's Opening at Maldun's Mill on Friday.

I felt I was getting somewhere: meeting people, building up a network of my own. Colombo had been the first break. I still wasn't sure why he'd been so helpful, in spite of what he'd said, but I was beginning to suspect it might really be disinterested goodwill. If it was, I felt a little overwhelmed. Possibly also a little disappointed. I wished, only for a moment but not for the first time, that I'd married Lance after all, and settled down to a respectable life in Winchester. If I'd done that I'd now be free, at twenty-five, of this everlasting speculation. I didn't like eyeing-up men, however secretly. As I successfully double de-clutched on the one-in-four hill at the top of Fraternity Street I remembered Aristophanes' bit in Plato's *Symposium* where he tells the story about all the four-legged creatures being chopped in two and rushing about forever looking for their lost half. Why (here I saw myself asking my father, who believes in these things) did God make us dissatisfied with just being one? I didn't need a partner to interrupt my life; why then did every social occasion present itself to me as a possibility of finding one?

If they had changed to driving on the right, the turn from Fraternity Street north on to the Lyonsness Road would be a hell of a lot easier than it is now. I was thinking about that, and about how I'd ditched poor Lance back in England, when I saw the hitchhiker. He hadn't stopped; he was walking up the road with his back to me and his thumb out. He had heavy boots and a shapeless green rucksack that looked as if it had been through the Second World War and back. I just had time to remember that this was Hy Brasil, where violent crime is unknown, and transport in rural areas tacitly consists of people giving each other lifts. I pulled up with a jerk, and skidded on to the verge.

He opened the door at once. 'Thanks.' I grabbed the rucksack as he heaved it in and pulled it over into the middle. It was heavy. At least it would make a barrier between us. He didn't look dangerous, only sweaty and dusty. He was fair and sunburned, with a lot of freckles. Although he was my age at the very least, I could see just what he must have looked like as a small boy. I wondered if he was old enough not to mind giving that impression; Arthur used to go to great trouble to cultivate a streetwise look.

He got in and slammed the door. 'Where's Lucy?'

I'd noticed already that hitchhikers in Hy Brasil take their rides for granted, and don't bother with an excess of gratitude. 'Oh, you know Lucy?'

'Of course. You're English?'

'How did you know?'

'As soon as you opened your mouth. Yeah, I've got it. You're the one writing a book about us.'

'A guidebook to Hy Brasil. Yes.'

'Have you ever been here before?'

Definitely hostile. Once again I cursed Colombo, or whoever it was, for destroying my anonymity so completely. 'No. My name's Sidony. I'm staying at Lucy's. You're a friend of hers?'

'Yeah.' Maybe he realised how surly he sounded, because he added, 'I'm sorry, I've had an unpleasant day. My name is Jared, and I really don't mind if you write a book or not.'

Already I counted that as remarkably civil, coming from him. 'Thank you, that's very kind. I'm not trying to be an expert, you know. It's just one of those guidebook series, saying things like where the Youth Hostels are, and what time the buses run.'

'At that rate it'll be about three lines long.'

'And other things. Potted histories and descriptions of places, stuff like that. Fairly standard.'

'Sounds pretty boring to me.'

'Well, you don't have to read it.'

There was a short silence. I took the next bend at thirty-five, then realised how sharp it was. Gravel crunched under the front tyres, and I dragged the wheel over. I saw my passenger – I'd forgotten his name already – clutch at the strap hanging by his ear. There were no seatbelts.

'Well, you shouldn't have annoyed me.'

'I'm so sorry.' He sounded it too, to my surprise. 'Truly, I am. I've had a horrible day. I don't lead a very sociable life anyway. And you're a guest. This is Hy Brasil. Freedom of speech, freedom of the press. You write what the hell you like. Bring the tourists in. You'll be doing us a favour. Personally I might feel like shooting them, but we need the money. You write away. Don't mind me.'

'I can't write and drive at the same time.'

'Not on our roads, anyway. Do you like it?'

'Like what?'

'Being here. I'm making conversation now, you see. Being polite.'

'Yes, then, I do like it. Do you live at Lyonsness?'

'No. Despair.'

The car shot up a straight stretch. 'Despair! Then you must be Robinson Crusoe! Peterkin told me about you. What did you say your name was?'

'Alexander Selkirk.'

'No, seriously.'

'Seriously, Jared Honeyman. And you seriously said you were called Sidney?'

'Sidony. It's a feast day; it comes just after Easter.'

'I like that. Are you called anything for short? Or does everyone call you Sidony?'

'Everyone except my brother. I wouldn't let anyone else shorten my name without my permission.' I glanced sideways at him. 'What's so funny about that?'

'Nothing. I'll remember, if I ever want to shorten your name, to ask your permission first.'

I ignored that, but anyway I was trying to recollect something else. 'I've got it,' I said suddenly. 'You were in the paper the other day. You got caught in the tidal wave, and you said it was "interesting, but you wouldn't specially want to do it again". That was you, wasn't it?'

'That was me.'

He was quite willing to talk about it, but you'd think he'd been in a completely different boat from Colombo. Colombo's boat had, according to the article, escaped by the skin of its teeth from a seismological cataclysm; Jared's boat had evidently found itself in a sea that was just a bit damper and bumpier than usual. I found that interesting, and tried to get Jared to tell me more.

We were driving past terraces of apple trees. The blossom had all gone now and the trees were green, but there were petals scattered on the ground like melting snow. Although I had my eyes on the road I was aware of him watching me. 'I do know,' I told him all at once, 'that I can't possibly know enough about the country to write the sort of book you'd want. But the offer was too good to miss. Sometimes you have to take risks, and say yes, even if you don't know how you'll do it. That must have happened to you sometimes?'

'Yes, that's happened to me.' He didn't take his eyes off me; I glanced at him sideways and encountered a steady blue-eyed gaze. I could feel myself beginning to blush, and changed gear hurriedly. 'So how would you describe it so far?' he asked.

'Hy Brasil?'

'Yes.'

'Not in any way you'd like, probably. Sometimes I seem to recognise things, as if I'd dreamed it all already. Like this bit.'

'This bit?'

'This road through the orchards. The apple trees. Meeting you like I just did. The way the sun makes patterns on the gravel. I keep having the feeling that it isn't new. People say autumn is melancholy, but I find it's the spring that feels so old. You think how many times it's happened, from the beginning of the world. That's how it feels at home, anyway.' I stopped. The uncanny impression of *déjà vu* went a little further than that, but I wasn't going to say so.

'Hy Brasil isn't very old.'

'No, I suppose not.'

'Not geologically or historically. Before Brendan came there was never anybody here at all. Right up until the nineteenth century there were arguments about whether the place even existed. Until there was a way of measuring longitude no one could say for certain whether it was here or not. A lot of people thought it wasn't.'

'And yet it's been written about for two and a half thousand years.'

'So? What does that prove? I should think more's been written about things that don't exist than things that do.' When I didn't answer, he added, 'Don't you agree?'

'I'm thinking about it. I suppose it depends on whether you believe in those sorts of things. Stories, I mean, and dreams, and stuff like that. I was looking at the Ortelius map. It's on the cover of a new book I saw in Finnegan's.'

'That's Brendan Hook's book. I never had dreams about this place until I went away to England. Then I did: homesick, I suppose. I guess it sounds daft to you, but the rest of the world seemed so unreal; I felt a long way away. I used to dream about Hy Brasil and then I'd wake up and wish I was still sleeping. Only at first, of course. How does it feel being a foreigner here? Do you mind it?'

I had to think about that one too. 'Yes and no,' I said eventually. 'I like feeling I can be whoever I want. I mean, no one here knows who I am or what I was like before.'

'But you know.'

'I can forget if I like. On the other hand, I don't like being lonely.'

'Are you lonely?'

'No. I mean, not superficially. People are very friendly. But sometimes I realise that no one else is seeing just what I'm seeing; then I look at myself in the mirror and I have this strange feeling I'm the only one like me in the whole world. I can't explain it really. Have you ever felt like that?'

'I never thought to put it like that. I felt very alone when I first went abroad, which I wasn't expecting because of the language being the same. But you can use the same words and have different thoughts.'

'Well, that has to be true of every single person,' I said practically. 'I suppose it helps that we both speak English anyway.'

'Of course it does. You can tell me what you dream about, which you couldn't otherwise.'

'Yes, maybe, but I don't think I will.'

'That's not fair. I told you.'

'You told me one thing. OK then, if you really want to know. Last night I dreamed I was about to have this lovely dinner: grilled trout and new potatoes and fresh peas, and a nice white wine, quite dry. I was just sitting down to it when I woke up. It was terribly disappointing. I'd only had cornflakes for supper because Lucy went to see *The English Patient* with Colombo. I expect that was why.'

'Well, I think that's both sad and significant. Someone should take you to Atlantis.'

'Oh? What's Atlantis?'

'It's the best fish restaurant in Hy Brasil. Which is to say, quite definitely the best restaurant of any kind in Hy Brasil, and probably the best fish restaurant in the whole Atlantic. It belongs to Penelope Hook, and it's in Lyonsness. It deserves at least two pages. I'm surprised no one's mentioned it to you already.'

'I'd like that. I can take myself, anyway, if I want to.'

'No doubt, but it wouldn't be the same, would it?'

'The difference isn't worth thinking about.'

'Yes it is. But in Hy Brasil we're more straightforward about being romantic. I noticed this a lot when I was in England. You come from the West Country, don't you?'

'Cornwall.'

'Of course,' he said, and out of the corner of my eye I saw him smiling. "Where the westering waters roll From drown'd Lyonesse to the outer deep." Isn't that right?'

'I don't know. Is that a poem?'

'If you don't know you should. We learned it at school. Tristan and Iseult. You believe in a lot of unreal things, don't you? Do you include love potions?'

I didn't answer him because I wasn't attending. We had come over the pass, and down below the sea sparkled in the sound between Lyonsness and Despair. I pulled up, forgetting him. 'Oh, wow! Look at that. Just look at that!' I opened the door and slid out into the bright air. I just stood gazing at the island and breathing in the smell of the sea.

'I live in the lighthouse,' said Jared.

'Do you? I sent a postcard of it to Arthur – my brother. We used to play lighthouses when we were little. We used to go to the Scillies for our holidays; I suppose that gave us the idea. We used to pretend the sycamore tree in the garden was our lighthouse. We used to make up shipwrecks and tempests. How does one get to Despair?'

'By boat.'

'Thanks a lot. I mean, is there a ferry?'

'No. You have to get someone to take you.'

'I see.' I waited a moment longer, then turned back to the car. 'Well, we'd better get on.'

'You can drop me at the Lyonsness turning, if you're going on to Ravnscar.'

As we lurched over the potholes he was busy writing something on the back of an envelope. I pulled up where he said, and opened my mouth to say goodbye. 'Here,' he said. 'When you want to come to Despair, phone that number and ask for Per. He'll tell you when I'm over. I've got a boat. All you have to do is ask.'

'Oh,' I said, staring down at the wobbly number he'd given me. 'Thank you very much.'

'My pleasure. I like you. I'd like to show you my island.' He was holding out his hand, and I shook it hesitantly. 'It is my island, you know. There isn't anyone else there so it must be. I'm sorry I was rude. I'll see you again, Sidony. Goodbye.'

He opened the door and jumped out before I could think what to say to that. I watched him running down the steep hill, his rucksack bouncing on his back. When he got to the corner he turned and waved, and then he leaped down off the road and was lost to sight among the trees. I stared stupidly at the empty road, and the white village with the sea behind it. Beyond it, the two peaks of Despair lay open to the sun, and the lighthouse at the top winked at me as if it were lit, though I knew it was only the sun catching the glass dome. I blinked, and shoved the recalcitrant gear lever into first again. As I ground slowly uphill again I switched on the radio. The Hy Brasil classical station was playing Mendelssohn's 'Fingal's Cave'. *Déjà vu.* I swore, and double de-clutched savagely. The Land Rover lurched across the muddy potholes on the road up to Ravnscar, while the sea glinted below.

TWELVE

ON THE GROUND floor of Maldun's Mill the outside walls had been laid bare to the stone. The inner walls and partitions were white, the carpet a tweedy grey. It made a good exhibition space, being pleasing in its proportions and unobtrusive in its colours. One space led through enticingly into the next, the whole arrangement of open rooms circling around the central shaft of the mill. The long windows on the north side looked on to the mill race, and when the place was empty the sound of rushing water percolated through into all its corners, just as it had done during the centuries when the ground floor of the mill had been used for very different purposes.

It was a pleasure to superimpose those images over the reality of the present. If you half-shut your eyes and concentrated on the shapes of the boulders in the stone wall, on the way they had been fitted together as if they had been deliberately formed for the space they now occupied; if you listened to the falling water that never stopped or faltered whether anyone remembered it or not, then the other images would come too, almost as strongly as if you could by a glance, a mere flick of the eye from the wall into the room itself, see the sacks of grain piled up in the corner, the winch and tackle, the trapdoor from the floor above. Over the sound of water you could nearly make yourself hear the grinding of stone on stone, the crank of the turning wheel outside, the water splashing from one paddle to the next.

But not quite. The past can't be present, except in the mind's eye, and that's only a delusion. Even if the past is caught, developed, printed, framed and hung on the wall it's still gone. The images don't take you back there; they only help you to remember. And what's the point of that, thought Nesta bitterly. She turned her face away from the wall, and faced the room. All those rectangular images, like tombstones in a cemetery, hanging there flat against the white walls. Why bother? There was a moment attached to every one, something which had once happened, but it was gone, and it couldn't be brought back.

She took a glass of red wine and trailed away up the stairs, leaving the President to stare intently at his reflection in the watery world beyond the window and carefully adjust his tie. Before Nesta reappeared the first guests had arrived, and Hook had chatted benignly to the Town Clerk of St Brandons and his wife, and then to the junior art master from the Academy, and to Ishmael Pereira's wife, to whom he endeared himself by remembering that she was one of the doctors at the new clinic in Lyonsness, and, even more impressively, being able to demonstrate that he'd thoroughly read the clinic's annual report.

Ishmael, meanwhile, ignored the company completely, and slowly toured the exhibition, examining each photograph with concentrated attention. Out of the corner of his eye Hook watched him disappear into the next room, and interrupted himself to say to Anna, 'Can we join your husband for a minute? There's something in there I'd like to watch him seeing.'

When they went through Ishmael was standing in front of a glass case mounted on a pedestal in the centre of the room. It had been cleverly lit: the goblet seemed to shine from within, illuminating Ishmael's dark face like the light in a Rembrandt painting. Of course the goblet, thought Hook appreciatively, was entirely correct for a Rembrandt, which made the analogy even more piquant. It was of green glass, with a crest impressed on the side depicting a galleon in full sail. Ishmael was wearing his grey Sunday suit, and he held his hat against his chest as if in homage to the beautiful object that lay before him. Hook, with whom Ishmael had worked closely when he'd been employed in the government's Finance Department, was quite aware that in fact it was no such thing. Ishmael paid homage to nothing but his incalculable Presbyterian God, and had never made a theatrical gesture in his life. He had taken his hat off at the door because that was natural to him, and he held it in that idiosyncratic way because he always did, especially when confronted with an item that interested him.

'Ah,' said Ishmael, looking up. 'There you are, m'dear. Hi-aye Jim. What do you think of our treasure, eh? I like the way Nesta's set it up. Clever.'

'Oh, she's clever,' said Hook.

He stood beside Ishmael and read the description that was discreetly pinned to the floor of the case:

Goblet of clear glass, with transparent dark green folded foot. Unusual print on bowl with impressed design depicting stylised galleon under sail. Venetian style, early seventeenth century. Unique decorated impression suggests a possible origin in the Low Countries. Raised May 29th, 1997, from Spanish ship *Cortes* (foundered October 31st, 1611), Ile de l'Espoir, Hy Brasil.

'Nesta will want to know what you think of this display,' said Hook. 'It was you that fished it up, I gather?'

'No, it was Jed Honeyman.' Ishmael looked at Hook dispassionately. 'You must have known that. The photo was on the front page of the *Times*.'

'And there it is,' said Anna, pointing. 'It's much clearer than it was in newsprint, too.'

Hook looked at the goblet in the photograph, clasped in the young man's hand. There was pathos in the image: when had a human hand last touched that smooth green glass? And whose? There had been a moment when someone had been alive, and thought, and hoped, and expected something other than the long drowned years that lay ahead. 'Full fathom five thy father lies . . .' no, that was inappropriate. It was a pity it had to be young Honeyman. The goblet was a lovely thing, pale green darkening towards its fluted base, almost as if the colour of the sea had washed off on it. The bowl was straight-sided, pleasantly asymmetrical, and slightly grainy. In the middle was the crested impression that had driven Baskerville into a state of almost unprecedented excitement. Apparently there were no known examples of a galleon impressed into glass. Possibly it was the specific whim of the Spanish admiral whose bones now rested in the submerged foothills of Despair.

'Of course,' said Ishmael, 'this is bound to mean that the project will go on.'

'Is that what you think, Ishmael?' said Hook softly.

'Yes. We've done six more dives since then, and we're finding—' Ishmael stopped abruptly. 'Good evening, Mr Baskerville.'

'Ah, Baskerville.' Hook turned to meet the chief museum curator and librarian of Hy Brasil, an old colleague of his who had at various times held less publicly known government appointments. Hook was a tall man, but Baskerville in spite of his advanced years and pronounced stoop, still towered over his President like a somewhat down-at-heel angel of death. An odour of age, unaired clothing and stale incense hung about him, as if he had recently been unearthed from a damp vestry. 'Now here's your exhibit. Rather pleasing, don't you think?'

Baskerville frowned over the glass case. 'It'll be safer in the museum.'

'Well, in a couple of weeks that's where it'll be,' Ishmael pointed out. 'But you can see how it makes a centrepiece for the photographs.'

Baskerville glanced disparagingly at the photo of Jared, and turned to the next. This was in colour, a composition of blues and greens, glass and sea. 'Very nice. But the goblet should be in the museum. The insurance for this was a nightmare, and the thing's beyond price anyway. Do you realise what it would fetch in America?'

'It's not going to America,' said Hook abruptly. 'We've had enough of that sort of thing.'

Ishmael and Anna quietly faded into the next room. The exhibition was filling up, and they were soon separated. Ishmael extricated himself from a discussion about the shocking state of road repairs, and obstinately returned to the photographs on the walls. In this section Nesta had returned to an earlier obsession of hers, in a series of studies of dry stone walls. Ishmael examined them with professional interest, as one who had both taken photographs and built walls. When Nesta appeared beside him, dressed strikingly in a robe of midnight blue, and a necklace and bracelets of silver and lapis lazuli, Ishmael said to her as if they were in the middle of a conversation, 'You've caught the balance there in the boulders. They look precarious, but they take the wind. The holes are the whole point. Anything that adapts to the wind acquires a certain grace, I think. Like sails.'

'Or sand dunes. Instead of just resisting it, you mean?' Nesta turned her back on the rest of the company. It was soothing to talk to Ishmael, although she soon stopped listening to his explanation of the mathematical properties of wind resistance. Instead she amused herself briefly, as she often did while men talked, by imagining what he would be like in bed. Since she liked both Ishmael and Anna the image she conjured up was less misanthropic than usual. She smiled at him charmingly, and said she remembered doing triangles of velocity at school.

When Jared saw them through the crowd his first thought was to join them, but he was waylaid by the landlord of the Red Herring before he got there. 'Did you see these?' said Ernest.

Jared looked at the photographs, in black and white, of lava formations in various parts of the country. He stopped for quite a time in front of a poster-sized representation of the Frenchman's Cave, in which the basalt pillars were highlighted by the afternoon sun, a study in light and form surrounding the opaque mass of the interior. If he looked at the photo with his eyes half shut the shape in the middle turned itself from black emptiness into an animal crouched between shafts of light. In fact all the photos in the section gave an ethereal quality to solid rock, which, said Jared to Ernest, was doubly artful because it was true: if you did touch them, all you'd actually feel was shiny paper.

'You're an intelligent young man, I believe,' said Ernest, 'But sometimes you make comments that would be remarkable in a child of six.'

'I'll assume that's a compliment. Hallo, here comes someone you should meet.'

Ernest turned round. 'But I have met her, with Colombo. A very fair young lady. Is she yours?'

'I don't expect she believes in possession,' said Jared. 'Sidony!'

The fair young lady started, looked round, and blushed. 'Oh, it's you. I thought you'd gone back to Despair.'

'I did, but I came back. Sidony, I gather you've met Ernest, who's the landlord of the Red Herring in Dorrado. You'll have to stay there, because it's the best inn in Hy Brasil. Ernest, she'll give you a write-up that'll keep you fully booked from now till the apocalypse. That is, if you're nice to her.'

'Ah yes, so you're the young lady who's writing the book.'

Jared tweaked her arm. 'He's worth talking to, but I'll come back presently and rescue you.' He winked at Ernest and wandered on, feeling unaccountably pleased with himself.

'The goblet,' Baskerville was repeating to the third passer-by that he'd managed to stop, 'should be in the museum.'

'It will be,' said Colombo. 'But it makes sense to have it like this first, the subject surrounded by images of itself, as it were. I like that. Is it security you're worried about? But here comes another subject. Hi-aye, Jared. Care to stand under the spotlight too?'

'Good evening, Mr Honeyman.' Baskerville turned stiffly

round, but ignored the hand that Jared extended to him. 'As you see, Ms Kirwan has the exhibit on loan as you requested. But it ought to be in the museum.'

'So I see,' said Jared, and strolled over. 'It looks pretty good, doesn't it? If you were fished up from the bottom of the sea and placed under a bright light, Colombo, I suppose you'd reckon it must be the resurrection?'

'As the fisher-up, I can't imagine where you think that puts you,' said Colombo. 'Mind you, there's been all sorts of people through here remarking on how beautiful you are. Perhaps you should be kept in the museum too.'

'What? Oh right, that picture. I suppose none of them mentioned giving me some money? Don't look at me like that; I meant a grant for marine archeology. Stop laughing, Colombo. I'm quite serious.'

'You don't have to tell me that. Mr Baskerville, now that the lad's produced the goods will he get his pay-off, do you think? I mean, if he's actually filling your cases at the museum with priceless objects, surely you'll write him a reference? You're on the Mayda Trust, aren't you?'

In the catalogue the first room was called simply 'stone', and the next 'water'. The first thing Sidony saw as she came through into 'water' was a green glass goblet in a pool of light, surrounded by three silhouetted figures, each one arguing from his corner like characters in a play. Even the words they spoke seemed to have been rehearsed a hundred times before.

'But it *won't* lie there for ever,' Jared was saying. 'Not now people know that it's there. If we're not allowed to get on with it now, this year, then someone else will. Someone from outside Hy Brasil.'

'They can't do that in territorial waters without permission.'

'Want to bet? And if the country really is going bankrupt, that's an argument for, not against, doing it now. First because who's to say the government won't sell the site to the Americans just to get the cash? And second, we're supposed to be encouraging tourists, aren't we? Well, you can't beat a salvaged galleon if you want to do that. It's the next best thing to Kidd's treasure. And if we in Hy Brasil salvage the stuff, we keep it here where it should be, in Hy Brasil. There's too much gone out of the country already, and that's a fact.'

'You can't argue with that, Baskerville,' said Colombo. 'No one made more fuss than you did when the Ravnscar treasure went to New York.'

'That was a wanton act,' said Baskerville. 'To disturb what had lain safe from the beginning of our history. Are you sure you're not doing the same though, Mr Honeyman?'

'You'd like me to have left it where it was, would you? You'd like it not to be here in this room now? You'd like none of these pictures to exist? You'd like it to lie on the sea bed until the end of time and no one ever see it again? At that rate none of us should ever try to make anything happen.'

' "Vacant heart and hand and eye," ' murmured Colombo. 'Isn't that it, Baskerville? "Easy live and quiet die." '

Baskerville looked at him from under formidable eyebrows. 'So you've been down there, too, MacAdam?' he said softly.

'I had nothing to do with what you're thinking of. I felt as badly as you, if that were possible. But I think I understand why it was done. It can't be changed, therefore it has to be forgiven. Everyone deserves that.'

'I don't know what you're all getting at,' said Jared irritably. 'We learned that poem at school, I think. But Colombo's never been diving in his life. No offence meant, but I wouldn't want to take him either. He's not the type. What's more I haven't done anything like what Lucy did, and never would, and I don't need forgiving. There's no comparison. I don't see how you could possibly make one.'

'We'll leave Lucy out of this!' cried Colombo. Sidony, who'd been apparently engrossed in the pictures on the wall, started, and they all saw her at the same moment. Colombo introduced her to Baskerville with such smooth aplomb it was difficult to believe the sudden flash of anger had been real. But they were all affected by it. Baskerville was unexpectedly affable, and agreed with Colombo that Sidony should visit him in his office at the museum. It must be useful to be a pretty girl, Jared thought cynically, as he leaned against the doorway that led through to 'earth' and watched them being so warily polite. He seemed to have become invisible to all of them; maybe it was just as well. But when Baskerville and Colombo went on into 'stone', Sidony said that she wanted to look at the rest of the photographs in here. She was unaware of Jared, and when she thought she was alone she breathed a big sigh, and stood in front of the goblet, and gazed at it thoughtfully. He stood quite still and watched her.

Eventually she looked up and saw him. She didn't seem startled that he was there, but just said, as if following a train of thought, 'I've seen it before somewhere, but I can't remember where.'

'No one's seen this one before,' said Jared. 'Except for the picture in the paper. It's been in Baskerville's workshop at the museum until today.'

'I've never been there. It must have been another one just the same. It had the same crest on it.'

'What?' She'd fairly caught his attention. 'You're sure of that? You're quite sure?'

'Of course I'm sure.'

'So it's at Ravnscar?'

'What? No, I don't think it was. I wasn't paying attention. I can't remember.'

'Sidony, you must!' He had her by the shoulder, but he seemed unaware of it. 'It's important. You've no idea how important it is. Please try to remember!'

'Ah, Sidony! We meet again.' Olly West was advancing towards her, both hands held out. Sidony ignored one outstretched hand and shook the other. Jared walked away abruptly. He found Ishmael and Anna getting ready to leave, and went outside with them. He was talking all the way, with excited gestures.

Nesta watched him go, and remarked, 'Something's got him going. And I don't think it's my work.'

'No m'dear, I don't think it is.' Hook looked out of the window, and watched Jared climb into the back of Ishmael's Grand Cherokee. Ishmael and Anna got in after him, the doors slammed, and they bumped away through the rutted car park. 'Well, I'm afraid I can't help you. Young Honeyman cuts me dead, at least, he did so quite pointedly this afternoon. I can't say I blame him, but it's a novel experience.'

'Take it to heart then, Jim. You've not been kind to him.'

'But you have, m'dear.' Nesta raised her brows at him. 'It's a very charming composition,' explained Hook. 'You've made the little devil look positively seraphic. I wouldn't be surprised if he ended up getting his money as a result.'

'I know you don't want him to.'

'But you do?'

'Why not, Jim? I just don't understand why not?'

'You don't need to understand, m'dear. I just wished you'd picked another subject, that's all. On the other hand I wouldn't want you to limit yourself. Would you like young Jared to raise the *Cortes*?'

Nesta looked him in the eye. 'Yes, Jim, I would.'

'Very well, m'dear. Never say I'm beyond influence. Next year he shall.' He put his hand on her shoulder. 'Here comes our tedious Baskerville. Say no more. Young Honeyman is forgiven, but he mustn't know that yet. But you, my love, may privately rejoice.'

Nearly everyone had gone now. Colombo was alone in the final section. He stopped for several minutes in front of the last photograph in the exhibition. He knew it well, so he'd hardly glanced at it this evening, though he'd taken the trouble to eavesdrop as the viewers shuffled by. The picture appeared to be of a naked man standing on the back of a whale. The form was simple: a straight line transecting a curve. A lot of people this evening had exclaimed at it. Most had noted the similarity between the photograph and the national emblem of Hy Brasil.

A few had speculated in detail as to how the photograph had been done. When members of the amateur camera club came by the discussion had become technical and complicated. Ernest had asked Colombo his opinion. 'Simple,' Colombo had said. 'It's a man standing on the back of a whale. Presumably she took it from a boat.' Cornered by the camera club in a body, he'd gone further and announced truthfully that he believed in miracles, and after that they'd left him in peace. Now that he was alone, he stood and contemplated the image one last time. It was early morning in the photograph. The man had his back to the rising sun, so that the light fell white across his back and shoulders, and his face was left in shadow. He was an image created in patterns of light and dark, seemingly without substance and devoid of personality, pared right down to form. The sky was soft as milk behind him. The back of the whale was smooth and black under his feet. It had also been extremely cold.

'Colombo? You're still here?' Nesta saw what he was looking at and smiled. For a moment their eyes met, full of laughter. 'Everyone's gone,' she said loudly. 'We're opening the last bottle. Come on through.'

The evening had been, predictably, a success. Over two hundred people had come, and two-thirds of the photographs had been sold. Hook opened a final bottle of red wine, and poured out glasses for Nesta, the gallery staff, Colombo and himself. 'So you'll give her a good write-up, MacAdam?'

'Not only good, but true,' said Colombo. 'I might even go back to the office and do it tonight.'

'You'll do it justice, won't you? Plenty of description, mind, and not just your own opinion. These reviewers always seem to think readers are going to be interested in their convoluted internal processes. But you're a reporter, MacAdam. You understand about facts.'

'I don't believe in facts,' said Colombo, 'But I'll describe everything as well as I possibly can. That I promise you, sir.'

THIRTEEN

LIKE ALL THE doors on the island, the door at Ravnscar was never locked. Colombo wandered into the kitchen and called out 'Lucy! Lucy?'

No answer. The papers on the long table had been tidied into piles at precise right angles at one end. The other end was bare, waiting for the next meal. There were new red candles in the pewter candlesticks, and fresh oranges in the fruit bowl. The round table in the window had been swept clean of crumbs. Simpkin the cat lay curled in a neat ball on the windowseat. Beside him was yesterday's copy of *The Hesperides Times* carefully refolded.

Colombo flung his jacket over a Jacobean carved chair, and went over to the stove. It was warm, and the coals glowed gently behind the glass door. There were brushmarks across the clean hearth, and the coal scuttle had been freshly filled. Colombo wondered vaguely what Lucy and Sidony were like when they were alone together: whether they went in for mutual housekeeping as a matter of course, or just sat over their wine discussing the vagaries of men. If that were the case, he would like very much to know what they said to each other, and how much either of them knew about how he felt.

However, that was not what he had come for. Yesterday he had bought a photograph, and ever since an impression had been tugging at his mind, and the maddening thing was that he couldn't place it. He hadn't gone to Kirwan's exhibition with the idea of buying anything. He only had three rooms in his apartment, and all twelve walls of them were full. He had been seduced, however, by a composition of blue and green, and a cleanness of line that seemed only possible in those cold colours. The subject was precise and yet surreal. It had the quality of dream that he associated with painting rather than photography. The two artists who sprang to his mind could hardly be more diverse: Dali and Hockney. Dali because of the precision of the dream, and Hockney for the intense clarity of tone and colour.

Colombo stood with his back to the stove while the warmth of it crept gently up his spine. He couldn't pick up his purchase until the exhibition was over at the end of the month, but he could recreate it in his mind's eye. Subject: a seventeenth-century glass goblet permeated by a background sea. Glass and sea together had come out the colour of the iris of the eye in a peacock's tail. The glass was translucent; the sea behind it was calm and opaque, an unreflecting milky blue. The goblet floated free, having dispensed with gravity, perspective and possibility in the simple erasure of whatever, in reality, must have been used to support it. But the trick was – he tried to think how she could have done it – the trick was, it hadn't been superimposed. The colour of the goblet was made out of the symbiosis of glass and sea. It had been all one photograph from the beginning, only somehow she'd taken the structural apparatus out of it. An angel in the image of a man, thought Colombo irrelevantly, could not really fly. He'd read somewhere, a long time ago, that a man would need to have a breastbone sticking out four feet in front of him if he were to begin to be a candidate for aerodynamics. And the wings could not, in nature, be additional to the arms. If a glass goblet could suspend itself against an ocean and fill up two-thirds of its area, then a man could surely become an angel without any physical inconvenience.

Kirwan had told Colombo all about the diving trip, and he'd seen the photo in *The Hesperides Times* six weeks before the original appeared in the exhibition. The goblet in the photograph was the one Jared had salvaged, no doubt about it, and yet

Colombo knew, was positively certain, that he had seen it before. The time and place hovered tantalisingly just across the borders of his memory. It was a long time ago. He must have been young. His father was in it somewhere. In Dorrado? Colombo mentally reviewed the crowded shelves of the Red Herring. There might well be goblets. Where there were nets, harpoons and glass fishing floats, and an outsize stuffed halibut in a glass case, why should there not be goblets? But no, it was not the Red Herring that he remembered.

Francis Morgan, Lucy's father, had a handwritten manu-script compiled by his grandfather, *Antiquities of Frisland: Being a Compilation of Legends and Artefacts of the Islands of Hy Brasil, 1855–1882.* Baskerville would literally have given his eye teeth to secure the four calf-bound volumes for the library archives, but Francis Morgan was not the man to part with his treasures, and his daughter, when approached persistently by an increas-ingly frustrated Baskerville, proved similarly recalcitrant. An unpleasant correspondence in *The Hesperides Times*, following a barbed article by Baskerville on the negative values of a *ci-devant* aristocracy in an age of revolution, had failed to move her. The *Antiquities* remained at Ravnscar.

Colombo looked at his watch. Twenty to five. He knew where the volumes were, on the bottom shelf between the desk and the window in the Great Hall, hidden behind the armchair whose faded leather still showed the worn patch where Francis Morgan used to lean his head, while he smoked his briar pipe and stared out of the window at the ever-changing sea. The bookcase was hardly a safe repository. If Baskerville only knew, he could have come and helped himself to the *Antiquities* any time this past forty years. But Baskerville did not know, and Colombo did. Lucy wouldn't mind. She might be hours, and he knew she'd say go ahead. She trusted him completely. Too completely, thought Colombo bitterly. He pulled back a dark-red curtain in a corner of the kitchen, opened a little door with a Romanesque arch, and took the private staircase up to the Great Hall two steps at a time.

The Great Hall smelt of woodsmoke and old ashes. Its main claim to fame was its sixteenth-century painted ceiling. The central panel depicted Poseidon mounted on a chariot driving six winged horses, with a ring of Nereids round him riding on dolphins, and the wine-dark ocean at his back. The god held the reins in one hand, and with the other he laid claim with a sweep of his trident to the empty archipelago of Hy Brasil. Six lesser panels bordered the main picture. The first was of a lush and fertile country, with valleys filled with apple orchards, and high pastures with cattle and goats. The second showed a busy harbour, with galleons three deep against the crowded wharfs. The third was of a snow-capped mountain with a plume of smoke at its summit, and a bright palace built among the many terraces of its southern slopes. The fourth depicted vast quarries dug into the mountainside, where men toiled with rollers and pulleys, and the rock was tricoloured; black, white and red. The fifth was a view of Poseidon's temple with its golden roof and classic portico, surrounded by a hedge of gold. The last panel was a picture of a meeting in a colonnaded market place, where men waited in decorous silence to cast their potsherds into one of the two amphorae in the centre of the frame.

Colombo had occasionally lain on his back on the thread-bare Persian carpet and studied the ceiling at leisure. Even now he wasn't in too much of a hurry to omit glancing up at it. He winked at Poseidon, and it pleased his fancy, as it always did, to imagine that the god winked back. He skirted the grand piano; the lid was open, and the score of a Chopin Polonaise left out on the rack. The huge leather armchairs and the horsehair sofa were untidily draped with rugs and cushions as they always were. The hearth was filled with cold ashes, and there were ring marks of red wine on the stone flags. Lucy's housekeeping was always pragmatic: in the daytime the Great Hall had nothing to do but retain the ghosts of past evenings, and hold out the promise of evenings yet to come.

Colombo stood over Francis Morgan's empty chair and

looked out on the view over the wooded mountain slopes to the sea. He was struck by a flash of memory: old Morgan in his chair, and Colombo's own father, Ewan MacAdam the Mayda ferryman, sitting across from him with his cap on his knee, imperturbably sipping contraband Scotch whisky as if he sat beneath Poseidon in a grand house like this every evening of his life. And he, Colombo, he'd been sitting too, on a pouffe with a woven pattern on it, all reds and blues and browns, soft and leathery against his bare legs. He'd had a treasure in his hand. He could remember the touch of it very vividly, the feathery strands between his fingers, and a long spine that felt like fingernails. And the colour, the vibrant blue-green eye at the tail of the peacock's feather. He'd forgotten until now that there'd been peacocks at Ravnscar, but it was coming back to him, two birds almost as tall as he was parading the courtyard, and himself waiting by the thorn tree, holding the housekeeper's hand, until the male displayed his gorgeous tail, and the house-keeper said, 'There you are, m'dear. Will you look at that now?' Then later the harsh peacock screams rose out of the summer dusk and in through the open window. The sound of his father's soft voice came back to him too, saying to Francis Morgan that there'd been talk, and he should perhaps beware, for what with this revolution people took strange notions, and the Pirate Kings, so they were saying, were speaking of coming up to Ravnscar to claim their own. And the old man gripping the arms of his chair, so that his pale skin stretched over his knuckles like bleached bone, and him saying . . . saying . . . saying what? Colombo couldn't remember, but even as a little boy absorbed with his peacock's feather, he knew what everyone knew, that the treasure was at Ravnscar, and Francis Morgan kept it, as all his ancestors had done before him for ever and ever. Whatever the treasure was: the four-year-old Colombo had had no notion about that.

Now he took his eyes away from the window with an effort, and looked round the faded room. The very same pouffe was still there, on the hearthrug. He remembered sitting in the middle of it as if it were his own particular island, but it had got much smaller in the last thirty-two years. There was a yellow ringbinder on it, labelled – Colombo went a little nearer to read the familiar spiky writing – *Chemistry Notes*.

Colombo was nearly three years older than Lucy, and had been in sixth year when she arrived at St Brandons Academy from Lyonsness Junior High, but he remembered quite well that she had been thrown out of the science department in her first term for attempting to burn the school library copy of *The Origin of Species* over a bunsen burner. She'd explained to everyone who would listen that it was a genuine experiment. Having read that copies of the first edition had been burned by Christian fundamentalists, she just wanted to find out how difficult it was to do such a thing. No, this did not reflect her opinion of the subject matter, because she didn't have one. She only read fiction. Colombo remembered quite well how she had held forth at length to an admiring audience during the lunch hour, when the less insipid sixth-formers, and the most adventurous juniors, used to skip school dinners, and go down to Caliban's for chips and black coffee. He also seemed to recollect that Lucy had sworn never to go to any kind of science class again. But it was definitely her writing. Intrigued, he picked up *Chemistry Notes* and opened it. He realised then what it was. Colombo had scruples, but only some. He stood listening for a moment. Not a sound. The house was empty. He read on:

Lucy Morgan: Chemistry Notes

So what did happen? How did I reach this impregnable state, immured in my castle as surely as Elaine was spellbound to her boiling bath? I've only told my story once. Io, Io, where are you now? A fortnight away, by mail, and that's two weeks too far. My dear and only friend, I miss you.

It took me four years to tell you, in snippets and rag-ends, and in the end you had the whole patched-up pattern from me. It's the place where I told you that I see most clearly now. I can't recall your face. The spider plant. Remember the spider plant, Io, the way it hung over our kitchen table in the apartment? I'm re-creating the whole room in my head just now. I'm sitting there again, inside my mind, at right angles to the rickety sash-window that reaches almost to the floor. I can see the cuttings in yoghurt pots you've set out in a row along the top of the bottom window, all leaning out as far as they can towards the sun. The window is wedged open three inches from the top. You complain about draughts, but I come from Hy Brasil where we're not so used to central heating. What do I see out of the window? A brownstone terrace, cars lining the road on both sides, the damp sidewalks embroidered with Fall leaves that kids have scuffled through and left grey lines among the gold. Why do I remember the Fall best, Io? Why not the piled-up snow, or the smell of spring and the young unfurling leaves on the peeling plane trees? I'm seeing the yard at the end of the terrace with the high black fence around it, where the preschoolers come running out in their recess. I remember those kids as a kaleidoscope of colours, the brightness of their sweaters as they run to and fro across the grey asphalt, squealing like gulls.

Indoors, I see our cramped kitchen with its sloping ceiling, its wooden shelves where the jars gleam. All those healthy foods we'd cook together, such lovely colours: orange lentils, yellow split peas, white basmati rice, soft brown flour, green mung beans, rich red kidney beans, pale butter beans, black-eye beans, brown rice, oatmeal, couscous, berrymeal . . . I can even remember the order they came in, ranked around the stove. You taught me to cook that way, Io. You taught me to do a lot of things your way.

And I remember how we talked. We sat one on each side of the yellow pine table, a bowl of fruit between us and coffee cups, wine glasses and crumbs, me nearest the window, and you on your own rush-bottomed chair behind the door. You could reach behind you and get another bottle of wine out of the rack without getting up, it was so squashed in our kitchen. We had a big sitting room next door, with sofas and Persian rugs and a sanded golden floor, but I remember us best sitting in the kitchen, the spider plant with its baby spiders hanging down from straw-coloured stalks just above our heads. I see myself turning my wine glass in my hands, and the sunlight catching the wine so it was like a liquid ruby inside the glass, between my warm hands.

What a weird story it must have seemed to be to you, Io, like a dream. But New York before I got there was like a dream to me, and my life there with you has become a dream again now. Is the past always a dream? It goes to the same place as dreams, I know that. My past now is just an unconquerable image inside my head. Maybe it's immaterial whether it really happened or not. But it's when I think about New York in Hy Brasil that I realise that Hy Brasil has not, could never be, a real place to you. Is that why you've never come? Is that why the two weeks between us can't be crossed, why we never reach one another now? What you are to me now, Io, is letters. When I come home and find an airletter in the box, and my address written in your familiar curly script, the kind they teach you in first grade in New York State, my heart glows. Once every couple of months or so, when a letter from you happens, my heart glows. Not at any other time, not now.

I have a woman living in my house. She comes from Cornwall, England. She is twenty-five years old, and she has an incredible accent, the sort they speak in a BBC costume drama, which is the kind of television we mostly import in Hy Brasil. She's very pretty in an English kind of way too: light brown hair that's not quite straight and not quite curly, blue eyes, and the kind of complexion that really does fit the

cliché about English roses: I'd never believed in that before.
But if she's a rose at all it's one of those wild, scratchy dog
roses with the windblown flowers that you can't pick. She
blushes very easily, and I can tell how much that annoys her.
It's easy to imagine her in a Regency pastel frock; she has – or
could have – that look of appealing frailty that would win an
audition for a Gothic heroine. I'd never dare say so. The fact
is she dresses every day as if she were on an expedition into
the outback. Maybe she thinks Hy Brasil is the outback. She
has thin delicate hands, with which she does anything
practical with great capability. I asked her if she played
the piano, and she reacted as if I were psychic. We went
up to the grand piano in the Great Hall, which luckily I'd had
tuned last winter, and she played me Chopin, which one
would think was unlikely to bring tears to one's eyes, but that
was the effect her playing very nearly had on me.

I like her. We talk, and there are moments when it's almost
like having you there. There are moments when I find myself
on the brink of telling her things about the past. I've only told
my story once, and that was to you, Io. I was watching her
while she played to me, and I saw her as both tough and
vulnerable. She likes being outdoors mostly, and if she's
indoors, she's usually reading. That means she misses much
of what goes on inside. There are a lot of things she doesn't
see. She's very efficiently collecting material about Hy Brasil,
but there are too many things she'll miss out, because she
doesn't understand the possibilities of her own role. Colombo
would fall in love with her, I think, if she could ever dream of
playing Elizabeth Bennett instead of Huckleberry Finn. I see
it like this because when we were talking yesterday she told
me Elizabeth Bennett was her favourite heroine in fiction,
and that when she was little she used to go about pretending
she was Huck Finn. 'Did you ever pretend to be Elizabeth?' I
asked her. She looked stunned. 'Me?' she said. 'Elizabeth?
No, not me.' I poured her another glass of wine so she

couldn't see me laughing. I couldn't look at her, it was too poignant: Elizabeth Bennett in denim dungarees and a khaki t-shirt.

But I find myself giving little things away. For example, she'd been telling me about her brother (whom incidentally I blame for inadvertently teaching her that really she's a boy) and I told her how I'd always been alone, only I'd had a friend all my life, and that he was dead. I even mentioned that he'd died at Ravnscar. I wanted to say his name to her, but it wouldn't come. That's private still, but I can write it now: Nick Hawkins. Nicholas. My love. Io, Io where are you now? Where is Nick now that Nicholas is dead? Io, I remember how when I told you it was afternoon when I began, and as I talked the shadows of the trees grew long outside, and the sun dropped behind the brownstone houses and twilight crept along our street like a curtain slowly drawn, and when I had finished it was dark.

What if I told her now? When I think of doing so I find myself thinking that she's English, a foreigner, she wouldn't understand. I never thought that about you, Io, and yet in some ways your world was far more foreign to me than hers. It's only the sea, really, that separates Sidony's home from mine, and in its own way that unites us, because the sea is the thing that we both know, from the beginning of our separate lives. But the sea also separates our worlds, there is no getting away from that. Shall I tell her why it was that Nicky died?

A door banged downstairs. Colombo unhurriedly put back *Chemistry Notes* exactly where he had found it, and went out to the landing. He leaned over the curved bannister rail of the great stairs, and called out, 'Lucy?'

She appeared immediately below him from the far door of the kitchen. 'Who's there?'

'It's me. Colombo. I didn't mean to startle you. I thought you wouldn't mind if I came up to consult the *Antiquities*.'

'Of course not.' Lucy was mounting the stairs. 'Are you finding what you wanted?'

'I haven't had time to look yet. Where's Sidony?'

'She went for her swim. She swims in Ogg's Cove every day. I think she's mad. I don't go in until at least July, but apparently the sea in Britain is even colder than it is here.' Lucy reached the landing and stopped. 'Are you in love with her, Colombo?'

'You know the answer to that. You know why, too.'

'You promised never to mention that in this house. And I've kept my side of it: I've never not made you welcome.'

'Do you think I've not kept mine?'

Lucy regarded him warily, her hand still resting on the bannister. In concession to the first heat of summer she had shed her usual tight jeans and white shirt and was wearing a faded red cotton dress and dusty sandals. Her skin was as smooth as a new sweet chestnut, and as always, she seemed to exude a certainty about her self that would, Colombo thought resentfully, prevent any man thinking for one moment that she ought to be thinner than she was.

'OK,' said Lucy. 'You have kept it. To the letter. I wish you wouldn't even think about it.'

'Sorry. My thoughts are my own.'

'I was hoping when you asked me to have your English friend to stay they might have taken another direction.'

'Do you want me to keep my promise or do you want me to answer you?'

'OK, forget it.' Lucy led the way back into the Great Hall. 'I suppose I vaguely hoped she'd make you happy for a bit.'

'That's kind. Rather like offering a soothing jelly to an ailing tenant, I suppose. I'd be careful how you dispense your vague hopes, m'dear, if your heart's too good for us.'

'Stop being melodramatic,' said Lucy crossly, going over to the bookcase. 'Which volume did you want?'

'Melodramatic! When I've been the last word in under-statement for five years! If we lived in a fair world I'd get a gold star and a packet of Smarties for good conduct. I don't know which volume I need to look through. Lucy, do you have any seventeenth-century glassware anywhere? I had a notion that I'd seen some once.'

'Do you mean the Jacobite wineglasses? Or no, they'd be eighteenth century, I suppose. Or the Venetian cristallo bowls? Or the Flemish flagons? They're all on the top shelf in the pantry.'

'I had an idea I'd once seen your father drinking whisky out of a green goblet with a crest on it.'

'A what?' Lucy let go the glass door of the bookcase and it swung to sharply.

'A green goblet. Do you remember it? Venetian, or possibly Dutch in the Venetian style, early seventeenth century. The point is— Lucy, why weren't you at Kirwan's exhibition last night?'

'It was a lovely day. I decided to plant out the tomatoes instead. Also, peppers, melons, cucumbers and squash. By the time I'd finished it was getting dark and I needed a bath. Which reminds me, while you're here you can help me lay out the hoses. It's so much easier with two. I could ask Sidony, but she helped me spread compost most of yesterday. You'll eat more of my food than she does in the long run. I'll look in at Maldun's Mill later this week. I don't like openings. If I'm going to look at pictures I want to look at them, not talk about nothing to boring people.'

'OK, I'll move your hoses. But Lucy, about this goblet – you should have come to the exhibition. You know that photo in the *Times* – the one of Jed salvaging treasure off the *Cortes*?'

'Yes? Oh yes, that was a goblet too, wasn't it? What about it?'

'Lucy, Kirwan arranged Jed's goblet in a glass case in the exhibition, with photos all around it of the sea, and one or two of the thing itself. But the point is, when I saw it close to, I remembered I'd seen it before. Here. When your father was alive.'

'You can't have done. Or are you suggesting Pappa threw it back into the sea for Jared's entertainment?' Lucy went through to the further door that led down the back staircase into the kitchen. 'Look for what you like, Colombo. I'll be downstairs.'

'Wait!' She turned back impatiently. 'Lucy, you *do* know. I can tell. What I'm saying is that there's another one. That's not so surprising. It could have come off the *Cortes* right after she went down. After all, there were survivors. You know how that American guy who did the blood-test survey reckoned that half of Lyonsness is descended from them. It's not surprising if they came ashore with whatever capital they could lay their hands on. And I *know* I've seen another of those goblets. I'm almost certain that I saw your father drinking whisky out of a green glass goblet that's the spit of the one in Maldun's Mill.'

'OK, OK,' said Lucy. 'Perhaps you did. So, I don't remember. If it's here it might well have ended up in the wine cellar. There's a lot of old bottles and glasses down there. If you're going to look you could choose a bottle of claret while you're at it. I take it you'll stay to supper, if you want a bit of time to look up goblets?'

'Well, if it's not a bother.'

'It'll only be pasta and salad,' said Lucy, who was an excellent cook and knew it. 'If you're staying the night you'll have to have the lower tower room. I've put Sidony at the top.'

She was right: the stone shelves in the wine cellar were crammed. They were carved out of solid rock, and at their widest stretched back several feet. Colombo searched diligently through the detritus of five hundred years of habitation, covering himself in the process with ancient dust and cobwebs. Half of this stuff should be in the museum, he thought, and wished he could get Baskerville down here. But Lucy hated Baskerville, and had never given anything to the Hy Brasil Museum which was Baskerville's life's work, except once, in response to an impassioned appeal from the frustrated curator, when she had donated a silver thimble that had belonged to her great-great-grandmother Josephine de Rosas. Unfortunately Baskerville had retaliated by displaying the tiny exhibit on its own in a very large glass case in the middle of the central hall. He had added to the label, 'owing to the unprecedented generosity of Lucy Morgan, mistress of Ravnscar'. Lucy couldn't keep the Pirate Kings out of the lower levels of the Ravnscar caves; they had their own entrance guarded by binding oaths of secrecy. But when they were due to conduct their ceremonies Lucy always barred and bolted the oak door that separated the Ravnscar cellars from the lower passages. It was a shame. Francis Morgan used to invite the Kings in afterwards for sweet Canary wine and macaroons, and relations had always been cordial. But Lucy would have none of it.

There was something about this goblet, too, that she was not saying. Colombo, who had made Lucy his especial study during the five years she'd been back from New York, knew quite well when she was lying. He was aware when he descended the cellar steps that she'd sent him on a wild goose chase. However, the search was not without interest, and Colombo had no scruples about making several notes and sketches to take back to Baskerville. He didn't expect to find any goblet, but even so his irritation gradually mounted. He had not lost his temper with Lucy for four and a half years, but sometimes the restraint had been an effort. The desolation of *Chemistry Notes* made him even angrier with her. She was sabotaging herself even more effectively than she was hurting him. 'Nick Hawkins. Nicholas. My love.' Damn her. Damn her. Damn her. The fifteenth-century Dutch pottery punch bowl he was holding slipped out of his fingers and broke into three pieces on the flagged stone floor. Damn Nicholas. Damn Lucy. And be damned to himself, for being caught up in this web of her making, and not having the wit to extricate himself, not even after five futile years.

FOURTEEN

Sidony Redruth. The Red Herring, Dorrado. June 22nd.
Notes for *Undiscovered Islands* (working title).

I'D BEEN meaning to come to Dorrado anyway. I didn't just leave
Ravnscar because I felt *de trop*. Lucy had insisted that she
wanted me there for as long as Colombo stayed, but her very
vehemence made me feel uncomfortable. I came home from
Ogg's Cove, where I'd been for a swim, to discover Colombo
and Lucy in the kitchen alcove playing chess. He seemed pleased
to see me, but for some reason I felt left out, and found myself
remembering, possibly not for the first time, how a week earlier
Jared Honeyman had said to me, 'I like you' and shaken my
hand. Neither Colombo nor Lucy seemed embarrassed, but then
there's nothing compromising about playing chess. It just
seemed an odd thing for two attractive people who were
obviously enamoured of one another to be doing together at
five o'clock in the afternoon. But after all, why not?

Supper, as usual, was delicious: tagliatelle with pesto, and
one of Lucy's homegrown salads. Colombo and Lucy were both
unwontedly silent, a bit *distrait*, I thought, so I didn't try to talk,
but concentrated on my food. Afterwards I said I'd go for a walk,
but when I stepped outside the fog had come down, and the
twilit woods were dripping and mournful. The invisible precipice on my right seemed to glower at me from its misty depths,
so that I started wondering if anyone had ever just walked

straight over it. Since Ravnscar had been inhabited, according to the legends, for over a thousand years it seemed statistically likely that they had. I see no reason not to believe in ghosts.

After a little while I went home. Lucy and Colombo had lit the fire upstairs, and were drinking Madeira in the light of it. Colombo poured me a glass, and I sat on the sofa enjoying the rich dark smell of it a good deal more than the taste. Firelight flickered softly over the painted ceiling, so that the god with the trident seemed to smile craftily down at me when I caught his eye. A log cracked violently and spat embers over the hearthrug. Lucy picked them up with the tongs and threw them back.

'So you bought Kirwan's photo of this goblet,' said Lucy after a long silence.

'Yes.' Colombo was leaning back in his chair gazing into the firelight, and hardly seemed to be paying attention.

'Things,' said Lucy. 'Treasures. Maybe it was better at the bottom of the sea.'

'Why? It's a beautiful thing.'

'Sure. And now it'll need dusting. I don't understand why people always want to have more things. One more object in the museum, one more picture in your apartment. Haven't you got enough stuff cluttering up your walls?'

'Most of us aren't drowned in treasures from birth. That's your misfortune, not mine.' He was turning his glass round like a kaleidoscope, not looking at her.

'Don't you be sorry for me!'

'I'm not.'

I looked from one to another, wondering what on earth was the matter, and whether they'd notice if I left. It occurred to me that on this foggy night my tower room would be cold. If I wanted to read in comfort I'd have to get into bed. It wasn't even nine o'clock yet.

'*O que é que há?*' said Lucy, in a voice that was suddenly gentle.

'Nothing,' Colombo said, but he still wouldn't look at her. He stared into the fire instead. He was wearing black jeans and a black polo-neck shirt, and against that sombre background his long hands, the right one adorned with its heavy opal ring, curled around the cut-glass tumbler like something out of a Medici portrait. The fact that he was unusually grubby, and had cobwebs in his hair, added to rather than detracted from the effect. 'Nothing. I just bought a photo. Would you rather I hadn't?'

'It's nothing to do with me. Buy as many photos as you like. Spend your entire life hunting for duplicate glass goblets. Find the whole set and invite Mr Baskerville and his cronies to dinner. I won't even comment if you'd rather I didn't.'

'Lucy,' said Colombo quietly, 'if it had anything to do with you, anything at all, it would be my pleasure to consult you about every investigation I undertake. As it is, I don't see why my interest in the *Cortes* treasure should have any power at all to upset you.'

I couldn't work out if he were angry, unhappy, or just bored. I don't suppose I'd ever be able to read Colombo's feelings. I think Lucy can, but at that moment she didn't want to try. Her own anger was palpable. 'It upsets me because you come here to hunt about my house for any odd bric-a-brac that takes your fancy, even if it isn't anything to do with you, and then you press me for explanations about things I know nothing about! Why hunt up the past and disturb everybody? OK, so you think my father had a goblet and now you can't find it. It probably got broken in the washing up. Why should I be interested in that? You don't care about what I'm trying to do here *now*. The truth is you're as cold as a fish; you wouldn't really share what you're interested in with anyone, even if she wanted to. What you say to me about myself: that's pure projection. It's you you're looking at. It's you that freezes everyone off.'

'Oh no,' said Colombo. 'Oh no, m'dear. *Quem vê caras não vê corações.* You of all people know that.'

They both know I don't speak a word of Portuguese. I put

my glass down, got up and went out. I don't think either of them noticed. First thing this morning I packed my night-bag, walked down to the road, and started hitching to Dorrado. Neither of them was up when I left. Colombo was sleeping in the room below mine in the tower, and when I crept down the spiral staircase his door was uncompromisingly shut. I left a note for Lucy on the kitchen table. That day I walked at least ten miles between the four rides it took to get me to the steps of the Red Herring, and I had plenty of time to wonder if I'd left too precipitately. I felt guilty that I might have made them feel guilty. It was a damp, depressing day, and I felt chilled, excluded and foreign. For the first time since I came to Hy Brasil I thought about what it was going to be like when I went home. As my footsteps crunched along the gravel road that wound around the slopes of Mount Brasil they seemed to echo against the mountainside as if there were two of me. As there always used to be. Sometimes I forget for a moment that it's changed. I forgot then, but as soon as I realised it, the moment passed. But it had happened, so I knew that in about a week's time I'd probably get a postcard from Arthur.

It was foggy dusk when I walked under the dripping sign into the bar of the Red Herring. Inside it was warm and filled with soft yellow light. A fire burned in the big medieval-looking hearth, and the light winked and blinked on polished wood, coloured bottles, faded prints, fishing floats and hundreds of mysterious objects that hung everywhere like in Aladdin's cave. The genie behind the bar was Moses in a leather waistcoat. It wasn't a lamp he was polishing, it was a pint mug. And Aladdin was there too, the only customer, in bleached jeans and a ragged blue shirt, standing with his back to me at the bar, a half pint in front of him. When he heard the door shut behind me he turned to look. It was Jared Honeyman.

'Hi-aye, Sidony,' he said. 'Welcome to Dorrado.'

I must have been tired after my long tramp, but for an absurd moment I felt tears against my eyelids, as if I'd just completed a long quest, and what he'd offered me was something more than words. It was wonderful to be there after a long day in the drizzle. The Red Herring is like an inn in a book. I'm writing this in a thin slip of a yellow room with chintz curtains that faces the harbour. I'm lying in my bed which is big and comfortable with a thick yellow duvet and stacks of pillows, and proper cotton sheets that smell of being dried outside. There is a flowered carpet, an old-fashioned chest of drawers and an austere wardrobe with a mirror, the door of which is wedged shut with a programme for the Dorrado Agricultural Show, Saturday August 23rd, 1995. It's half past three in the morning and I am filled with wellbeing so that suddenly everything I see and touch pleases me. It has been a most unexpected evening.

I had a bar supper with Jared. We sat in the inglenook, one on each side of the fire, at the end of a long slate table that used to be a shove ha'penny board. Jared was interested that I recognised it, and I said I reckoned that the only reason there was shove ha'penny in Hy Brasil was because the West Country sailors must have brought it here. He told me the Honeymans came from Porlock in the eighteenth century, and now he was their last surviving male descendent in Hy Brasil. Jared had steak and kidney pie for supper and I had plaice and chips.

By this time the bar was filling up, but no one disturbed us in the inglenook. We both had treacle pudding. The food here is all real, not bought in frozen from the Cash and Carry.

Jared told me about Mrs Silva who does the cooking, and from that we got on to other families in Dorrado, and I found out a great deal. Colombo, for instance had occasionally spoken of 'my sister', but it was Jared who told me he had seven of them, all married but one, and more nephews and nieces than Jared had bothered to count, though he was able to tell me the names of nearly all of them. Colombo's only brother is a Jesuit priest in Brazil, but all his relations on his father's side are Scots Presbyterians, a dual heritage which accounts, Jared told me, for Colombo's fatalistic streak, as well as his ability to see both sides of everything. But then, he said, everyone in Hy Brasil is a bit like that on account of living under a live volcano. I asked how he knew Colombo, but the question seemed to puzzle him: he had always known Colombo.

When I said I wouldn't have coffee in case it kept me awake, Jared mentioned that there was a gig at Da Shack as it was Saturday night, and if I liked a bit of dancing there was no reason why we shouldn't wander down there later on. This sounded like excellent copy for the book, so I said yes at once. Jared said if he was going to dance he'd better not have a second helping of pudding, so I bought coffee for us both. He's very easy to talk to. No one in Hy Brasil has shown more than a perfunctory interest in where I come from, and so far I've liked that. There's a certain perverse freedom about feeling as anonymous as possible. But when Jared started asking me I found myself telling him a great deal. I told him about the travel writing competition, and how I really shouldn't be here at all. He laughed, but said on the contrary, he saw it as precise proof that I should. When I asked why, he said, 'Kismet', and refused to explain. He told me about diving off Spitzbergen, and about marine salvage, and gannets. We seem to have read a lot of the same books when we were young. He doesn't remind me in the least of Arthur, but in a way it was like having Arthur there.

Da Shack looked most unpromising from the outside on a foggy night. It's a long frame-built shed down by the harbour, badly in need of a new coat of yellow paint. The place was already full of people, and Jared knew them all. They weren't all the same age as us. There were people older than my parents, and people who looked barely old enough to drink (you have to be seventeen in Hy Brasil). You'd never have got such diversity together in a place like Da Shack at ten o'clock on a Saturday night in England. This is a foreign country. For a moment I felt so shy I just wanted to run, but to my relief Jared didn't sit down with any of the groups who greeted us, but led me up half a dozen steps to a raised platform at the back. There was a small table looking over the floor below that still wasn't taken, and we sat there. I looked around at the dark green walls covered with old advertisments: The Bisto Kids, Coleman's Mustard, Horlicks For Night Starvation. An antique canoe hung above our heads, and between us and the band stood an old-fashioned scarlet petrol pump with a notice on it saying, 'Motor Car Fuel Only: contains lead'.

Jared pointed out various people to me: three of Colombo's brown-eyed sisters were there with their husbands, there were various Gunns, Hawkins, Pereiras and Kidds, most of whom seemed, from Jared's rather involved account, to be cousins of his by marriage. Then there was an alarmingly sexy-looking woman with long blonde hair whom I understood, from what he didn't say, to be an ex-girlfriend. I began to feel extremely visible, though no one took much notice of us except to smile and wave at Jared. But my father is vicar of a small village, and I knew quite well that no detail about me would have been missed by anybody. I began to blush, until I reminded myself that I was a writer, an objective observer of life to whom this whole scene was merely excellent material. But I wished the band would come back and start playing again, so we could all get lost again in sound. To my surprise when the waitress came round to us Jared ordered water, and I did the same. The water in Hy Brasil is delicious. When I told Jared so he smiled and said,

> *Srotha teithmilsi tar tir,*
> *rogu de mid ocus fin,*
> *doini delgnaidi cen on,*
> *combarty cen peccad, cen chol*

(I'm copying it out. It didn't sound like that but I got him to write it down for me afterwards.)

'What's that?'

'It's the inscription on the drinking fountain in the market place in Dorrado. It comes from an old Irish poem about a voyage to Hy Brasil.'

'And what does it mean?'

'As well as I can tell you, it means, "The soil in that country is watered by sweet, gentle streams. The natives drink the best cider and wine. They are a fine people and full of integrity. Sex there is not a sin, and no one need feel any guilt about it."'

'Are you sure it means all that?' I asked suspiciously.

'I'm not an Irish scholar, but that's what I'm told.'

At last the band started playing again. They weren't young. Jared said they'd been together since the sixties, and to look at them you'd think nothing had touched them since, but there was nothing fossilised about their music. They were pretty versatile. The saxophonist alternated between a tenor and a soprano sax, the guitarist between lead and rhythm, one of the singers also played the fiddle, and then there was a drummer and a wild-looking guy playing an electric piano and a synthesiser. It was mostly old-fashioned stuff, but funky rather than nostalgic. I liked it. I sipped ice-cold water and listened, and suddenly everything changed, like in a dream, into one of those moments of intense happiness which you recognise and know that this is it, this is what you're alive for, and this makes it all worth it even if you die tomorrow. I didn't care any more if we were watched by half the world. The band broke into 'Love Shack'. I looked up and caught Jared looking at me with something that might have been surprise, but I didn't have time to tell, because he jumped up and held out his hand to me, and we went on to the floor and danced. And that's what we did until three o'clock in the morning. I love to dance. I get wild. It takes brilliant music for me to really know I've got a body, and those elderly-looking hippies had everything it takes after all. They played 'Mustang Sally', 'Chain of Fools', 'Do you Love Me?' and lots more. Sometimes if the music is great I dance with my eyes shut and get really into it. I did that last night at times, and other times I found myself looking at Jared. Jared dances the way I do, crazily.

His tattered shirt came undone and flapped madly. When the band began to play *I Only Have Eyes For You* I hung back; in fact it wasn't at all unpleasant to get close to him. He has a good sense of rhythm. But all through the evening every time I looked at him I'd find his blue eyes fixed on me, with that naked look one can't help recognising, and can't help remembering either that one has a certain power and occasionally men are vulnerable to it, and sometimes one ends up hurting them. But when it's happening it all seems worth it, and in the end, too: however it ends I think, as far as I can tell so far, it still stays worth it.

I got out my pen and paper just now so as to write this all up for the guidebook, but I can't even remember the name of the band. I'm on to my second bound notebook, but I'm worried that what I'm writing is the wrong sort of book. Certainly I can't put Jared Honeyman into a guidebook to Hy Brasil. Imagine how furious he would be.

That was last night.

When I came down at ten this morning Ernest said there was a message that I was to go to Maria's house for breakfast. 'I'll run you down there,' he said. I said that was hardly fair, as he was doing himself out of a customer, but he said he had a mind to go himself. It was only when we arrived that I realised that Maria was Colombo's sister, the one who's married to the harbour master. Maria was at the stove making an endless succession of pancakes. Her sister Maeve was dishing up Spanish omelettes and two more of the family were dispensing hot bread and coffee, while a mob of dark-eyed children milled about the table under their feet. About a dozen people from last night were sitting round the kitchen table, including the entire band. The babble of talk mingled in a friendly way with the smells of coffee and fresh bread. The table was covered with blue and white china and in the middle there was a big bowl of oranges looking almost luminescent in the sun from the open window. Jared was wedged in at the end of the table, rapidly demolishing a bacon sandwich. When Ernest and I appeared he said, 'Good, you got her,' with his mouth full, and moved up to make room for me.

I wondered as I ate if Colombo were still at Ravnscar, and, if so, whether he and Lucy were having a cheerful breakfast in the alcove of the kitchen window, then remembered that would have been hours ago if it had happened at all. I looked at Colombo's sister Natalia, leaning across her tattooed and silent husband, in order to tell the lead singer from the band how it was she knew that Father Browne's housekeeper was feeding him entirely out of tins, so that the poor man never saw any fresh meat or vegetables from one month's end to another, which would account for his terrible complexion, and in the middle of the summer too. I thought how if Colombo wasn't at Ravnscar he might have been here. I remembered the day Colombo brought me to Dorrado, and how he'd never mentioned his family, but taken me to his god-mother's house on the hill to have tea. I looked at Maria who was breaking more eggs into a big blue-and-white bowl and arguing with a man I didn't know about fish quotas, and it occurred to me that Colombo had shown me a very different country from all this. Then I thought about Lucy, living alone up at Ravnscar, and I wondered if she'd ever been to Da Shack, and if she had, why she'd never mentioned it to me.

Next to me Jared was telling Ernest and two of the MacAdam sisters' husbands about a document in the Spanish National Archive that told how the *Cortes* was commissioned to sail from Seville to Panama with a triple order to supply the existing colonists, to lay claim to new land and to seek for treasure. 'The irony is,' he was saying, 'That the *Cortes* went looking for treasure and now she's turned into treasure. What's lying off Despair is nothing less than a microcosm of Spain, 1611. We were down there a couple of days ago and we found the complete rim of an olive jar. And we've got other sherds that might be part of it too. God knows what's lying under the sand, but we don't even have a vacuum pump. And no one even wants to know.' Jared had told me just the same thing, last night, and it occurred to me that if I spent more time with him I was going to hear him telling people about the *Cortes* fairly often. That was the first time I'd caught myself making any assumption at all about Jared. I looked down. He was spreading butter lavishly on hot rolls. His hands were very unlike Colombo's, being square and brown, the fingers cracked and roughened by outdoor work and seawater. There's nothing elegant about Jared, but he has a look of sturdy capability which makes an odd contrast to his unpredictable temper. I wondered which impression was the deceptive one: maybe he's just paradoxical.

I listened to the cadaverous-looking man who played the guitar telling me where the band had toured in England fifteen years ago, until Jared put his hand on my shoulder and said, 'You'd like to see the back of the mountain, wouldn't you, Sidony?'

'The back of which mountain?'

'Brasil. Marco here says we can borrow his jeep. You ought to see the coast north of here. It's something else.'

'Jared borrows cars like other people borrow a pound of sugar,' remarked the guitarist.

Jared grinned at him. 'You'd like that, wouldn't you, Sidony? You're not busy?'

'No, I'm not busy.'

Only, of course, I am busy, or ought to be. It's time to turn over a new leaf, literally, and get back to where I'm supposed to be:

The west coast between Dorrado and Ogg's Cove can hardly have changed since the basalt skeleton of Hy Brasil first heaved itself out of the sea five million years ago. Certainly, once the old Dorrado whaling station is out of sight, history has made no impression on it. The only signs of habitation are the two parallel tyre tracks that mark where a vehicle has been this way before, and they stop abruptly where the angle of the hillside steepens to an alarming thirty degrees. The ride's an uncomfortable one, heaving and bumping over rock and marshland, but the surroundings are spectacular. In June the grass slopes are pink with thrift, and the rounded outcrops of basalt gleam in the sun as if they hadn't hardened yet into solid rock. The track stops where the grassy terrace peters out, and from then on one walks over bare rock. The basalt is rough and rounded like the barnacled back of a whale, as easy to walk on as paving stones. In the cracks between the rock swellings the grass is lush and studded with spring flowers: early purple orchids, lousewort, tormentil and milkwort. We passed a few of the feral goats which people keep telling me have become a pest on Hy Brasil. Their ancestors were left on the islands by passing sailors, so there would always be a supply of meat when their ships came back. The sea thumps lazily against the invisible rocks below, and white gulls swoop and glide, their cries echoing against hidden cliffs. One can see the islands that guard the entrance to the bay of Dorrado: Gwionsay, Bjornskerry, Tegid Voel. To one's right the slopes rise upwards into the mist that hangs over the summit of Mount Brasil. It's an active volcano; all this could be swept away tomorrow, or a hundred years from now.

Jared said, when I asked how one lived with a thing like that, that it was more like living with a person than a thing, and when I asked how, he said all volcanoes had personalities, and the way people dealt with them in the past was to think about how they were feeling rather than what they might do. I said that wasn't very scientific, and he said that living with anyone, which was what I'd asked him about, was an art not a science and Shakespeare knew what he was talking about when he said that, 'Oft the teeming earth Is with a kind of colic pinched and vex'd By the imprisoning of unruly wind Within her womb.' The metaphor is particularly pungent, he said, insofar as the smell is in fact remarkably similar. Even after living with Arthur all my life it sometimes takes me a while to realise I'm being teased.

I look at what I've just written and I think, who'll read that, tomorrow or a hundred years from now? Will people come here because I wrote this, or will they sit at home, gentlemen in

England now abed, and read what I've written rather than come here? Jared would rather they stayed away, but I'm trying to keep Jared out of this. In that last paragraph I failed completely. I realise for the first time that the reason guidebooks are so boring if you happen not to be in the relevant place, is because they don't have any characters, and travel books, which do, are mostly lies anyway. Everyone I've met who knows the inside story of a travel book has told me it's nearly all a lie. Is it a lie to say what flowers there were, and how old the rocks are, and leave out Jared? It's certainly a distortion. At the moment my commissioning editor in Islington seems very far away, and Jared is very present, much more of a reality than she will ever be. I think I should get two different-coloured notebooks, one for what I'm supposed to be writing, and one for what I'm really thinking about.

Jared and I sat on a rocky outcrop looking out to sea, due west in the direction of the northern peninsula of Newfoundland. I remembered the map that Peterkin had showed me in the Pele Centre, on which all the area around us was coloured in with grey spots. I mentioned this to Jared. He said Hy Brasil was very like Iceland, in that volcanic activity was usually chronic rather than fatal; it would leave nasty scars but it wouldn't necessarily be what finished you off. I told him how my mother saw Surtsey rise out of the sea; she just happened to be flying to Reykjavik on the right day. 'Lucky,' said Jared.

'Yes. She used to tell us the story; it made quite an impression. What happens when an island gets made: fire and steam and melted rock. Indescribable really.'

'I'd say it had been described quite often.'

'Where? In the *National Geographic*?'

'Well, yes, that too. Or how about like this:

"Below the thunders of the upper deep;
Far far beneath in the abyssal sea
His ancient, dreamless, uninvaded sleep
The Kraken sleepeth . . ."

'I can't remember the next bit. Hold on. Yes, I've got it . . .

> "There hath he lain for ages and will lie
> Battening on huge sea-worms in his sleep,
> Until the latter fire shall heat the deep;
> Then once by men and angels to be seen
> In roaring he shall rise and on the surface die."'

'Is that what they taught you on your oceanography course?'
'No, I learned that in Ogg's Cove Elementary School.'

'You seem to have learned a lot of poetry at school. Much more than we do. You know, that in itself would be my mother's notion of Utopia: a country where all the children learn loads of poems by heart at school. She's an English teacher.'

'We were doing a project on the volcano,' said Jared. 'I remember a lot of red paint.'

We were silent for a bit, looking out to sea. I thought of something I'd meant to tell him. 'Oh, by the way, Jared, you remember I said I'd seen that green goblet before?'

He sat up at once. 'Of course I do. What about it?'

'It suddenly occurred to me when I was cleaning my teeth this morning where it was. There was a wineglass just the same – with the same crest and everything – with lots of other junk, on a shelf in the Pele Centre. It was when Olly West showed me round his office.'

'*What!* You mean that man . . . Sidony, are you sure?'

'Yes. At least, I think I'm sure. It had a crack in it. I wasn't noticing particularly at the time, but now I think about it, that's why I recognised the one in Maldun's Mill.'

'*Where* did you say it was? In the main office?'

'No, in his little office. The one on the right as you go in. There's a whole lot of bits and pieces on the shelf above the seismology journals.'

'You're absolutely positive?'

'Well, yes. At least, you're making me think I'm not. But it must have been like, because I'm sure that's why your goblet seemed so familiar. Why? Has anyone taken treasure off the *Cortes* before now, do you know? I suppose they could have.'

'There were survivors.'

'Well then, I suppose it wouldn't be so odd. I mean wine-glasses . . . did they have sets of things in those days?'

'The story goes that eleven people got off. It must have been a hell of a night.'

He didn't say anything else for a long time. I divided my attention between the sweeping gulls and his frowning profile. Eventually I said, 'Jared?'

'Mm?'

'In return, will you tell me about Lucy?'

'Lucy? What about Lucy?'

'I think she's lonely,' I said. Though before I spoke I hadn't formulated the idea, I knew as soon as I said it that it was true. 'I've stayed with her nearly three weeks now and I like her a lot, and I can tell. I know Ravnscar is home for her, but most people couldn't stand it. Sometimes she talks about New York and I wonder why the hell she came back here at all. She had a life. She talks to Colombo more than to anyone else, but usually on the phone. When he actually turns up they seem very tense together. She knows who everyone is, but she doesn't seem to have any friends. And yet she's kind and hospitable and friendly, and we talk a lot, but there's this great big emptiness in the middle. I like Ravnscar. I love staying there and I'll never forget it. But sometimes since I got to Dorrado yesterday – was it only yesterday? – sometimes I've just wanted to cry. I think I've been getting lonely myself. Missing something. Missing out on life, that's what it feels like. That's what it's like with Lucy; it's been rubbing off on me. I can't explain.'

'You can cry if you like,' said Jared. 'I don't mind.'

'I don't want to cry *now*.'

'You'd rather I told you about Lucy?'

'Yes, please,' I said, and waited.

'I'm younger than she is,' he said at last. 'I was only thirteen when it happened. But what I know isn't just gossip. I was up there quite a bit. My mother used to work there.'

'At Ravnscar?' This was a new piece to fit in.

'Yes. After my father was gone my mother got a job there. Cleaning. I was nine when she started. In the holidays she used to take me up there with her. We used to go by bike: an hour to get up there in the morning and ten minutes downhill to get home. We used to take the back track, past where the Pele Centre is now. Old Morgan was alive then. I was scared of him to start with, but one day he caught me reading Hakluyt's *Voyages* in his library in the Great Hall. I thought he'd be angry, but he wasn't. He talked to me and after that he said I could go in there whenever I liked and read what I wanted, but I was never to take anything away. It was a bargain. We each kept to it until he died. But after that it was just Mrs Lock – she was caretaker after the old man died and Lucy went away – and she didn't believe me when she found me back there after the funeral. She said if she caught me again where I had no business to be she'd call in the peelers. She would have, too. And by that time I'd been in trouble already. Borrowing boats without leave. It was only borrowing, Sidony, apart from the petrol; I'll admit the petrol. It was just I needed to have a boat, and we had no money. I didn't feel good about stealing, but there are worse things. Henty says so, in a book called *Hold Fast for England*. The captain says that the worst thing is to be a liar, and he wouldn't keep any young officer on his ship who told a lie. 'Upon my word,' he says, 'I would rather a boy were a thief than a liar.' That comforted me a lot, as I'd never felt any great need to tell lies. But Mrs Lock made it pretty clear to me I was no good, and I never went near the place again until I came home last year, and Lucy and I got to be friends again.

'But when everything happened my mother was actually in the house. I wasn't. I was supposed to be at school in Lyonsness, but I wasn't there either. Oddly enough I was up on the volcano.

It was the same day I climbed down into the crater, just by myself. I used to do things like that around then. Crazy things, daring myself how far I could go. I'd probably have killed myself one way or another, only when I turned fourteen Ishmael came from St Brandons to live at Ferdy's Landing. He and Anna were living in a caravan while they built the house. That was when he bought the boat I've got now, just before Rachel was born. I was upset at first about them taking over the place, but they were kind to me. Very kind, you could say, because if you want the honest truth I pinched Ishmael's boat one night, and he caught me coming back. I thought he was going to hit me and I just went for him. He could have mashed me to pulp one-handed, but he didn't. The end of it was he hired me to crew for him, and after that things got better. But it's Lucy you wanted to hear about, not me.'

'I'm interested in all of it.'

'I'll tell you about Lucy. Maybe she'd mind, but I know she could trust you even if she did mind. You know Penny Hawkins?'

'Yes, Colombo took me to see her. I thought I might have seen her this weekend, being in Dorrado.'

'No one sees Penny at the weekend. That's when Jim comes home.'

'Jim?'

'The President to you.' I glanced at him in surprise. He sounded so bitter; I wondered if it was just because of not getting a grant for the *Cortes* or if there was something else. 'Oh, our Jim mingles with the peasantry all right, but not on weekends. That's his time off. You'd never guess he was a Dorrado man, would you? But he is; that's why he can afford to ignore everybody on the west coast. Ignores his wife too, except at weekends. I don't know why she stands it.'

'Maybe she loves him.'

'And yet Penelope Hawkins isn't a fool. Anyway, you weren't asking me about Jim. Penelope had a cousin, Lem

Hawkins, who lived at Ferdy's Landing. His son was Nicky Hawkins. No one's told you about him?'

'No.'

'It must have been strange to be Lucy. She lived alone with her father up at Ravnscar. I don't suppose he took much notice of her. There were housekeepers, not always the same one, but I remember them all the same way: ugly and fierce. I was scared of Ravnscar when I was a little chap. Lucy went to school in Ogg's Cove with the rest of us. When I started school Lucy was the oldest girl and Nicky was the oldest boy. They used to bully us little ones. Our house was nearly a mile from the school. I was only five when I started, but I had my own bike and my Pappa taught me to ride it so I could go to school. But Nicky was mad at me for that – he was twelve and he hadn't got a bike – and every day he and Lucy used to throw my bike in the nettles. I never told anyone – you know how you don't when you're small – but I was always all over nettle stings. When I get stung now I always think of Nicky Hawkins. But later on everything changed, and I saw quite a different side of him. Back then he and Lucy always stuck together. There's not many left of the old landowning families now – the original Pirate Kings. Most of them went down when the Brits took over, all but the Morgans up at Ravnscar, and the Hawkinses dwindling away at Ferdy's Landing.

'Lem Hawkins was a friend of my father's. Later my mother told me that after my father was gone Lem gave her money. We had nothing, you see, because they confiscated Pappa's business, and he'd put everything into that, so I guess we needed help, but Lem was going bankrupt himself. He used to come sometimes after I was in bed and talk to my mother. About my father, I suppose.

'Anyway, Nicky's mother left his father and took Nicky away with her out of Hy Brasil. Lucy went to Lyonsness High and after that it was OK at school. I can remember the day Nicky Hawkins came back to Ogg's Cove. His father was away by then, and the house was all boarded up. Nicky was seventeen. He came off the boat, went straight to Gunn and Selkirk and got the keys out of them, and moved back into Ferdy's Landing. It must have been just the next day or so I was over there – I used to fish off the rocks up there – and there was smoke coming out of the chimney and the boards taken off the windows. I spied around a bit, and there was Nicky dragging all the furniture and cushions and stuff out into the sun and spreading them to air. I wasn't sure it was him. He looked grown up to me – thin and dark with long hair that fell over his eyes – not at all what I remembered. I wouldn't have let him see me, but then Olly West came round and was talking to him, and so I came out from under the trees and joined them. I doubt if Nicky was pleased to find a ten-year-old hanging about, but he learned pretty soon that I was useful. He used to pay me shillings to wash his dishes and chop kindling; I even used to cook for him, mostly baked beans or egg and chips. I was only a little chap but I'd had a much more practical education already than he ever had. I needed the money, and also I was interested. I could remember Nicky being just another kid at school, and now he was living in his own house all by himself like a boy in a book. I don't think he was ever nice to me – he used to call me Friday and that made me furious – but I was fascinated by him. So I used to hang about.

'So did Lucy. She was pretty circumspect at first. Nicky wasn't exactly hospitable – not a word in his cheek for anyone who happened to call on him. Of course folk started happening by just so soon as the news got about, but they weren't asked in. The one who was a real menace was Olly West. Always coming by with tins of spam and trying to make Nicky talk. I was there when he said Nick could always confide in him. Nicky was stripped to the waist, splitting logs, at the time, and the way he cleaved those pine trunks I'd have run a mile if I thought any of his feelings were directed at me. But Olly wouldn't notice a nuance if it sliced him through the brain. It was me that suggested booby traps, and we did some of that. I don't think Olly thought it was anything but an act of God, but he laid off his daily visits after a while and I think Nicky was grateful to me.

'But Lucy . . . I'd have seen her off too, if I'd been told, and I wouldn't have asked for my shilling either. I didn't think we needed any girls. But Nicky wasn't me, and he wasn't ten years old. We'd been sweeping the chimney, I remember. It had a starling's nest in it. I was in the kitchen afterwards sweeping up the soot and the doorway darkened and in came Nick with Lucy and he said, "Put the kettle on, Jed. We've got company." And as soon as Lucy could see after the bright sun outside she said, "Christ, Nick. This place is *filthy!*" I was scunnered but he just smiled that secret smile of his, with his long hair falling over his face and hiding his eyes, and said to me I'd better wash out the mugs in hot water. Well, I didn't, but she stayed and had tea all the same, and after that there wasn't any peace. At least, that's not fair. It wasn't that she made trouble, it was just that she changed everything.

'It wasn't just the shillings.' Jared threw down the bits of moss he'd been absentmindedly pulling apart, and spread his hands wide. 'The thing was I adored him. The fantasy I was living in came, ironically enough, out of the library at Ravnscar. The old man was gently escorting me through all his boyhood favourites: Ballantyne, Farnoll, Henty, Kipling. Not ideal mental equipment for a poor post-colonial boy from a dysfunctional family, but there it was, and there was Nick. I thought Nick was the hero of my very own adventure story come real. I was in my private, temporary heaven, with a supply of shillings thrown in, when along came Lucy.

'If I'd had any arsenic I guess I might have put it in the tea. As it was, I just waited on them, like the little mermaid. The summer went by and I used to make the tea and light the fire and go fishing off the rocks for Nicky, and on the whole I was happy. And then one morning – it was very hot; I can remember I was just wearing my grey shorts and a straw hat, but I had a new leather belt with a knife in it that I'd just got for my eleventh birthday – I came over from Ogg's Cove with the milk for Nicky, and I couldn't open the door. It was barred on the inside. I banged and there wasn't any answer. So I left the churn on the step, and I climbed in the window. The kitchen had got much cleaner since Lucy was around. It was quite tidy now, but there was nobody in it. So I stood at the bottom of the stairs and called out "Nicky!" It was dim up there, with the curtains still drawn on the landing, and then I heard voices. I could hear Lucy up there with him. Nicky came at last and leaned over the bannisters. He looked very brown in the dim light. "I've brought the milk," I said. He asked how I got in, and I told him. "Well, then, you can just get the hell out of here the same way," he said. "And if you find a door locked on you, it means keep out. So get that."

I'd like to say I never went back. But I did. I got used to Lucy being there too. At least, I suppose I did. Anyway, they got used enough to me. They didn't try to pretend she wasn't sleeping there, but Nicky made me swear an oath on his grandfather's Bible that I'd never tell. Come to think of it,' said Jared, suddenly turning to look at me. 'This is the first time I ever have.'

'I don't think it matters now,' I said.

He touched my hand briefly. 'No, I don't think it does. In fact, even then it began to matter less. School started again, and the following year I was at Lyonsness. Nicky lived at Ferdy's Landing for two years. I still used to visit him a lot, but I didn't want his money any more. I could get more mowing the lawn up at Ravnscar. I saw Lucy around up there, of course, but she never mentioned Nicky to me. I knew she was still going to Ferdy's Landing though. I knew most things that went on in Ogg's Cove.

Then this American guy came to Hy Brasil. Cosmo Ashton. Lucy met him at some party at Government House. He'd made his money in oil, in Texas, and he was living in the

Bahamas. He'd started setting up marinas there as an investment, and he had this notion he was going to develop Dorrado as a high-class marina for yachts crossing the Atlantic. He had surveyors out there too, to see if Dorrado harbour could be developed as a deep-water facility for cruise liners. Oh, he had all sorts of plans. Anyway, he used to come to Ravnscar. He was a big, fair, soft sort of a man; I didn't like him. He smelt of money. He used to come up in his Porsche and take Lucy out. I don't know where they went. Kidd's Hotel, probably. I wouldn't eat an unpeeled banana out of that kitchen myself, but I don't suppose Cosmo knew anything about that. Old Morgan was failing fast by this time. He was still alive, but shaky on his pins, and thin as a skeleton. His face was all bones and staring eyes. He still used to recommend books to me: *The Mutiny on the Bounty*, Cook's *Voyages*. That was the last one. By the time I'd got to Hawaii old Francis Morgan was dead.

'But Morgan was still dying back then, and Cosmo was coming to the house. I think Cosmo fancied himself Master of Ravnscar, an oil baron disguised as Pirate King, and Ravnscar could certainly have used his money. I don't know what old Morgan thought about it. He must have considered what might happen to Lucy when he was gone. Nicky's father was a bankrupt. Officially Ferdy's Landing should have been sold, I suppose, but I don't think anyone ever offered for it. Nicky would never have left quietly if they had. But there was Nicky, nineteen years old and on the beach, apparently living on nothing in Ogg's Cove. And there was Cosmo, working for a big company, rolling in money up to his white neck. And there was Lucy, nineteen years old and as beautiful as her mother had been, as least that's what my mamma used to say, and totally incapable as far as anyone knew of earning tuppence.

'She was very quiet, always, but I don't think Lucy was ever shy. She used to laugh a lot, but she wouldn't share the joke. She'd put her hand over her face and laugh without telling anyone why, and people used to find that disconcerting. They were right too; she probably was laughing at them. I think she must have seen Cosmo for what he was. But Lucy was always terribly practical. She likes money, you know. It may seem odd to you, knowing that house, but when we were little Lucy never had any money either. I once pinched a threepenny bit off her. She never knew it was me – and for God's sake don't tell her now – but you'd think she'd had her grave robbed, the way she went on about it. It was meant to be for our school charities' collection, but she wasn't going to put it in there any more than I was. Also, she wanted to go to America. She told me so, one day when we were in the kitchen at Ravnscar. I was having my tea break and she was waiting for Cosmo. She was wearing make-up, I remember, and a tight black jumper and a very short black skirt and leather boots. I wanted to remind her about Nicky and Ferdy's Landing, but of course I didn't say a word. Would she have listened to me if I had? I doubt it, but I've wondered about it a bit more often than I'd like.

'Well anyway, that's more or less the end of the story.'

'Jared! You can't stop there!'

'I'm not going to, but the next bit's rough. I wasn't there, I told you. I was up on the volcano. She'd agreed to marry Cosmo. The night before the announcement appeared in the *Times* she spent at Ferdy's Landing with Nicky, but obviously she didn't tell him what she'd done. He must have read it later the same day when he went over to Ogg's Cove for his groceries. Lucy and Cosmo were up at Ravnscar. Nicky came up to Ravnscar. He had a shotgun. Did I tell you that? He burst into the Great Hall. Lucy was there, and her father, and Cosmo. Nicky shot Cosmo dead.'

'Oh my God!'

'Lucy tried to hold him, but he pushed her away, and ran. Out of the front door and on to the cliff path. And he threw himself over the cliff.'

'You mean he was killed?'

'Of course he was killed. And that's it. You asked me about Lucy,' said Jared savagely. 'Well, now I've told you. That's it.'

'Oh, no!' I found I was shivering, on the verge of tears. 'Oh no! Jared, that's terrible. It's appalling, tragic.'

'No.' He seemed determined to be hurtful. 'Not tragic, melodramatic. Because that's how you like to see it. But you're not reading a book now. You only see it that way, anyway, because it was at Ravnscar. If the same thing had happened at the back of Water Street on a Friday night you'd just call it sordid.'

'But it happened! Oh Jared!'

'Well, even if it is a tragedy it isn't yours, and it's all over now. You don't need to take on.'

I thought about a thirteen-year-old boy climbing down by himself into the crater of an active volcano, and made an effort to pull myself together. 'Shall we walk on?' I said to him.

I was in the act of standing up. There was a grinding noise, like giant mill-wheels. The rock moved. I was flung sideways, and fell down hard. The basalt was rough under my palms. My hands were sticky. When I looked there was blood. I struggled to my knees. Something huge crashed into the sea behind me. Water smacked against the cliffs; there was a long slithering sound of soil and stones and rushing water. I dared not move. The waves against the cliffs were much too loud, as if some monstrous thing had surfaced and the island itself was being sucked into its wake. But the rock under me stayed still. Something warm touched my back. 'Sidony?'

'Oh!' But I wouldn't lie there whimpering in front of him. I made myself sit up very slowly. There were smears of blood on my grazed knees. I looked up the mountain and there was a strip like a scar split open less than a mile away. I remembered the seaquake that had made headlines in the *Times* only a couple of weeks ago, and how I'd been fool enough to feel sorry that I'd missed it. I'd never felt so unsafe in my life as I was feeling now. 'Oh!' I pressed my hands to my cheeks and one of them came away with a smear of blood on it. It was silly but I couldn't stop shaking. We sat on the rock and he put his arm around me, and I leaned against him and shut my eyes until I felt a bit better. 'I'm sorry.'

'It's hardly your fault,' said Jared. He was looking back up the mountain. 'I think maybe we'd better go back.' He touched my cheek with his finger. 'Do you have a hanky?'

'No.'

'Nor do I. Well, it's not bleeding much. You must have fallen against the rock.'

'Jared, the rock *moved*.'

'Yes, it was quite a tremor.'

'I suppose you're used to it?'

'No,' said Jared. 'I'm not. If you're ready, I think perhaps we should go back.'

'You know what?' I said. 'I think you must be the least hysterical person I've ever met in my life.'

He smiled at that. 'Well, I'm glad I can make an impression some way. But even so I think we'd better go.'

I stood up shakily, but I wouldn't accept the hand he held out to me. All the way home I distrusted the ground under my feet, and that made everything in the world suddenly frightening in a way it had never been before. But Jared didn't say anything and neither did I. When Arthur and I used to tough it out like this it was always Arthur that gave in first. I knew it wouldn't be like that with Jared. Not only would I never be able to beat him, but I had a humiliating suspicion that he wasn't even playing. For some reason I was thinking of a picture in a book I'd had when I was little, of a dark neverland appearing down below in the middle of a crinkly sea, under twinkling stars. It was the beginning of a new chapter, and the caption, in curly writing, read 'THE ISLAND COMES TRUE'. I swallowed, and planted my feet firmly in Jared's footsteps as if that would keep the earth tame and quiet under me until I got back home.

FIFTEEN

PETERKIN SAT WITH his back to the window, reading the most recent catalogue of earthquakes in the New Madrid seismic zone. It made the Mid-Atlantic Ridge seem comparatively torpid. Hy Brasil had been geologically quiet for nearly a fortnight. Peterkin yawned and put down the printout. Globally it was a quiet day. It was a quiet day in the office too: the monitors on Mount Brasil had nothing to report, and Olly West had left the moment Peterkin arrived, at nine o'clock in the morning. The thermometer was already over 80°F, and Olly had been anxious to get down to Ogg's Cove and his breakwaters. Peterkin had his employer's measure by now: if nothing of interest was occurring underground he'd sunbathe for the rest of the day. It was nearly noon, and a regular scorcher. Peterkin had opened all the windows and the door, but still the office was as close as an oven. The fan in the ceiling turned desultorily, barely disturbing the knot of flies that buzzed against the ceiling. Outside the sky was metallic blue, and the land quivered in the haze. Wearily Peterkin clicked on PRINT, and the printer disgorged the latest reading from Mount Brasil. Peterkin picked up the paper, glanced at it, and threw it on the table. No earthquakes. Nothing. He yawned.

'Peterkin!'

He stopped mid-yawn, and swung his chair round. Jed? Hi-aye. I wasn't expecting . . .' The words trailed away.

Jared had a shotgun. Aimed at him, Peterkin. Peterkin's jaw dropped. 'Jed?'

'Sorry, old chap. I didn't mean to startle you.' Jared crossed the threshold and came right in. He lowered the gun. 'Listen, Pete.'

'What the hell do you think you're doing? Is that thing loaded?' Peterkin could hear the squeak in his own voice, and tried to make it firm and deep. 'Jared! Put that down!'

'No,' said Jared. 'Now look, Pete, it's like this. Olly's got something here that doesn't belong to him. I need to find it. It's nothing to do with you. I didn't want to bring you in, only at night there'd be the burglar alarm, and I don't know how to fix those things. So I had to come now. I have to force you to let me.'

'But Jed . . .' Pete looked hurt. 'You don't have to point that thing at me. God, don't you remember . . . You don't think you can't trust me?'

Jared held the gun so it was pointing at the floor just in front of Peterkin's bare feet. 'Think, man. This is your job. I'm not about to lose it for you. Olly's your employer. If you help me, and it gets out, you're done. Think of that!'

'You always used to leave me out when things got real,' said Peterkin sulkily. 'Seems like it's not changed much.'

'For Christ's sake, Peterkin, what do you think this is? Cowboys and Indians? Stop wasting time. When's Olly due back?'

'God knows,' said Peterkin, reminded of his other grievances. 'He's on the beach. And if you'd come at night you'd probably have got him not the alarm anyway. After that second earthquake he was trying to do a round-the-clock watch single-handed. He was wanting me to start at two in the morning as well, but Pappa said I should say no if he wasn't giving me time and a half. Which of course he wouldn't. The crazy thing is there're all these professors and experts and what-have-you from all over the world phoning up more or less begging to come in and do shifts for nothing. But he won't let them.'

'Typical. Anyway, I know where he is. I saw him. That's

why I'm here. Now stop changing the subject and listen. Either I hold you at gunpoint while I search, which won't be comfortable for either of us, besides taking twice as long, or we can take that bit as read. That means you quit moaning and co-operate. Suppose you stand there at the window, keep your back to the room. That's right. Now you won't see a thing, which means you can quite truthfully say you didn't. If I find what I want and get clear away you never laid eyes on me at all. Got that? And if anyone comes up you'll see them at the bend in the road, and there's nothing to stop you having a fit of coughing, say, which I can't help overhearing, but you won't know about that because you were at the computer and you never saw me slip by. But if there's trouble and I'm caught, and it's obvious you couldn't possibly have missed me, you're not involved because I forced you at gunpoint. No one could lose you your job for that. More likely give you a medal. Got that?'

'Yes, but . . .'

'Shut up, Pete. You're wasting time. No, don't look round.'

'I could help you, if you told me what . . .'

'Shut up!'

Peterkin subsided, and looked stonily out of the window. Heat shimmered over the curve of the road fifty feet below. He could feel the sweat running down his back inside his shirt. There were small movements behind him, the familiar click from the latch on the door of Olly's inner office. Then silence. Five minutes, ten minutes. The door clicked again, and Peterkin took a deep breath. Jared's voice came from just behind him.

'There we are. That didn't hurt, did it?'

'You could have trusted me!'

'I did. There's a phone six inches from your right hand. I'm off, Pete. You never saw a thing, remember that. And if anyone says anything's missing, you don't know a thing either.'

'Well, I don't, do I?'

'Don't take a huff, old chap. That's the whole . . . what's that?'

'Fuck!' Peterkin's eyes were riveted on the bend in the road. 'He's coming up! I'd know that gear change anywhere! That's Olly.' Even as he spoke an ancient blue Ford came out of the trees and reached the hairpin bend. 'He's coming!'

'So long, Pete. Mind, you never saw a thing!'

Out of the corner of his eye Peterkin saw a figure flit past him into the sun, like the shadow of a passing bird. He turned back to the empty office. Automatically he picked up the chart from Memphis, Tennessee and sat down in front of his computer, his eyes glued to the paper as if every fault line on the planet had exploded into action on the very stroke of noon.

Jared crawled into a shady cleft three hundred feet above Hogg's Beach, where a shrunken waterfall trickled over slabs of bare lava. He unslung his gun, which had not been loaded, and his knapsack, stuck his head under the thin stream of water and drank thirstily. Then he sat down, took off his hot trainers, and dabbled his feet in a fern-lined pool that lay six inches below its usual watermark. Below him the beach glinted in the full blaze of the sun. He could see no one on it, but a solitary swimmer was slowly crossing the bay, parallel to the grassy shore just below where he sat. It didn't matter; he could get back to his boat – which was hidden, as it could only be during a flat calm, in one of the inlets off Brentness – through the lava channels without anyone seeing him.

Nothing moved, not so much as a bird. The land seemed stunned by heat. He pulled off his damp shirt, and used it to wipe the sweat out of his eyes. Even in the shade, dressed only in cut-off jeans and a green sunhat, it was far too hot. He began to undo the straps of the knapsack.

It was far too hot. At three o'clock in the afternoon the sun showed no sign of relenting. After the blinding heat outside, the apartment was as cool as a cave, and Nesta entered it gratefully, threw her bag down on the sofa and kicked off her sandals. She needed a drink. There were two messages on the machine. She pressed the button and listened while she poured herself a glass of juice.

'Sweetheart. I'm letting Pereira take me up to Ferdy's Landing this afternoon. He insists I take notice of his communications project which will apparently employ upstanding citizens in their thousands and tens of thousands. It sounds ghastly to me, but then I'm not looking for a job. I think really he wants to show me his computers. Pearls before swine, but I daresay they'll give me tea. I adore you, but don't wait dinner.'

'Nesta, this is Jared Honeyman. Listen, there's something I need to talk to you about. It's urgent. Very urgent. I'm at Lyonsness 263, Per Pedersen's. I'll stay here till you call back. If you do. I hope you do. If you're not back tonight I'll go home, because of the gannets, but in that case, can you leave a message here? I do need to talk to you urgently. That is, if you don't mind. It really is quite urgent.'

Nesta refilled her glass, and wandered over to the window while she replayed the messages. The city shimmered in the heat. Beyond it the sea shone like polished oilcloth. She smiled as she listened. Then she curled up on the sofa, picked up the phone, and began to dial a number.

Baskerville sat on a high stool at his workbench in the museum, examining a barnacle-encrusted lump of rust through a powerful magnifying glass. There were no windows in here, but the heat had infiltrated from the exhibition rooms in the front of the building. Baskerville had removed his black jacket, which hung over the back of his chair looking like an undertaker's mute, and had rolled up his grey shirtsleeves to expose two skeletal forearms overgrown with thick white hairs. His braces, startlingly, were scarlet. He was frowning so intently over his work that his eyebrows met in one straight line like an untrimmed hedge. The phone rang several times before he moved to answer it.

'Baskerville here . . . Yes? . . . Oh yes, Ms Kirwan. What can I do for you? . . . Keys? . . . What keys? . . . I don't have the keys to Maldun's Mill . . . Oh, those keys . . . I don't know about that . . . It shouldn't be removed from its case . . . There's the insurance . . . The insurance was a nightmare . . . You want to photograph it again? . . . Now? . . . I suppose it couldn't wait? . . . No . . . No . . . Technically that's true . . . Yes, technically, I suppose it does belong to young Honeyman . . . He seemed willing for it to come to the museum . . . I had assumed . . . Yes, technically, I suppose he can . . . Only a photograph? . . . Who wants this photograph? . . . I see. An artistic inspiration. Well, I suppose these things do happen . . . So Honeyman isn't there? He doesn't want to take the thing back? . . . No . . . No . . . So you're going down there now? . . . Alone? I'm not sure that's wise, Ms Kirwan . . . Very well, very well . . . Yes, I have them here . . . I suppose technically . . . naturally I'm anxious . . . Oh, very well . . .'

Two green glass goblets side by side. Not quite identical, but certainly twins: they belonged in a time when no two things were ever quite the same, though the differences were hardly measurable. Of course the first one to come ashore was marred by the long crack in its bowl. God knew when that had happened: on the night of the shipwreck, perhaps, or at any time in the intervening three hundred and eighty-six years. The second goblet was unflawed as the day it left the hands of its maker. But apart from that one obvious difference, the likeness rose, clear, striking and unassailable, so that from a few feet away the two goblets were precise mirror images of one another. It was when you came closer, to within inches, that you began to see that each one had its own characteristics. The ring at the base of the sea goblet was not exactly parallel to the foot; the glass bowl of the land goblet was marginally grainier; the impression of the galleon on the sea goblet was about a milli-metre off centre, compared with the land goblet.

The shutter clicked with a flash. 'OK. I'm coming in a bit nearer.' Nesta, with her eye to the camera, brought the lens a mere foot away from the goblets. 'Bring the light down a bit. A couple of inches. Not as far as that. Back a bit. Down. Yes.'

She took two more shots, and lowered the camera. 'OK. You can put that light away now.'

'Before my arm drops off,' agreed Jared, putting the hot spotlight down cautiously on the floor, and unplugging the flex.

Nesta screwed the lens cap back on. 'Well, we should get some half-decent pictures out of that.' She put down the camera, and surveyed the two glasses once again. 'And now, my lad, I think you'd better tell me all about it.'

'I just did tell you!'

'You've told me nothing I can't see with my own eyes, except what you told us all that day on the boat. All right, so the other goblet belonged to Nicky Hawkins, and he kept his matches in it on the mantelpiece at Ferdy's Landing. Nothing wrong with that, assuming he wasn't the vandal who put that crack in it. But when Ishmael got to the Landing the glass wasn't there. And quite clearly when you fished it up he'd never seen anything like it before in his life. So where's it been all these years? And how did you find it, when up until now you obviously hadn't a clue where it was? And whose is it now?'

'It's Nicky's.'

'No, Jared. We bring nothing into this world and it is certain we can carry nothing out. Nicky's dead.'

He looked away from her, and stared at the two goblets. Now the bright light was gone, they looked ordinary again. Two wineglasses on a stand draped with a white linen cloth. It was hard to see what all the fuss was about. Jared bit his lip. Two wineglasses. A memory surfaced: Nicky's brown hands cupping the green glass, Nicky's face illuminated by the candlelight from the table, Nicky swilling a pale liquid around the bowl, watching something dissolve that wasn't sugar, Nicky holding the glass to his lips so that he could taste. 'A sip, Friday, only a sip. It's spiked. None of that sniffing that you don't like. This is easier stuff for a little chap.' A mouthful of bitter apples. That was all.

A warm hand touched his bare arm. The slightly musky scent that was part of Nesta Kirwan came suddenly very close to him. 'Poor Nick,' she said. 'He was a friend of yours, wasn't he?'

Under the sign proclaiming MALDUN'S MILL: ART GALLERY. CRAFTS. GIFTS. CAFÉ, a white board said CLOSED in uncompromising black letters. Twenty to eight. Two vehicles remained in the car park: a 1958 black Citroen DS and a BMW motorbike. Baskerville's ancient Jeep pulled up beside them. Baskerville climbed out stiffly, like an ungainly spider, and strode over to the entrance. The door was unlocked. He slipped inside. The main hall was deserted, the entrance desk closed up for the night, the archway to the shop barred by a steel sliding door. One light was on, shining through the alcove at the far end from the room where the goblet was. There was no sound at all.

Baskerville moved silently across the hall, and peered in.

He saw two impossible things at once. The goblet had duplicated itself, and both of it stood on a white linen cloth on the stand in the centre of the room. And Nesta Kirwan and Jared Honeyman were locked in one another's arms a foot away from it.

Baskerville contemplated both phenomena without drawing attention to himself. During that time he was able to establish, according to the clear evidence of his senses, that the goblets were separate realities. In fact they were indubitably two. Moreover, the embrace, though incontrovertibly intimate, was not precisely amorous. There was no kissing. When it ended, and young Honeyman wiped his eyes with the back of his hand, swallowed, and said, 'I'm sorry, I didn't mean to make a fool of myself', it only confirmed Baskerville's revised impression.

'You haven't,' said Nesta. 'On the contrary. I'd say you were a charming and admirable young man. If we've finished here, I think we should put all this back where it belongs. I'm hungry. Have you any plans for dinner?'

'Dinner? No. I mean, all I have to do now is pick up some stuff I left at Per's and return his bike. Then go home.'

'We could go to Atlantis. You've eaten there before?'

'Atlantis?' said Jared. 'Yes, Lucy took me there on her birthday. But I don't think . . . I didn't bring any other clothes over, it was so hot.' He glanced down at himself. 'Would they let me in? And even if they did . . . To be honest with you, I haven't got enough money for Atlantis.'

'This is on me. I'm sure you need something to eat, and you look very fetching. I'm still waiting to hear all about your day, remember. No, you don't have to start thanking me, I'll enjoy it.' Nesta turned round to pick up her camera case. 'Christ! Who's that?'

'Only me,' said Baskerville, strolling forward. 'I knocked at the door but apparently you didn't hear me.'

'What on earth are you doing here?' demanded Nesta. 'You didn't think I was making off with the treasure, just because I needed to borrow the keys?'

'No,' Baskerville glowered down at them both. 'I was worried about you working in here alone after hours. I'm surprised the gallery agreed to it, given the security risks. But I see now you're not alone after all.' He fixed his chilly gaze on Jared, as if he'd caught him *in flagrante delicto*. 'I'm not at all sure that this was wise. You didn't tell me that our goblet had a mate.'

'No,' said Nesta. 'There was no reason why I should. Jed traced it, and he suggested I did some photos of the two together. It'll make a good story in the *Times* next week.'

'May I look at it?'

Nesta looked enquiringly at Jared. Jared hesitated, cleared his throat, and said sullenly, 'Since you're here, I suppose there's no reason why not.' He watched Baskerville lean forward, his hands clasped behind his back, and peer closely at the land goblet, then at the sea goblet, and then at the land goblet again.

Jared seemed to change his mind about something, for he suddenly said in a much more conciliatory tone, 'Do you want the light on it again, sir?'

'Please.' Baskerville groped in his pocket and brought out his magnifying glass. When Jared held up the spotlight again he grunted, and continued his survey. He put out his hand and very gently turned the goblets round. Jared held the light as steadily as he could. 'The same,' said Baskerville at last, and sighed deeply. 'Indubitably from the same workshop, by the same maker. Both genuine. Both original. This is an exceptional discovery.' He turned suddenly and fixed his piercing stare on Nesta. 'Why was I not informed of it?'

'I came to do a job for a client,' said Nesta. 'I only saw what it was an hour ago. Mr Honeyman is still my client. It would be quite unprofessional of me to give you information about that. But both goblets will be coming to the museum. Won't they, Jared? That's what you said?'

Jared was carefully winding up the flex from the spotlight again, but he stopped and looked up. 'Yes, it was. I found both those goblets, Mr Baskerville. I've given the first one to the museum. By right of salvage it's mine, but what the hell would I want to keep it for? I've got glasses at home if I want something to drink out of. And I mean the second one to end up in the museum too. I'll bring it to you soon enough. So what's the problem?'

'I'd be interested to know where you found the second goblet.'

'That'll all come out. I'll tell the whole country, just as soon as I can. It'll all be in the paper.'

'And why not now?'

'I can't say now. But very soon I will.'

'Whose is it?'

'It belongs to a friend of mine.'

'Lucy Morgan?'

'I'm not saying more. But I will. I'll tell the whole story the moment that I can, that I promise you.'

'And why not now?' Baskerville leaned over the stand and glared down at him. 'Why not now? What have you discovered about the treasures of Ravnscar?'

'Look,' said Jared, facing him. 'This is nothing to do with Lucy Morgan. Nothing. You can leave her out of it.'

'You had the run of that house, didn't you, Honeyman? It must have been interesting for a young boy, especially one with a romantic disposition. I expect you indulged in all manner of exploration.'

'Look here, Mr Baskerville, I don't know what you're getting at, but this goblet didn't come out of Ravnscar. And yes, maybe I have been exploring, a bit more recently than you probably think, and maybe I have found out some things I didn't know before. Why should that bother you? Is there anything I might discover that you'd rather I didn't know? I'm bringing stuff into the museum. Isn't that what you want? Why do you suppose I'm doing it?'

'He's right, Mr Baskerville,' put in Nesta. 'You've no reason to doubt his motives. He's only doing just what you're doing. You both like digging things up. Oddly enough I'd say you were both much too idealistic about our history, besides being obsessed with antiquities. Really, you know, you should see Jared as an ally, a colleague even. In fact,' Nesta grinned in sudden mischief, 'Possibly even your successor. We're all mortal. You should cultivate him. Don't you see he'd make an awfully good job of it?'

Baskerville, clearly unamused, ignored her. 'Explain yourself, young man. What could you possibly discover that I'd rather you didn't know? It's the withholding of information against the public interest which concerns me.'

'I'm not withholding anything,' said Jared. 'At least, I shouldn't need to for more than a week. I just have to consult somebody first. The glass isn't mine to give. I need to talk to a friend.'

'Lucy Morgan.'

'I tell you, that goblet does not belong to Lucy Morgan.' Jared picked up a shoebox, and began to fold the cracked glass carefully in bubblewrap.

'Wait!' Baskerville laid a bony hand on Jared's arm. 'Where are you taking it now?'

'Away.' Jared shrugged off the cold grasp, and faced Baskerville. 'Look, sir, you really don't have the right to ask me. This is about something else. Not to do with finding or keeping treasure, but something that somebody did. When I've dealt with that I'll bring this to the museum, safe and sound. I promise. But I can't now.' He put the goblet gently into the box, and spread his hands, trying to make Baskerville comprehend. 'It's nothing to do with treasure. It's just something I have to sort out about the past. My past, I mean, not history. If you can't understand me, then you'll have to trust me, or lump it. I didn't ask you to come here, and I had every right to ask Nesta, and do what I've just done.' He turned away, and slid the shoebox into his knapsack, wedging it carefully among various other objects that were already in there.

Under Baskerville's jealous eye, Nesta replaced the sea goblet in its case, and locked it. 'Your keys, Mr Baskerville.' She turned to Jared. 'Jed, if you could put these lights and things in the car, I'll lock up here and take the Mill keys back to Mr Rodrigues. Do you want to go on down to Atlantis and get a table? Ask for one by the window, if there's still one free.'

Jared shouldered his knapsack, gathered Nesta's equipment together, bid Baskerville a wary goodbye, and departed.

'Ms Kirwan,' Baskerville began at once, as she had known he would, 'Where did that young man get that goblet? Has that Morgan woman sworn him to secrecy? Or did he steal it?'

'I don't know,' said Nesta. 'It's not my business and I didn't ask. But I can tell you one thing for sure: Jared is neither a thief nor a liar.'

'For sure?' said Baskerville. 'Oh, no, I don't think so. He had a reputation for being light-fingered, I believe, even as a child.

He has a record, you know. I daresay you'll recall he's been inside, and I believe there've been some questions recently about drugs. My guess is the police know a good deal more about him than either you or I. He's plausible, I can see that, and evidently he's learned a way with women. I wouldn't let him impose upon you, Ms Kirwan, if I were you.'

'My God, Mr Baskerville, talk about a serpent's tongue! What did the poor boy ever do to you? No, I'm not going to listen to any more.' Nesta swung her camera case on to her shoulder. 'Come on, I'm locking up now.'

Halfway to the door she swung round on him. 'You know, Mr Baskerville, I don't understand this at all. You were one of the four. So was Jack Honeyman. What the hell happened to that? If you've forgotten, I could swear to it that Jared hasn't. Are you sure you don't owe him something? Is that what it is, Mr Baskerville? Is it conscience? Think about it. I mean what I say. Jared coming home should be the very thing you dreamed of. He's doing the same work as you. He cares about the same things. He's his father's son too; think what his father was to you. How do you reckon Jack Honeyman would expect you to treat his boy? Jed was never in trouble until his father went away. He did as well as he could. And he's not in trouble now, unless someone else makes it for him.'

'Ms Kirwan, I'm perfectly willing to work with him. I have worked with him. Against the advice of our President, I might add, a consideration which I'm sure will carry some weight with you. I could wish Honeyman were a qualified archeologist, but I'll admit the work he's done on the *Cortes* has been meticulous. You can't accuse me of prejudice. I would just be interested to know where he found that goblet.'

'He's promised to bring it to you. That's all that concerns either of us. I'll admit, I don't know where he got it, or what he's up to, but my guess is that a glass goblet wasn't the only thing he found. Maybe one day we'll hear more. Meanwhile, I suggest that we each mind our own business.'

Baskerville bowed. 'As you say, ma'am. May I wish you a very pleasant evening at the Atlantis.'

Nesta opened the door of her car, and watched him as he hunched himself over the steering wheel of his Jeep, and jolted away over the potholes into the gathering dark. Then she swung her camera on to the back seat, and set off the other way, through the twilit terraces of ripening apple trees towards the twinkling lights of Lyonsness.

SIXTEEN

Sidony Redruth. Ravnscar Castle. July 18th.
Notes for *Undiscovered Islands* (working title).

I HATE IT when you think you're not waiting for anything, but every time the phone rings you realise that perhaps you were. I'd been helping Lucy in the garden all day, weeding and watering, and I'd just come in to be in the shade for a bit and get myself a drink. The tiles on the kitchen floor were cool under my bare feet. I pulled off my sunhat and ran my hands through my sticky hair. I didn't mind being hot and grubby. It reminded me of childhood, playing in the garden with Arthur. I even had scars on my knees, just as I had always had then, from climbing the fir tree that grew by the stone gateposts of Ravnscar. I felt as if I'd abdicated temporarily from the adult world, and when the phone rang half of me didn't want to be dragged back. The other half felt that familiar sinking thrill in the pit of my stomach, but I wouldn't let myself think the thought that came with it.

'Hi-aye,' A male voice, not one I knew. 'Is that Miss Lucy?'

'No. She's in the garden. Do you want me to get her?'

'Well now . . . You'll be the young English lady? You could maybe take a message for her?'

'Sure.'

'Per Pedersen, you can tell her, with a message from Jared—Jared Honeyman, that is – but you know our Jed, now I think about it. You were with him not so long ago at the Midsummer dance in Dorrado. Isn't that right?'

'Yes,' I said cautiously. 'Yes, I know Jared.'

'Of course, so you do. If you could say to Miss Lucy that Jared is needing to get hold of her as soon as possible. He was trying to phone her from here yesterday all through dinnertime, right up to three o'clock. She was out, seemingly?'

'We took a picnic to Hogg's Beach. It was so hot.'

'Indeed yes, the weather is terribly hot. You won't be used to that?'

'It gets quite hot sometimes in Cornwall.'

'Yes, I suppose it would do. So if you would say to Miss Lucy that Jed wishes to speak to her urgently, about a matter he needs to discuss. And maybe she could call back and leave a message for him here?'

'I'll tell her to do that.'

After I'd put the phone down I stood still for a minute, staring through the window at the blank white heat outside. My head ached; I didn't feel as eager to go back out as I had three minutes ago. Lucy was potting on fuchsias in the greenhouse. She wouldn't mind or notice if I'd gone. It was too hot to do anything really.

Too hot. An idea occurred to me. 'Go where you like,' she'd said. 'Look at what you like. There isn't anything secret.' Well, why not now?

I followed the cellar steps down from the kitchen, through the first cellar with the garden tools and fishing tackle, and through the wine cellar below that. My guess is there's a small fortune in liquor underneath Ravnscar, but it isn't the sort of thing I know much about. The most precious wines, including the vintage madeiras in oak casks labelled Sercial, Bual, Rain-water, Malmsey, and Amontillado, along with the Napoleonic brandy, are kept in a special low-roofed vault guarded by an iron-studded door with a huge sixteenth-century lock. At least, it would have been guarded, if the door had been latched to, and the key turned and taken out of the lock. Nothing is kept fastened at Ravnscar. I crossed the uneven flagged floor of the main cellar between double rows of barrels, all neatly labelled in faded ink. I reached the second door at the back, and turned the heavy key in the lock. The bolts were already drawn back. I couldn't get the door open, until I figured out it had been unlocked all the time. When I turned the key back and lifted the handle it opened surprisingly easily. I took the torch from the stone shelf and switched it on, and picked up the ball of string. The end of the string was fastened to an iron peg hammered into the wall.

With the torch in my right hand, and the string unravelling from my left, I climbed carefully down to where the three identical passages branched out. St Joseph's chapel was to my left. I picked the middle passage, because I could already see more steps descending. They went down a long way. I remembered Lucy saying I'd need a jumper, and wished I'd thought of it. When the steps stopped I was aware of the living rock under my feet, shiny and cold. I could feel myself coming out in goose-bumps. The passage forked, and I chose left. Then left again. The distances weren't very long, but already I'd used more than half the string. Suddenly there were no more walls in front of me. I shone the torch around. I was in a bare oval space like an empty crypt. The dome was like an untamed version of St Mark's in Venice, bright red and yellow rock with gleaming stalactites hanging from the roof like carved ivory. In one corner the walls were built up with loose boulders. The rest was solid volcanic rock, Mount Prosper from the inside. I saw the dark mouth of another entrance directly across the chamber from the way I'd come. By the time I reached it my string was almost gone. It was a much thinner passage, but when I shone the torch upwards I couldn't see the roof; the yellow beam reflected on mica far above my head, then petered out into the dark.

The string ended about ten feet into the passage. I thought for a moment, and felt in my shorts pocket. There was nothing there but a yellow plastic ring from a hose joint. I tied it to the end of the string, and laid it on the floor so I couldn't miss the little yellow blob on my way back. I left it, and went on. The passage took a sharp turn down. I felt bereft without my string, and tried to remember what the way back would be if I didn't have anything to guide me. It boggled my mind trying to think of it backwards, and I gave up. No one was about, and who would ever want to move a piece of string anyway? Three more steps went down in front of me. I followed.

Suddenly the roof was so low I had to stoop, and the walls curved inwards. I knew I could only go as far as the next fork; without a string I dare not risk anything but the straight way. I was beginning to think it might be quite nice to turn back.

There was a door in front of me. A plain oak door with an iron handle. No lock. It had some sort of graffiti on it. The writing was old-fashioned and spidery. I held the torch up close. It was part of a poem:

Look not thou on beauty's charming –
Sit thou still when kings are arming –
Taste not when the wine-cup glistens –
Speak not when the people listens –
Stop thine ear against the singer –
From the red gold keep thy finger –
Vacant heart and hand and eye –
Easy live and quiet die.

I read the message and wondered who had scrawled it there. It felt like some sort of a challenge. I took hold of the door handle and very slowly I turned it.

The chamber beyond was not empty. When I shone my torch slowly round it lit upon furniture: four heavy, carved chests, a great chair with curved legs crossing each other and a high back like a throne, draped in red velvet. Around it, the stone benches carved out of the thickness of the wall were also lined with long red velvet cushions, embroidered with golden tassels. There were several black candle holders five feet high or more, with burned-out candles still inside them. Everything was circular: the chamber itself, the curved benches, and the ornate carpet in the middle of the floor, with rounded patterns on it in red and black and gold. And the white things in the middle of the carpet – my torch jumped in my hand – the white things in the middle of the carpet. I swallowed, and focused the light, and made myself look at them properly.

A skull and crossed bones. Real ones. They weren't white, in fact, but faded grey. I could see the squiggly lines across the skull. The teeth were yellow and had gaps in them. The long bones looked old, a bit worm-eaten at the ends. As far as I could tell they were human thigh bones. I looked down on them, and wondered who it was. Who it had once been.

Thank God the string was there, exactly where I'd left it. I was up the steps again, and across the bare chamber. The string led me faithfully round the first turn, and round the second. I must be almost at the bottom of the staircase. I reached the place where three roads met. A looming grey shape slithered out of the right hand passage and barred my way, holding his lantern high over me in one white fleshless hand. I shut my eyes and would have screamed, but my mouth was too dry. I leaned back against the wall and merely whimpered, shielding my face with my arm against the eldritch light.

'Good afternoon,' said the ghost. 'Miss Redruth?'

The smell of the grave still clung to him. I opened my eyes and saw him through a cloud of smoky mist. He wore ancient black like a Victorian butler. I stared at his lantern, mesmerised. It wasn't a candle inside. It was a small electric bulb. It was one of those battery lanterns they sell in the supermarket in St Brandons. I lowered my eyes cautiously to his face. I'd seen it before. In Maldun's Mill, staring avidly at a green glass goblet in a white case. 'Mr Baskerville?' I heard my own voice come out somewhere between a whisper and a squeak.

*　　*　　*

He was the oddest person to entertain to tea. About halfway through I decided I quite liked him. The smell was really nothing worse than badly-aired clothes. He had a grey look about him, but he was not unclean. He ought to wear a bit of colour, but presumably there was no one in his life who would suggest it to him. He said he preferred Lapsang Souchong, and I made it in the Hester Bateman teapot. He continued to apologise with rusty old-fashioned courtesy for having startled me, until I told him there was no need to say any more about it. He ate two ginger biscuits. I would have been less nervous if I hadn't expected Lucy to walk in any minute. I had a feeling she wouldn't approve, but what could I have done? One thing that a West Country vicarage has in common with the castle of Ravnscar is that hospitality is compulsory, and as far as that goes I'm my mother's daughter. I just couldn't bring myself to tell him to go away. He was working on an archeological report on the lower caverns of Mount Prosper, apparently, and the path at the bottom of the cellar steps was a useful short cut. He wouldn't let me fetch Lucy, which I very much wanted to do. He said there was no need to disturb her. I thought there was; never before have I found afternoon tea so nefarious.

Even so, I began to enjoy our conversation. He said he'd visited Cornwall as a young man, but when I asked when that was he said, 'Long before you were born. In the Dark Ages, m'dear,' and his lips stretched out in a thin white line which I realised was a smile. He seemed to remember Cornwall well, however. We had an interesting discussion about chambered cairns, of which of course there are none in Hy Brasil. That led us on to the Phoenicians and the tin trade, and we somehow got from there to the Renaissance explorers. He mentioned the goblet we'd looked at together at Maldun's Mill. 'The interesting thing about that particular goblet,' he said, 'is that it has a duplicate. Long before Mr Honeyman salvaged the one you saw, its fellow was brought ashore, probably by one of the survivors from the wreck. But then, no doubt you've seen it. I expect Miss Morgan showed it to you?'

'Lucy? Oh, no, she hasn't got it. It's not *here*.'

'I think if you ask her you may find that it is. So she didn't tell you about it? It's an interesting story.'

'I'm sure Lucy doesn't even know about it.'

'But you do, I gather?'

'Me?'

'Forgive me, m'dear. I thought when you said "not *here*", you meant you'd come across the story, or even the goblet itself, somewhere else. These things get about. It would be an interesting legend to write up in your book, would it not? You must come and visit the museum sometime. I have some intriguing notes on possible artefacts from the *Cortes*. You know the story goes that the screen in St Bride's church at Ogg's Cove is made from timbers from the wreck? Possibly the goblet is in Ogg's Cove too. I must speak to Father Segato about it sometime. Perhaps you've met him? He may be able to tell you where it is now, if you're sure it isn't at Ravnscar. I'm sure he'd be delighted to help you in any way he could.'

Staying silent, after what he'd just said, was tantamount to lying, or, if not that, a very uncivil way to treat a guest. The second goblet had nothing at all to do with Lucy, I was certain about that. I couldn't be incriminating anyone except possibly Olly West, which I didn't care too much about, especially after Jared had been so indignant, and to what more reliable authority could I mention my find than the curator of the National Museum of Hy Brasil? All this flashed through my mind during the time it took to swallow half a ginger biscuit. I said, 'I have seen it, in fact. It isn't here. It's in the Pele Centre. I saw it on the shelf in the little office when Olly West showed me round. I don't think he realises what it is. He didn't mention it.'

Baskerville's expression didn't change. He sipped his tea, and stared out of the window into the blazing heat outside. I didn't like to interrupt his thoughts. I don't think either of us moved for nearly five minutes. 'Well, that's very curious,' he said at last. 'And what do you think of our earthquakes? It isn't what you're used to, I'm sure. Nor are we, as a matter of fact. This has been the most unstable year since 1958, I believe.'

Not long after that he said he must be getting back. He told me to give his regards to Miss Morgan. I suppose I should have escorted him as far as the wine cellar door, but I just didn't feel like another descent into the nether regions. I shook his chilly hand at the top of the stairs, and listened to his footsteps gradually echoing away, down into the dark.

I didn't think any more about Baskerville until the following evening, which was the Saturday night that Penelope had invited me to dinner. It was almost two months since she and Colombo had promised I should meet the President, and by the time the invitation did come I'd more or less forgotten about it. I'd never completely believed I'd get to dine with James Hook on one of his quiet weekends in his own house, and I had been amazed when Penelope finally phoned. Lucy seemed to think it was quite normal, but when I was about to set off, she did seem a little more agitated than usual.

'Sidony!' she said, when I came downstairs. 'Turn around. Let me look at you. Oh m'dear, you see you can look pretty if you try. It's a pity Henry Tilney isn't going to be there. But where has that dress *been*?'

'Nowhere. Not since I came.'

'I can see that. Rolled in a ball in the bottom of your rucksack I suppose.' She was dragging an ironing board out of the cupboard. 'Is your mother like you, or are you the despair of her, or both?'

These things never seem to me to be worth arguing about, so I allowed her to have her way with me, and even let her lend me a gold chain with a star on it to hang around my neck. When she was satisfied she tossed me the Land Rover keys, and off I went.

When the door opened I did a double take. It was Maeve standing there: Colombo's sister Maeve whom I'd met at breakfast with Jared the day after the dance. I felt so relieved to see her: in the two hours it had taken to drive from Ravnscar to Dorrado I'd worked myself into quite a state of shyness. I think it was Lucy and the ironing that set me off. Maeve said nothing at all about my unusual appearance – not knowing me she probably didn't realise how unusual it was – but greeted me as if I were an old friend. I felt bereft when I realised she was leaving me at the drawing-room door, having announced me by both my names to whoever was in there. I must have looked as panicked as I felt, because she gave me a little push from behind, and whispered, 'It's OK m'dear, he won't eat you. He won't have to; there's a smashing dinner coming up. I should know. I'm the cook.'

The President didn't eat me. On the contrary, he was extremely affable. I sat on the edge of my chair sipping dry sherry, and remembered I needed to stay sober enough to drive home over those mountain roads in the dark. I wished Colombo were there, or Lucy, or Jared. I doubted if Jared ever ironed anything; he wouldn't see the point. I wondered if he ever felt shy, and discovered that I had no idea. On the other hand, I was fairly sure that Colombo would not feel shy under any circumstances, and one only had to look at him to know he would never dine with his President in an unironed shirt. I tried to imagine Colombo shirtless, ironing, but I couldn't conjure up a domestic setting for him at all. Meanwhile the President was talking about a new programme of Study Abroad scholarships, and student exchanges at the University of the Hesperides. I did my best to look intelligent. 'Travel for the young,' he was saying. 'I'm all for it. Personally, I never want to stay in a foreign hotel again as long as I live, or shake hands with another royal personage, or be photographed again with balding men even older and uglier than I am in ill-fitting suits. But to the young all things are no doubt new.'

'Sweetheart, I don't think they send the young to diplomatic functions.'

'No, such tortures are reserved for desiccated cynics like myself. The young are merely offered the means to do what they will, and in another country. But youth should have its opportunity, youth should rule. Old age should merely mete and dole unequal laws unto a savage race, but at least the current arrangements allow us the occasional transient opportunity to feast our eyes upon a pretty face. I never thought that young women should be immured at home. We have a pro-active equal opportunities policy in Hy Brasil, Miss Redruth. In fact there are more women employed in this country than there are men. You will no doubt have observed the preponderance of women in the public sphere.'

'I thought the reason so many men didn't have jobs was because there's no more fishing. And the women don't usually get the highest-up jobs, do they?' As soon as I'd spoken I felt I'd said the wrong thing, but he seemed delighted with me.

'There you are, my love,' he said to Penelope. 'I detect an articulate member of the opposing party.' He turned to me. 'Never let it be said, m'dear, that we lack an opposition. The young naturally assume that role without any prompting from above. My grandchildren displayed a flourishing instinct for contradiction from the age of eighteen months. My son and his wife tell me that this is normal and healthy, from which one deduces that there is no need whatsoever to foster any artificial systems of controversy. The young will automatically oppose the old, and in the end the young, God help them, will overthrow us all. And when they do so they will know that they are old. Don't look so dismayed, m'dear. Bear with my weakness; my old brain is troubled. Have you noticed much dissidence among our young?'

'No,' I stammered. 'No one seems to talk about politics much at all.'

'No, the burden of government is of little weight to those

who never felt it. Never mind. Which of us was born to be appreciated, after all? Hy Brasil won't always have me, the young it will always have with it, unless of course we all encounter our apocalypse simultaneously in the immediate future. Our volcanological problems must be an added source of interest to your researches? I hope I don't express myself too blasphemously, m'dear? I understand you come from a godly household.'

'Well, Jim dear,' interposed Penelope, 'I think perhaps you do.'

At that moment the double doors at the far end of the room swung open, and Maeve, in a white apron, announced, 'Dinner is served.'

Maeve was right: the food was good. The three of us sat at a long table with a silver epergne in the middle of it, lit by six white candles. The President sat at one end, under a portrait of himself as a young man, and Penelope at the other, under a painting of a white horse with a docked tail. 'Is that a Stubbs?' I asked her.

It was, and for about twenty minutes she and I talked about horses. I felt grateful for the three years of horse mania I'd put in between the ages of nine and twelve, undeterred by Arthur's teasing. Penelope said I should come in daylight sometime and have a tour of the stables. But when we had all finished our soup and had started on the *boeuf en daube*, she interrupted herself. 'But I mustn't go on. You wanted Jim to tell you how they took the NATO base on Mount Ailbe, didn't you?'

I looked nervously at him. 'Well, it would be really interesting. If you're sure you don't mind.'

'M'dear, Jim always loves to talk about himself. Don't you, sweetheart?'

'It's my pleasure, m'dear. So what would you, Miss Redruth? The story of my life, and the particular accidents gone by since I came to this isle? Or no, that would be too much. You'd like to know about the Trojan Horse?'

'If you don't mind telling me.'

'Not at all, not at all.' He wiped his mouth on his napkin, and took a sip of wine. The Trojan Horse. Yes, indeed, that was the crux of the matter. I came back from the Americas in '58 with just twelve men, and we were landed secretly at Hogg's Beach one freezing February dawn. We hid first in the lava field at Brentness, and then we moved up into the caverns under Mount Prosper. Under the house where you're staying now, in fact, m'dear. The caverns of Ravnscar remained our headquarters for the next two months, while we recruited local support. Lemuel Hawkins was our agent to the outside world. He lived at Ferdy's Landing, and through him we kept our communications open, mainly by sea. It was Lem who first drew my attention to Jack Honeyman.

'Yes, Honeyman was the key to it all. He had no record of political activity, though he was known to be a staunch Union man, a creature almost unheard of in Hy Brasil. It was a Union of one, in fact, and totally irrelevant to the man's own life. He'd had his own business from the day he finished his apprenticeship. I knew nothing of that, of course; he was only a lad of sixteen when I had to flee the country. But Honeyman was known as an eccentric. He had the only subscription in Hy Brasil to the *Socialist Worker*. Always more than a week late, of course, because it came from Southampton on the ferry. But the Honeymans always took strange notions into their heads, and Jack's politics were a standing joke in Ogg's Cove, nothing more. Obviously NATO didn't take him seriously, because he must have been vetted pretty thoroughly, or they'd never have let him in. But let him in they did. Of course they were desperate men. Desperate men, Miss Redruth. You know why?'

'Because of the drains, you mean?'

'That's it in a nutshell. Drains were their downfall. Hell hath no fury like a backed-up drain, and the mountain would keep moving. NATO had their own personnel for everything, or should I say everything but a shifting sewage system. Even men who control the fate of a planet must shit.'

'Sweetheart, we're at the dinner table.'

'Sweetheart, I know. But still the young lady hangs upon my tale. Within yards of the control room, as I say, there have to be the usual offices. Now, the sewage system had been put in at the beginning of the war by the British, when Mount Ailbe was an Allied base. They had problems with it even then. It was a single system, you understand, so that all the drains fed into one main sewer, which led to the treatment system, which was then outside the base. The original pipes were fireclay; when NATO expanded the base after the war they used concrete pipes. So you see all the pipes were rigid, and liable to crack even in small earth movements. Also, the main drainage system wasn't designed for two hundred personnel. Trouble!

'The other problem was the gradient. The Brits designed it to be around one in forty, but there was a problem with subsidence under the treatment plant. What with one thing and another, the drains kept getting blocked. And so we come to Jack Honeyman, Plumbing and Drainage Expert. He was only twenty-six, but his business was flourishing and his reputation went before him. No other man understood so much about the uncertain ground on which we stand. No other man in the country could or would guarantee a reliable septic tank. In desperation, NATO called him in. Scorning and fearing any local interference, they had previously gone ahead in their own fashion, and made what Honeyman described as a right pig's ear of the whole thing. He did his best, but every time he did a repair the drains would promptly collapse again somewhere else. In the end he told them that the only possible solution was an entirely new system.

'Six months of red tape and backed up drains ensued. At last the go-ahead came from High Command. The job proved to be a large one. Jack had to start again at the very beginning. He couldn't use local labour. NATO provided the brawn, but Jack's was the brain, and Jack's also was the white van that went through the perimeter fence every day, past the guard posts, and right up to the main building complex. They got so used to his passing that after a while they failed to see him any more. Everyone knew that Jack Honeyman was all right.

Jack was thorough. Jack, in all innocence, demanded to see the plans. He had to know where the existing pipes were, you understand. His plan was to replace the single system with a series of individual septic tanks, each serving a section of the base. Each mini-system was to have some flexible pipes built into it. The beauty of the arrangement was that one blockage wouldn't disrupt the drainage system of the whole base any more. It was a typical Honeyman solution. Jack was one of these small-is-beautiful chaps, ahead of his time you might say.

'He had to look around the place. Escorted, of course, always escorted. And never within too close range of the control room. Of course he knew perfectly well where it was that he wasn't being taken. But he would never have done anything about it, if it hadn't been for Lemuel.

'I used to slip into Dorrado occasionally. I had a wife and child, neither of whom I'd seen for ten years, and that was quite an incentive. It was Lemuel who pointed out Jack's white van to me one night in the streets of Dorrado. We made our plans, and he began talking to Jack. Jack listened. Remember he'd been reading the *Socialist Worker* in solitude ever since he was old enough to write a cheque for the subscription. Lem encouraged our Jack to come over to Ferdy's Landing of an evening and talk politics. A month of this, and the time seemed right to let him know that the caverns of Ravnscar were no longer uninhabited. Lem swore him to secrecy, and brought him up to meet us. Jack was a Romantic. In five minutes I knew that we were sure of him. It took Jack a week longer to realise the same thing, and then the planning began.

'April 9th, 1958. Jack drove his white van in as usual, carefully packed with a load of pitch-fibre piping. Heavy stuff, I can tell you, if you happen to be underneath it. Which we were, three of us: myself, Lemuel Hawkins and a gentleman from Hy

Brasil who had been decorated several times over for his distinguished career as a sapper in the Second World War. You know Fernando Baskerville. In fact he was just telling me you'd had a pleasant cup of tea together yesterday.' The President offered me another glass of wine, and I shook my head. While he poured one for himself, he remarked in an offhand manner quite unlike his usual style. 'The bravest man I ever want to know.'

'Fernando was the deputy librarian in St Brandons library. He kept a low profile after the war, but he was then and always has been totally committed to the cause of independence. I think there is almost nothing he would not have done to achieve it. I'm an egotist, m'dear; I daresay you've noticed that. But Fernando was something else: a patriot. Every revolution must have one, and he was ours.

'So Jack Honeyman drove his van into the base as usual, and his papers were cursorily checked at the gate. He opened the back doors as usual, and as usual the guard glanced in at yet more sections of flexible piping. We crossed the tarmac under the eyes of a dozen sentries with sub-machine guns and pulled into the loading bay. The chance came when the shifts changed, and Jack got us out of the van and into our hiding place. He was white as a sheet, and that worried me, but he stayed cool enough. He was the one I didn't know, you see. The one who didn't belong. If he failed us, killing him wouldn't have saved us, not in there. We were in his hands. But he came through. Oh yes, Jack came through. It only took about three minutes to get us out of the van and down the manhole. Then we were hidden inside the obsolete sewer, the one that had cracked open in the first place. God save me from an active life again.

'Jack went home at the proper time, and waited with the rest of our men. He'd played his part. In 1958 there wasn't a sophisticated internal alarm system; we'd already crossed the wires that were hooked up to the control room. We had the whole night to work in. We were inside the perimeter sentry patrols, and we didn't need to go any nearer the manned section round the control room. We'd studied Jack's plans, and we knew exactly where to find the access points to the drains. We weren't short of drain rods: I've never seen so many as they'd got piled up in there, after all the trouble they'd had over the years. We used Satchell charges with plastic explosives. In those days you could get anything like that from US army surplus – just buy it on the open market – with no questions asked. They were ideal for the job – you can carry them in a pocket like a lump of clay, and yet one of those things will take out a whole block – all you have to do is put in your detonators on the spot, attach the charges to the leading edge of the drain rods, then very carefully thread them through the system. That way you can lay your explosives at the strategic points. They're radio controlled; Fernando fixed the detonators with a different frequency for each section. And of course the methane in the old sewage system would give an extra boost to an explosion.

'In fact the control room probably wouldn't have gone right up if we had blown up the place – the drains just didn't get quite close enough, and the room itself was embedded in solid concrete – but we banked on them not taking the risk of major explosives going off all round, and we were right. We kept a watch for internal patrols and had to duck out of sight of a couple. That was all. Slow and cautious, that's what we had to be. Silent. We knew the layout. We knew where Jack had stored the rods. We knew from him just where to go, and when we got there Baskerville knew what had to be done. By the morning of April 10th the entire sewage system of that base was mined.

'Fernando was in charge of the detonators. Lem and I stood guard with tommy guns. We knew they daren't rush us, because Fernando would have got his explosion in first. There was a benign phone system – for ordinary calls. We tapped into that. We called HQ and told them we could blow their base to atoms at the touch of a button of our own. We were prepared to negotiate.

'It took them a little while to realise we were serious. In fact we had to blow up a section of offices at the edge of the complex before they fully understood that we meant what we said we'd done. We gave them four minutes to evacuate the rooms first. After the explosion they did begin to talk.'

'Sweetheart, you should explain to her it wasn't quite as simple as that. If you hadn't had the Americans behind you, you'd never have got the Brits out.'

'If she wants to hear all that tedious stuff, would I be the man to deny her? Penelope is right, m'dear. Nothing is ever quite as heroic as it looks. Possibly the White House was a little less surprised than Westminster by our tactics. The British colony of Frisland was becoming something of an embarrassment at a time when so clearly the North Atlantic was destined, by those who believe in manifestations of destiny, to become territorial waters. I'm not suggesting that we hadn't talked to anybody at all. We had no army of our own, so some form of tactical alliance was obviously essential. The point is that we won. A bloodless revolution. I am delighted that we're able to welcome you to the independent nation of Hy Brasil.'

I watched Maeve clear the plates and set out summer pudding and a jug of cream on the table. My favourite. Was it my imagination, or did I notice a touch of disapproval in the rigidity of her back as she walked away and shut the door behind her? I felt a totally irrational sense of solidarity, and maybe it was this that emboldened me to clear my throat and speak. 'The bit I don't understand, though, is that I keep hearing that John Honeyman was exiled for being a British agent. I heard that he had to leave the country in 1979 and he's never been heard of since.'

'Poor Honeyman. You'll have realised by now that he was a man who could quite easily be persuaded. Yes, too easily swayed. Too easily wrought to the point of action. And once he was in, he was in deep. It's a sad story. From May '79, you see, British policy in the Atlantic began to harden up again. The Falkland situation didn't happen out of the blue, whatever the media liked to suggest. No, imperialism may go into remittance from time to time but in my experience it never quite goes away.'

'But I thought Honeyman was a Marxist?'

'Honeyman was a disillusioned man, m'dear. I told you he was a Romantic. He expected more from a revolution than it was able to deliver. Because we'd used him he mistakenly assumed that he had a further claim to power. Certainly he began to make a nuisance of himself almost from the moment of our success. In the late seventies the British opposition was already making plans for after the election, and in Hy Brasil they found our disaffected hero ready to their hand. Typical Honeyman, he went in deep, and shortly afterwards, sadly, an example had to be made.'

I helped myself to pudding. It reminded me of home, and that made me feel tough. I wasn't going to give up yet. 'So what happened to him in '58, after the revolution?'

It was Penelope who answered, and I had a feeling she was trying to steer the conversation into a different direction. 'He went home to Ogg's Cove, and carried on with his business. It must have been a couple of years later that he married Josie O'Hara. We went to the wedding. It was a happy marriage, as far as anyone outside can ever tell, though I know they were upset about not having any children. And then suddenly after all those years that wheat-headed baby came along, and of course he was the very apple of their eyes. A different kind of child might have been spoiled, I suppose, but he was an independent little chap, and his parents were sensible people. But I do remember how Jack used to take him out fishing in that boat of his when really the child was much too young.'

We had our coffee in the drawing room. Before that Penelope directed me down a wood-panelled passageway, and I passed one open door before reaching the bathroom at the end. I glanced inside. It was a comfortable-looking den, with a deep armchair, a television set, and book-lined walls. Opposite the doorway, at the desk, there was a lit computer screen. I would never normally have done such a thing; my mother would have been horrified if she could have seen me, but somehow the events of the last day or two had strung me to an unusual pitch, as if I'd almost started to believe I was living in a James Bond film. God knows what I expected to discover, but I took two furtive steps into the room until I was near enough to read the writing on the screen. It was an email message, and it said:

Hi Pappa,
Tell Mamma Martha sent L.L. Bean Catalogue snail mail this a.m. Summer schools finish today, thank God. Supposed to leave for Santa Barbara mid-week. Kids have chicken pox, so flight will probably be hell. Not even sure if we can smuggle them aboard in all their pustular glory. Meantime James Jr. threatens to drop out of school, and Tara writes me to say she's come out as lesbian and is moving in with her friend. Her bank direction, so that I can continue her allowance, arrives in the same mail as their mother's letter saying why all this is my fault. What possessed me that I'm putting myself through all this TWICE? No final dates yet on European trip. May fly HB from Frankfurt after Germany conference mid August. Love to Mamma. Brendan.

I returned to the drawing-room feeling slightly ashamed of myself, and assuaged my conscience by talking to Penelope about the propagation of fruit trees. This led to a lecture from the President about the democratic way to run a cider factory. I was feeling vaguely troubled, and I felt I needed time to think about why. I wondered how Jim had known that I came from a godly household. Surely no one would bother to have a dossier on me? I had an idea I needed to be careful, that in some intangible way the ground was shifting under my feet. It's very difficult to be careful when you don't quite know what of. The

President asked me about my book. Surely he can't be worried about that? He said he'd like to read the proofs. Why? Or was he just being polite? Somehow I don't feel at present that life is very straightforward. Even back here at Ravnscar, the place no longer seems to be quite what it was at first. Lucy had gone to bed when I got in. I wish there were someone in Hy Brasil that I knew well enough to be able to wake them up in the middle of the night. But I don't know anybody here nearly well enough for that.

SEVENTEEN

ON SATURDAY EVENING the offices of *The Hesperides Times* were almost deserted. Friday night was the climax of the week; the paper was in the shops in St Brandons at opening time on Saturday morning, and across the country by midday. Weekend work was desultory; much of it was coverage of rural events, and so Saturday was a good time to work in the office in peace and quiet.

In the main office the monitors stood like tombstones in the slatted light of the streetlight shining through half-closed Venetian blinds. A bright light drew the eye onward through the open door into the sub-editor's office, and within its bright circle two intent figures studied a paragraph of white print on a blue screen. Colombo scrolled slowly to the end, watching the other's face to see when he was ready to go on reading. Baskerville sat hunched on his stool like a hawk on a dead tree, his famous predatory profile, subject of innumerable *Times* cartoons, highlighted against the dark wings of his stooped shoulders in the black pinstriped jacket he'd been wearing for the past forty years. He was frowning, but that meant nothing. Baskerville usually frowned. Colombo took his forefinger off the cursor, and waited patiently for the verdict, while he re-read his own words. A pithy piece of work: he was pleased with it. His contact in the Finance Department had provided him *sub rosa* with some rather interesting statistics that seemed to contradict the official breakdown of the GNP for 1996–7. Tidesman, without making any overt statement, had achieved, Colombo thought, just the right note of ironic ambiguity.

'Tidesman,' said Baskerville eventually, 'should not be young.'

'You expect him to do something about his age, sir?'

The old man slewed round on his stool, and looked Colombo in the eyes. Colombo met his gaze squarely. 'You asked my opinion, MacAdam, and you're getting it. You need to remember that Tidesman is a hundred and twenty years old. He's learned discretion. Treat him with respect. Tidesman knows a lot more than he tells. That's his secret. A young fellow like you, you're too impatient. You're asking him to say too much.'

'You think he should read like the Delphic oracle?'

'The Delphic oracle was a demented virgin. We don't have room for that kind of exploitation nowadays. Nothing inspired, nothing cryptic. Isn't that your style, MacAdam? You're not attempting the oracular?'

'No. And since I'm neither demented nor virgin, possibly that's just as well.'

Baskerville's laugh cracked out like a whip. Colombo was used to it and didn't flinch, but he flushed when Baskerville said, 'Crossed in love but not without consolation, eh? Don't let them get you down, MacAdam. Oh yes, Tidesman's an old man. He knows the most unexpected things. Don't underestimate him. That's your trouble, you're not letting him speak for himself.' Baskerville dropped his voice to a harsh whisper. 'He has his own voice. That's the problem with your generation. They've not been taught to listen. You have to learn to wait on him and see what he tells you.'

'I'm a reporter with a job to do,' said Colombo. 'Not an altar boy in an esoteric mystery ritual.'

'It's a pity,' replied Baskerville. 'The Kings would have you. No denominational prejudice there. You wouldn't reconsider?'

'No.'

'Of course,' remarked Baskerville. 'You speak in ignorance, since you choose to know nothing about it. But then you're a Papist, and so is Francis Morgan's daughter. Possibly you're well suited, for a more iconoclastic pair it would be hard to find. But she won't have you, and you won't force her because these days it's not considered a viable method of operation. Just as well for you, MacAdam; that house has no luck. So there we are: you approach Tidesman with unprecedented arrogance, and Morgan's daughter has sent our treasure out of Hy Brasil, and you condone the act.'

'No. I've told you before I think she was wrong. The treasure didn't belong to the Morgan family; it belonged to Hy Brasil. It was an arrogant act, if we're speaking of arrogance, to give it away.'

'Curiously enough that's exactly what Tidesman said about it.'

'I remember that he did. I wasn't in his confidence then, but on that occasion I agreed with him wholeheartedly.'

'Ah, now this is better. If you always approach him with respect, the way you're doing now, his voice will sound more clearly.' Baskerville shifted painfully and turned to the screen again. 'And what does Tidesman know of profiteering? Tidesman works with our government and not against it. That's why he's still here.'

'You wouldn't want him to keep silent if government were wrong?'

'Or if MacAdam thinks it wrong? MacAdam should be very sure of his facts if he values his position.'

'I think I'm careful enough,' Colombo gazed at the screen. 'There's no connection between me and Lucy Morgan, you know. I don't know who told you that there was.'

'No, none,' agreed Baskerville cordially. 'I know that. I'll tell you one thing I ought not, and that's very unusual for me. But you're a promising young man, though much too obstinate, and I wouldn't want to see you come to grief. It's this: Nicholas

Hawkins was initiated, a sennight before he was killed, in the secret chamber under Ravnscar. You know what that means?'

'I don't know anything about it and I don't want to. And Nicky's death was an accident. It was no one's fault.'

'So MacAdam is to be judge of that too?' Baskerville laid a claw-like hand on Colombo's knee. 'I'm warning you for your own good, young man. Keep away from Ravnscar. It's an unlucky house.'

'It's not my house. I don't know why you're warning me.'

'I do so because you may be getting into deep water, meddling in too many matters that don't concern you. Don't think I don't know why you asked my opinion tonight. You think all this is a game, young man, but it isn't. If I cared to say what I know, it wouldn't be your work at stake. It might possibly be your life.'

'Is that a threat, sir?'

'No, as a matter of fact it's not. I ask you to respect Tidesman, because I've a fondness for him. I say keep clear of Ravnscar, if you don't want to tangle with the Kings. There are those who may be under oath to avenge a brother. But I won't give you away, even if I do know where you're going tonight. I won't talk to the President about you, so long as we have Tidesman in common. And that's in your hands, Mac-Adam, if you can keep it there. So take care! That's all I have to say: take care!'

'Ssh!' said Colombo. 'There's someone coming up the stairs. Do you want me to print this out? I don't want it on screen if we've got company.'

'I'll see it in print soon enough. Modified, if you take my advice.'

A voice was already calling out from the main office, and it accompanied its owner without ceasing into the room. 'Colombo? Colombo? Ah good, this is fortunate. I had hoped to find you here. Ah, Fernando, well, well, long time no see. I can only spare you a few minutes just now, I'm afraid, but we'll meet at the Mayda Trust meeting next Tuesday. I've been putting together some new proposals. You're going to find them extraordinarily stimulating. Colombo, this is the latest Pele Centre press release. You'll want to make it a major headline, of course, after the unusual amount of seismic activity we've had this month. The tables of figures are the measurements of magma movement underground given from the two installations on the southern flank of Mount Brasil. You'll want to print them in full. The text gives a further breakdown of the figures relating to the two seismic events recorded earlier this month, and consequent predictions of further volcanic activity. You won't need to change anything. It can go in just as it is, on the front page. And I've included a photograph of myself. You won't need to bother about getting a new one. I know how busy you must be.'

'I'm not the editor. I'll leave it on his desk for you.'

'West!' barked Baskerville.

'Yes, indeed. If you want to read my proposals in advance . . .'

'I hear you've sustained a robbery.'

'A robbery!' Olly West stared at him. 'I hardly think so. As you know my house is never locked, but mother doesn't go out. No, no, you've been misinformed, my dear Fernando. I haven't been robbed.'

'I'm talking about your office.'

'My office? With the new burglar-alarm system? No, no, I'm glad to say it's not possible. I've just had it fixed. The company were appallingly inefficient, selling me the wrong components and then trying to cover up their own mistakes. I was on the phone to them every day, and in the end it took months to get it working properly. But it's installed now and in full working order. I had the police in Ogg's Cove busy checking it all last Sunday afternoon. No one could break in. Of course we have all sorts of expensive equipment in there . . .'

'And other things,' interrupted Baskerville.

'Yes, and now I have a new assistant. Allardyce had to go,

I'm afraid. He had terrible problems working with other people, that was the trouble. I advised counselling therapy, but he wouldn't take any interest. It was a pity, as he had an official training in volcanology, but one must take other matters into consideration when appointing personnel. Now I'm training up young Peterkin. He has no background, of course, but . . .'

'West! I'm telling you that you've been robbed. Are you saying you haven't even noticed?'

Olly West stopped talking for a moment, but he still didn't meet Baskerville's eyes. 'Of what have I been robbed?'

'A green glass goblet. And other things. Perhaps I should tell you that I've spoken to the thief. The *thief* – the emphasis Baskerville placed on the word made Colombo look at him sharply – 'the *thief* informs me that he also found other information – "something he has to sort out about the past" – do I make myself clear to you, Mr West? I was told that a glass goblet "wasn't the only thing he found". Are you sure you aren't missing anything important, Mr West?'

Olly glanced at Colombo, but his gaze slid away at once when he saw that Colombo was looking at him. 'This is ridiculous, quite ridiculous, my dear Fernando. A green glass goblet? I don't even have such a thing, to my knowledge.'

'No, you don't, not any more. But until two days ago it was on the shelf in your private office.'

Olly West shrugged. 'Well, there are various things up there I haven't gone through lately. I wouldn't know. Who says it was there?'

'An independent witness.'

'You're lying!' The man's mood changed so fast that Colombo jumped up, clenching his fists, as if to protect the old man who sat perched imperturbably on his stool. Olly West bent over Baskerville and hissed at him, 'If you've broken into my property, or if you've instigated any kind of robbery, I'll have the law on you! You'll be hearing from my solicitor, Mr Baskerville. This is an outrage!'

Baskerville wiped a drop of Olly's spittle from his forehead, and said, 'No, Mr West, I have not broken into your office. And if I had, what kind of law could you invoke against me?'

There was a short silence. Colombo looked from one to the other, his eyes bright and alert.

'I suggest you go home and check your inventory,' said Baskerville. 'Let me know what you find.' He stood up stiffly. 'And if I hear instead from your solicitors . . . Well, perhaps the time has come. But if I fall, West, know this: I do not fall alone.'

'In my opinion,' said Colombo, striding up and down, 'the old man's going senile. I would to God that's all there was to it. He's been very good to me; I wouldn't be where I am now if it wasn't for him. And after all these years I still can't decide if West is God's fool or Machiavelli's prize pupil. What a pair! After half an hour of witnessing a duel between those two I can't even imagine what's real any more.'

'M'dear, sit down, and stop pacing up and down like a tiger, or I'll start thinking we're in a cage. I'm about to dish up. You'll feel better when you've eaten. You can pour the wine now if you like.'

Colombo fetched the open bottle from the hearth, and came over to the table. It was laid for two, and four green candles burned in the centre of it. The table was polished wood, the china dark green, the napkins maroon. Silver winked in the candlelight. Nesta brought a steaming dish from the oven and placed it on the mat between them, between the bread and the salad. 'Thank God for civilisation,' said Colombo, by way of grace, and sombrely helped himself.

'Listen, m'dear,' said Nesta presently, laying down her fork. 'About Jared. . .'

'Baskerville didn't tell Olly who it was. He only told me when that serpent in sheep's clothing had taken himself off. He didn't say a word about following you to Maldun's Mill either. He's being pretty cagey. But the thing was . . . Nesta, he's putting it all on to me. He said if Tidesman presses the government too hard – he's talking about my articles on the economy – he said, if I go too far, a scapegoat will be found. He was talking about Jed. He said to me, "Do you want his blood on your hands?" *My* hands, Nesta! Can you credit it? Basically he's telling me to stop being controversial or someone's going to do for Jed. Does that make any sense to you? Does any of it make any sense at all?'

'M'dear, I'd better tell you. There's something else.' Nesta picked an olive out of her salad and ate it. When she'd delicately spat out the stone, she went on, 'Jim called me from Dorrado an hour before you got here. He'd just had Baskerville on the phone to him. Baskerville told him everything he knew, I think, even that I'd taken poor Jared out to Atlantis and given him dinner. Jim wanted to find out what Jed had told me.'

'And what *had* he told you?'

'I didn't think it mattered. Jim asked if Jared had mentioned anything else. If he'd found anything else *at all* – those were his words – at the Pele Centre.'

'And had he?'

'Yes, Colombo, he had. Jed told me he'd found letters that had once been Nicky's. He took those as well. He didn't tell me what they were, but he said, "I have to sort all this out, you see. There's someone I need to talk to."'

'Ah!'

'You know who!'

'I can guess. Lucy phoned me at the office today. She asked if I had any idea why Jared was leaving urgent messages all over the place for her to contact him. She thought I might have been in touch with him. I said no, as far as I knew he was incommunicado on Despair.'

'I did think it might be Lucy, when Jed said he had to talk to someone. Because he did say, "it's all stuff to do with the past, but Olly isn't going to get away with this". And with the letters being Nicky's, I guessed that Lucy might be involved. But where Olly comes into it I just don't know.'

'You told Jim all that?'

'Yes, m'dear, I did. I don't think Jim was particularly interested in the letters. You know I won't let Jim hurt Jared if I can possibly stop him. But even less will I let Jared hurt Jim.'

'I see,' said Colombo drily. 'Conflicting loyalties.'

'Yes, my love. Just like you.'

'Touché,' said Colombo, and reached for the cheese.

He was silent for a long time after that, brooding over his coffee, and staring out of the window at the slowly darkening evening.

'You're exhausted, Colombo. Come to bed.'

'I need to have a shower.'

'Have one then, and come to bed.'

When he came through into the white bedroom she'd turned out the light and drawn back the curtains, so that they could look out on to the pale night sky and the lights of St Brandons glowing like a starlit pool surrounded by the outer dark which was the sea. Colombo went over to the window and stood there naked, breathing in the cool salt breeze that the night brought with it. When he turned back to the room, darkness had crept in so that all he could see was the faint outline of the white bed. He felt his way back and got in beside her. The sheets were cool and clean against his skin. She always had them clean; he'd asked her about it once and she'd told him yes, naturally she had clean sheets on Saturday, for him, and then again on Sunday, before Hook came back from Dorrado. It was no trouble, she said, and it would hardly be civilised to do anything else.

Nesta's cool common sense was balm to his soul after the tortuous agonies of love. On the other hand, sex with Nesta was anything but cool; after the frozen wastes where he and Lucy together seemed to dwell, it was like coming in from a winter day to a blazing fireside. He put his hands out to her and met her hands. She was laughing, he knew. She always laughed at sex, and in the faint light from the window he thought he could see her smile. He rolled over on to her and kissed her. Her hands moved down his back and he shut his eyes. For a moment he thought of the yellow file labelled *Chemistry Notes* and the vision of loneliness that had haunted him ever since he read it. He shoved the thought away, and obliterated Lucy from his mind the way he had to do every Saturday night. It seemed as wrong to him to think of one woman while making love to another, as to go straight to Mass after a night of fornication. It actually disrupted his life a good deal more to go to church on Wednesdays than to forget about Lucy for one day out of seven. But then it was only fair that illicit pleasures should be paid for, even if his method of accounting was unorthodox.

Before he finally fell asleep he heard the clock from St Brendan's Cathedral striking three. After that he was dreaming, and somehow Jared was in the dream. They were in a small boat sailing through the turbulent darkness on the far side of Despair, and Jared was telling him to bale, to bale, to keep on baling. But the boat filled slowly as the melting rock poured in and burst the seams, and he knew he could only save his own life if he woke himself up, and left the other there. Then he was looking down on Hy Brasil from far above, and all the islands were drowning in red lava, everyone except for him, and he knew that he should go down with them, because if he did not the end of his beloved country would be entirely his own fault, and then he would have nowhere to go, but would wander the empty seas forever, outcast until the end of time. He woke up, hot and shuddering, and remembered where he was. He reached out for Nesta. She was cool and soft-skinned in his arms, still half asleep, but she responded to him as he could always trust her to do. He was wide awake then, making love to her all over again, so that just for a little while he was not alone any more.

EIGHTEEN

Sidony Redruth. Ile de l'Espoir. July 20th.
Notes for *Undiscovered Islands* (working title).

STANDING ON THE jetty at Lyonsness, I thought about the way that islands get moved. Look at Juan Fernandez, for example, which is in the Pacific, at 79° west, 33.4° south, at least three hundred miles west of the coast of Chile. Defoe shifted it without compunction to the mouth of the Orinoco in the Caribbean, to 60.4° west, 9° north. He did this in order to provide a suitable mainland only thirty miles off, and consequently a supply of savages, which he needed for the plot. I call that fairly cavalier behaviour. Swift, on the other hand, is disingenuously vague about bearings, when Gulliver discusses what might have happened 'if I had not made bold to strike out innumerable passages relating to the winds and tides, as well as to the variations and bearings in the several voyages'. Well, indeed, supposing he hadn't, what then? Then if you go back to the old maps, right up to the nineteenth century, real islands keep vanishing because there was no accurate way of determining longitude, and for the same reason unreal ones keep appearing. Also, on old maps, islands are proportionately huge, not the tiny dots they are in a modern atlas. That's not wrong. The maps are meant to be a picture of the islands as they are inside one's head. They're drawn to the scale of their significance.

I thought about all this while I looked across at the mists that wreathed around Despair. If I didn't know it was there I wouldn't have been able to see it at all. I don't think I'd ever fully grasped before how the existence of Hy Brasil could have remained the subject of serious debate for so long: it was 1865 when its place on the Purdy chart was last disputed. I considered the world in 1865, and it seemed incredible that such an incontrovertible fact as an archipelago could still have remained unproven. There was a white boat moored just below where I stood. Its name was painted on the side: *Cerberus*. Inside it were two cardboard boxes and a thing that looked a bit like a gas cylinder. I stared down at it, and remembered how when Marco Polo came back after all those years and described his travels, they didn't believe him. I think that must be one of the worst things in the world: to tell the truth and not to be believed.

'Sidony?'

I looked up, and there was Jared. He put a bulging carrier bag down on the quay. 'Were you waiting for me?' he asked.

'No,' I said, surprised. 'I was just looking round.'

'You said you wanted to come over.' I must have looked blank, because he pointed at the boat moored at my feet. 'That's my boat. You said you wanted to go to Despair. I've been expecting you to get in touch.'

'I do. But I wasn't . . . I didn't know you were over today.'

'I'm not done yet,' he said. 'I've still to fetch my washing. It's in Per's washing machine.' He waved towards a new bungalow built on a mound at the end of the town. 'It would be a good day to come,' he added. 'A friend of mine killed a sheep. This is all mutton.' He indicated the carrier bag. 'So I could feed you pretty well.'

'Well . . .' A great many thoughts were going through my mind. The first was that I hadn't heard from him at all for a month. After the night at Da Shack, and our walk, and the earthquake, I'd expected him to get in touch. He hadn't. My second thought was that no way was I going to show any enthusiasm for his company if he didn't make it very clear indeed that he wanted me around. Another thought was that I genuinely did want to get to Despair, and the best chance of doing that was with Jared. Finally, I remembered that I was, first and foremost, the writer of a book, and that meant seizing every opportunity, whatever my personal inclinations. 'I suppose I could come today,' I said at last. 'You'd have to bring me back again, though. Wouldn't that be a bother?'

'There's no point coming back today. The mist's down. Come for a day or two at least. As long as you like. It'll probably be clear again tomorrow.'

'I suppose I could,' I said doubtfully. 'I'd need to get my stuff.'

'You've got the Land Rover?' I nodded. 'You can do it to Ravnscar and back in an hour and ten minutes. Half an hour to get yourself sorted, say? I'll be here again at . . .' He looked at his watch. 'Three. Can you do it by three?'

He gave me a note to give to Lucy, but of course I'd forgotten that Lucy would have to come back to Lyonsness with me to retrieve her Land Rover. On the way she took it upon herself to warn me that I was more attractive than I realised, and that Jared had been living on his own for over a year. I said I didn't foresee any problems. She exclaimed that she never meant for one moment that I wouldn't be safe with him, more the other way about if anything. I was indignant, and she gave me a tangled explanation from which it emerged that she was fond of Jared, she'd known him since he was a baby, and although she'd seen him get into a lot of trouble, she'd also seen him be very good to his mother. 'Mind you,' added Lucy, 'his mother had been more than good to him. But most boys of eighteen don't think of that.'

'What happened to his mother?'

'She got iller and iller all that winter and then she died. Jed went back to college after Easter, then the first weekend he was back in St Brandons he ended up assaulting a policeman. They sent him to jail for six weeks. He took the boat to Southampton the same day he got out. He didn't come back for almost eight years.' Lucy slowed down as we came into Lyonsness. 'It's nothing to do with me,' she added, 'but I'd rather you didn't hurt him.'

'I don't intend to.'

'Intend!' repeated Lucy derisively. She pulled up on the quay with a jerk.

After all that, the sight of Jared sitting patiently reading the cricket section of the *Times* in his boat, which was now level with the jetty, disconcerted me: he looked self-contained and very far from vulnerable. As soon as he saw us he folded up the paper and leapt ashore.

'Lucy! I didn't think you'd be there! Did you get my message?'

'Hundreds of messages,' said Lucy acidly. 'Everything short of SOS. But I wasn't in. So what's up?'

'I can't tell you here.' He looked from me to her, and back again, like Paris trying to reach a tactful compromise. 'I need to talk to you. Come over to Despair. I can bring you back in an hour or two.'

Lucy looked at her watch. 'Can't. I have to be in Ogg's Cove by seven. I'm going to hear Song of the Sea play at the Crossed Bones.'

I was momentarily disappointed. I'd forgotten about the gig, and I'd really wanted to go. The tapes Lucy had played me were brilliant. But maybe there'd be another chance.

'Tomorrow?' asked Jared.

'Tomorrow I'm opening the Scouts' Bring and Buy sale in Dorrado, and having lunch with Penny. And in the afternoon we're watching Lyonsness play Dorrado.'

'Day after tomorrow?'

'Oh, Jed! All right. Suppose I'm here at eleven the day after tomorrow, and you can take me over for lunch? Then Sidony can come back with me if she's had enough of you. Will that do?

OK, see you in a couple of days. But if the weather's horrible I'm not crossing the sound. Be nice to her. She likes tea at four in the afternoon. I hope you're up to it. Be firm with him, Sidony. See you.'

The crossing excited me. As soon as we were a couple of hundred yards out we couldn't see land at all. It was just ourselves in a small hollow of visibility surrounded by cloud and sea. The mist in my face was like damp fingers, and I could see little drops of water congealing on my jacket. I'd looked down on the tide race through the sound very often from Ravnscar. Now, with the tide just turning, the water close to me was still and green, but I could see little upwellings where the current was just beginning to set the other way. Jared said another quarter of an hour and we'd have really begun to feel it, but at this time of year it's possible to get across most days. He has a mooring in a little bay at the end of the white strand. He dropped me off at the lighthouse jetty, and we unloaded my bag and his shopping. Then he took the boat round to the mooring. I walked along the top of the beach through wet marram grass, and watched him row ashore in a little pram dinghy.

In one of my favourite books when I was small, the characters step into a picture, and into another world. Landing on Despair was like that. It slopes towards the south-west, so on a clear day you can see the whole of it laid out from Ravnscar. Some days it's flat like a backcloth, other days it comes much closer and is three-dimensional. As we walked up the hill, loaded with bags and boxes, I had this strange idea that I was seeing myself as a little figure inside the picture, but part of me was still outside. As we went up the fog grew thicker, as if we were vanishing ever further out of sight of the world I'd come from. It took me a while to take in, maybe I still haven't quite, that I really am here, not there. I'm sitting here on solid ground, on the island of Despair.

The lightkeepers' houses are built in a row with their backs to the northeast and the cliff, and their faces on to a walled yard. Jared lives in the house next to the tower, which is the smallest. The family houses are boarded up. He has a big kitchen living-room downstairs, and two bedrooms upstairs. One bedroom is full of diving equipment, and various bits of an engine laid out on newspaper. The other room is for sleeping in, presumably; the door was shut so I didn't look. I wasn't sure whether there'd be a bathroom or not, but there is a very cold one in an extension at the back.

The kitchen is cosy. It has a cast-iron wood stove which is lit most of the time because he uses it for cooking, and a table by the window with a red oilcloth over it. I'm sitting at the table now, writing. Behind me there are shelves full of books, mostly on marine archeology, navigation, seabirds, and cetaceans, in that order, but also some volumes of selected poems, ranging from John Donne to Medbh McGuckian. On the other side of the room, underneath a big army blanket, there's a huge sofa with no springs. At one end of it there's a pile of cushions built into a kind of nest with books and scraps of paper all around it. There isn't any other furniture at all. The whole room is warm and bare and clean. I like it.

I'm amused by the girlie calendar from Trink's garage that's hanging above the table. He has marked the days off with green crosses. SUNDAY JULY 20th. I suppose it could be quite easy to lose count all by one's self on an island. The only other picture is a print of Millais' *Boyhood of Raleigh* on the wall above the sofa. I didn't mention the calendar but I asked him about the picture.

'We had it at home,' he said. 'I let nearly all the things go because I'd nowhere to put them, but I did take that. I wish I'd kept more now. Someone would have lent me a space to store stuff for a few years. But I didn't. Didn't think of it, I suppose.'

He put a hunk of mutton in a big pot to boil, and then we went up to look at the gannet colony. It's strange being at the top of the cliff when you can't see down. You just hear the echoes going very deep below you. A gannet close to is a large yellow and white bird, very like the never-never bird that rescues Peter Pan when he's marooned on the rock in the mermaids' lagoon. I told Jared this, and he told me about the blood samples that he and Per had taken in the spring. This hasn't been done before with gannets, but it was very successful, and proved that these birds originated from colonies in the Scottish islands. Apparently when you take a blood sample from a gannet you have to insert the needle into the capillary tubes in its armpit. One of you has to hold the bird, and stretch out the wing, and the other sticks in the needle and gets the blood. You put the blood into sealed vacuum flasks, until you've got all your samples, – they did twenty birds this year – then you take the blood home to the centrifuge machine, which Jared says looks a bit like a coffee grinder, and you separate the plasma, and you put it in the freezer compartment at the top of the fridge, and as soon as you can you get it across to Lyonsness and put it in Per's deep freeze. Then you call the university from there, and it's picked up and taken back to the biology department where they do the DNA work.

I want to see the view from the summit of Despair. Jared says he thinks the mist will clear by morning. He's cooking supper now. I'm hungry, and the mutton smells good. It's getting very warm in here. The window is all steamed up with cooking, and I can't tell any more which are the drops running down the inside of the glass and which is the fog on the outside. I watch Jared wash half a dozen newly dug potatoes under the tap, and add them to the pot. I'm a bit sleepy. He's whistling as he peels a couple of onions. I watch him drop them into the pot whole. I recognise the tune as a song my mother used to sing: 'Let him go, Let him tarry, Let him sink or let him swim, He does not care for me And I don't care for him . . .' Presently he opens a tin of baked beans and tips that in too, and stirs everything round with a large wooden spoon. I watch him take a spoonful of mutton stock and taste it. 'Do you like salt?'

'A bit,' I say cautiously. After a moment's hesitation I add, 'You know there's a rosemary bush in the corner of your yard?'

'Yes, what about it?'

'You could put in some of that.'

'Oh.' He looks at his stew as if it might answer him, like at the Red Queen's dinner party. 'OK.' He puts the spoon down. 'How much, do you reckon?'

'I'll get it if you like.'

Ferdy's Landing. July 23rd

That was barely thirty-six hours ago. I need to describe what happened after that – I think I must, for my own peace of mind – but I just don't know how to begin. At the beginning, my mother would say, and go straight on through until you get to the end. I shall try; it would help a lot to sort my thoughts out. It would make more sense than crying anyway.

We had a stupid argument after supper. It began because we were talking about library books, of all things. He said it was far more important to return books to a library than not to steal money, because everyone has a right to access to books, and it's a serious crime to take away knowledge that should be held in common. I said that you couldn't possibly judge what other people needed their money for, and it was wrong to take what didn't belong to you, never mind what it was. He argued that it would be right to take works of art from a secret collection that was stored away in a vault after being bought on the black market. I said abuses should be stopped by constitutional methods, and it was arrogant to take the law into one's own hands. He replied that it was irresponsible not to act in the face of injustice. He said supposing I were being assaulted in front of my brother, what would I want Arthur to do, start phoning my solicitor? I said that was a sexist example. He said women always said that when they couldn't defend themselves against logic. I lost my temper. I didn't think his arguments made sense anyway; he seemed to be coming from some illogical position between Marxism and piracy. He said I'd been brainwashed by a Protestant-capitalist-imperialist value system. I can't remember exactly how it happened, but it seemed to me he was being rude about my father, and as I say, I lost my temper.

In the end I said I wanted to go to bed. He produced a roll of bedding, and asked if I wanted the sofa or an inflatable mattress on the floor. 'The sheets are almost clean,' he said. 'No one's used them except Colombo.' The mattress was an old-fashioned one without a foot pump; I was surprised he had the breath to blow it up, he looked so angry, but I suppose a diver has to go on breathing deeply whatever his emotions. As soon as we'd made up the bed he went away.

The mattress was cold, and wobbled uncomfortably whenever I moved. I seldom quarrel with anybody, except Arthur of course, and I couldn't understand why the end of such a good day had gone so wrong. Being alone, I began to cry.

The next thing I knew he was there beside me, with his arm around me over the heap of blankets. 'I'm sorry,' he was saying into my hair. 'Sidony, m'dear, I'm sorry. Truly, I am. I didn't mean to be horrible to you. Honestly, I didn't.'

I hardly ever cry, but when I do start I find it difficult to stop. I should have stopped then, because if the cause was that he wasn't being nice to me, then I should have been instantly better now that he'd changed his tune. I don't know how it was: I think perhaps I'd been feeling lonely for a long time. When you're by yourself in a foreign country it's very rare that anyone comes near enough to touch you. If I'd looked him in the eyes I'd probably have ended up howling, so I turned my face into his chest instead. He was wearing a red flannel nightshirt that smelt as if it had been stored in a musty cupboard; presumably he didn't usually wear anything in bed on a summer night. I tried to pull myself together, but he said I didn't have to, and then I did let him cuddle me, and went on weeping, rather like Violet Elizabeth Bott in *Just William*.

Presently Jared said, 'M'dear, I'm getting cold. Could we go upstairs? It's a lot more comfortable.'

That brought me round at once. 'No! If you think it's OK to upset me so I cry, and then use that as an excuse to get me into your bed, then you've got another think coming, because I won't!'

'I don't! Of course I never meant to make you cry! I'm sorry. I said I was sorry. Look, come upstairs and I promise I'll make no attempt whatever to seduce you tonight. It's nice up there. I'd like to show you. Please.'

It was much warmer in his bed, under a thick duvet that smelt faintly of Jared. 'Look,' he ordered me. 'I wanted you to see out.' There was a small square window in the north wall, right behind the bed and on a level with it. I lay on my front, and leaned my elbows on the sill, with the bedcover tucked around me, and my shoulder touching his. 'Look,' he repeated. 'The mist's away.'

Below us the ground sloped away to the cliff top twenty feet away. We could see right over it into a moon-washed sea that licked the lava skerries with long white tongues. The skerries were fantastically high, jagged at the edges and sharp as monsters' teeth. The ocean was grey and silver where the moonlight caught it, black under the shadow of the cliff. The brightness of the moonlight varied like breathing going in and out, but then I realised it wasn't the moon that was changing; it was the lighthouse: two long flashes and two short, fading into nothing and then coming round again. We seemed to be suspended offshore like an eagle hovering over a world composed of contrasts and sharp edges, inked-in shapes in an ice-clear spectrum of black to white. It was a pitiless, cold-blooded world, composed as a Dürer etching. I wriggled closer under the duvet, and he put his arm around me and held me tight. 'It's nice, isn't it?'

It wasn't the word I'd have chosen, but, framed as it was by the square window, it felt magical to be so very nearly inside a world so alien. Without the window frame, if the magic were suddenly to become real, it would be terrifying. 'Is it like that under the sea?' I asked him.

'Yes and no. Under the sea there're colours. But the dimensions are like, I mean: not feeling earthbound. That part's the same, only with the sea it's real, not just looking out, but being able to move around in it and touch things. It's nice. I'd like to show you one day.'

I gazed and gazed, while little draughts crept in between the window and the frame, and ran lightly over my face and arms. The rest of me was very comfortable. It was getting harder to keep my eyes open. When I couldn't keep awake any more, I squirmed back under the covers and closed my eyes. I was just aware of his warm body curling itself around my back, but right after that I fell asleep.

In the night I must have rolled over because when I woke I was looking straight into his eyes. He was leaning on his elbow looking down at me; he must have been watching me while I was asleep. 'Morning m'dear,' he said, and kissed me. I wasn't properly awake; I responded with a fervour that I'd almost forgotten I could feel. I've been so busy with that damn book I haven't had time to think about loving anybody. I expect I surprised him, but he liked it, because the next moment he was holding me very tight and stroking me and kissing me passionately. I touched him back, and I could feel his erection hard against me. But after a while he drew away, and buttoned up his nightshirt again. 'I keep my promises,' he said. 'Maybe we'd better get up.'

Hoist with my own petard, I reckoned. If you promise not to seduce a person you can't very well, according to the strict letter of your bond, behave in a provocative manner and then ask her if she's changed her mind, because that's precisely what seduction is when you think about it. It briefly crossed my mind that I hadn't promised not to do anything to him, but then I decided I'd be tempting him to break his word, which wasn't fair.

'Would you like some tea?' asked Jared. 'There's something in the other room I want to show you.'

I let him go. There wasn't much else I could do with any dignity. After he'd gone I rolled over on my front and looked out of the window at the pale morning. The skerries in their beds of foam looked like the teeth of a drowning dragon. On the floor next to me there was an upturned fishbox, which served as a bedside table. I leafed through the books: *The Mariner's Handbook, Surveying in Archeology Underwater*, a book of poems called *Fishermen with Ploughs, Maritime Archeology, Pottery from Spanish Shipwrecks 1500–1800, The Gannet, Spanish Armada Tonnages*, a recent volume of the *International Journal of Nautical Archeology and Underwater Exploration, The Selected Poems of Percy Bysshe Shelley, The Naval Tracts of Sir William Monson, A Voyage to Virginia in 1609* and a photocopy of *The Rhyme of the Ancient Mariner*, a dozen pages stapled together. I flipped through and read:

Alone, alone, all, all alone,
Alone on a wide wide sea!
And never a saint took pity on
My soul in agony.

That was all the books. No fiction. Underneath Monson there was a looseleaf notebook with pencil diagrams on the first page that looked like geometry. I turned the page. There was writing in neat italic script, unusual for a man, but I was beginning to recognise the distinctive calligraphy of Ogg's Cove Elementary. It said:

A candle burning underwater

Sea-green   light   incarnadine
          pearl   incandescent
          mica   incorruptible
abyss   (St Elmo's fire)
he is   flame/sulphur
sea deep   (pearls from sand)
eyes
Sea-green light//   The Serpent
His eyes//incandescent   Leviathan
Dull eyes/   Kraken/squid
Sea green//unseen//deep

whale/blood/incorruptible/he is/he sees/scars

Dull eyes seeing unseen from the abyss
The sea flames green
Sand in a dying shell is incandescent pearl
A candle burning underwater

The rest of the notebook was blank. Lying next to it was a small brown paper bag. Idly I glanced inside. It contained two unopened packets of condoms, and a receipt. I hesitated for a moment, and then I took out the receipt and read it. It said:

20/7/97 TRINK'S GARAGE
FISH ST, LYONSNESS
PHONE LYONSNESS 632

petrol 2 galls	£4.03.09d
AAA batteries 4	£1.13.04d
frsh frt 1	.07d
cdby dry mk	.03.06d
frlite cdms	£1.02.04d
Total	£7.01.06d
CASH	£7.01.06d

THANK YOU FOR SHOPPING AT TRINK'S

I knew for a fact he'd bought petrol after he'd said he'd meet me at three, because he told me so. Well.

I picked up *A Voyage to Virginia in 1609*, and opened it where the place was marked with a torn-off corner of the notebook. It said:

> During all this time the heavens looked so black upon us that it was not possible the elevation of the Pole might be observed; nor a star by night nor sunbeam by day was to be seen. Only upon the Thursday night Sir George Somers, being upon the watch, had an apparition of a little, round light, like a faint star, trembling and streaming along with a sparkling blaze, half the height upon the mainmast and shooting sometimes from shroud to shroud, 'tempting to settle, as it were, upon any of the four shrouds . . .'

I could hear Jared coming up the stairs, and I was glad I was reading something I didn't have to put quickly away. He brought me a mug of tea, put his own down on the front page of *The Ancient Mariner*, and went into the other bedroom and came back with a small cardboard box. He placed it in the middle of the bed, and got back in under the duvet at the foot of the bed, where he sat crosslegged facing me.

He took out something wrapped in bubblewrap, and gently unrolled it, and held it up. It was the glass goblet I'd seen at Maldun's Mill. No, it wasn't. It had a crack in it, right down one side of the bowl, the same as the other goblet, the one on the shelf at the Pele Centre, only this one wasn't greasy and dusty. It shone like new, like the one from the bottom of the sea. 'Jared! Can I look? Which is it? Where did you get it from?'

It was heavier than I expected. I turned it round, and there was the crest with the galleon. It was like the halfpennies they have in Hy Brasil which have Drake's *Golden Hind* imprinted on one side, only it wasn't as neatly etched as those. It was more the impression of a ship in motion: lines and sea-colours rather than nautical detail. I touched it, and felt the curves of the sails under my finger. 'Better than in a glass case,' I said. 'More real. But which one is it, Jared? How did it get here?'

'It belonged to my friend Nicky.'

'Nicky Hawkins? You didn't tell me that before.'

'No. But this one was his. It was cracked then. He had it on the mantelpiece in Ferdy's Landing.'

'But did Ishmael . . . ? What about . . . ? This is the one I saw in the Pele Centre, isn't it? That one had a crack in it too.'

'I'll tell you. But I want to show you more first. Put that down a minute.' He delved into the box, and handed me something else. It was a brass polished cone the shape of the volcano, about two inches long, with rings etched around it and some measurements along the side. The base had threads so it could be screwed on to something. Considering it was so small it was quite a weight. 'You know what that is? No? It's the top of a shell, the kind they used in the First World War. Nicky's great-grandfather picked it up at Gallipoli. It was one of Nicky's treasures.' I started asking another question, but he ignored me. 'Now this.'

He passed me an ebony snuffbox with a delicate oil painting of a ship in full sail on its lid. 'That's not a galleon,' I remarked.

'Of course not. It's a British ship of the line, about 1805.'

'Oh yes, I've seen the *Victory* in Portsmouth.'

'So have I. The snuffbox belonged to Nicky too. He used to keep his dope in it. Now these.'

He dumped a bundle of papers into my lap, loosely tied together with string. Letters slid out as I picked it up. I recognised the spiky italics immediately, and I couldn't help seeing the first words:

My darling,

I can't come tonight. The bloody President's coming to dinner and Pappa says I have to be dutiful. Tomorrow, maybe.

I've thought about what you said. I don't know. Sometimes I think there's a fate on me, and I must let you go, or I'll add your ruin to our own. Maybe you should go away from here, my dear love, while you still can . . .

I pushed the letters back together. 'No, no. I don't know why you've got them, but Lucy would never want me to read these.'

'I don't mean you should. I didn't read them either, and I wouldn't. But you must understand: these belonged to Nicky. All these things are Nicky's.'

'But the glass is the one I saw at the Pele Centre . . .'

'Sidony, I found all this at the Pele Centre.' I must have looked blank, for he reached over and took my hands as if that would make me understand him. 'The glass was on the shelf, just where you said. While I was there I thought I'd just check what else was up there. And on the end of the shelf there was an old shoe box, do you remember seeing that?' I shook my head. 'Well, it was there, covered with dust like the other junk. When I looked inside I saw the shell head, and the snuffbox, and so I knew it was more of Nicky's. Then I looked at the papers, and of course I knew Lucy's writing right off. I didn't even have to look inside. Sidony, you realise who had to deliver all those letters?'

I shook my head at him, still bemused. 'You mean you *stole* it all out of the Pele Centre?'

'No! It was Olly stole them out of Ferdy's Landing. After Nicky died the house was boarded up. No one moved anything until Ishmael bought the place, and that was all of two years later. I tell you Olly must have taken them. He must have gone into Ferdy's Landing!'

'And now you've taken them out of his office?'

'Those things are Nicky's, Sidony! What was that man doing in Nicky's house? What the hell was he after? Olly West doesn't know a thing about the *Cortes*. He always says the past means nothing to him, he's only interested in the future. It's true, he really does, though I know it's hard to believe anyone could be that stupid. He wouldn't know when 1611 even *was*. He's the last man to go around pinching antiques.'

'Well, that would figure. If he'd known what it was he'd have taken more care of it. But why would he want Lucy's letters?'

'He didn't. I thought at first he'd planned to blackmail her, but that don't fit. There's nothing secret about what happened with Nicky. Nothing left to hide.'

'I wouldn't *dare* attempt to blackmail Lucy.'

Jared grinned suddenly. 'God, nor would I! No, that won't wash. But there's something . . . Ever since Olly got here – that's just before Nicky came back – I'm not sure. No, I can't explain it. But what I do know now is that Olly West must have been into Ferdy's Landing after Nicky died, and he took away these things from there. I don't know why. But they're not his.'

'They're not yours either, Jared.'

'That's what I'm telling you. All these things belonged to Nicky.'

'So what are you going to do with them?'

'I've thought about that. Listen, Sidony. There's only one other person who'd recognise all this, who'll know where all these things belonged just as well as I do. No one else ever got invited into Ferdy's Landing. This is why I have to talk to Lucy. Otherwise it's only my word against Olly's. But she and I both . . . That's *proof*.'

'Of what? Why do you need proof?'

'I want to know why Olly West was after Nicky's things. He didn't need an antique goblet or a shellhead from Gallipoli. What did he want? I want to know what happened after Nicky died. You know Olly tried to buy that house himself, but Ishmael came in with a better price. No one else wanted it – the heir was a distant cousin, well, it was Penelope Hook, in fact. You know her, don't you? Nicky was very touchy about anyone meddling, you know. He kept all his papers in his father's tin army trunk, and the only time I ever tried to open it he boxed my ears. Did anyone ever do that to you? It really hurts. I never touched the thing again. I don't know what he kept in there.'

'Do you think Lucy knew?'

'I don't know that either. I've never mentioned Nick to Lucy since I came home. But now I must. If Lucy'll back me up, I'm going straight to Gunn and Selkirk with all this lot, and they can chase up West. I didn't think before, I never thought what happened to Nicky's things. When he died I was . . . upset, I suppose. And later I tried not to think about any of it any more. But now I want to know. I think he'd want me to find out.'

'I suppose Penelope might have cleared out some things?'

'Penelope? In which case . . . No, I reckon Olly got there first. Penny would have known not to leave the goblet. But you're right. We have to consider that.' He frowned. 'Sidony . . .'

'Yes?'

'These letters . . . I've never talked to Lucy about any of it. We've never mentioned the past. When she comes tomorrow . . . I'm quite glad you'll be there. I mean, before I explain all the other stuff I need to give her back the letters, and tell her I need to talk about Nick. But . . . well, I've told you how it was. I'm not sure I'm just the right person to hand over those letters. I mean, maybe it would be better if someone else gave them to her. Someone she trusts who isn't anything to do with the past. Maybe someone who isn't a man.'

'Well, there's quite a few of those around,' I said tartly. He flushed, and I instantly took pity on him, and laid my hand on his knee. 'Jared, it's OK. Don't be upset. It's just my natural reluctance to get involved. But you've both been very kind to me. I'll do it.'

He nodded, and started putting Nicky's treasures back in their box. I got out of bed. 'Sidony? That promise I gave you. It was made for one night. You do realise that, don't you?'

I could only hope he'd attribute my obvious embarrassment to a becoming modesty, but actually it was guilt, because I'd looked through his things, and therefore knew more about his intentions than I was supposed to. 'Yes, you were quite clear about that,' I said, as I went downstairs to find my clothes.

We continued in perfect amity until we were washing up after the largest breakfast I'd eaten since Easter 1993, when Arthur and I stayed in a bed-and-breakfast on Arran, this being my brother's attempt to cheer me up after the break-up of my first serious relationship, which happened to be with my Fiction 1700–1900 tutor, just six weeks before my finals. I was explaining to Jared how I really wanted to stay longer in Hy Brasil, only my deadline was October, and I hadn't much more money. I told him how Lucy had refused to go on charging me, and that I was paying her in housework and gardening instead, 'So I should just about manage until September, but that's all.'

'If you really did want to stay you would,' argued Jared. 'You haven't *got* to do anything.'

'I've taken an advance from the publishers and I've already spent most of it.'

'So? There's nothing to stop you putting a manuscript in the post, is there? If you really meant it about wanting to stay here you'd find a way. You're going home because that's what you want to do most, only you won't admit it. You'd rather not deal with the fact that you have a choice.'

'There's no employment here. I can't see much choice.'

'You mean you won't. You just think in straight lines because you've been told it's morally good not to do anything different. There's nothing really stopping you doing whatever you like.'

'Such as?' I demanded, as I dried a plate.

'Well, for example, you could decide not to go away at all. You could decide to forget your book and marry me and live for ever on Despair. It's your choice.'

I dropped the plate.

I knelt down and very slowly picked up the pieces. I'd have

been less startled if he'd thrown a bucket of cold water over me. My face was burning, either with embarrassment or fury; I wasn't sure which. It seemed to me a thoroughly underhand example to use. It wasn't a statement or a question. I could have dealt with either of those, but I didn't know how to casually ignore a conditional hypothesis which suggested in equal proportions a sentence to life imprisonment and a garden of earthly delights. I stood up with my back to him and as I laid the broken shards on the table I looked out of the window.

'Jared, who's that?'

'What?' He caught the sharp edge of fear in my tone, and was beside me in a flash. There were men in green uniforms coming up the hill. They had guns. The only place I ever saw men in uniform with guns was in Milan airport. My mother's father got out of Poland in 1939. Perhaps my reaction was atavistic: if there'd been anywhere to go I would have run. I trembled, and my legs felt weak. Maybe I couldn't have run.

'Christ!'

'Who is it?'

'Fucking coastguards!' He was at the cupboard. *Coastguards?* In Cornwall coastguards give you weather reports. Jared took a long double-barrelled gun from the top shelf. And a box of cartridges. 'Can you aim a shotgun?'

'Of course I can't! I've never even *touched* a gun,' I backed away. 'I'm *English!*'

'Fuck.' He clicked something and the barrel of the rifle went down. He took two cartridges from the box. 'Get away from the window! Get upstairs!'

'Jared, you can't shoot people! What are you *doing?*'

'They're not taking me! Get upstairs!'

'No!' I grabbed the gun by the barrel. Luckily he hadn't clicked it back yet. 'No! You mustn't shoot anyone! You can't! Especially not coastguards or police. You'll get into terrible trouble! Jared, you *can't!*'

The room went dim. There was the shadow of a man at the

window. Jared wrenched the gun away from me, locked the barrel into place, and raised it to his shoulder, pointing door-wards.

The door was opening.

'Jared, *No!*'

I took him by surprise. He was just aiming the thing. I snatched it from him. Suddenly the room was full of men. I fled behind the open cupboard door. Jared tried to break for the door upstairs. They closed in. The moment they touched him he went berserk. If the police came after me I think I'd try to be civilised and polite and hope that would soften their hearts. But as soon as the big guy laid a hand on Jared he lashed out. He fought like a cornered cat, struggling wildly until they knocked him off his feet. I saw him hit the floor face-down with a crack, and then they were on him and had his hands handcuffed behind his back. It took them about twenty seconds. It was their efficiency that appalled me: it was like a reflex. They'd obviously been trained to deal very easily with anyone like Jared.

I couldn't see his face. Very quietly I backed from the cupboard to the stove, and I slid the shotgun in between the back of the stove and the wall. It fell with a noise like a poker rattling in a grate. No one noticed. I think however long we live that that was probably the best turn I'll ever do him.

The green uniforms were everywhere, all through the kitchen, into every shelf and cupboard. I heard them thumping up the stairs, heavy footsteps on the floor above, voices shouting from room to room. They took no notice of me. When they turned to the cupboard where I was standing one jerked his thumb at me and signalled a question to the big guy who was still standing over Jared where he lay on the floor. He just shook his head. I wasn't even worth wasting words on, thank God.

They came flooding back from upstairs. When I think about it now I think there were no more than half a dozen altogether, but it felt like an army. One had something in his hands. Not Nicky's box, nothing like that. Just some plain plastic packages, the sort you get Chinese ready-meals in at the supermarket, only they were blank on the outside.

They dragged Jared to his feet. They didn't ask him to get up, they were deliberately rough with him; I'd never seen that before. Where he'd fallen one side of his face was bruised and swelling. He didn't say a word, but there was a defiant sullenness about him that made the big guy shove him so he staggered against the other one, who hit him hard on the side of the head with his clenched fist, as if Jared had fallen on purpose. I was the one that flinched, not Jared. He was half-dazed, though, and when the man thrust the packets into his face and shouted questions at him, he just shook his head as if he were too weary to reply.

I stared at the packets. I could hardly take in that this was real. It was like a nightmare where things that you know keep turning into something else, and just for one moment there was a question in my mind. I'm not sure if there were doubt in my face, but when I looked at Jared I caught him watching me, and he gave me a tiny shake of the head, which wasn't dazed at all but very clear. I believed him; I do still, and I always shall. I *know*. But what those men were saying was that they'd found the stuff in his possession, and he didn't try to deny it. I was the only witness, and even I could see there wasn't any point. I said nothing, and when they took him away I did nothing. What could I have done?

The whole thing took about a quarter of an hour. When they'd gone it seemed so quiet. My legs were shaking, and I sank down on one of the chairs at the table. I held up my hand and watched how much it shook. My thoughts were clumsy and slow, all the more so because of the urgency I felt. After a minute or two I got up. It occurred to me that the heat from the stove might do something to the gun. I wasn't sure if it were dangerous for a loaded shotgun to get hot or not. I took the poker, and leaned down over the back of the stove. It seemed fairly cool down there. I managed to push the gun along with the poker until I could reach in from the side and get it. I had to take it by the barrel, which I did extremely gingerly, making sure it wasn't pointing at me. I was trembling so much it was quite difficult to do. I was nervous that something might explode, though I've never heard of a gun exploding unless you pull the trigger. When I got hold of it I found it heavier than I'd expected. I lifted it cautiously over the hot water pipes. I had an idea that I ought to unlock the barrel again as there were two unused cartridges in there. When I examined the top of the gun I could see the lever you pressed sideways to make it go apart. I pushed it very gently with my finger, just in case it might be the trigger after all, even though I knew it wasn't, and to my relief the thing slid back and the barrel went down, just like when Jared had loaded it. I could see the cartridges tucked in at the top. I considered for a minute, and then very warily I took them out.

I felt better when I'd put the gun away. Gradually I was working out what to do. I was in the middle of picking up his books, smoothing their pages and putting them back on the shelves as closely as I could to their right order, when I heard an engine burring away like a distant sewing machine, in the direction of the sound. Even so, I waited until I'd tidied up a bit more. It was lucky he didn't possess very much. They'd left the open shelf of pans untouched, and they'd never even got to the cupboard; the only damaged thing in the kitchen was the shards of the plate I'd broken which were still lying on the table. I didn't face going upstairs.

The next thing was the key. I put off looking, because my worst fear was that it might be in his trouser pocket. His sea jacket was hanging on the back on the door. There was nothing in the pockets except the wrapper from a bar of chocolate, a pencil and a set of allen keys. My heart sank. Then I saw it: an ignition key hanging on a nail in the frame of the back door. Thank God.

As I ran down the hill I studied the sound apprehensively.

There was a froth of white water in a v-shape just to the left, between Despair and Lyonsness. I prayed that for the next hour or so it wouldn't start doing anything else. High tide yesterday had been around three o'clock. Right now it was eleven twenty-three. So it must be coming in. That meant the water would be flowing both ways round the island, presumably, until it met in those nasty-looking white horses. There wasn't any noticeable wind. There didn't seem to be any reason why things would change, but one thing I knew was that you never knew.

The dinghy was lying upside down at the top of the beach by the jetty, where I had helped to carry it. I untied the rope that held it down, turned it over and dragged it down the beach. It scraped unpleasantly on the stones at the top, but I couldn't lift it by myself, so I had to hope it didn't matter. I got the oars fixed into the rowlocks, shoved off, and scrambled in. Luckily I can row: my parents aren't into boats but Arthur and I often used to hire a rowing boat from our local beach for an hour or two on a summer afternoon. I came alongside *Cerberus* quite neatly, and climbed into it. I had to tie the dinghy to the boat while I found the boathook and fished around for the mooring. The rope was wet and weedy and tried to slip out of my hands, but I fixed the painter of the dinghy on to it with several half hitches, until it seemed secure enough.

With a sinking heart I turned my attention to the engine. Turning on the ignition was no problem. But as I'd feared there was one of those horrible cords you have to pull with a jerk to make the thing start. We have one on the lawnmower at home. It used to be Arthur's job to mow the lawn. It was a family joke that the refinements of gardening were beyond him. I will never think of running a lawnmower as unskilled labour again. I pulled the cord as hard as I could a few times and nothing happened. I studied the engine a bit more closely. There was a lever underneath where the cord came out. I remembered about the choke, and I tried pulling it. I jerked the cord again and this time there was a small noise. Encouraged, I did it again. And again. It got better after a while and then suddenly it died with a sort of gasp.

I guessed I'd flooded the engine. Quite likely they'd beat up Jared. They'd lock him in prison. This wasn't England. They might be torturing him at this very moment to make him confess to what he didn't do. I was crying, but I ignored it. I made myself wait five whole minutes by my watch. It was the longest five minutes I ever want to live through. I felt so incompetent: this sort of thing just didn't happen to people in books. At last I took a deep breath, picked up the handle, and gave the cord one almighty jerk. The engine roared.

I turned the throttle down with trembling hands. I pulled on the painter until the mooring rope came up again. I can untie a bowline without difficulty. The boat was floating free. I knew how to go into forward because I'd seen Jared do that yesterday, though I hadn't been paying much attention. I turned the lever, and the boat suddenly shot forward. I grabbed the tiller just in time before we hit the rocks, remembered to shove it the opposite way from where I wanted to go, and got the bows pointing into open water. Next thing I knew I was out of the bay and into the sound.

I felt the current at once. It was trying to make me go east, towards Lyonsness. Maybe it would win: my heart was in my mouth. In the end I had to point nearly west to keep on going straight across. But when I did that it worked: I found I could aim exactly for the spot I wanted. There was no mist now, but the sound seemed to have got twice as wide as it was when Jared was there, and the middle of it felt very exposed. I could see the Atlantic stretching away to the north-west, and for the first time in my life I didn't like it. But by the time I got to the other side I was already growing accustomed, and when I lowered the throttle and came carefully round the rocks into the bay at Ferdy's Landing I was breathing almost normally.

There was a small pale-brown girl with a halo of black hair, dressed in nothing but a pair of pink dungaree shorts, sitting on the end of the jetty fishing with a rod and line. When I came alongside, which I thought I did rather well, she got up and took the painter from me, and tied it to a ring with a neat clove hitch. I switched off the engine. 'Hello,' I said. 'I'm Sidony. Is your father in?'

'In the kitchen, Pappa and Mamma both. Where's Jared?' She watched me gravely as I tied the stern rope to a ring. I could see her looking at my knot, but she didn't comment.

'He couldn't come,' I said. 'I need to talk to your Pappa about it.'

I was glad she didn't come in with me. All the more so, in that when I walked into that orderly kitchen where Ishmael and Anna were drinking coffee over the remains of their lunch, with three abandoned places at the table between them, as if this were an ordinary day and the world were still a normal place, I instantly came very close to tears. But Ishmael and Anna were almost strangers to me, and I controlled myself. I must have looked awful, though, because I didn't have to tell them something was up. They were kind, and brought me in at once and sat me down at the table. I was surprised how calmly they listened to my story. Ishmael interrupted me with questions twice. I described the big coastguard to him as well as I could. I told him how they'd brought the packets in as if they'd found them upstairs. 'But they were never there. I *know* they were never there. It was a set-up. Jared never had any drugs anywhere.'

'How do you know?' asked Ishmael. 'Had you searched his house too?'

I stared at him in shock. 'Of course I hadn't! But I still *know*. Don't you believe me?'

'Oh, I believe you. All I'm saying is, you've no more evidence than I have. You say you know Jared. How? I think I know him too. But you can't prove him innocent, and nor can I. Not that way.'

He seemed so cold about it. I couldn't help it, the tears were spilling over and running down my cheeks. 'He never had drugs,'

I reiterated. 'Jared never would. But even if you could prove it, he did hit those policemen, or whatever they were. I saw it.' I was sobbing openly now. 'And they'll send him to prison for that, just like they did before. And supposing I hadn't been there, he might have shot one dead. He might easily have. And now they'll lock him up. That's what he's scared of, of course he fights. And when we were talking before and I asked him what he was afraid of, he said the thing that frightened him most in all the world was being locked in, not able to get out and being in the power of people he couldn't trust. That's what he told me and that's exactly what they'll do to him. They'll hurt him. I *saw* it. I saw them hurting him on purpose, and they'll do it more, now they've got him. And he won't give in, he'll fight them, and they might do anything to him then. And you're his friend. He said so. That's why I came here as fast as I could. And I've already wasted a whole lot of time trying to work that fucking engine, and if you won't do anything but ask me silly questions you're going to waste a whole lot more!' I'm ashamed to say that then I buried my head in my arms on the table, and fairly wept.

Anna came and put her arms around me. 'It's all right, m'dear,' she said. 'We're his friends too. You can trust Ishmael, he'll get him out. But he needs to think.'

After a minute or two I sniffed and swallowed, and accepted a cup of coffee. Ishmael sat at the end of the table, frowning. But when he spoke to me again his voice was kind. 'I won't waste time. I don't think he'll find a better friend than you, but maybe I can deal best with the next bit, and I promise you I will.' He smiled at me suddenly. 'M'dear, it's all right. I'll do whatever I have to, I promise. Can I ask you one or two more questions?'

'Of course.' I wiped my nose on my sleeve, and Anna passed me a tissue. 'Just because I make a fuss it doesn't mean I can't think. Just ignore it.'

'I don't think you make a fuss,' said Ishmael. Then he said, 'What's Jared been doing this past week? Has he been finding out anything he didn't know before?'

I stared at him. 'I'm not sure. At least . . . there's Nicky's treasures. Is that what you mean?'

'Nicky's treasures?'

I explained. 'But they searched the house, and the box was right there by the bed, because Jared had been showing them to me, but they never said a word about it.'

Ishmael didn't seem to be listening. 'How did he get into the Pele Centre?' he asked abruptly.

'He didn't say.' I hesitated, and added, 'He wouldn't, I think. We don't seem to agree about stealing.'

'Would anyone else know he'd been there? Has he talked to anyone?'

'I don't know.' A thought occurred to me. 'I suppose Peterkin might have an idea. He'd know Jared, wouldn't he?'

'Peterkin's brother was Jed's best friend at school,' said Anna. 'Pat's away from Hy Brasil now. Pete was always tagging after them both. He'd do more or less anything Jed told him to. He wouldn't shop him, though, unless someone really scared him.'

'Yes,' said Ishmael. 'There's Peterkin.' He pushed his chair back from the table, and stood up. 'All right, m'dear. I'm not going to waste any more time. Now listen, what we're going to do is this . . .'

NINETEEN

JAMES HOOK SAT at his desk, while behind him gulls wheeled in the wind beyond the plate glass window. Three letters lay on the desk before him, all written in an elegant italic script, even though they were inscribed in pencil on cheap lined paper stamped at the top: *Government Jail, St Brandons, Hy Brasil.* He read them over again, frowning. The first said:

> Dear Per,
>
> About the gannets: I hate to have to ask but if the project stops now that's four months' work pretty much down the tubes. My notes are on the second shelf down on the right hand side of the stove, behind the table. About half the chicks are already ringed – it says in the notes which nests – the rest need doing as they get big enough. I collect dropped fish from round the nests daily to check on species of fish prey. See notes for details. Like I told you, now the main gannet stuff is done I'd just started a general record of successful breeding this year on fulmars, Leach's petrels, kittiwakes, puffin, ringed plover, dunlin and tern (latter doing much better this year). You don't have to bother with all that if you don't want to. It says in my notes how far I'd got. And I keep an eye on the spotted sandpiper's nest above the mooring – remember I showed you.
>
> Thanks. I'll give you my pay. I hope it won't be for long.
> Jared.

MARGARET ELPHINSTONE

The second said:

Dear Sidony,
I hope you're OK. I've been worried about how you'd get off the island. It was rough on you. I'm sorry.

I can't write much and it can't be private. But what I said to you just before that happened – I mean it. Only I shouldn't have said anything about being on Despair, because I can understand why not, in the long term anyway, but the other bit, that was the important part, and I would do that *anywhere*, supposing you wanted it. *I mean this*. Please could you give Lucy the message which I mentioned to you?

I hope I won't be here long. Please don't go away before you've seen me if that's possible. If not, leave your English address with Lucy. *Please don't forget*. If you do have to go away, please don't forget, even if other things should happen to you away from here, that I still need to talk to you. Even if it's a while, I'll be in touch. I don't know who reads this, so that had better be all.

Love from Jared.

The third said:

Dear Ishmael,
I'm in the jail. I don't know why. I don't know what to say that will get past the censor. But if you can think of anything, please do. They say I can't see anyone, but maybe *you* could ask. I guess I need your help.

Jared

PS I can't see what it should have to do with the *Cortes* but maybe you could keep an eye on things there too?

'Hands!'

The bodyguard appeared at the office door. These two can

go,' said Hook, and pushed over two letters with their envelopes. 'See to it, will you?'

'Yes sir.'

All Jared could see from the high barred window was a patch of deep blue, and the shining gulls that wove across it, tossed by a wind he could not feel. It would be wild on Despair today, all sun and wind and dancing sea. The air would smell clear as water, fresh off the Atlantic, and the wind would try to whip his notebook out of his hand as he worked. The gannets would huddle face into it, barely turning their heads as he walked among their nests. But when they took to the air they'd let the wind take them and fly free, way out over the ocean, as far as the eye could follow. The island was just where it always was. Only he was missing. He shut his eyes and thought about his island as it was when he was not there.

Yesterday he had gone round every yard of the coast, visualising it inside his head, remembering the name of every rock and precipice. Yesterday the patch of window had been dull grey, and recalling Despair had been comforting. Today was different. Today was the sort of day that he had always found impossible to spend indoors, and he felt dangerously active. He wasn't likely to start screaming or hammering at the steel door of his cell, but he understood how people could. He caught himself staring out at the patch of sky again. He shut his eyes.

They weren't letting him have any books. He'd tried asking for a Bible when secular reading matter was refused, but they weren't taken in by that ploy, and said no. Yesterday they'd allowed him to write three short letters, and then they'd taken away the paper and the pencil again. They said he'd do better to take his time to re-consider. That meant he wasn't to be allowed to read, or write, or see anybody, until he confessed to what he hadn't done. He'd hesitated before writing the letters. He'd demanded the means as a right, but when to his surprise it was conceded, he sensed a possible trap, though it was hard to see how he could have incriminated himself or anybody else. He wasn't at all sure his letters would get posted. He doubted if any of them were quite what his jailors had been hoping for.

The only satisfaction he'd given them so far, if it did satisfy them, was that he'd been extremely sick. The cell still smelt. Even being in here all the time, and presumably relatively oblivious to the smell of himself, he was unpleasantly aware of it. Maybe it was the bang on the head that had caused the sickness; maybe it had been the long drive over mountain roads, lying on his face on the floor of a police van that smelt of petrol, with his hands cuffed behind his back; maybe it was the effects of being interrogated under bright lights in a small hot room, for what felt like hours although he had no way of knowing, with pains shooting through his head, and having to try hard all the time never to say yes to what he hadn't done, even when they kept changing the questions. Maybe it was just simple fear. They hadn't threatened him with anything specific, yet.

He hated being sick. Compared to other things that might happen it was trivial and humiliating, but it had left him feeling weak. No one had come near him all that night, but next morning, when he'd asked to have the basin emptied out, they'd refused, and left him with it for the next forty-eight hours. Now everything, including himself and the pyjama-like prison clothes he was wearing, seemed to smell horrible, but he wasn't sure any more how much of it he was imagining.

Same problem with the bucket, not that he'd eaten anything much after he'd vomited away the breakfast he'd had inside him when he came in. Yesterday some of his appetite had come back, however, and he'd eaten the nameless stewlike substance that had been pushed in through the slit in the door.

The warder on the afternoon shift on the fourth day had responded at last to his request for a toothbrush. Jared had a hunch the man was acting against orders, but naturally he didn't ask. No toothpaste, of course, but he still had a sliver of soap that he'd hidden from the first day, when they'd let him have a bowl of warm water to wash. The taste of soap was better than the taste of sick.

The first couple of days, after they'd finished questioning him, he'd surprised himself by sleeping most of the time. His head had been pretty sore. It was harder to sleep now. He wasn't used to having no exercise. He'd examined every inch of the cell, out of a kind of desperation, because he knew there'd be nothing to find and there wasn't. The bed was a solid platform along one wall, about two and a half feet wide, covered by a thin mattress with a stained cover and two shrunken grey blankets. There was a small shelf beside it on which stood a plastic jug of water and a plastic cup, and under the window there was a stained plastic bucket. That was all. A central light was let into the ceiling, controlled from outside the cell. The first forty-eight hours it had been left on all the time, and then someone had switched it off, to Jared's relief, and since then it hadn't come on again, so that at night the soothing dark crept slowly in and wrapped him round as if to comfort him.

The floor space was a little larger than the size of the bed. The wall opposite the bed was of uncoated concrete blocks, and had obviously been put in later to divide this cell from the next, the two having originally been one. That would figure: Jared knew that when Hy Brasil was a British colony the prison had been built to accommodate twenty prisoners, and the whole outfit had conformed to British standards. In fact it had never been more than half full before 1958. For a few years after that it had been shockingly overcrowded, but for the past twenty years or so it had hardly been mentioned in the news at all.

He had been in this place before, for six weeks in fact, and occasionally since then in dreams. The main difference was that last time he hadn't been alone. What he remembered best was playing cards all day with a man called Starkey, one meaningless round of two-handed whist after another, but it was better than doing nothing. Starkey used to cheat, as if it mattered, but at the time it had become more and more irritating. Not that Jared had lost his temper; no stakes were involved so there was nothing seriously unfair about it. The days had been no more boring than a long sea voyage, and in some ways more comfortable. It was the injustice, and the being locked in, that had upset him. That, and the lack of privacy just two weeks after his mother's funeral, and a bare week since he'd packed up everything in the house at Ogg's Cove, locked the front door and the back door for the first time in his life, and handed the keys back to Ravnscar estates. He'd intended to come back to college, and try to make a new life for himself, but it hadn't worked out that way. Eight years had passed since then, but finding himself incarcerated between the same concrete block walls, it was all coming back to him as if it had only just happened. He could have done without that.

This time, however, he was completely alone. Sometimes he heard voices in the corridor, but never close by. The sun shone in a small bar across the ceiling from dawn until what he guessed was about two hours later, so he deduced that he was somewhere along the north-east wall.

This was the seventh day. They had questioned him twice more, but not for two days now. No one had come. Sometimes he'd panicked. It was too hot in here, and the window didn't open. At night he'd wake up in a sweat of terror, imagining or dreaming that the ceiling was coming down lower, and the walls were closing in all round him. It was in the small hours that he came closest to despair, and found himself believing that maybe he wasn't going to get out, or at least not soon.

The law of Hy Brasil said that no one could be kept in prison without trial, unless they were awaiting trial. How long was it possible to await a trial? Jared didn't know. Perhaps for as long as the President pleased. It was in the middle of the third night, not before, that he found himself thinking about his father. Had Jack Honeyman ever been in here? Had Jack Honeyman ever got out of here, if he had been in? It was only when he thought of that that Jared broke down. But when he did cry, he did so in complete silence. If anyone were out there listening, they would never have the satisfaction of knowing they'd reduced him to that.

In the daytime he never gave way at all, because now and then eyes would appear at the slit in the door and look at him, and he was determined they would never see anything that it would give the government the slightest pleasure to hear about. During the day he usually sat cross-legged on his bed, either staring at the small barred square of sky, or with his eyes shut. Luckily there were some resources that they couldn't take away from him.

He knew a lot of poetry by heart. Up until today his recall had been fairly random, but he decided now that he needed some kind of a system. In fact all sorts of approaches were possible, since he had no idea what he knew until he remembered particular bits of it. Having been denied a Bible, he took a perverse satisfaction in beginning there. Ironically, he had carried off the school Scripture prize for Bible Recitation for six years running, as well as the largest number of undischarged detentions. The sun had still been on the ceiling when he started this morning, and now his stomach told him it must be around dinner time, and he was still no further than the Psalms:

> If I take the wings of the morning,
> And dwell in the uttermost parts of the sea
> Even there shall thy hand lead me,
> And thy right hand shall hold me.

The last lines meant nothing to him, but he repeated the first two twice more, and the four walls of his cell receded just a little. *If I take the wings of the morning.* Scripture twice a week, Old Testament and New Testament. The classroom at Ogg's Cove, with the morning sun and the sound of the sea coming in both together through the open window, and the voice of Miss MacIlwraith droning through the Pentateuch. The first day he'd gone to school he'd come home and told his parents that it had been all right, but he didn't think he'd go again. Even when they'd explained to him over and over again he hadn't really understood. He went, sure enough, every day, on his new red bike that his Pappa had taught him to ride, but when he got there he forgot that he had to stay inside, and he'd wander off when no one was looking, down to the beach usually, or sometimes up to the green slopes of Mount Prosper. He had no memory of ever being brought back.

The day he did remember was the time that Miss MacIlwraith stood there with a red face talking very loudly, telling him he was bad, and that she'd make him learn, once and for all. There was a terrible threat in the way she said it, although he didn't know what the words meant: *once and for all*. She'd taken one of the girls' skipping ropes and looped it round his bare leg, and round the leg of the table, round and round and round, and then she'd tied a knot in it, a hard knot that he wasn't able to undo, even if she'd not been standing guard to make sure he didn't try. Then she went on teaching the class, without looking at him.

He'd sat there, not sobbing aloud, but weeping in silent abandonment until the bell for dinner went and she finally untied the rope and let him go. He could remember the feel of the tears coursing down his face and dripping off his chin. He'd cried like that without stopping in front of the whole class, and he hadn't cared what they'd thought. He could feel the rope, not very tight, but firm around his calf, and the cold shiny feel of the table leg against his skin, and he was utterly devastated. When she untied him at dinner time he shot away out of the door, on to his bike, and straight back home.

His Pappa had been angry. To begin with Jared thought the anger was with him, and that frightened him, being unprecedented. But it wasn't that; he could remember his mother saying, 'No, Jack! Jack, wait, no!' and his Pappa shaking her off and going out to his van, and just before he slammed the door he'd said, 'I'll give that woman a piece of my mind. And that headmaster. That's no way to run a school. No way to treat a child.' And he'd driven off. His mother had taken Jared by the hand and led him indoors. He couldn't remember what had happened after that.

School had had some good bits: nature study and poetry. The poem for the week had been pinned up on the noticeboard in the corner. They had to copy it out in their best writing and take it home to learn. Learning poetry was easy.

Four and twenty ponies trotting through the dark
Brandy for the parson, baccy for the clerk,
Laces for the lady, letters for the spy,
Watch the wall, my darling, while the gentlemen go by.

Every spring at school they grew hyacinths in jars of water on the window sill, and collected tadpoles which slowly turned into frogs. Sometimes the tadpoles ate each other. The first piece of scientific research he'd ever done was after he asked Miss MacIlwraith when frogs had come to Hy Brasil. She didn't know, but his Pappa took him to the library in St Brandons to find the answer. There wasn't one, exactly, but they found the first mention of frogs in the Rev. Archibald Fitzroy's *Fauna of Frisland* published in 1856. Jared could remember the feel of the heavy leatherbound volume in his hands, and the delicate accuracy of the etchings. It was the beginning of an enchantment.

See he comes, the human child
To the waters and the wild
With a fairy hand in hand
From a world more full of weeping than he can understand.

Each year he'd made his way further up Mount Prosper. By the time he was nine he'd climbed right up as far as the precipices just below the summit. By the time he was nine other things had happened too.

The heart's echoes render
No song when the spirit is mute:—
No song but sad dirges,
Like the wind through a ruined cell,
Or the mournful surges
That ring the dead seaman's knell.

But he was getting out of order. Shelley had come into his life much later. The approach now was to think of the very first poems he could remember. 'I remember, I remember . . ., Away down the river A hundred miles or more . . ., His helm was silver And pale was he . . ., And naebody kens that he lies there . . .' Back, and back, and back. And away back beyond all of that, an image of a coal fire burning in the grate of a cast-iron stove. The sounds of the wind in the chimney and a low voice singing. The red light flickering through the darkening room, over the white nappies hanging on the drying rack over the fire, over the shiny surface of the black kettle on the stove, over the hands that held him close, and shining on the plain gold ring that he sometimes tried vainly to prise off her finger:

I love my little laddie
You're just like your daddy,
I love my little laddie
I love you 'cos you're mine.

There was a sudden grating noise. Jared opened his eyes. The steel door swung open. He felt cold all over, and his skin inside the loose shirt prickled. Then he saw who it was, and he jumped to his feet and hugged him.

'Ishmael!'

It was all he could say, for a moment. Ishmael took him by the shoulders and looked him searchingly in the face. 'Jed? Are you sick? You've been sick?'

'No, not now. I'm sorry I can't open the window.'

'Look at your eye!' Ishmael turned him to the light. 'Who did that? Look at you. Where you're not purple you're white as a sheet. They beat you?'

'Beat me?' Jared touched his bruised face. 'That was when they took me. That's all.'

Ishmael, still holding Jared by the shoulder, turned to the warder at the door. 'All right. Lock us in, then, and go away.' The door closed. 'Half an hour, Jed. Sit down. There's a lot I need you to tell me.'

Jared was looking puzzled. 'You can't have got my letter? They only let me write it last night.'

'No, I haven't had a letter. Your girl – Sidony – came straight over to Ferdy's Landing after they'd taken you. It's taken me this long to get someone to let me see you. But I haven't wasted my time. Jed, we don't have long. Tell me everything, as straight as you can. You've had time to think. What have you done that anyone wants you in here for?'

'I haven't been smuggling drugs, for a start.'

'You don't need to tell me that. So what have you been doing that I don't know about?'

'Ishmael, about Sidony . . . Was she all right?'

'Oh yes, she's all right. Upset about you, of course, but then she's in love with you, so it's only what you'd expect.'

'Really? Did she say so? Do you really think she is?'

'Yes. No she didn't. Yes I do. But we can't waste time on that now. Listen, Jed, I got you a lawyer.'

'Gunn and Selkirk?'

'No. They have other interests. I got you my own. Utterson. But it's best if this doesn't come to court. We don't want you up on a drugs charge when we know you'll be framed anyway. What I need you to do now is to tell me everything you did at the Pele Centre. Yes, Sidony told me about that. Go over it carefully, Jed. It's important.'

He listened intently, and only interrupted Jared once. 'You don't need to lie about that. I've talked to Peterkin. He's sore –

oh, not at you, the fool – but Olly sacked him. So would I have done. Couldn't you have found a better weapon for armed robbery than a forty-year-old shotgun?'

'Just how many weapons do you think I've got?'

'All right. Go on.'

When Jared had finished Ishmael said, 'So you only searched the shelves? You didn't look in his desk?'

'No. Why should I? I'd found what I was looking for.'

'You didn't touch the safe?'

'What safe?'

'There's a safe in the far corner behind his desk.'

'Is there? Maybe I noticed it. I didn't really look. Why should I? How do you suppose I'd break into a safe?'

'With difficulty. So these are the facts: you broke into the Pele Centre and took an antique goblet and some worthless bits and pieces that once belonged to Nicky Hawkins. You did this because you're obsessed by Spanish treasure and you thought you owed it to a dead friend. No, don't interrupt. For some reason this has put the wind up quite a lot of people in high places. So much so that they arrest you on a trumped-up charge and won't let you speak to anybody. Did you read all the papers you took away?'

'Of course not! I told you, they were Lucy's letters to Nick. Who do you think I am?'

'Never mind. I've read them all. Don't look like that. It's quite simple. As soon as Sidony told me what had happened I took her back to Despair, and I collected that box of Nicky's things. I thought someone else might get there all too soon if I didn't. I also searched your house, while Sidony was tidying up, in case there was anything else. Nothing. I read the letters you'd taken as soon as I got home. They confirm a few things about Nick Hawkins that I'd guessed already, but nothing new. There must be something else. The only person who's in a position to know just what you took or didn't take is Olly West. But Colombo says he didn't even know he'd been robbed until Baskerville told him.'

'*Baskerville* told *Olly*? The fucking viper.' Jared stared at Ishmael. 'But how did he find out about the Pele Centre?'

'Well, Jed, I wouldn't say stealth was your strong point. Now listen. I'm beginning to see my way. I'll have you out of here as soon as I can. But it won't be tomorrow.'

Jared's eyes dropped. 'Do you really think you will?'

'Sooner than if you're tried for possession of hard drugs.'

'Ishmael, I've thought and thought about it. I can't prove it. They could send me down for years if it comes to that.' Jared's voice cracked.

Ishmael regarded Jared's downbent head. 'That's why I won't let it come to that.' He touched Jared's arm. 'I'll get you out, I promise. Don't worry.' He glanced at his watch. 'Ten minutes. Right, tell me this: when you used to hang around with Nick at Ferdy's Landing, how much did you know about his drug smuggling?'

Jared went very still.

'Tell me, Jed. There isn't much time.'

'I can't,' said Jared hoarsely. 'I promised not.'

'Look at me!' commanded Ishmael. Reluctantly Jared raised his eyes. Ishmael gripped his shoulder. 'Jared, the man you promised is dead. Nothing you say or do touches him now. If you don't speak you'll probably die too, in here, and quite soon, and I won't be able to save you. What matters most?'

Jared stared at the concrete wall. Ishmael glanced at his watch, and waited. He was about to speak again when Jared suddenly began to talk in an expressionless monotone, apparently addressing the wall in front of him. 'It was only every few weeks or so. Nicky didn't have money for anything regular. And hardly ever in winter, because the weather had to be right. The tip-off was easy: just a phone call. The rendezvous was west of Brentness. You line up the Despair light and the tip of the Ness. Two degrees north of west. It had to be there; it's the only place on the north coast that's not visible from Despair. The light was still manned then, remember. Now it's automatic it must be a lot easier. We used Nick's dory. No lights, of course, until we were round the Ness. Then we'd signal. I never went aboard. I had to stay with the boat. They'd lower a ladder for Nick, and he'd go up with the money, and then he'd come back after quite a long while – I used to get pretty cold – and they'd lower the stuff down after him. It was mostly dope to start with; the bricks came in big square bales. Then it got to be more cocaine each time, until it was hardly worth bothering with the dope at all. The coke came in a couple of fifty pound sacks, heavy duty plastic. We'd get it back to the Landing and take it up to the house on the wheelbarrow. Mamma never knew I was out; I used to wait till the sitting room clock struck eleven – I could hear it through the ceiling – and climb out my window and down the pear tree. I used to keep myself awake reading with my torch under the bedclothes. Mamma was always in bed by half past ten. The scariest part was cycling over the mountain without lights. Once I was with Nick I was never scared, though I damn well should have been. We went out on some bad nights, and it wasn't much of a boat. I didn't think anything of it then; I trusted him, you see. Though sometimes on the way back it was me that had to steer. In summer it would be dawn, and that made it easier.'

Ishmael glanced at his watch. 'The name of the trawler?'

Silence.

'Jed, it's life or death. I mean it. The name of the trawler?'

Jared hid his face with his hand. '*Santa Perpetua*.'

'Registration?'

'Panama.'

'Captain?'

'I don't know.' Jared turned towards him suddenly. 'I truly don't! Nicky never told me anything. If I asked him anything he'd say I was just a kid and curiosity killed the cat. I only know what I saw. And now I've told you all of it.'

'Just a kid,' repeated Ishmael grimly. 'So. Who bought the stuff from Nick?'

'I don't know! He never told me anything like that!'

'You never saw anyone at Ferdy's Landing? No visitors? From St Brandons, maybe?'

'No! No! I don't know! I've told you everything I remember!'

'OK, OK. The warder'll be here any minute.' Ishmael looked at his watch, and then searchingly at Jared's face. 'You're all right, Jed? They've not hurt you any more than what I can see? No? Well, Anna gave me a basket of food for you, but they took it off me. I hope you see some of it. And I couldn't bring in any papers of any kind. But Sidony told me to send you her love, and she's sorry she wasn't more use to you.'

'But she was! She did all that anyone could! Tell her please. Tell her . . . Oh, never mind. Send her my love. Tell her I wrote her a letter.'

The key turned in the lock, and the door swung open.

When Ishmael had gone they came in and searched Jared thoroughly and ungently. Afterwards he lay curled up on his bed, shocked and shaken. It was a long time before he could begin to think himself away, and when at last he was able to form the images inside his head, it was under the sea that he conjured up, a dim, free-floating world with no boundaries, no malice, no words. Gradually he stopped shivering, and began to be sleepy. He was almost gone when a sudden jerk recalled him, and he sat up suddenly.

The plastic jug and half-filled cup slid off the shelf and fell to the floor with a clunk. He stared down at the widening puddle on the concrete. There was a sudden huge booming from underneath, a roaring like the wind, and from deep inside the building came a long grinding groan, as if the place itself were being stretched in agony. The floor dropped. He was still in the shock of it when huge cracking noises started exploding all round him. 'Oh, Jesus, no.' His whisper was lost in the din. He jumped up, reeling on the uneven floor, looking for somewhere to shelter, but knowing there was nowhere at all. He hammered desperately on the door, but the noise of his fists was drowned in an avalanche of falling sound. He fell back, knuckles bleeding, and curled up tight on the bed, pulling the blankets over him, and covering his head as much as he could with his arms.

TWENTY

Sidony Redruth. Ravnscar Castle. July 28th.
Notes for *Undiscovered Islands* (working title).

I SAT OPPOSITE Lucy at the round table in the window, just as I had the first morning I was at Ravnscar. So many things were unchanged: the pile of magazines, Ginger curled up purring next to me, the Cluedo set next to the toaster on the shelf behind me, the trolley with its tray of spreads and home-made jams. Some things were different: a chess set in a wooden box now lay on top of the Cluedo, the date on the two-day-old copy of *The Hesperides Times* said July 26th, 1997, and the yellow file had gone from underneath the magazines. It wasn't grey outside; it was a wild mix of wind and light, and there were white horses right across the sound. On another day I'd have wanted to be out there, down on the shore with the sun and the flying wind and the breaking waves. But the other thing that had changed was me. When something is terribly wrong, when you're hurt or bereaved or afraid for a friend, then a dead weight sits at the back of your head, and though you might not be thinking of it all the time your body knows that life isn't right. You feel like an alien looking out on a world that used to be normal. I'd been feeling like that for a week now. It was bad, but it would be worse to be locked in and not knowing what they were going to do to you, especially if you were more frightened of that than of anything else in the world.

A bundle of old letters lay on the table between us, loosely tied with string. 'I didn't look at them,' I told Lucy again. 'Nor did Jared, except just to see what they were. I promise.'

'I don't think I'd care any more if you had.' She pushed her fringe back wearily, quite unlike her usual vigorous gesture. I wished for the hundredth time she'd just get her hair cut, at least at the front if she wanted to grow the rest of it long. 'Olly West is a total bastard,' she repeated. 'I don't know what we do about Jed, but I can't help being quite glad that man hasn't got these any more.'

'You *knew* he had your letters?'

'Oh, God, yes. I've known ever since he took them. I told him I didn't give a damn. He could publish them as a serial in the *Times* for all I cared. But Olly's not one to take no for an answer. Just on his own he's enough to drive a girl to America, even if nothing else had happened at all.'

'Did you know about the goblet?'

'No. Oh, I'd have recognised it if I'd seen it, but I've never been into Olly West's private office. I don't go near that man if I can help it. That goblet used to be at Ravnscar, you know. My father kept it for whisky, which he didn't drink often, but he never used it for anything else.'

'So how did it get from Ravnscar to Ferdy's Landing?'

She didn't answer. This is stupid, I thought. I'm sick of treating her life story as if it were the Eleusinian mysteries. After all, I've told her all about me. Aloud, I said, 'Maybe I should tell you that I know quite a lot about you and Nicky Hawkins.'

'Jared told you?'

'Yes. Why not? He isn't sworn to secrecy. And being your friend, naturally I was interested.' It's odd how a completely normal statement, or so it seemed to me, can sound so sacrilegious. I'd said it now, and I was feeling irritable because I was worried about other things. I plunged on. 'You know what? I think you ought to talk about yourself a bit more. All this reticence just isn't healthy. Keeping it to yourself the way you do: well, it can't be doing you any good.'

I waited to see if she'd walk out, or hit me. She did neither. She stared down at the letters, biting her lip. Then she swept them off the table and put them on the bench beside her, out of sight. 'You're not the first person to tell me that. My friend Io – the one I shared my apartment with in New York – she said just the same. You want to know how Nicky came to have that goblet?'

'Yes.'

I'd almost given up waiting by the time she answered me. 'When we were young, Nicky was my friend. My only real friend you could say. I was hurt when he came back to live at Ferdy's Landing and didn't visit. I went to see him. He wasn't very friendly. The only person he'd have around was Jed. Jed was just a kid, but kind of wild, I guess. In the end I talked Nick into coming up here, but when he arrived I didn't really know what to say to him. He said could he look round the place again? We'd played hide-and-seek all over, you see, when we were kids. So I got to showing him around, and we were kind of remembering stuff, and we started talking. We were in the Great Hall, and the goblet was there by my father's chair. Pappa used to have a dram sometimes late at night. It was left from that.

'Nicky said, "That's the goblet from the *Cortes*, isn't it?" And I said, yes, and I asked him how he knew. He told me the story.

'It was in the year 1703, when Roderick Morgan was Master of Ravnscar, and James Hawkins lived down at the Landing. They were both buccaneers, of course, but Morgan was abreast of the new era. He'd been educated in England, and he corresponded with Pepys, Addison and Defoe. He married an English captain's daughter. His sons all went to Eton and his daughter married an earl. He built himself a trading office and warehouses down by the new commercial harbour in St Brandons. It was he that commissioned Queen Anne Terrace to be built – you know – the street just down from Government

House, overlooking the harbour. Number One was to be his town house, and the others were the first spec-built houses in Hy Brasil. They say Roderick Morgan was a bit of a dandy. His wig and snuffbox are in my father's dressing-room, if you want to look sometime. He had several ships, and if nearly half of them had log books and bills of lading for anyone to read – well, who was going to ask questions about the rest?

'Hawkins was a different character altogether. He'd lost his right hand in a skirmish off the Orinoco River, and instead he wore a hook.'

'Oh come on, Lucy. Not a hook! You're not asking me to believe that?'

'I'm not asking you to believe anything; I'm telling you the story. He sailed his own ships, and there was nowhere in the seven seas he hadn't voyaged and plundered. They say he took a British man o' war just out from Trinidad, though he only had six men and a jolly-boat, and he made his prisoners sail it home under his own command. When the top peak of Despair heaved over the horizon, he made every man of them walk the plank. They say he was marooned for a year on Ascension, when his crew mutinied because he wanted to sail them out of the Atlantic. When the mutineers got home to Hy Brasil their wives took pity on Hawkins, and forced their men at gunpoint to go back south and fetch their captain home. The acting captain was a woman called Laura Lee who was Hawkins' mistress down at the Landing. She bore him ten children, I believe, and in the end he married her, but I've heard too that he had as many descendents over again in ports from Rio to Riga, at least that's what they say. Drink was his downfall. Drink, and lust for treasure, and the cards.

'He used to gamble with Morgan, in winter when they were both at home. Dice, cribbage, picquet and two-handed ruff. They say in Ogg's Cove that maybe Morgan marked the cards. I don't believe that, but it was known he had the luck of the devil; they used to say it was the devil's luck went with the treasure of

Ravnscar, and maybe it still is. So the years went by, and Hawkins gambled away his treasures and his land. Even the house at Ferdy's Landing was held under mortgage. Hawkins was a desperate man.

'The green goblet was his talisman. When he played he'd drink from that cup and not from any other. He'd wear his black hatband, and a certain patch over his eye, and odd stockings, and the green goblet was the one cup he'd drink from. He thought it held his luck in it. The night came when he had nothing left to pledge. It all belonged to Morgan. So Hawkins pledged his green glass goblet, and Morgan dealt the cards, and they played. And Hawkins lost, so Morgan took the goblet away with him, back up to the castle of Ravnscar, and he put it on the table in his room before he went to sleep. And the next morning Morgan was found lying in his great four-poster bed – the one I sleep in now – with his throat cut. What's more, all the deeds of the mortgages were gone from Morgan's desk, and Hawkins' notes of hand, and no one ever saw them again. There was nothing left written to prove that Hawkins owed Morgan anything. So Hawkins got back all he had lost, all except for the glass goblet which hadn't been touched. It was still there on the table by the bed. So it stayed up at Ravnscar, and it never left the castle again until Nicky Hawkins came home.

'Nicky told me all that. I said to him, "Well, maybe you should take it back." I didn't say, but we both were thinking, that all the land and ships that James Hawkins once owned were gone now anyway, everything but the old house at Ferdy's Landing, and that was pretty much falling down. Nicky said no, the goblet had been won in fair play, and it could only be got back the same way again. "Do you play cards?" he asked me.

' "Only beggar-my-neighbour," I said to him.

'He thought that was so funny. I was offended, but not much. Where would I have learned to gamble, for God's sake? "All right," Nicky said. "I'll play beggar-my-neighbour with you, and the winner takes the cup."

'So we played. At first I was winning, and I thought the game was mine. Nick only had one card in his hand. A knave, it turned out. He got a queen back from me, and then he went on winning, and so it went, to and fro, until I'd lost all my cards. So I gave him the goblet, and he took it back to Ferdy's Landing. He kept it on the mantelpiece with a couple of matchboxes in it.'

It seemed an odd way to put it, so I asked, 'Why two matchboxes?'

'One with matches in, of course, on top. The one underneath was always the same one. Bryant and May Safety Matches. He kept other stuff in there.

'A few days later I went to Ferdy's Landing. I felt we'd more or less got back to being friends again. Not quite. The place was filthy. Jed was there, sweeping the floor. After a bit Nicky sent him off, and then he said, "I've got a pack of cards too. Do you want to play beggar-my-neighbour again?"

'"What for?" I asked.

'He said, "How about every time anyone loses cards they take off something they're wearing, and how about every time anyone wins any they put something back on?" Strip beggar-my-neighbour, in fact. I looked at him. As far as I could see he was wearing jeans and a t-shirt. Maybe pants underneath, though with Nick one couldn't be sure. He was barefoot. I was wearing eight separate garments. I agreed.

'I guess we both cheated. Nobody won. In the end we both lost something we were possibly just as well without. We never finished the game anyway. But that's neither here nor there. It was the goblet you were asking about.'

'Can I ask you something else?'

'Ask what you like. I might not answer.'

'Did Nicky have any secrets?'

'Of course. Don't we all?'

'I'm not sure. I'd have to think about that. But what I mean is, do you know what Nicky kept down at Ferdy's Landing that would have made it worth while for Olly West to break in there?'

'If Olly were a different kind of character, I'd say the answer to that was pretty obvious.' She gave me a speculating look. 'Jed didn't tell you Nick was a dealer?'

For an uncomprehending moment I imagined Nicky foxing the cards at beggar-my-neighbour, then I remembered the matchbox. 'Oh, you mean *drugs*?'

'So Jed didn't say? Poor kid. Nicky made him swear on a skull right on the stroke of midnight, down among the broken graves in the Hawkins vault under St Bride's Church, that he'd never breathe a word to a living soul. I was there. Only Nicky knew how to frighten Jed. Give that boy threats or orders and you could be damn sure he'd go off and do the opposite. But try giving him nightmares . . . Like I say, Nicky knew how to handle Jed.'

I didn't want to think about Jared's nightmares, so I said crossly, 'But how could Nicky deal drugs stuck out at Ferdy's Landing?'

'Don't you know anything? They came by sea, of course. A secluded anchorage, miles from the nearest village, open to the west, close to the main sea routes from South America through to Europe . . . What more could you ask? Nicky didn't have a bean. He had to live somehow. When his mother left his father she took Nick back home with her to Colombia. Nick wasn't short of relations on his mother's side, so it wasn't hard for him to fix up contacts. It was a good time too. The market for cocaine was expanding fast. Most of it got sold on, and ended up in Europe, but a bit stayed right here. All Nick needed to do was drop into St Brandons once a week and do a little obvious shopping.'

'Were you involved?'

'Oh, no. I didn't approve, to tell you the truth. But what else could he have done? It's in our blood in this country; it's only the product that changes. I suppose I did do some things I wouldn't do now.'

'But . . . I thought it was *papers* Olly West was supposed to have got hold of. Ishmael thought the government were worried because Jared had taken papers, but there were only your letters, and you wouldn't have written anything important . . . what I mean is, anything that would be important to anyone else. Ishmael thought there might be other documents in there, that Jared hadn't looked at, but there weren't, only letters from you.'

Lucy frowned. 'Nicky kept his private papers in his father's tin army trunk. He kept his accounts in there too. I can remember him doing them. There were a lot of used envelopes with money in, in various currencies. And notes about his contacts, all in code. I remember us making silly jokes about the codes. And there were some family papers too. I think he kept some of the stuff underneath sometimes, too. But that was hidden in various places at different times.'

'The only time Jared ever tried to open that trunk Nicky boxed his ears. He said it really hurt.' I looked tentatively at Lucy. 'Can I ask you . . . is it true you cheated on Nicky in the end?'

'If Jed told you, I'm sure he told you the truth.'

I found this enigmatic, and took my courage in my hands and said so.

'I don't mind you trusting Jed,' she answered. 'I'd ask you to take what some people say with a pinch of salt though.'

'You'd rather I didn't talk about it?'

'Here.' Lucy got to her feet so suddenly that I jumped. 'I'm going to let you read something. Wait here.'

I sat at the window looking at the trees tossing in the wind. In less than five minutes I heard her thumping down the private staircase again. She ducked under the red velvet curtain that hid the door so that it swirled out into the room, strode across to me, and thrust a single sheet of worn paper in front of my eyes. 'Read that!'

To Lucy Morgan, Mistress of Ravnscar, from the ancient order of Pirate Kings of Hy Brasil. Midnight, August 30th, 1984.

Inasmuch as our sworn brother Nicholas Hawkins of Ferdy's Landing was beguiled to his untimely death, we hereby swear vengeance on the author of his betrayal.

We pronounce this doom: that, if the woman who brought about the death of our brother uses her devious arts on any man again, her evil fate will fall, not on herself, but him. To be beloved of her is a perilous road, and the man who treads it will do so to his own destruction. So she willed it once. So let it be, so long as she shall live. This we swear.

As heir of Ravnscar she is sworn to preserve our safety and our secrets. If by making this doom known she brings the forces of the outside world to bear upon us, she knows already the fate that must befall her.

I read it through twice. '*Crap*,' I said. 'Lucy, that is the most ridiculous load of sadistic sexist *crap* I ever read in all my life.' I'd have torn it up, but she snatched the thing away from me.

'Sidony, you can't do that! OK, it's all you say it is. Sure, it sucks. But this is Hy Brasil you're in. Maybe it's also true.'

'I wouldn't let myself be put upon by anything as revolting as that anywhere on this entire planet! If it's crap in Penzance or Islington, it's crap in Ravnscar. You surely aren't going to take any notice of that poison pen kind of nastiness. They're usually written by frustrated spinsters, anyway.'

'Now who's being sexist? And they don't have women in the Pirate Kings.'

'Looks to me like that's their problem.'

'Sidony, it's nice of you to be angry. It's nice of you to care. But I'm telling you it's different here. They mean what they say. Don't you understand? I've had to live with their judgment for the last thirteen years.'

'For Christ's sake! You're not telling me that's why you won't go to bed with Colombo? You wouldn't let those wretched Pirate Kings do that to you? You must be nuts!'

At that point she lost her temper too. 'Nuts, you think? And what would you feel then, if Colombo just happened to fall over the cliff? What then? You'd say then you didn't want to live on that sort of planet and therefore it hadn't really happened.'

'I wouldn't say anything of the kind, because it damn well wouldn't happen! No one's going to push Colombo off anything! If you mean Mr Baskerville, he wouldn't, because he likes him. he talked about him when we were having tea and it was bloody obvious he thought Colombo was the rising hope of the stern unbending *Hesperides Times*. Lucy, you can't *do* this to yourself! I mean, I know what happened was awful. I think you're really brave; I don't think I'd ever have faced this place again if it had happened to me. But you can't let it ruin the rest of your life! Of course Colombo wants you! There's nothing wrong about that. I bet he's frustrated as hell. I would be. I don't see why you have to push him off all the time! You'd probably be a lot happier if you didn't.'

I waited for her to shout back. That's what Arthur or Jared would have done. Instead she collapsed into a crumpled heap, buried her head in her arms on the table, and burst into hysterical sobbing. I never felt so little feminine solidarity in my life. I didn't want her. I wanted Jared, but Jared was in prison. But I couldn't just tell her to shut up. I took one reluctant step towards her.

There was a faint sound, like an explosion far away. I didn't exactly hear it, but in a strange way it seemed to vibrate inside the walls. Ginger, curled up on his cushion next to me, sat up, ears pricking. The red curtain rustled, but there was no wind. Ginger leapt off the windowseat and shot underneath the stove. Lucy felt it too. She raised her head, and sat quite still, listening intently. 'Did you hear that?'

'I heard something.'

'Strange,' said Lucy. She rubbed her eyes, and looked at me. 'I'm sorry, I didn't mean to weep. I'll be fine now. I think it's because you remind me of Io. I haven't heard from her all this summer.'

'Do you miss her?'

'More than anybody in the world.' Lucy stood up, and I knew she was going to put the kettle on. Our habits were becoming one another's. As if she knew what I was thinking, she said, 'You've quite a temper, haven't you? I'll miss you when you go back to England. Very much.'

TWENTY-ONE

THE PRIVATE LOUNGE at the Red Herring is permanently booked on Mondays for Whist Drives, on Wednesdays by the Dorrado Poems and Pints Meeting and on Thursdays for practice by the West Coast Madrigal Singers. On Fridays and Saturdays it accommodates customers who want quieter surroundings than the live music and crowds downstairs. On Tuesdays and Sundays the room is available for private functions. Its popularity might seem unaccountable, since the furnishings are Spartan, and the decor given over exclusively to British Railways and Steamship Company posters. Combined with a cracked brown linoleum floor, an institutional wall clock with a loud tick, uncomfortable benches, small round stained tables at just the wrong height, and a lingering smell of ancient cigarettes, you'd think the posters would create an unsettlingly transient effect, suggesting as they do that customers are there to catch something that might be leaving at any minute. But in Hy Brasil a British Railways waiting room is a novelty and a joke, and when Ernest's grandfather opened up the room in 1910 he knew exactly what he was doing. Its popularity has never waned.

No one had booked the lounge tonight. Colombo's sister Natalia helped in the bar on Sunday evenings, and the landlord was using his private room himself. He had three companions. They sat with their heads together at the table nearest the window, their backs to the empty hearth. On the table was a jug of cider and three pint mugs, and a glass of orange juice.

'The point is,' Colombo was saying, 'that the prison's in a dangerous condition and it's been evacuated. All that end of the industrial estate between Port o' Frisland and St Brandons' Dock is damaged, though I heard they're allowing the cider factory to open again tomorrow. Today the whole area was deserted except for the surveyors, the earth sciences people, Tommy Zakis who won't move out of his bus and police patrols on the lookout for looters. Apparently the epicentre was on a direct line between Mount Brasil and Port o' Frisland. Five point six on the Richter scale. There've been two more minor tremors, and the road to the Point is still cordoned off. I was down there this morning, strictly unofficially. I got my photos and I even got an interview out of Tommy in exchange for a bag of groceries. I looked at the prison, and the concrete's cracked all the way down from the roof. You can see daylight up above if you look in at the main door. Thank God it didn't happen in the town. They've moved all the prisoners into the old British fort at the Point, right on the far side of the damaged area. What I'm saying is, the fort's cut off from everywhere else, with the road still more or less impassable.'

'Great,' said Ishmael. 'Just like Alcatraz.'

'God help the poor souls,' said Per. 'They'll all get bronchitis in that place. Is it the dungeons they've put them in? I don't think our Jed will do very well underground.'

'No, but the point I'm trying to make is that there's no modern security system in the fort. I'm saying there might be a possibility of going round by sea without anyone knowing.'

'What were you thinking to do when you got there?' asked Ishmael. 'Disguise yourself as a minstrel and sing outside his window? If he has a window, that is. Or dress up as his mistress and carry in a basket of freshly baked bread with a file in it, and then take his place?'

'Oh, all right. But you can't just ignore the earthquake. It seems providential to me.'

'So what isn't?' said Ishmael. 'Anyway, Providence has given

St Brandons a nasty shock, when everyone's been assuming for the last two hundred years that the fault was only on the west side.'

'Nicely put,' said Colombo. 'Tidesman could use that. You wouldn't mind?'

'Use what?' said Ishmael, but didn't wait for an answer. 'My guess is that security is as tight as it ever was, if not more so. They knew how to build a jail in 1812. It's probably more secure than the new one. Even if there were a way to get him out, what would be the good of that? Where would he go? Would you ship him out of the country? How? Through customs at the airport? On the ferry? Or would you hide him in Hy Brasil? Where? Under Ravnscar? Or maroon him permanently on Tegid Voel? Do you think that's what he wants? No, he has to go free. Free to live his own life in his own place. It's not getting him out of there, it's getting him his rights that'll free him. That's why my plan is better.'

'Can it be done soon?' said Per. 'If he's locked up alone, the way you describe it, it must be bad. And in an earthquake too. That would be an upsetting thing to happen to anyone. I'm afraid that if he gets rattled he'll fight, and then they'll have a real charge to fasten on him. You know what he's like.'

'No,' said Ishmael. 'I don't think he will. He wasn't rattled when I saw him. And maybe he's not alone now. They won't have the same accommodation in the fort.'

'It seems to me,' said Ernest, 'that Jared must look after himself just now. Ishmael has a plan, or he wouldn't have asked us to meet. I'm intrigued; you seem to have picked an interesting set of conspirators. Isn't it time to tell us what you want?'

'Yes.' Ishmael looked round at them. 'For a start, I picked you because you're Jared's friends. I'm hoping you may be willing to take a small risk on his behalf. I also chose you because this isn't just about Jed. He's been framed on a drugs charge: you know that. It's a lie, but the drugs themselves are real. They're here. Make no mistake about that. I don't think any of you, wherever your loyalties may also lie, believe that our economy should be maintained by illegal traffic in drugs. I know Colombo doesn't. He's written about it; he's even tried to drown himself in his attempt to find out what's going on. Well, I guess I can offer you the best scoop you're ever likely to get. That's why I picked you. I picked Ernest because I know he agrees with me on the drugs issue, and also because he's bound by an oath to Nicky Hawkins. I picked Per because he was Jack Honeyman's friend, and since Jack disappeared he's been as good a friend to Jared. I picked all of you because I think you're capable of carrying out what I have to suggest. Am I right? Do you want me to tell you my idea?

'Very well, then. We have to act fast. The earthquake was providential, but not in the way Colombo thinks. An earthquake was the one thing that could have given us enough time. Now, listen.'

Colombo stood in the dark, listening. It was a clear night, and the sky was full of stars. There were more stars in the sky in Hy Brasil than anywhere else he'd been on earth. The Milky Way arched over him like a broad road, until it disappeared behind the looming blackness of Mount Prosper. The trees below were hushed and silent, without a breath of wind. He could hear the faint beat of the waves along the shore.

There were small sounds in the building behind him, and a faint rectangle of light along the edges of the blacked-out window. He felt again for the gun inside the holster at the back of his belt. He didn't like having it. That moment when Ishmael had opened the safe in his office, and brought out those sleek black weapons, small enough to be children's toys, Colombo had felt cold inside. But he'd had to admit he did know how to use a hand-gun; his brother-in-law, who was in the coastguards, had taught him when he was sixteen. So now he was in temporary possession of a nine millimetre Glock semi-automatic, with instructions to fire if necessary, on guard outside the Pele Centre, now deserted for the first time since Saturday's earthquake. If Ishmael was right, it probably wouldn't be left unattended for very long.

They'd waited in the cover of the wood until Olly West finally drove away in his rusted Ford. In the dark of the wood they'd been invisible even to each other, dressed in black from head to foot, three of them with their faces smeared in black. Just before they'd gone in Ishmael had said softly, but they could hear the smile in his voice, 'In we go, then. Four black brothers.' It seemed to Colombo an extraordinary moment for anyone to feel amused; he'd never seen Ishmael like this before.

The break-in had been easy. Ishmael had been to visit Allardyce, and he'd had a quiet word with a friend who worked in Ogg's Cove police station. He'd opened the door with two keys, one for the yale and one for the mortice lock, and as soon as they were in he'd keyed in the code number for the alarm system and switched it off. 'No point being complicated when you can be simple,' he'd said. They'd brought rolls of blackout material borrowed from the cellar at Ravnscar, and it had taken less than five minutes to tape up the windows that faced on to the road.

Ishmael had ordered Colombo out to his post. Ernest had already found the safe in the small office, and was examining the combination lock. 'I hope to God you're right, and Olly didn't change it after Allardyce left.'

'You can bet Olly never guessed Allardyce knew. It wouldn't have occurred to him that the man would watch him through the back window with a telescope. And all Allardyce ever took was Olly's so-called confidential report on himself, and even then he returned the original as soon as he'd copied it. Go on, try it.'

Two turns to the right. Twenty-three. Three turns to the left. Nine. Two turns to the right. Forty-eight. The lock had clicked, and the metal door swung open. Colombo had caught a glimpse of a chaotic jumble of heaped-up paper, and then Ishmael had looked round and seen him still standing there.

'Man, what are you doing? They'd court-martial you for this! Out!' Colombo had been startled, as he hurried back to his post, by the speed and efficiency with which Per was already at work on the filing cabinets in the main office. Per just glanced at Colombo as he passed, but Colombo read in that quick look that his own dereliction from duty had been noted. He'd always seen Per as a gentle, methodical man, but maybe there was a streak of ruthlessness in more people than he'd realised. He was aware of being found wanting in this unexpected atmosphere of military discipline. Possibly an education in English Literature and Journalism had not covered everything. But he knew his reactions were quick, and he could keep watch. His hand closed again on the grip of the gun, and he walked quietly across the turning circle so he was standing directly above the silent trees, listening intently.

There was a rustling down in the wood: a night bird perhaps. A tiny breeze came in from the sea and riffled through the summer leaves. Over to the east he could see the yellow glow from the lights of Lyonsness. He looked back to the closed door. He longed to look inside again but he'd got the message now very clearly. For the tenth time he looked at the luminous dial on his watch. Fifty minutes. When the door did finally open, the light had been carefully switched out first.

Someone whispered, 'Colombo?'

He could tell from Per's voice that they'd done it, even before he went on: 'Got it. Time for photos. I'll take over here.'

As soon as the door clicked to, the light flooded on again, so Colombo stood blinking, momentarily dazed. The work counter with the printer on it was dragged out into the middle of the room. In the space where it had stood the carpet was rolled back, and a section of loose chipboard had been lifted away. In the gaps between the joists below there were swathes of plastic covering. A section had been torn away, and inside there were – Colombo's heart jumped – small plastic packages, identical to the one Jed had picked up on Despair.

'My God!'

'Camera,' said Ishmael, and thrust it into his hands. 'We may not have long.'

While he took his photos, Ishmael and Ernest went through into Olly's private office. Colombo glanced in once, after he'd taken a photo from the main office doorway. He saw the safe gaping open. There were papers inside, and more papers piled up on the floor.

Ishmael looked up and saw him watching them. 'Are you done?'

'Not quite. I'll get a couple with the whole room in. So there's absolutely no mistaking it.'

'Get on with it, then.' Ishmael bent over the safe again, hiding its open door from view. Five minutes passed.

'I'm done.'

'OK.' Ishmael stood up. 'Samples. As many as we can get in those bags. Then we put everything back.'

But it was Colombo and Ernest who replaced everything. Ishmael was back in Olly's office, crouching in front of the safe, sorting rapidly through piles of paper, tossing some into a big black holdall, and piling up the rest on the floor. He came through when they'd finished. The office looked vacant and orderly as if it had never been touched. 'That's that, then. Ernest, get this stuff out of here, and the camera. Cache it where we said. You and Per keep watch. If we're interrupted, give the signal, but don't wait. The evidence is more important. You know what to do if I can't follow.'

They turned out the light and stripped off the blackout. The door stood open. Ernest and Per slipped away with their burdens into the edge of the wood. Ishmael waited until he heard the low whistle that meant Per was back at his post, and then he touched Colombo's arm and led the way back into Olly's private office. The blackout was still up in here. Colombo closed the door and switched on the light. Ishmael jerked his thumb towards the piled-up papers. 'We got the current stuff. All there, in Olly's writing. It's the other connection we still want. The desk's not locked. You try there.'

Colombo sat down in Olly's revolving chair. His hands were shaking, he noticed vaguely. They'd done what they came to do, nearly, and Ishmael was right. It was unlikely the place would be left unguarded for long. The word was almost certainly out by now that Ishmael had bribed his way into the prison and seen Jared. They should have been here two days ago, but the earthquake had kept the Pele Centre continually in operation ever since it happened. Olly had had to accept assistance from the University Geophysics Department, or rather, he'd been ordered to place his resources at their disposal. The place had been full of academics all weekend, day and night. Ishmael wouldn't have been the only one waiting for them to go away. Colombo leaned back, and felt the gun pressing against him, inside his jacket. He wished he were somewhere else.

While fear flittered at the back of his mind his hands were busy, and part of his mind was concentrated on the task in hand. The papers he was looking for would be fifteen to twenty years old. He flipped quickly through the laser-printed white sheets that filled the drawers. Nothing typewritten in the first drawer. The second held stationery and a bag of boiled sweets. The third was a mess of old invoices and handwritten accounts. The bottom drawer was a random mass of typewritten and hand-written paperwork. Colombo knelt down, and began to leaf through the sheets one by one. They all related to a controversy at a scientific institution in London back in the seventies, and didn't seem to be relevant at all.

'Ah!'

Colombo looked up. 'Got something?'

Ishmael held up a thin sheaf of papers. 'I think we're there. Take a look at this.'

Colombo stood up. There was a knock on the window. They both stopped dead. Per knocked again, and they heard him through the opening, 'Lights! Lights on the back road!'

Four minutes, Ishmael had said, if they sighted a light at the turn. Time for plan one. Get everything back. Papers in the drawer. Colombo stuffed the wodge he'd set aside in his jacket pocket. Drawers closed. Chair in place. Waiting for Ishmael. Ishmael piling up the papers. Deliberate, slow motion, almost. Colombo longed to hurry him. Papers in the safe. Door closed. A twist to the lock. 'Get the light off.' Click of the switch. Blackout ripped from the window. Material tumbling into his hands, covering his face, all over the place. Then he heard it. The gear change at the turn. Fifty yards away. He was shaking, couldn't get the stuff bundled through the window. Ishmael seized it from him and shoved it into Per's waiting arms. 'Out the door, man! Go!'

Through the hallway. The open door. Into the night. Lights on the hairpin bend. Turning his way. He'd be transfixed if they caught him. The light swinging slowly round. Himself running, feet pounding on the gravel. Into the dark. Off the edge of the road and into the forest. The safe dark. Uneven ground, knots of roots and branches snapping under his feet. The path suddenly vanishing. A shock of ground hitting him in the back. His hands scrabbling for purchase among prickling pine needles. Something hard pressing into the small of his back. Sweet Jesus, that gun! The safety catch was on, but even so . . . He rolled over fast and sat up. Lights and the sound of the car behind him. Slamming doors. Lights. Then voices on the road above him. A flood more light.

Colombo wriggled further into the shelter of the trees. Where was Ishmael? Had they left any traces? Any minute the search might start. He'd be caught here like a grounded duck. There was a sapling right by his head. Holding on to it, he pulled himself shakily to his feet. Like an idiot he looked once towards the lights behind him. The Pele Centre was lit from end to end. When he looked back into the wood again all he could see was green spots dancing in front of his eyes. Feeling his way with his hands, he part-ran part-slithered down the hill. Pine trees kept coming up to meet him. Barbed branches leaned across and swiped his face. The ground got steeper, gave way under him. He shot down a bank and fell feet-first on to the road, at the edge of the second hairpin.

Ernest ran out of the trees and grabbed his arm. 'Where were you? Come on!'

They were under the trees, moving downhill fast. Ernest lit the way ahead with cautious flashes of his pocket torch. 'Ishmael?' gasped Colombo.

'Yes, yes. Come on, man!'

And then they were out of the trees, on the bare hillside. The night was cool and smelled of salt. Stars blazed. They stopped, and over his own shuddering breaths Colombo heard the soft beat of the waves. Below the arch of the Milky Way came the regular flash of a brighter light. Two long, two short. The lighthouse was keeping its watch over the empty dark space on which it stood, the abandoned island of Despair.

TWENTY-TWO

Sidony Redruth. Ravnscar Castle. July 29th.
Notes for *Undiscovered Islands* (working title).

'I DIDN´T MEAN to get involved,' I said to Anna. 'But I knew I had, even before I got his letter. He'll get my answer today if they give it to him. I don't know: I suppose I must love him or something.' It was unlike me to speak so intimately to someone I'd known for hardly more than a week, but it had been an intense time, and I'd spent quite a lot of it at Ferdy's Landing.

'Well, why not? You have to get involved with something or someone in the end, or you might as well be dead. This bit of trouble will soon get sorted out. You can tell your parents you've made a fair choice. I know Jed; he has his faults, but they're all on the surface. The point is he'll be kind to you, and he's guileless: he couldn't lie without you knowing it. He won't change when things get tough. You're an Episcopalian and so is he; at least that's what his poor mother brought him up to be, though she was raised Catholic herself. Sex'll be good: he'll usually notice how you feel and he's obviously very healthy. Also he's the kind of man who'll love his children. I don't see how anyone could expect more than that.'

I couldn't reply for a minute, she took me so aback. This was leaping to far more conclusions than I'd ever, except possibly in my wildest dreams, begun to consider. Because people in this country speak English, one tends to assume they think the same thoughts we do. Wrong. Sometimes I realise I've strayed into another world. I didn't know what to say; political correctness just wasn't in it. It's occurred to me several times that there's a distinct lack of feminist consciousness in Hy Brasil. At last I said tentatively, 'I suppose one might also hope that a person was going to be interesting to talk to.'

'All the time?' said Anna. 'That's asking quite a lot.'

'Well, I think it's important.'

'Then I hope you're interested in salvage,' said Anna. 'And gannets. And money, or rather the lack of it. And listening to odd bits of poetry.'

I must have been in a weak state; when she mentioned the bits of poetry my eyes filled with tears. I looked down so she wouldn't see, and said, 'You do think Ishmael will get him out?'

'You can trust Ishmael.'

She was certain about that, even if I wasn't. I didn't say anything. Anna filled up my cup. Espresso is to Anna what tea is to Lucy: a panacea for all life's ills. I wish it were that simple. I could hear the shrill voices of Eva and Susanna through the open back door. They were in the tree house that burdened down the battered hawthorn tree outside the garden gate. Presumably Ishmael was the kind of man who loved his children, since Eva had told me that it was he who had made the tree house. I don't think our father ever knocked a nail into a plank in his entire life, but I think Arthur and I were just as lucky all the same.

Anna pushed a tin of flapjacks across to me, and said, 'You're serious about Jed, aren't you?'

I wriggled uncomfortably. What right had she to ask? Or I to answer, if it came to that? He wasn't here.

'Because in that case,' she went on, as if I'd spoken, 'I think perhaps I should show you what it is that Ishmael's taking to Government House.'

That puzzled me. 'But I know, don't I? I mean, he told us? The drugs and stuff from the Pele Centre? Everything he needs to prove it was Olly not Jared? And like I said, I promise I won't tell anybody until it all comes out.'

'Come into the office. Bring your coffee.'

I'd spent a fair amount of time in Ishmael's office this past week. It had a vacant look about it with the computers switched off, and Ishmael gone. I looked round at the blank screens. I'd hate to work in a place where you couldn't see out of the window.

'Sit down.' I sat obediently in Ishmael's office chair. Anna passed me a brown A4 envelope. 'I'll leave you to read these. Come through to the kitchen when you're done. Just shut the door when you leave and it'll lock itself.'

The sheets inside the envelope were fresh photocopies. The originals had been on smaller sheets. They were mostly documents with official letterheads, typed on an old-fashioned portable typewriter. There were also three long handwritten letters, each covering several pages. My hands felt cold and my stomach hollow. I had no reason to feel anxious, but it felt like a premonition. Anna closed the door quietly behind her. I raised my head and looked round the empty office. One of the skylights was open. I could hear the penetrating squeals of the little girls outside. I bent my head and began to read the first letter.

November 29th, 1979
Dear Lemuel,
As you requested, I am committing to paper the information I gave you yesterday, on the understanding that you take no further action than to deposit my statement, with the supporting evidence, with Messrs Utterson and Utterson, not to be referred to until November 29th, anno domini 2029, at which date the documents will be delivered into the hands of Jared Alan Honeyman, presently of Ogg's Cove, if living, or his heirs at law, if deceased. In the absence of any living descendants of John Alan Honeyman, formerly of Ogg's Cove, the papers are to be destroyed, unread, by the lawyers, as agreed. I cannot emphasise too strongly the necessity of placing these documents in safe hands as soon as possible; it is not too much to say that the peace, and

possibly the independent status, of our nation depend upon your immediate discretion in this matter.

I write under constraint, as you know. Your misapprehension as to the part played by myself is understandable, if unfortunate. I thought we knew one another a little better than that. As things now stand, it behoves me to clear my own name, for posterity if not in the eyes of my contemporaries. It is an honourable name, and although no one else now bears it, I would not see it ultimately dishonoured in the person of its last representative. In the immediate future the best we can hope for is silence.

As Librarian of our city library, I have, as you know, undertaken certain private enquiries for the government during the last twenty years, in cases where my expertise and access to information were relevant assets. It was with some reluctance that I agreed to compile a dossier on the post-revolution activities of John Honeyman, owing to natural feelings of loyalty towards a former comrade in arms. However, I was, and still am, persuaded in my own mind that my first duty is to my country. I enclose a xeroxed copy of the document in question. The evidence is incontrovertible: John Honeyman joined the Communist Party on February 4th, 1962, just two months after such affiliation was pronounced by our government to be illegal in the state of Hy Brasil. You gave it as your opinion yesterday that it was the mere fact of official prohibition that caused Honeyman to take this step. I find it difficult to believe that a man of even moderate sense would indulge in such an irrevocable step merely as an act of defiance against constituted authority. Jack never made any secret of his socialism, but an enquiry into his private actions has forced me to the reluctant conclusion that his apparently naïve idealism was in fact a carefully constructed façade for more subversive political activity.

Whatever Honeyman expected, or whether in fact he had

considered the matter seriously at all, inevitably demands were placed upon him. I incline towards your belief that he didn't realise what he was getting into. Unfortunately, however, the dossier includes incontrovertible proof, in the form of two intercepted letters in his own hand, of Honeyman's seditious correspondence with agents within the Soviet bloc. I do not need to explain to you, of all people, the sensitive nature of this kind of contact in Hy Brasil. Heroism is one thing, patriotism another; anachronistically perhaps, I believe in both. The fact remains, my dear Lemuel, that our nation exists courtesy of the White House, and did so from the moment you, Jas Hook, and I laid our mines in the NATO sewers. The government of the USA was prepared to bargain with us, as we had calculated, because it was in their interest that this nation should no longer remain a British outpost. Certainly we may well wish we were not totally dependent on their goodwill towards us; a wish changes nothing. We have no army. Our defence rests with the two hundred employees of the Hy Brasil Coastguard Service, and the benign attitude of the major power in the Atlantic since 1945. Repudiation of Moscow was a foregone condition. You know as well as I do the pressing reasons for our President's apparent volte-face, in terms of his former left-wing connections, once he was firmly instated.

Honeyman's implicit defection was potentially a serious embarrassment. You and I know all too well what it is to become an icon of revolutionary change within our own lifetime. The compensations may be gratifying in their way for a man of a less retiring disposition than myself; the burden is at times too wearisome. But heroic status also confers a certain immunity from the just enforcement of the very authority we risked our lives to set in place. Hook dared not arraign Honeyman for his socialist affiliations, because Hook himself gained the unanimous support of the people, in '58, through a public manifesto that was overtly socialist in principle. If Honeyman were allowed to defend himself publicly, he would be able to point out, with truth, that Hook had reneged on every point within the '58 manifesto, beginning with the first principle, that there would be free elections held in this country at a minimum of every four years.

That was why Hook asked me to prepare the false dossier. As a genuine socialist Honeyman could have become a martyr in the eyes of the people; as a British Loyalist he would merely be seen as a traitor. Ironically enough, it was simply a matter of twisting the evidence a little. Public opinion had looked askance at Jack for his continued adherence to *The Socialist Worker* after the Revolution. Was it not a British publication? Did it not arrive every week on the ferry from Southampton? It certainly didn't uphold a primary loyalty to one's own nation. I felt some compunction, but the fact remained that Jack had made himself vulnerable in the first place. He was one of those who'd fight for a lost cause just because it was lost. He'd turn in the moment of triumph for the sole reason that victory confers authority, and Jack would fight against institutionalised authority whoever upheld it. I should qualify that: he would fight against any *immediate* institutionalised authority. A totalitarian state in another hemisphere he was apparently able to regard with complacent and ill-informed idealism. I'll say no more on that; I can still respect the friendship that you felt for him.

Very well. You have here all the documents that confirm what I have written so far. You demand that I also tell the story that has not been written. With this I acquiesce, for the simple reason that I wish to clear my own name, in our history, as it will be read by posterity, if not in my own lifetime. I swear to you, Lemuel, that I believed Hook when he said the only possible solution was to exile John Honeyman for life.

Honeyman was arrested at 11.30 p.m, on December 24th,

1978, at his house in Ogg's Cove. He was at home; the arrival of the police was clearly utterly unexpected. He was immediately detained in the prison in St Brandons. A closed enquiry took place, inside the prison. I was not present. It was reported, eventually, that Honeyman pleaded guilty to espionage, sedition and treachery, in the face of proof positive that he was in the pay of the British Secret Services. Moreover, it was announced that he had a more immediate connection with the new British government then coming into power. The British general election in May 1979 was a just cause for anxiety for a post-imperialist ex-colony in the middle of the Atlantic. It was an emotive moment to reveal the contents of the false dossier on John Honeyman. A verdict of exile for life was pronounced.

On the evening of August 6th, 1979, Hook required me to be present at a final interview with Honeyman. I had no wish whatsoever to confront Honeyman again. We had been comrades, as I say, and although my first duty must always be to the security of my country, I could wish it had not demanded the sacrifice of a man I had respected.

I was with Hook in his office. Honeyman was escorted to the door, and sent in alone. I was shocked at the change in him. He'd been in prison eight months. I have never enquired what means were used to extract the plea of guilty, or whether indeed it was extracted at all. Lemuel, these papers must be placed in safe hands, as you promised, immediately. Only when I have your word that they are deposited in the vaults of Utterson and Utterson can I be certain that I have not, by writing this, precipitated my country into the horrors of insurrection and civil war. I had no idea, that I swear, what Hook intended. To cast me as witness was, I cannot help but feel, an act bordering on the diabolical. It is, and will always remain, my word against his. As I write, I am aware of the lack of authority in the words I inscribe. All I can give you is my sworn word.

I didn't even see him do it. I was looking at Honeyman, and Honeyman was looking at Hook. I saw Jack's face change, and I swung round, but too late. I heard the shot before I saw the pistol in Hook's hand. He said – I can quote verbatim; I'm unlikely to forget – 'So, Fernando. We have various possibilities. Either you did this, or I did. Either one of us acted in self-defence, or in cold blood. Or he seized the gun and did it himself. Or it never happened at all. I've shocked you, I can see. I think it's only fair, perhaps, if I offer you the choice.'

What choice was there, Lemuel? What could I have done? If we'd had a revolution at the end of '79, it would have meant civil war and very likely, given the tenor of the new government at Westminster, a British invasion. I think the only choice I had was to put my country first. Hook knew that, of course, which is why he chose me. And of course he explained to me that he had had no choice either. Exile, he said, was a romantic notion, but in an age of modern media and telecommunication, no longer a serious long-term possibility. The fact was that Jack, if given the chance, could tell his own version to the world, and what he had to say would come straight back to Hy Brasil. There was bound to be trouble if the man tried to contact his family, as he inevitably would. Jack, said Hook, hadn't the necessary ability to let go and move on.

And so I chose that it never happened at all. Three men knew the truth: myself, Hook, and his bodyguard Hands. It was Hands and I who had to dispose of the body. We chose the far side of Despair as being the most remote coast in Hy Brasil, well out of sight of any settlement. And I'll admit to thinking the place appropriate, because it was Jack's own fishing ground. We weighted the body with stones, and put him overboard about a mile out from the island, right on the edge of the deep. So that's where he lies, if there's anything left of him. I enclose no evidence for that part of my story. There is none. You only have my word for it.

I also enclose documentary proof of a flight made from St Brandons airport to Heathrow on August 10th, 1979, by a passenger carrying a new passport (he'd never been out of the country before) which identified him as John Alan Honeyman; citizenship, Hy Brasil; sex, male; d.o.b. 6/1/32; height, 5′ 9″; hair, light brown; eyes, blue; special peculiarities, none. There are no further records following the arrival of flight BA333 in London.

It's been a terrible thing to write this down. It haunts me, Lemuel. It's three months ago now, and still it seems like yesterday. Hook has a new carpet in his office. My God, it makes me sick to tread on it. But no doubt I shall serve the man to the end of my days, or his. I have no other choice.

You will inform me, if you please, as soon as these papers are safely deposited with Utterson and Utterson. I shall not rest easy until I know they are locked in that impregnable vault, and unattainable for the term of fifty years.

In spite of all, I am, sir, and hope to remain,

yrs,

Fernando Baskerville

I read the letter through twice. When I put it down my hands were trembling. I stared up through the skylight. The children in the tree outside were shrieking with laughter. A gull flew across the rectangular patch of blue above my head. After a bit I turned to the other papers, and read them through.

There were two letters in Jack's own writing. Unlike his son's flowing script, his handwriting was crabbed and sloped backwards, as if it wasn't something that came easily to him. But the content showed an ease of expression that was already familiar to me. The letters struck me as being extraordinarily innocent. He wrote to a Soviet agent as if he were a drinking partner in the Crossed Bones. He wrote his thoughts, or so it seemed to me, about why the state of his country seemed wrong to him, and how it upset him that promises had not been kept.

As if political promises were ever kept! It struck me that if a man genuinely trusted to that extent in the natural goodness of other people, even the ones employed by a totalitarian system, he was pretty well foredoomed to die, unless history had the decency to leave him alone.

The typewritten sheets were official communiqués, without either an addressee or a signatory. There was a copy of the paper confirming Honeyman's CP membership, and a contradictory statement about his affiliation with MI5. The dossier consisted mainly of a record of intercepted letters and tapped telephone calls. There was an official notice that prisoner J.A. Honeyman had been discharged on August 10th, 1979, and taken in a closed police van to St Brandons airport, and placed, still in custody, on Flight BA333 to Heathrow. Attached to that with a paper clip was a letter from British Airways confirming the details of Flight 333, and that the passenger had in fact travelled on the relevant date.

After I'd read it all, I turned back to Baskerville's letter. Then I read Jack's letters again. I felt cold and sick. It had never come home to me before that I lived in a world where this sort of thing could really happen. Whatever had really happened. Even with all the evidence sitting there in front of me, I realised I could only make up my own mind about that. It was all words, not proof. But behind it all there had been a real person, and all one could say for certain was that he had gone for ever.

I sat there so long that in the end Anna came back to look for me. Then I put the letters back in their envelope, and watched her open the safe, and replace them carefully exactly where they'd been. 'There's no need to mention this to Ishmi,' she said to me. 'In fact, better not.'

Back in the kitchen she made me more coffee, which I accepted although I felt quite jittery enough already, and as we talked I began to feel calmer, as if I were back in the real familiar world again. We didn't discuss the papers; Anna made it obvious that she wasn't going to do that. She talked about her girls, and how fond they were of Jared, and how now that Ishmael was so often busy, it was nice of Jared to take them out in his boat sometimes, fishing with handlines.

'Jared used to crew for Ishmael, didn't he?' I asked her.

'That's how we got to know him. It began the night Jed pinched our boat. Ishmi guessed who it was, when about midnight he found the boat gone. Olly West had warned him about Jed. So he sat up and waited. Jed was only fourteen. Sure enough, just after dawn, Ishmi saw the boat coming back. He watched Jed cut out the engine, to be quiet you see, and bring her in alongside and moor her. He was just creeping away up the jetty when Ishmi jumped him. He fought like a cat, Ishmi said, hardly Queensberry Rules, and he wouldn't seem to understand when he was beaten. In fact he bit; Ishmi still has the scar on his left hand, if you look closely. I was shocked by that, though Ishmi wasn't, but then nothing shocks him really. So Ishmi, with his hand all bleeding, dragged Jed into the caravan, and woke me up. We managed between us to calm him down a bit, and in the end we got him to talk to us. When Ishmi said maybe the best solution was to try him out as crew, I was doubtful. Rachel was still a baby; we were broke because all our money had gone into Ferdy's Landing; Ishmi was working part-time at the coastguards; and we were trying to build a house at the same time. I didn't think we needed a delinquent boy on our hands as well.

'But it worked fine. Ishmael was impressed by his seamanship, and at sea, he said, Jed would do as he was told, though on land it was a different matter. And Ishmi liked him. You don't notice the difference in their ages so much now, of course, but even before Jed went away he seemed to grow up pretty fast. With his mother being ill he had to. But Ishmi always liked his company. Jed could – still can – make him laugh. That isn't always easy to do, but Jed seems to know how. Ishmi liked Jed's poems; he was amused by all that. Apparently when there wasn't much doing out there, he'd say to Jed, "Let's have a poem, then," and Jed would always

produce one. Even Ishmi learned a few lines by heart, the bits he
liked best. He'd repeat them to me later, and then he'd laugh.
What was that one he liked again? I know:

> Then out spake brave Horatius,
> The Captain of the Gate:
> "To every man upon this earth
> Death cometh soon or late.
> And how can man die better
> Than facing fearful odds,
> For the ashes of his fathers,
> And the temples of his Gods . . ."

I'm sure Jed could tell you the rest of it. Ishmi used to say it
sounded pretty good against a bit of weather. The two of them
always got on. They've a fair bit in common. Ishmael had a
rough time growing up himself.'

'Where did he grow up?'

'Tuly. You've not been to the south islands?' I shook my
head. 'Well, Tuly's mostly rock, as you'll see if you go there.
They live by fishing, but the fifties and sixties were hard times,
with the depression. The story is that Tuly was uninhabited
until the 1780s, when a Bristol slaver out of the Gold Coast was
wrecked on the west side of the island. They say that the
prisoners had escaped from the hold and overwhelmed and
killed the whole crew, before they reached the Caribbean, and
they were trying to sail the ship home to Africa, but of course
they didn't know how to handle a three-masted brigantine, or
navigate in deep waters. So they fetched up on the Tuly rocks, in
daylight and fair weather. They say not a life was lost that day.

'Anyway, that's Tuly, and the folk there have kept pretty
much to themselves ever since. A few comings and goings, but
not much. Too much inbreeding. They're nearly all Pereiras,
after the old landowners – absentee, of course – who laid claim
to the island, and took rents from them. And then in the sixties

the fishing suddenly boomed, and from being the poorest community in Hy Brasil suddenly they were one of the richest. That's all gone now. The population's lower than it's ever been, down to forty-seven since last month, my sister-in-law was telling me on the phone. They had another family move away three weeks ago.

There's always been trouble about sending their kids to school on the mainland. Just after the Revolution it was finally agreed that Tuly Elementary would teach up to Junior High. Occasionally a girl would come over after that to do two years at St Brandons Academy, but never a boy. The boys all went straight into the fishing. Ishmi was the first boy ever to leave the island to go to school. That was in '72. You've seen the hostels for the island children up by the school in St Brandons? Like two fortresses, boys on one side, girls on the other. The first week Ishmi was there they held him out of a third storey window, hanging by his ankles, and they wouldn't haul him back in until they'd made him call himself all the names they knew that are used to describe the folk from Tuly.

That was only the beginning. The kids didn't like him because he was clever, and that didn't fit the image they had of Tuly. But after a bit he got better at fighting back. Then there were the chess championships. He was international class, you know, on the television and everything. And he could play cricket. The first year we all just thought he was too damn *good*. But when he came back after the summer he'd grown his hair thick and matted like a Rastafarian, and he started wearing jeans with holes slashed in them, and no shoes, because one of the less libellous things they taunted him with – which isn't true – is that the Tuly folk go barefoot. That was a typical way for Ishmael to deal with it – I know that now – and it worked. It's against school rules not to wear shoes, but Ishmi gets away with breaking rules, maybe because he only does so when it's important. He was still getting straight As for everything, but you'd never have guessed it to look at him. And if the boys still had it in for him, it soon became fairly obvious that the girls didn't, not that he took any notice of them. By that time he was going out with a singer from one of the clubs on Water Street. After the first year the other lads learned to leave him alone.'

'So you were at the Academy then too?'

'I was two years below him. I knew who he was. He says now he knew who I was too, but I have my doubts.'

'So how did you get to know him?'

'I didn't, until I came back to St Brandons in '83. I qualified in London, after I did my first degree in medicine at the university here. By that time Ishmi was working in the government Finance Department. He was a real whizz-kid, working with the President and everything. It was just when the fishing was starting to go down. Ishmi had lots of ideas, but it was the red tape and graft that finished him. In the end he just couldn't stand it any more. But back in '83 we were both in St Brandons. I met him again at the consultant surgeon's Christmas party, and he recognised me from school. Naturally I remembered him, though he'd changed his image somewhat since I'd last seen him. We went out a few times, and I discovered he hadn't got so respectable after all. They have good clubs – great music – downtown in St Brandons. We were both into that. And then I happened to mention I'd always wanted to see whales close to. I never had, even though I grew up in Dorrado. My family were farmers, and we didn't have a boat. So Ishmael asked a friend of his, Per Pedersen, if he could borrow his Shetland model – that's the same boat Per sold later to Toby Ready at Ogg's Cove – and he took me out from Lyonsness to the far side of Despair. That's when he first told me he was thinking of moving out of town and setting up on his own. "A computer and a boat," he said, "If I had both of those I reckon I could make a living." I said it sounded pretty good.'

'Did you see whales?'

'Indeed we did. We saw humpbacks, which is what we'd hoped for. And not just that. M'dear, we saw a sperm whale.

Truly. Now that's rare, once in a blue moon if you're lucky. And it sounded right close to us, fifty yards from the boat maybe. We were rocking in the wake of it. I shall never forget that moment, not in all my life. They come up to look, you see. Curious about us, like us about them. We saw it so close you could see the scars on its skin. They say the sperm whales dive deep, right down into the abyss, where they feed on the giant squid. They say the scars you see are from those battles. Picture that: those two huge creatures fighting a mortal duel, locked together down there in the dark. The sperm whale surfaced again; we saw it blow. They rest a while on the surface after diving down so deep. It blew, and then it floated there, for all the world like a lump of shining land. And then it dived, a slow roll over and out of sight, down into the deep.'

'Oh! It must have been magic!'

'I guess it was. I think I was fairly out of myself just seeing it. I know Ishmi was. He's not one to act by what he feels, not usually. He tends to have it all worked out first. But on that occasion, not. So that was our beginning, in the bottom of an old wooden Shetland model, with a couple of lifejackets underneath us to make it slightly less uncomfortable. It was a very fair day, and we were far enough out to drift, but he had to keep reaching up to shift the tiller so as to keep her head into what swell there was. Not very romantic, I'm afraid.'

'I think that's extremely romantic,' I said truthfully.

'Well, we did get married three months later. It usually happens that way in this country.'

I wondered briefly how on earth Anna thinks we organise things at home. She's worked at a big teaching hospital in London, and yet she seems to have this notion that contemporary rural life in England is accurately depicted in Mrs Gaskell's *Cranford*. I looked at her across the table, and tried to imagine what she'd been like fourteen years ago. When I first met her I'd had an impression of a fairly formidable woman, definitely somebody's mother, with angular features and an overly authoritative manner. I could imagine her telling her patients exactly what they ought to do. Now I noticed for the first time that she has beautiful brown eyes with long lashes, and a slightly downy skin that looks as if it would feel soft like apricots. I like the way she treats her children. She talks to them as if they were reasonable beings, but supplies them at the same time with a demonstrative affection that too many people reserve only for cats.

Suddenly I answered the question she'd asked me nearly two hours ago. 'Yes,' I said. 'I am serious about Jed. I don't know what that means exactly. I don't know what will happen.'

'No one ever knows what will happen,' said Anna. 'That's the deal. But I reckon it only means one thing, the same thing it always means. It seems odd to me that you seem to find it so surprising.'

There was a sudden sound of wailing from the tree outside, and a moment later a grubby weeping child appeared at the door. 'She pushed me down the ladder! She won't let me in!'

Anna swept her youngest-born on to her knee, and rocked her in her arms. 'Sounds like you'd better leave her alone until she changes her mind,' she said.

'But it's not fair!'

'Nor is life,' said Anna, cuddling Susanna in one arm, and reaching for her coffee with the other. 'I wouldn't let it worry you.' She looked over her daughter's curly head and continued, as if we hadn't been interrupted, 'You seem to have a curious idea that it can't possibly come to this, or that for some reason it shouldn't. But with Jed it will. He'll want this sort of set-up, and he'll have fewer mixed feelings about it than most men do. He hasn't got a family to run away from. You must see that by now.'

'I suppose I do,' I admitted. 'Maybe it's myself who's a bit harder to understand.'

'Is that all?' said Anna. 'Well, I wouldn't let that worry you. The whole thing seems fairly obvious to me.'

TWENTY-THREE

A THIN DRIZZLE hung in the air outside the President's plate-glass window. St Brandons was awash with cloud, which had sunk down on the east coast of Hy Brasil and now lay sluggishly, apparently too exhausted to drift any further. In front of it the President lolled in his chair, absentmindedly doodling a black-and-white maze on the notepad under his right hand. Opposite him, Ishmael had drawn up one of the upright chairs to the other side of the desk. He sat with his feet firmly planted on the floor, holding a leather file open on his lap. He had taken various papers and photographs out of it, and laid them on the desk in front of Hook. The President didn't seem to be paying much attention. He was gradually filling in the walls of his rectangular maze with thick black ink.

'So,' said Hook at last, and laid down his pen. He picked up one of the photographs by one corner and held it to the light. It was a black and white image of the main office in the Pele Centre, with the desk pulled out, and an area shaped like an open grave where the floorboards had been pulled up. It was possible to make out the plastic packages stacked within. One corner of the picture was badly over-exposed. 'I've seen better photographs,' remarked Hook.

'I think its interest lies in its subject matter.'

'Oh, come,' said Hook. 'You can't separate subject from technique in photography, surely you know that? There's no connection between image and fact except what a consummate artistry can convey. In this case the perspective is distorted, I would say, by excessive nervous tension on the part of the photographer. In other words you didn't take it. I think I know who did, but perhaps it would be more tactful of me not to ask. Your methods of acquiring information seem to have been unorthodox, Pereira.'

'But effective,' said Ishmael. 'As you see, I have conclusive proof that the Pele Centre is the centre for the drug trade which we knew existed somewhere on the north-west coast. The astonishing fact about it is that an intensive campaign by government coastguards over the past two years failed to uncover a shred of evidence pointing to the Pele Centre. I've been aware for years that West was an obvious suspect.'

'I seem to recall you had doubts about him.'

'Remember I was the financial advisor on the Planning Committee when West's proposal was first mooted? I asked then why he'd picked the old quarry on the west side of Mount Prosper. Why not the Ogg's Cove side of the watershed, where the unit would literally look out over Mount Brasil? Half a mile over the ridge, and they'd have their main object of study right there outside the window. But no. He wanted that quarry. Why? You can't see Mount Brasil from there, but you do get the best possible view of the north coast, from Brentness to Despair. Why did he want that? The Committee dismissed my objections. I was the financial expert, not a planner.

'But I kept my eye on the Pele Centre from the time I moved to the Landing. Mine is the only house from which you can see it. When West worked late shifts we'd see the lights up there. The other thing we see from Ferdy's Landing is the coastguards patrolling between Brentness and Despair. I suspected West, but there was an obvious problem. West has no boat. If, as I guessed, the stuff was coming ashore somewhere between Ogg's Cove and Lyonsness, who was bringing it? What kind of boat could cross the Atlantic, land on our shores away from any harbour, leaving no trace at all, and then vanish?

'There had to be a shore contact with a boat. I made discreet enquiries about all the boats that work regularly out of Ogg's Cove and Lyonsness. I was quite aware that the most likely suspects were individuals who owned their own boats, who operated them from secluded harbours, and who fell into no clear category of work. That put myself and Honeyman at the top of the list. Honeyman was obviously out. He's only been back in the country a year, and I've been aware of an active smuggling trade for much longer than that. Also, you don't find a successful drug smuggler selling a first edition of Raleigh's *History of the World* at auction because he can't afford to buy underwater surveying equipment. You certainly don't have to fetch him afterwards from the Crossed Bones at Ogg's Cove because he's drunk himself into a state of maudlin and voluble regret on seven pints of draught cider. You can't tell me the government doesn't have a dossier on Honeyman. You can't tell me either that it fits in any respect the profile of a large-scale drug dealer.'

'Circumstantial evidence, Pereira. I'm not sure you'd convince a jury.'

'I know what would. Of course I should have been treated with far more suspicion than Honeyman, because a very few enquiries would have told the government that I had the income to match the supposition. You could tell your jury, too, if you didn't know me very well, that I also have the personality: cold, competitive, devious, tough. And I live at Ferdy's Landing, a far more logical landing place than Despair, since it's not only on the mainland but also at the end of a serviceable road. Everything, in fact, pointed to me, but of course I had the best of reasons for knowing that it wasn't me. You can also see, if you have any idea what paranoia is, and I think perhaps you have, why I had a strong incentive to discover the real operator.'

'I remember now: trust was never your strong point, Pereira.'

'If Hogg's Beach or Ferdy's Landing were being used on a regular basis I'd have known about it. I could also rule out

Brentness. On a calm day you could land a cargo with difficulty. How many calm days do we get in a year? And when it was landed, what then? You couldn't get a vehicle anywhere near the place. That left Lyonsness and Ogg's Cove.

'Everyone knows about Olly West: naturism and break-waters. He's down on Ogg's Cove beach every day of the year, often at the most peculiar times. Sometimes on his bike, sometimes in that blue Ford, which he parks at the end of the jetty by the coastguard station. Everyone knows he loads fertiliser bags full of rocks into that van and dumps them on his breakwaters. And who takes any notice? The only record of his activities in the police station in Ogg's Cove is a petition from the townsfolk requesting that he be compelled to refrain from cycling down the main street on market day with nothing on.'

'The petition was granted. I understand he undresses now as soon as he reaches the sand dunes.'

'Yes. Well, if he was my man, there were certain things I had to find out. First, who were his contacts and how did he get them? Second, if the stuff was brought, as I suspected, in ships that anchored just out of sight on the edge of the deep, whose boat was flitting the stuff ashore? Third, perhaps most impor-tant, what was his motive? He ran a thriving above-board business, apparently, and he's certainly not an addict. I thought I knew the answer to all three questions. As it turns out, I was right. But I needed proof.'

'I'm sure your zeal for justice is commendable. Some might say that such activity exceeds the responsibilities of a private citizen.'

'Not according to our constitution. And then Honeyman takes a green glass goblet and a box of worthless oddments that once belonged to Nicky Hawkins from the Pele Centre, and as soon as the word gets out, he's locked in the jail. Not just in jail, but solitary confinement, and I'm told he can't see or commu-nicate with anyone. Why?'

Hook opened his mouth to reply, but Ishmael ignored him.

'It was the connection with Ferdy's Landing and young Hawkins that gave me my clue. After Hawkins died the house was shut up for months. Penelope Hawkins took a few family heirlooms, and the rest was cleared out and sold by the auctioneers. It was more or less empty when I bought it.

'I've paid some attention to West. In some ways he does have the right personality profile. And yet I'd be amazed to hear he does drugs himself; there had to be another reason. I realised early on that the veneer of guileless eccentricity is somewhat less than skin deep. But it wouldn't have worked for him if it wasn't also the truth. West *is* the fool that he seems, but not quite in the way one first thinks. Jared said to me that the man must be certifiable because he didn't know that St Brendan came before the Pirate Kings. I don't think that would pass muster as an IQ test, but it confirmed my own opinion about the muddled state of West's mind.'

'There I would certainly agree with you.'

'Thank you. The other thing that made me wonder was his stubborn refusal to co-operate with the University in monitoring the volcano. I didn't want to make too much of that, as I can see how it springs directly from the man's insecurity in his own profession, but after the Port o' Frisland earthquake two days ago I was sure I was right. I went to see West myself then, and I tried to say to him that it was madness, given a state of seismic emergency, not to pool his resources with the University. I suggested using graduate students, if he didn't want staff, and mounting a twenty-four-hour watch. His response was offensive, and hardly relevant. It was at that moment that I decided to raid the Pele Centre.'

'Without any legal authority whatsoever,' remarked Hook.

'True. So this is the story, as I pieced it together: West hears that Nicholas Hawkins is dead, and a few days later he breaks into Ferdy's Landing. He knows exactly what he's looking for. Three things. Firstly, he's known for some time where Hawkins gets his money. My suspicion is that he was blackmailing the boy. In which case, he'll want to check there's nothing left in the place that might incriminate him. Secondly, he thinks there may be something in this for him. Sure enough, he finds Nicky's papers that tell him, when he breaks the code, exactly whom he needs to contact in order to start up a lucrative trade of his own. Thirdly, he's at pains to remove all evidence of the goods. The last thing he wants now is an enquiry into Hawkins' past dealings. He removes every contraband article from the house. My guess is that he looks in the glass on the mantelpiece, and finds it contains a good deal more than a box of matches. He puts the glass in the box along with everything else.

'West's as cunning as they make them, but there are things he doesn't see. He comes back from Ferdy's Landing with his haul, and disposes of it carefully. But an old green glass, and a little black box with a ship on it? Take out the contents, and it's the same to him as a couple of jam jars. Spring cleaning's not his strong point. He shoves them on a shelf and lets the dust gather. And a shell from Gallipoli? God knows what he thought he'd got there. But he examined it, no doubt, and found it wanting. Have you ever seen inside the man's house? Yes, you probably have. The point is, he's quite clearly never looked at a created thing aesthetically in his whole life, and that was his downfall.

'There's a moral in that, no doubt,' murmured Hook.

'Of course, all the enquiries I made could easily have been duplicated by official investigators. I discovered that some of them had been. But what about the invisible boat that evaded the most stringent coastguard patrols? The obvious solution was corruption among the coastguards themselves. I know most of those men pretty well. Well, you can see from the paper just by your left hand exactly what I found out. And here is the confirmation, from Olly West's safe. You recognise the signature, sir, of course?'

Hook took the paper, glanced at it, and shrugged his shoulders.

'It wasn't hard to work it out: all West needed to carry on

Hawkins' trade was access to a boat. He might have taken over Hawkins' boat, but West's no sailor, and what's more the boat itself was beyond repair after being left all winter after Hawkins died. It was pretty well derelict long before that; apparently Pedersen had done some work on it the year before, and he told Nicholas he was risking his life every time he took the thing to sea. Of course that didn't stop Hawkins. In my view the unforgivable thing was using the child to crew for him. He knew it was dangerous, he knew it was criminal, and he knew the boy was all his mother had. Luckily I think that Honeyman was, even at that age, basically incorruptible.'

'Evidence, man, evidence. Could you tell that to the jury?'

'Certainly I could. But back to West. Why turn to smuggling? This is 1985. He's been in Hy Brasil five years, and he's applied for and been refused resident status twice. He's made three attempts to get it by marriage, but he couldn't bring any of the women to clinch the deal. He hasn't a work permit; he's here on sufferance, with his visa renewed every six months, because he has some sort of income coming in from the UK. Now he's trying to get government backing to start his seismological centre. Why on earth would he sabotage his status here by turning to a highly dangerous illegal trade? If he were caught, the best he could hope for, as a British citizen, would be deportation, the worst, judicial sentence under the law of Hy Brasil. Well, as it happens, I've read the government dossier on Oliver West. He *was* threatened with compulsory repatriation after demands from the British consulate that he be returned to the UK to answer charges of blackmail and embezzlement. I began to see his motive. I suggest, sir, that West had an interview with – shall we say a senior government official? – in the spring of 1985.'

'And your proof?'

'I'll tell you. Why would such an official listen to West? 1985: The fishing industry is in dire straits. Hy Brasil has just refused again to join the European Community. Unemployment in rural areas is escalating. The truth is – and probably only you and I know just how true this is – the country's on the verge of bankruptcy. In fact it's my belief you'd talked to West even before I handed in my resignation. I'm now a good deal clearer than I was then why my own remit should suddenly have become impossible. I know my policies were right; why were they so suddenly rejected – not even rejected, in fact – just lost somewhere in the system? I suggest that West bargained for life-long residency, government grants to start up his centre, all the capital support he could wish for, and permanent indemnity against repatriation. In return he offered a prestigious scientific project, but, more importantly, a regular source of secret revenue, and, to safeguard the government against exposure, himself as the fall guy. He was in a strong position, because not only did he have the contact, but he also knew that the government wouldn't dare make a direct link even if they knew how.'

'I admire your imaginative abilities, Pereira.'

'He gets the go-ahead. The next thing he needs is a boat. As it happens, he knows something about the private life of Chief Coastguard Ready at Ogg's Cove that makes a useful bargaining counter. If necessary I can reveal what it is, but it would cause several people pain if I did so, and I'd rather not. Ready is indecisive at first, but then the government suddenly issues him with a second boat, along with somewhat ambiguous orders about excise patrols and a fifty per cent bonus for two men to put in some occasional unofficial overtime.

'Hawkins' drug traffic was small-scale and spasmodic; it began through family contacts. West built it up from there into a regular, expanding business making serious money in an international market. After all, he had government funds to invest, and with the massive profit and almost instant returns, the trade grew like a toadstool, overnight. For twelve years West and the government have held one another in a fine system of checks and balances. Its basis is power and need, certainly not trust, but the profits are equally welcome to both. Would you say that was a fair analysis, sir?'

Hook laid down his pen, and regarded his maze, apparently with satisfaction. Certainly it was very symmetrical. 'You've been very busy, Pereira.' He sighed. 'I have, of course, reposed a good deal of trust in you, from time to time.'

'I hope you'll continue to do so, sir.' Ishmael shifted the papers on the table. 'My only object is to serve my country to the best of my ability. It would, of course, be a shock for you to discover that government personnel and resources had been diverted to an illegal and immoral trade, one, moreover, which you have yourself denounced on numerous occasions.' Ishmael picked up the letter with the signature he'd just indicated. 'Naturally, if it came to your attention that coastguard patrol boats had actually been engaged in the trade they were employed to suppress, you'd do your utmost to stamp out all corrupt elements.'

'Of course, Pereira. I'm surprised you find it necessary to ask.'

'If the ringleaders within the system could not be traced, the lesser agents would be relieved of excessive responsibility, and new senior officers appointed. You might want to set up a committee to implement this.'

'Possibly I might.'

'It would seem sensible for that committee to be given authority over the Customs and Excise Department, in order to implement more effective preventive measures.'

'Indeed it would.'

'The same committee could also undertake the immediate prosecution of West on behalf of the government.'

'I suppose it could.'

'The man is still at large. But without government connivance he can't leave the country. You will of course want to mount a police search and coastguard patrol immediately to bring West in.'

'Doubtless I will.'

'I think your ideas on the subject are very sound, sir,' said Ishmael. 'You'd need to pick the right chairman for your committee, of course: a man you could trust, whose discretion you could always rely on.' He picked up the letter with the signature, and put it carefully back in his file.

'Enlighten me,' said Hook. 'Twelve years ago you handed in your resignation, and you told me that the joys of government employment had permanently palled. What brought about this change of heart?'

'Call it a triple stake in the future.' Ishmael began to gather the papers together. 'I should tell you that copies of the relevant documents – only the relevant ones, mind you – are already with the editor of *The Hesperides Times*.'

'You underrate me, Pereira. You didn't need to tell me that. And now, I suppose if the government were at all strapped for cash, you'd encourage it to invest more liberally in your telecommunications projects? Jobs for all, wasn't that the idea? I suppose if I let you you'd produce a new budget next week?'

'I think it will take a little longer than that, sir. But yes, I do have some proposals.'

'And supposing I say no to them?'

'That is of course your prerogative, sir. There are a couple of other small matters we need to settle today.'

'Don't tell me. Is it a man or is it a fish? Dead or alive? I thought we'd come to it. Young Honeyman?'

'Yes.' Ishmael took another envelope out of his folder. 'Now that we've proved Olly West was the shore contact, presumably the government will immediately release Honeyman with an appropriate apology.'

'Not so fast, Pereira. You've proved your case with West. You have him. Sweep him from the board. But I'm not so sure that you're in a position to trade your other pawn. You've just told me yourself that Honeyman, unlike West, was actually involved in the trade under Hawkins. And he has a record. I think it could be quite difficult to argue a case for him now.'

'I don't think it's necessary. What I can tell you is why he's come close to paying for the theft of a glass goblet with his life. I think if I do that you'll understand why he must be innocent.'

'His life?' Hook raised his brows. 'Isn't this becoming just a little melodramatic? Whoever do you think has threatened his life?'

'Was Mr Baskerville involved in any way with West's smuggling activities?'

'Fernando? The idea seems risible, but then, as you say, government investigation seems to have been remarkably inept, so I can only suppose now that anything is possible.'

'You know that he was not. And yet when his suspicions grew, after he talked to the English girl, that Jared had stolen papers from the Pele Centre, he telephoned you. That call must have considerably startled you, sir?'

'Dear me. Do your private enquiries include tapping the public telephone lines? And yet you, like the rest of us, are subject to the law, Pereira.'

'My sources of information were entirely legal. It was easy to find out that Mr Baskerville, and others, were deeply concerned about the papers that Jared found in the Pele Centre. As it happens, you were all quite wrong. He never even noticed West's safe, let alone attempted to open it. All he found was Lucy Morgan's letters to Nicky Hawkins. And Lucy Morgan says that yes, West did attempt to blackmail her, in exchange for sexual favours, but, she said, he got nowhere, because she told him he could read her letters to anyone he liked but nothing on earth would prevail on her to go within a yard of him. I think in Mr Baskerville he found a more susceptible victim. The thought would never have crossed my mind, however, if Jared hadn't been thrown in jail, or even if I'd been allowed to see him.'

'My sources tell me that you did see him.'

'You know that now? Yes, I paid my way in. If I'd failed I'd have appealed to the UN in Geneva.' For a moment the mask of politeness slipped. Ishmael said with grim emphasis, 'I would, and I will, do whatever is necessary to make sure *this* Honeyman does not disappear.'

Hook glanced at him sharply, but said nothing. His pen remained poised over the blacked-in maze.

'Jared knew nothing,' said Ishmael. 'Framing him was simple. The mistake your men made was to ignore the English girl. She came to me, and I drove her at once to Lyonsness police station. She made her statement, and I took her, with two detectives, straight back to Despair. We found everything just as she'd described. We were still there when the two special agents turned up to search the place, and we were able to tell them the job was already done. It wasn't drugs they'd been sent to look for, was it? If you'd wanted a straightforward search for evidence of smuggling, the coastguards could have done it when they arrested Jared. But evidently they'd had orders not to do that.

'So it wasn't just about framing Jed, was it? You didn't know, until Baskerville called you, that Lem Hawkins had discovered, and left written evidence, of what happened to Jack Honeyman. That evidence was supposed to have been deposited in a solicitor's vault, and left unread for fifty years. Instead Hawkins kept it in a secret hiding place in Ferdy's Landing. Perhaps he had other plans; I think it possible he would have talked to Jared when he came of age. But within months of John Honeyman's disappearance, Hawkins was tipped off, possibly by Baskerville, that his own life might be in danger, but that's a guess. Hawkins took the ferry to England the same day, without returning to Ferdy's Landing. He knew he was ill before he left, and six months later he died in an English nursing home.

'I imagine Ferdy's Landing was searched after Lemuel Hawkins left, but you didn't know about the old smugglers' hiding place. We found it when we were working on the house five years later. It had six pounds of cocaine in it. I took them out to sea and scattered the stuff overboard. Far less did you know that West had taken those letters from Nicky's tin box at Ferdy's Landing. You never knew that the box contained a complete confession written by Baskerville, and that West has been blackmailing Baskerville ever since. When Kirwan confirmed to you that Honeyman had taken documents from the Pele Centre that it had obviously upset him to find, I think you decided that Honeyman would be arrested on a false charge, tried in a closed court for drug dealing, and that once he was safely sentenced, and in legal custody, probably for life, he would quietly disappear.

'But you had a new problem: you suspected I had this.' Ishmael held up the brown envelope he'd been holding. 'You didn't know, but I may as well tell you now, that I didn't find it on Despair, but in the safe at the Pele Centre. But I know quite well it's the reason you agreed to talk to me today in private. You understand now that Jared knows nothing about it. If he disappears, in fact, it will be for no reason at all.'

'You expect me to trust you a great deal. I should like to see those letters.'

'Certainly, sir.' Ishmael took the letters out, and placed them on the table: three long handwritten letters, one in different handwriting from the others, and a sheaf of typewritten documents. He watched Hook pick them up, one by one, and read them. Hook's face registered no emotion of any kind.

Ishmael said, 'Of course, the welfare of the country is the most important thing to both of us. That's why we both welcome the breaking of this pernicious drug ring. We're both dedicated to preserving the peace, and to taking positive steps to build up the economy. It's understandable, but regrettable, that the government arrested the wrong suspect. The least embarrassing tactic now will be to release him with an official apology. That can be done immediately. There's no need to complicate the issue.' He swept the letters off the desk, and put them back in their envelope. 'This is sensitive material. Perhaps too sensitive even for the government's private archive. I'm quite willing to relieve you of it, and we need not mention it again. I certainly won't discuss it with anyone else.'

Hook gave him a swift look. 'You swear to that, do you, Pereira?'

'If you like. But first it's only fair to tell you that there are other witnesses who have copies of these documents, and who know as much as I do. It's not good policy to place too much responsibility on one man. They too will agree to remain silent.'

'And naturally you won't tell me who they are.'

'No, sir.'

'Very wise. But it's hard to trust to a proxy oath, when you don't know your principal.'

'I'm not sure that you have a vast choice in the matter, sir. But I'm willing to swear that so long as Jared Honeyman has his freedom, no citizen of Hy Brasil will refer again to these documents during your lifetime.'

'Ah, so there's the sting in the tail! You'll publish them when I'm dead?'

'I'll never publish them, sir. I swear to that.'

'And I'll never be rid of you again, either, will I, Pereira?' He gave Ishmael another swift glance. 'Do you know what fear is?'

'Of course. What man doesn't?'

'You surprise me. Tell me one thing, since we're conversing here so frankly. I'd be interested to know if you're using Honeyman to acquire power for yourself, or your own power to acquire Honeyman?'

'Neither. Power isn't mine to possess. I want to see things done justly. I hope I'd be as fair to a stranger as to a friend. Naturally when a friend is unjustly treated I feel it more. As I see it, it's simply a matter of knowing who your neighbour is.'

'A remarkably cryptic reply, Pereira. But I see hope in it, since it appears to admit your President on equal terms to your scheme of justice.'

'It wouldn't be justice if I didn't.'

TWENTY-FOUR

Sidony Redruth. Ravnscar Castle. July 30th.
Notes for *Undiscovered Islands* (working title).

TODAY I CLIMBED Mount Brasil.

I'd known from the day I arrived in this country that this is
something I would do. What I could not have known was how I
would feel about it, and why. Before I left England, my future life
in Hy Brasil was a total blank. I'd read what I could find about the
place, but I had not the first notion what it would actually be like.
That was why I wasn't exactly looking forward to it. I wasn't
dreading it either. I had no feelings one way or the other. The only
thing I was sure about was that I was glad of the break from what
seemed then to be my real life. It was like walking into a book, or
into a dream. Once I was in it, it seemed to be all there was, and it
was everything I'd left behind that became unreal.

When I set out to climb the mountain I didn't tell anybody
where I was going. I was afraid because of the earthquake
warnings. I need to clarify that: earthquakes and volcanoes had
not the power to bother me, in my present mood, so much as the
fear that someone might be cross with me, and tell me off. I knew
it was irresponsible to climb an unknown and precipitous mountain all on my own. It would have been bad even if it hadn't been an
active volcano which might erupt at any minute. I would have
been warned off even if there hadn't been three significant
earthquakes along the fault line in the last two months, all within

thirty miles of the crater. My insurance specifically ruled out mountaineering, not that I intended any serious climbing, but no one could argue that Brasil wasn't a mountain. I was selfish and irresponsible and not keeping the rules. I knew this, and I felt accordingly guilty, as I deserved to do. But I went.

As soon as I'd started on the steep and narrow way I felt better. I'd parked, at six o'clock in the morning, in the lay-by off the Lyonsness/St Brandons road where I'd so often passed the signpost that said simply 'Mount Brasil summit 7 miles, 7098 feet. Monte Brasil 11.2 quilometros; altura 2163 metros'. That gave me a start of nearly two thousand feet, this being the highest point on the road. It was an ideal day for walking, sunny with a small wind. I climbed laboriously through the terraces. The apples were ripening red and yellow on the trees, and the wild flowers fading. Sometimes I'd find what seemed like a path, with dried-out footsteps or goat prints, and then it would fade away, and there'd be another dry-stone wall built into the mountainside. I'd weave to and fro across the hillside, looking for ways round, and then I'd give up, and scramble cautiously up the terrace walls, doing my best not to dislodge the stones. Even in the cool of the morning it was hard work. Sweat dripped into my eyes, and trickled down between my breasts under my shirt.

I came to the end of the terraces, and passed a row of white beehives on a sunny slope. I stopped just beyond them to look at the map. The path from the lay-by was marked as a clear dotted line. Well, it had been as clear as that, for the first fifty yards. I looked at my watch and then east. The sun was half the length of my thumb over the horizon, and still east enough to be north of where St Brandons lay to the south-east. I'd never walked in a country where a compass didn't work before. It was more disconcerting than I'd expected. But the weather couldn't be better, and it was forecast to stay that way. I folded the map, which hadn't told me anything I didn't know already, and put it away. Then I took a deep breath, and struck out in a straight line up and west through steep woods of birch and aspen, mixed up with tree heathers as tall as I was, all in flower now with the bees buzzing over them. Hy Brasil has its very own species of tree heather, *Erica hybrasiliensis*. It pleased me to assume that this was it, though to be honest I wasn't at all sure.

Everything up here was damp from the cloud that had only lifted that morning, and the grass under my feet was lush and green. Presently there were no more trees, only tough grasses and bog myrtle, which gave off a sweet-sharp scent as I pushed my way through it. Above my walking boots my bare legs were soon scratched and flecked with drops of blood. Where there were outcrops of basalt I scrambled on to the rock and walked over that. Soon there was more rock and less scrub, then even more rock, and after a while the myrtle was gone and the short grass only came in patches. It was like walking over a huge rounded pavement with giant cracks in it. Presently I stopped for a drink of water. I ate some chocolate and an orange. I'd done two hours.

When I'd eaten I lay on my back and watched the thin herring-bone clouds far above. They were hardly moving. I thought about not being allowed to visit the prison. I don't think they can refuse to let people have visitors in England, but I don't really know. He has a window. I asked Ishmael that, and he said yes. All you can see from the window is the sky. I lay there and thought maybe he's seeing this same blue sky, and the small high clouds so far above the earth they don't even feel the wind up there. But if he can see them, it'll only be a little square, not the whole arch of heaven like it is from here. Presently I got up and went on. The air was sweet and clear, like a draught of chilled wine.

The wind grew keener. I stopped and put my jersey on. There was no more grass. Between the smooth billows of rock there were loose stones, and clumps of moss. And flowers. I hadn't expected flowers where there was no grass, but there were small pink saxifrages and alpine lady's mantle, and a little white flower I didn't know. They looked very fragile among the loose stones. I trod between them carefully. Presently I saw steam rising, like vapours from a dragon's nest. Soon there were trickles of steam everywhere. I came right up to one, and there was a perfectly round pool, rust red, rimmed by ferns and mosses, with water bubbling up from the bottom. It smelt like matches. Cautiously I dipped my finger. Hot. I took it out fast, and walked on, sucking my scalded fingertip.

The earth under my feet turned red and grainy. There was nothing growing now. The rocks were a shambles, flung everywhere like the blast from an explosion. It was hard to pick my way. I passed more hot springs, reeking of sulphur. The steam caught in my hair and turned to beads of water which dripped down my forehead into my eyes. The great boulders made me feel very small, like a mouse scurrying through the rubble of a devastated city. I sat by a hot spring to eat my lunch. The sound of water, flowing away in a steamy stream, sounded cheerfully normal, so I could almost make believe this was an ordinary stream in a benign and English countryside. I could think that, just so long as I listened, and felt the sun on my skin, and didn't let myself look round.

I climbed slowly on, until I came to the bottom of a jagged lava outcrop, where I needed my hands to pull myself up. When I'd struggled to the top I looked back. I was above the hot springs. I could see now what I couldn't before, how the springs curved across the face of the mountain in a continuous ring of steam and sulphur. I hadn't realised how close together they were until I was through.

My feet were getting warm. As soon as I noticed I bent down and touched the rock on which I stood. It was hot. I thought for a moment that I might turn back. I'd never stood on hot rock before. Then I remembered Colombo telling me, not long after I arrived, how when you walked on Mount Brasil you felt the heat coming through your boots. So it was quite normal. I looked at my watch. Four hours. It couldn't be much further. I nearly got out the map again, but I knew by heart what it said.

Without a compass it had nothing more to tell me.

Climbing up among the loose rocks, I began to feel a bit frightened. The smell of sulphur was getting stronger, and there were no firm footholds. I'd broken every rule in the book, coming up here by myself and not telling anybody. I don't know if it was guilt, the sulphur, or the altitude, but I felt breathless, and I had an odd notion that I wasn't judging things properly. Yet at the same time everything seemed twice as clear as usual: the shapes of the rocks, the clump and slither of my boots as I searched for footholds, even my hands searching for holds looked more alive, almost as if they weren't part of me at all. The conviction grew on me that it would be sensible to turn back. I reached a false summit, and looked at the waste of rock behind me, and the foreshortened waste ahead, and I thought seriously about turning. But it really couldn't be far now. When I set off upward again, almost without willing it, I was suddenly quite certain what I was going to do. I intended to make it. I was still scared, but not undecided any more. I felt serene.

In the end the crater came as a surprise. Another difficult scramble, another false summit – but it wasn't. I'd reached the edge. The mountain fell away below me. I was looking down into a great bowl-shaped hollow. The rocks were stained yellow with sulphur, and tails of steam rose and escaped, with a faint hissing like a thousand spouting kettles. The ground under my boots was so hot I had to keep shifting from foot to foot. The bottom of the crater was red and gravelly, and quite dry. It looked frighteningly empty.

He'd come up here, all by himself, the same as I had, and when he'd reached the crater he'd climbed down into it. He'd been thirteen. I'd been eleven. Probably the very same day that Jared had climbed into the volcano, and Nicky Hawkins had shot Cosmo Ashton and thrown himself over a cliff, I'd been in the vicarage garden with Arthur, playing, as we usually did, that we were in danger. Nothing would have induced me, now, to do what Jared had done. Even so, I raked the rim of the crater with my eyes, and tried to work out where one could possibly start. About forty-five degrees from where I stood there was an edge of lava that looked fairly solid. Maybe one could get enough grip on those toothed edges. But if the rock came loose, or broke . . . I looked down into the cauldron at my feet and shuddered. I wondered how far down he'd got. Out of the wind, with the sun beating down on steaming rock, it must have been terribly hot in that enclosed symmetrical space. From the bottom the sky must be a round circle of blue far above. It would be like climbing right out of the world, to go down there. I acknowledged that I would never, ever, under any circumstances, have done it.

I noticed something else close to the top of the lava spur. I wished I'd brought the binoculars after all instead of leaving them in the Land Rover because they were so heavy. I'm always doing that, but I can see more than most people with the naked eye anyway. I screwed up my eyes against the sun, and made out a cylindrical shape with something sticking out at the top. It must be one of the monitoring stations from the Pele Centre, wedged on to a ledge a little way below the lip of the crater, just as Peterkin had described. I began to walk slowly along the edge, looking down into that hot empty space all the time. Presently I found another monitor, outside the crater this time, so that I was able to walk right up to it. It looked absurdly makeshift, but when I examined it I realised that it was half embedded in a solid concrete foundation, and where it was exposed every join had been carefully soldered. It must be completely weathertight. It was just what Peterkin had said: an oil drum with a plastic pipe sticking out of the top, which must have the radio mast inside it, and a miniature solar panel. It seemed odd to think there was a computer in there busy doing calculations.

I'd been so awestruck by the crater that it was only now I began to pay attention to the view. Standing on the eastern lip, I could see right across the foothills and plains to St Brandons. A smudgy haze hung over it, but otherwise the coastline from Lyonsness to the far south was sharp as a knife edge. The southern islands were lost in mist, but Despair was clear and flat as if it had been cut out of cardboard. It was a little different from the shape I knew so well from Ravnscar. The southern aspect of Mount Prosper seemed like quite a different mountain from the one I knew. Instead of the steep scarps and plunging woodland of its seaward side, it curved up from the watershed in a long supple ridge, a bit like the view of a horse's neck when you're in the saddle. From where I stood I could see the pass quite clearly. The metalled road over to Ogg's Cove glinted in the sun. It was the highest pass in Hy Brasil, at over four thousand feet. I'd only gone over it once, the first day I went to Ogg's Cove, before I'd found the back track that led from Ferdy's Landing over the north-west shoulder of the mountain. I stared at Mount Prosper for a long time, learning it, and then I turned east again. I spent a long time tracing the roads, and the places I knew, some because I'd been there and some from reading the map.

I couldn't see the west coast from here. I'd have to walk round to the south side of the crater to get any view further round. I started to do just that, but after a while I began to realise that the distance round the lip of the crater was much further than it looked. It was slow going, over hot gravel and lava boulders, and it might take me an hour or more to circumnavigate the whole thing. I stood looking south towards Dorrado, and wondering what to do. I could hear a sound like a distant sewing machine, and a moment later I saw a helicopter buzzing across the flank of the mountain that snaked down towards Dorrado bay. It disappeared behind the ridge, but a few minutes later it came back again, hovering over the sunlit slopes like a wasp over a honey jar. I looked at my watch. Ten past three. I wasn't going to have time to walk right round the crater. I turned back, scrambling along the lip until I reached the place where I'd come up, and set off down. It was a tough haul back, over rocks, past the hot springs, down through stones and scrub, into the trees, down through the terraces.

By the time I reached the Land Rover it was half past six. Twelve-and-a-half hours. My legs were shaking with exhaustion,

worn out by the endless thud, thud of the long trek downhill. I
leaned on the metal door and shut my eyes, too tired at first even
to get my boots off. I'd pushed myself to my limits, further than
I'd expected, but no one need ever know. I'd been wicked, gone to
the very summit of where I shouldn't, and got away with it. No
one could be angry with me now. I reckoned there was only one
person I'd ever feel like telling. The thought surprised me, and I
quickly added to it: of course, if the subject came up, I'd also tell
Arthur. Feeling strangely disloyal, I bent stiffly to unlace my
boots.

Ravnscar Castle. August 1st

If it hadn't been for what happened the evening before, I'd never
have attempted it. I'd only have known Mount Brasil as a
tourist, safely shepherded along the correct route, if there is
such a thing, by some experienced person who'd make sure I did
it the right way. In retrospect I'm glad it didn't happen like that,
but if Lucy hadn't shaken me to the core, the way she did, I'd
never have gone up there on my own, and I'd never have known
what I'd missed. All the time I was climbing I kept going over
and over what she'd told me. When I finally reached Ravnscar as
dusk was falling, I'd accepted it, because there wasn't really any
choice. I realised I didn't want to lose her.

I'd got back from Ferdy's Landing late on Wednesday
afternoon. Lucy was in the garden, so wouldn't have heard
the phone if anyone had rung. I'd half hoped there'd be a
message from Colombo. Ishmael still wasn't back when I'd left
the Landing, and I was desperate to hear what had happened. I
couldn't tell Lucy about the Pele Centre yet, but there were
some things I was at liberty to ask. When she did come in, her
mind was on the supper; she gave me an onion to chop, more as
a sop to my pride than because she needed my help. I can tell
Lucy thinks I can't cook.

I thought for a minute, then I put the onion down and

turned to face her. 'Lucy. I found out something today. About Jared.'

'Oh?' Lucy looked round, knife in hand. 'You mean . . . nothing about drugs?'

'Drugs? No. I know he had nothing to do with drugs.'

'I'm pretty sure he never had anything more to do with it than what I told you,' said Lucy. 'Only he did grow up with the idea, thanks to Nicky, and since all this business started I have sometimes wondered . . . No, never mind. So it's not that?'

'No.' I picked up the onion again, and looked at it without really seeing it. 'I found out today,' I said slowly, 'that Jack Honeyman didn't go into exile. I found out that he wasn't a British agent.'

Lucy put her knife down on the chopping board, and turned to look at me. 'So you found out that? You mean Ishmael did find Lem's letters after all? But surely he never showed them to *you*?'

'What do you mean? What are you talking about?'

'You've been at Ferdy's Landing all day, haven't you? That's where the letters were, in Nicky's tin trunk. Was the trunk still there when Ishmael bought the house? I've wondered sometimes if Ishmael knew, if he'd found those letters. He's never breathed a word to me, but then why would he?'

'Do you mean you *know* about those letters?'

'Wait a minute,' said Lucy. 'Suppose you tell me just what you've seen?'

I hesitated for a minute. This was getting too close to the boundaries of my promise, but I reckoned I still didn't need to mention the raid on the Pele Centre. I told her exactly what I'd read.

'Yes,' said Lucy. 'They're the same ones. So Ishmael's had them all this time? But why should he show them *now*?'

'You *knew* about them?'

She must have caught something in my tone, because suddenly she looked sulky, like a defiant teenager being told off by her mother. 'Of course I knew. Nicky told me every-thing. His father had a hiding place inside the chimney at Ferdy's Landing. A sort of seventeenth-century safe, you might call it. Nicky found the letters there when he was clearing it out. He needed to use the hiding place himself, you see, but when he looked there were still some old papers of his father's in there. He read the letters about Jack Honeyman, and then he showed them to me. He asked me what I thought he ought to do about it. I said do nothing. In my experience nothing is usually the wisest thing to do. Nicky took a bit of persuading, but I pointed out to him he didn't want to draw attention to himself, for various reasons. There was no bringing Jack back, and who could Nicky have appealed to anyway? Only the government, and you can't expect them to call themselves to account, can you? No, I reckoned it was all dead and done with, and best let lie. So Nicky put the letters at the bottom of his tin trunk, and we forgot about them, more or less. He couldn't hide them in the chimney again, because Jed knew about that place. He found it one day when he climbed up the chimney to clear a starling's nest. Jed knew what Nicky kept in there. I don't think he'd have looked for anything else, but as Nicky said, you never knew with that kid what he'd think of getting into next.'

I stared at her. 'Lucy, are you telling me you *knew* all those years ago that Hook shot Jared's father, and Baskerville dumped his body at sea, and all this time you've never said a word about it?'

'Well, it's hardly like that. I didn't say a word when Nicky was alive, because that's what we agreed. And why should I say anything when I came back from New York? Who to? What for?'

'To Jared, for a start. Jack was his father.'

'Come on, Sidony. Jared was just a kid.'

'All the more reason why he needed to know. And his mother too. Jack Honeyman's wife – she wasn't just a kid, was she?'

'But no one could have expected me to . . . Maybe she was better not knowing. At least she could still hope.'

'My God, that's about the cruellest thing I ever heard! I can't believe it! You *knew*! You knew all the time. When Jared's mother was dying, you *knew*! And when Jared came home last year . . .'

'Hang on a minute! When Josie Honeyman was dying I was in New York. And when Jed came home last year it didn't even cross my mind. Supposing it had? What then? What if I'd said to Jed then, "Oh by the way, your Pappa was shot and dumped at sea eighteen years ago, and Mr Baskerville and the President did it." What then? What then, Sidony? You can be damn sure he'd have rushed off and done something silly. He might well have ended the same way, if I'd told him. Talk about cruel! That would have been the cruellest thing to do!'

'You *knew* all the time! You knew about Mr Baskerville!'

'Didn't I always tell you I couldn't stand the man? Well, now you know why.'

'I still can't believe you *knew*!'

She just couldn't see why I was so shocked. In the end she got fed up with me. We ate our supper in total silence. I had no appetite. I said I'd probably go out early tomorrow, and she heaped coals of fire on my head by saying, 'Take the Land Rover if you want. I'll be here all day anyway. I need to make jam before all that fruit goes off. And I want to harvest the peas.' I'd liked to have refused, but it would have sounded childish, and also, I'd have been stuck.

Driving home through the twilight, I thought about Lucy. She hadn't been at the forefront of my mind all through the day, but somehow, during that long tramp, I seemed to have reached some kind of resolution. Lucy was Lucy. I couldn't blame her for that. If I did, I'd only lose a friend. I couldn't change the past.

The light was on in the kitchen. When I went in she was sitting at the long table writing out labels. There was a delicate smell of herbs and cooking meat. In front of her, neatly arranged on trays, there were about forty pots of jam. She looked up and smiled when I came in. 'I hope you're hungry. Cally Simpson came by with a couple of pigeons so I roasted them. But you've caught the sun! Wherever have you been?'

I hadn't even meant to tell her, but I instantly did. Her mouth dropped open. 'You didn't? You went up *there*? Today? But – no, you didn't hear the radio. What time did you leave?'

'Quarter to five.'

She was looking at me with a fascinated horror that I couldn't interpret. 'It was on the news at eight,' she said. 'Then they kept flashing warnings right through *Good Morning Hy Brasil* and *The Old Grey Folk Café*. Red alert. They're picking up a harmonic tremor on the west side of the mountain, which sounds to me like something which would give delight and hurt not, but apparently it's not quite like that. Anyway, they're advising everyone to keep off the mountain. They can't stop you because it's a civil right here to go wherever you like except into someone else's house. The Right of Free Access. Then they even had a piece on it at eleven o'clock on *The World at One*, which means everyone in Britain must have heard it too.'

'Oh dear.' I sank into a chair because my legs were trembling. 'Oh dear. I *knew* I was bad. But I've done it now.'

'Good for you.' Lucy's mood changed so abruptly that my carpet of guilt seemed suddenly to be swept from under my feet. 'Good for you! I'd never have guessed you had it in you. I've never been to the top actually. What's it like?'

'You've never been?' It was my turn to be astounded.

'No, why should I? Is there boiling lava?'

It was one of the friendliest evenings we'd had together. We were both relieved that everything was all right between us, and we tacitly avoided controversial subjects. After I'd had a long soak in the bath, she brought down a book of etchings, Reid's *Art Rambles in Hy Brasil, 1871*. He'd drawn his picture of the crater almost from the very spot where I'd been standing. There was the jagged edge of lava on the far side of the crater, exactly as

I'd seen it. I assured Lucy that it really did look like that. I was ravenous, and with Cally Simpson's pigeons she'd surpassed herself. After supper I could hardly move. I was falling asleep at the table, but I felt too warm and comfortable to want to go away. Lucy poured us some Madeira.

The knock on the door, when it came, took both of us by surprise.

'Colombo?' said Lucy. 'But no, that's not his knock. But who . . .'

She went over and opened the door. 'What? What the hell do you want?' I heard her say. 'What, now?'

She let him in. Of course, she didn't know. I almost screamed. It was Olly West.

He looked quite manic. Lucy was alarmed, I could tell. Maybe she thought he was drunk. I must have gone white. I'm pretty sure he only had to take one look at me to realise that I knew. He looked from her to me, and back again. I felt a pang of sheer terror. I didn't know what he was after. Why here? Why us?

'Ah, Lucy,' he said, 'And Sidony. I think you'll understand the reason for this little visit.'

Lucy stared at him. 'I haven't a clue. What do you want?'

'You've kept your secrets very well,' said Olly. 'I've known, of course. I've been aware of what you were doing all the time. Up until now I've minded my own business. But in the interests of public security, as a responsible citizen and a leading business man in the area, I feel I have a responsibility to the public. Matters have gone too far to be tolerated further. Private blackmail is one thing, but there comes a point when these activities become a serious threat to public peace and security. I believe, indeed I have ascertained, that Hy Brasil has retained the British constitutional right of citizen's arrest. I must ask you to accompany me to the police station, Miss Morgan.'

'What the hell are you talking about?'

'I'm talking, as you must be well aware, about twelve years of systematic blackmail, Miss Morgan. Yes, you look startled, Sidony. Bear in mind you have a duty here as witness. There has, of course, been constant speculation among less privileged stratas of society within this area concerning Lucy's apparently abundant source of income. She put herself through college in the United States, or so she says, shortly after the events in question took place. And the upkeep of the castle of Ravnscar must be a heavy burden for a young woman. I've not felt called upon to interfere . . .'

'Oh yes you have. After I got back from New York, you felt called upon to interfere almost every bloody day. It wasn't until Colombo threatened to knock you over the parapet that you finally stopped pestering me. You know damn well you did everything you could think of to get the privilege of being responsible for the upkeep of this place! I haven't forgotten you getting down on your knees at this very table and saying you were in love with me! I haven't forgotten how you said you wanted to marry me! How could I forget? I've never felt so sick in all my life!'

'Lucy, I stopped coming here because I discovered exactly why you didn't want me to participate in what you called your very private life. I regard your subsequent rejection of me in the light of a lucky escape. Once I was aware of your emotional incapacity for forming an adult relationship I could only feel grateful to all my friends who warned me against having anything to do with you in the first place.'

'Bullshit! The reason I didn't want you is that I do, in spite of everything, retain some faint instinct of self-preservation. Everyone knows you're always sucking up to vulnerable women who've got money. Well, you never keep them very long, do you? I wonder why?'

'Lucy, I prefer to believe you're still capable of some rational communication. I know you have problems; you may remember I even bothered to find a therapist who'd be able to help you, and small thanks I got for that. Rest assured my eyes are opened, and my attentions to you will never, thankfully, be renewed. I thought better of anything I felt for you a long time ago. No, I come here today as a public representative, in the cause of public justice. I come to tell you, before a witness, that your secret is no longer a secret. The President himself now knows that you retained letters belonging originally to Lemuel Hawkins, and that after the death of Hawkins' son Nicholas – and I make no mention of your responsibility for that – you have systematically blackmailed Mr Baskerville, a respected public official of this government, for the last twelve years.'

'I *what*?'

'Blackmail. An unpleasant word for an unpleasant offence. I took what steps I could. You've been bluffing Mr Baskerville, haven't you, Miss Morgan? Those letters, addressed, I believe, by Lemuel Hawkins to your father, unaccountably disappeared from Ravnscar over four years ago. You didn't tell Mr Baskerville that, did you, Lucy?'

'You're out of your box!'

'No, you didn't tell him, and your silence has been lucrative. Perhaps I should have had more compunction. It was I who removed those letters, Lucy. I still loved you then. I wanted to turn you back from the ruinous course which you were determined to pursue. Of course, as you recall, I tried to talk you out of it. I tried to make you see that money gained by evil means would never bring you happiness. I offered you an alternative. In fact I offered all that I have. You spurned me, but in the interests of justice and the public good I removed the letters. You must have noticed that, Lucy, but you never spoke. I've kept those letters in a safe place all this time, but now I fear the time has come when in the interests of justice I am forced to reveal the unhappy truth. For your sake I've put myself in danger, as accessory after the fact. I think my compunction will be understood. The only course open to me now is to make your actions public.'

'Olly!' said Lucy. 'Get out of here. Go on! Just get!'

I'd never seen her look so formidable. To my surprise he didn't quail. Instead, before either of us could move, he strode across the room and grabbed me by the arm, where I was still standing thunderstruck, holding on to the edge of the table. 'Oh, no, Lucy. You can't intimidate me now! Think of your friend here! She is the witness of what I have to say. Have you told her how you deliberately suppressed the truth? How you've pretended friendship to young Honeyman all these years? And yet you knew who murdered his father, and you didn't hesitate to make what profit you could from that? Have you told Sidony what you've done? Does she know how you and Nicholas Hawkins involved young Jared in smuggling drugs? Was she aware of any of that when you encouraged her to get into Jared's bed? Did you tell her how he'd been using the contacts Hawkins gave him? Does she know who arranged for him to be where he is now?'

'You're lying! It's a lie from beginning to end, and you know it!'

'Oh, no, Lucy, I think not. I think when I take you down to Ogg's Cove police station, our government will be glad to reward me for bringing a criminal to justice at long last.'

I think Lucy began to have an inkling of what he was up to at the same moment as I did. I didn't believe Olly for a moment. Lucy still didn't know, of course, that he'd been busted. I wondered when he'd found out. Nor did she know, as I did, who employed him. Olly must have discovered the raid, and since then he'd probably found out just what Ishmael and Colombo had been doing today. He couldn't hope that Hook would protect him. Hook would save his own bacon first. Unless Olly could offer another, more profitable scapegoat, and point out to Hook that he could then still have a faithful servant at the Pele Centre ready to command? Why would Hook accept Lucy instead of Olly? Would Baskerville let that happen? Maybe Baskerville would; there was no love lost between him and the house of Morgan. They already had Jared. If Olly offered Lucy too, as an alternative sacrifice to himself, what was in it for them? The answer came to me, even while I struggled to free myself from Olly's predatory grip. Ravnscar. They'd get Ravnscar, and all its treasure. No doubt Olly had already suggested it. The man must be desperate, but he was still trying to twist his way out.

Lucy ran across to her desk by the window, and picked up the phone. Her hand was on the dial. The emergency number in Hy Brasil is 111. She dialled one. Olly let go of me, and was across the room like a streak of lightning.

Lucy screamed and dropped the phone. She ran for the door. I heard her scream again, in the conservatory. The outside door banged.

Olly put the phone back on the hook and turned to me. 'She can't go far,' he said. 'I think you'd better accompany me instead. You witnessed all of that, didn't you? I think we should tell the police all about it, don't you?'

He was advancing on me slowly, round the table. Both the door through to the conservatory and the door into the tower were behind him. I backed away from him, towards the stove.

There were two doors I could possibly reach. The back stair to the Great Hall. But if I went upstairs, he'd follow. Chase me through the house. I'd have to run across the hall, down the main stair, back through the kitchen. The other door led to the cellar. He might not think of that.

I could feel the warmth of the stove at my back. I ran forward and dodged round the table. I was at the cellar door. He threw himself on to the table and swung his legs over it. I hadn't bargained for that. I tugged the door open and shot down the stairs.

He was after me. I darted across the first cellar. My sandalled feet clattered on the worn out steps. Louder footsteps echoed just behind.

Into the wine cellar. My arms stretched in front of me, feeling the dark. I made for where I thought the door was. I met stone wall and groped along it. There was wood under my hands. I scrabbled for the handle, and flung the door open. The torch was in its place on the shelf. There was a crash from the wine cellar. I glanced round, shone the torch. He'd tripped over a cask and fallen headlong. Wine spurted over the stone flags like blood.

A plan jumped into my head. He was still getting up. I prayed to God he wouldn't find the light switch. He obviously didn't know the place. But he'd know about the caverns. Deliberately I darted back into the wine cellar and flashed my torch, behind the casks.

He was after me. I dodged, found the other door. Flung it open. Flashed the torch. Into the little dead-end vault where Morgan kept his Napoleonic cognac. Torch out. I threw myself back against the wall, just out of arm's reach of the door.

It worked. He followed. Stumbled into the dark right by me. I cowered from the image of groping hands. He passed me.

I nipped back through the door and slammed it to with all my strength. I felt for the great iron key, and using both hands I turned it. It locked with a clank. I tugged the handle. Locked. Well and truly locked. I pulled out the key. It was cold in my hand.

He guessed. It must be pitch dark in there. He was back at the door. In the beam of the torch I saw the handle turn. Had I really locked it? I held my clenched fist tight against my face, watching. The door didn't budge. He started banging. I ran, clutching the torch and the key.

Up the stairs. Into the cellar. Up the stairs. The kitchen desk. The phone. I picked it up. My hands were trembling so much I could hardly dial. One-one-one. The torch was still on. I switched it off.

'Hy Brasil coastguards. Can I help you?'

'Oh,' I said, hearing the shake in my voice. 'Oh, please. I've just caught a man. In the cellar. Oh, please, please come.'

TWENTY-FIVE

COLOMBO LEANED BACK against the sofa and inhaled luxuriously. He breathed out very slowly and achieved one perfect smoke ring. It hovered for a moment between him and the pale light outside the window, then vanished. He closed his eyes. It had been quite a day.

Presently he picked up his pipe again. He had bought it years ago in an antique shop in Amsterdam, and he was fond of it. It was made of blue-and-white earthenware, with a round bowl and curiously flattened stem. The contents were last year's home-grown from his brother-in-law's greenhouse, Hy Brasil's best. He tapped the ashes out of the bowl, pressed down the green weed, and breathed in again. The dry leaves glowed. He held his breath for a moment, eyes half-closed.

His story would be in Saturday's *Times*, on the front page. President's orders. He remembered his editor's face, when he'd put the phone down after the call came through, and he laughed softly. And when Colombo had shown him the negatives, still damp from processing . . . All he had to do tomorrow was look over the layout. Not that design was any of his business, really, but this was his scoop.

So that was it. He had no compunction at all about Olly West. He'd never liked the man, and since the day when at Lucy's request he'd ordered the fellow to stop pestering her, he'd despised him as well. Olly had tried to poison Colombo's mind against Lucy, and when Colombo had finally hauled him off the premises, Olly had accused Colombo of trying to fling him over the precipice, and had subsequently attempted to sue him for damages. Luckily, Gunn and Selkirk had persuaded him he didn't have a case. No, Colombo wasn't going to agonise over Olly. Olly had been in this racket up to the neck, and he must have known that Jim would dump him if things got tough. Maybe they'd arrested him by now. Ishmael had said he couldn't be found. If that was Jim dragging his feet, Ishmael would probably know how to apply a bit more pressure. The case was in the bag now, anyway.

The other matter was more complicated. Until he'd read Lem Hawkins' letters, Colombo had banked on the possibility that Baskerville might not be seriously implicated. In one respect Colombo was in total agreement with his President: Jared should not see those letters. If Jared knew the truth, the country would become untenable either for Jared or for Baskerville. Hook, Colombo had no doubt, would find his own way out of it, as he always did. It was hard to see how that could be done, however, without sacrificing one man or the other. In Colombo's view both Jared and Baskerville were irreplaceable: ironically enough, for many of the same reasons. Hook had sworn Ishmael to secrecy, but would Ishmael find a way round that? Those letters should be kept in government archives, unattainable, at least until Hook and Baskerville were dead. Twenty years? Thirty? What would Jared be like then? Or himself? Or Ishmael? Would Jared ever forgive them?

What would he, Colombo, feel if it were him? Hard to imagine. His own father, Ewan MacAdam, had died suddenly of a heart attack, in the square near the fountain on a balmy Tuesday evening in May, on his way to a Dorrado Horticultural Society meeting three years ago. It was a brief and public way to die. His body had been brought back to his house and laid in a coffin in the front room that looked out over his prize roses to the jagged islet of Tegid Voel. On the following Saturday every man in Dorrado had followed the coffin to the churchyard. In the small house at the back of the town, which had once contained nine children, Colombo's mother now presided alone over a determined world of grandchildren, photographs, visitors and cats. Colombo didn't visit as often as he should, because weekends were complicated, but he retained a childlike assumption, he realised, that there was still a home to go back to.

The Honeymans had rented their house at Ogg's Cove from Ravnscar Estates. It was right above the beach, a stone cottage with a fuchsia hedge around the garden, standing on its own about half a mile out of the town. Colombo had probably only been in it once or twice. When he'd slept the night on Jared's floor a couple of months ago, and had lain sleepily watching the sweep of the Despair light, two long, two short, across the walls and ceiling, he'd found himself remembering the Ogg's Cove cottage. There was a picture on Jared's wall that had reminded him of it. Twenty years, thirty years. Would Jared ever forgive them? How much did he think about the past anyway? There was no way of knowing. Colombo shook his head, and raised his pipe to his lips again. It couldn't be helped. Jared would surely understand by then, if it did come out, that none of them had had a choice.

He wasn't feeling sleepy: the last two days had held too much for his mind to stop working over all that had happened. He was feeling mellow, however, and quite ready to put all action behind him. Just now it would be a huge effort even to stand up and draw the curtains. Anyway, there was no need. His apartment was on the fourth floor. In daylight it looked over a roofscape of tiles and chimney pots, with beyond them a small glimpse of the sea. All that was visible now, from where he lay on the floor, was the reflection of the street lights in the sky, pierced here and there by the faint pinpricks of the brightest stars. If he stretched out his right arm he could switch on the lamp, but he couldn't be bothered to do it. If he did, the windows would blank out and the velvet-soft night sky would vanish.

He thought about going to bed. If he fell asleep on the hearthrug it wouldn't be for the first time. The view from the sitting room floor pleased him. His crammed bookshelves stretched up and up to the ceiling on both sides of the fireplace. There was just enough light to see the figures in the Chagall reproduction over the mantelpiece: the round white moon, the naked white-winged angel, the pale face of the tumbler, the eye of the red horse. No limpid blue, not in this light, but he could imagine it almost as well as if it were there. Above him he could see the angular pattern of the window panes cast by the street lights, at odds with the other pattern of the moulded cornice and the rose in the middle of the ceiling. 1902. They could be bothered to make ornamental ceilings in 1902, even on the fourth floor. He thought about the men who'd carefully plastered the ceiling ninety-five years ago. Ragged-trousered philanthropists, no doubt. He inhaled again.

The bell rang. The sound had barely permeated his consciousness when it rang again, insistently, as if someone were leaning on the bell push. Then it stopped, but it was followed immediately by a banging on the door. Colombo stood up groggily, ran his hands through his hair, and went and opened the front door. '*Lucy!*'

'Oh.' She tumbled through the front door, and literally fell on his neck. 'Colombo! Oh, thank God you're here!' She burst into tears.

He shut the door with one hand, led her into the sitting room, sat her on the sofa, and took her in his arms. 'What's happened? M'dear, what is it?'

'I came straight here.' She was shivering so hard her teeth were chattering. 'Colombo, this place *reeks* of dope.'

'You shall have some. M'dear, what is it? What's happened?'

'Olly,' Lucy said, and began to weep afresh. 'He came to the house. Olly West!'

'Oh, Jesus! Lucy, what did he do to you? What happened?'

'He didn't do anything. I ran away.' She choked back tears. 'I ran into the dark. Along the cliff path. The path Nicky went. I didn't mean to. I didn't think. I just ran, right along the top of the gorge past the stone bench. I couldn't see. I was at the brambly bit. I slipped. I couldn't tell where I was. I think it was that bit – you know – where the path gives way, just where it turns back into the wood. Right by the edge. It was dark. I couldn't see to climb up again. It was slippery. Wet with dew. I didn't dare move. I thought . . . I thought . . .' She buried her face in his shirt and wept without restraint.

If she heard the things he murmured into her hair, she gave no sign of it. Her hands were very cold. He felt her arms up her sleeves, and they were cold too. She was frozen. 'Lucy. Lucy, m'dear. Tell me. It's all right now.'

He had to bend very close to hear her. 'It was the old path. The one that's worn away. I couldn't see to get up again. I didn't dare move. There wasn't anything to hold on to. I just waited. I thought I'd have to wait till light. But gradually it was easier to see. I was below the edge, but only just. About five feet down. It was barely a ledge I was on. It was all crumbly. I was scared I'd fall. But I knew if I didn't move I'd just get stiffer and tireder until I fell off. I couldn't have kept hold, not all night. So in the end I just went for it. I climbed up fast so I couldn't think. I couldn't see to hold on. I did slip, but by that time I'd got my arms over the edge. I grabbed hold of a bit of tree and I pulled myself up. And then I just lay there for a long time.' She sat up, her hands against his chest, her tears still falling freely. 'Why did I run like that? Along there, of all places? I must have been mad. But he scared me so! He scared me.' She gave a convulsive shudder, and buried her wet face in his shirt.

'But you came here.'

'I went back in. Because of Sidony.'

'Sidony?' His voice was suddenly sharp. 'Was she there too?'

'She'd gone. He'd gone.' Lucy was sobbing again. 'Colombo, I looked all over the house. Everything was left just as it had been. And there wasn't anybody there at all!'

'So what did you do?'

'I didn't know what to do. I got in the Land Rover and I came straight here.'

'You mean when you ran away Sidony was there with Olly West? And when you came back there was no sign of either of them? How long were you out there?'

'I don't know. It felt like forever.'

'Lucy, don't cry! Wait!' He came back a moment later with a full tumbler. 'Drink this. You'll feel better.'

'What is it?'

'Claret. Drink it. That's right. Now tell me from the beginning.'

He listened, interrupting her sometimes with anxious questions. When he'd got the gist of it he pressed her hands around the glass again, and made her hold it. 'Finish this. I won't be a minute.' He switched on the lamp and picked up the phone.

'Ishmael? Ishmael? Thank God you're there . . . . Did I wake you?'

Lucy closed her eyes and drank. She couldn't stop shaking, and the glass clattered against her teeth. The drive was fading away into nightmare; she couldn't remember any of it clearly. Colombo's voice went on, sharp and urgent. He was talking about her.

'Yes, she's here. She's all right. No, well, I don't think she was in any state to think of that. No, she's all right.'

So Ishmael thought she was a fool, or worse. Lucy supposed it didn't matter any more. Just at the moment nothing mattered. She took another gulp of wine. Colombo's voice changed. She raised her head quickly, listening hard.

'She did?' Suddenly, amazingly, he sounded gleeful. 'No! . . . Oh, brilliant! . . . Oh, well done Sidony! . . . She's there? . . . Can I speak to her? . . . Is it really?' He looked at his watch. 'Good God, you're right. So it is . . . No, no, that's fine . . . In the morning then . . .'

At last he put the phone down. 'It's all right. Sidony locked

Olly in the wine cellar. She called the police, and then she called Ishmael. Olly's in the cells, and Sidony's in the spare bedroom at Ferdy's Landing. I hope she's sleeping better than he is.'

'She did what?' Lucy drained her glass. 'Explain, Colombo! Tell me everything!'

'I will. Are you all right? I'll get you some more wine.'

'I don't need more.'

'I do.'

He came back with the rest of the bottle and poured another glass. While he told her what Ishmael had said, he re-filled his pipe and lit it. When it was going nicely he handed it to her, and took back the glass. Presently they swapped again.

Lucy stopped shivering. She was beginning to feel warm again, enveloped in a drowsy sense of well-being. Colombo's story pleased both of them, and so he told it her again. She laughed, and wriggled down against his shoulder. He passed her the pipe again. It reminded her of Nick. She was sad about Nick, but the bad parts seemed very far away, now that she was warm again. And the good was suddenly very close to her, as it had never been since the day he'd died. She'd not again lain like this, curled up against a man's comfortable body, since that last night she'd been with Nick. She reminded herself vaguely that she had to be wary, that always, whenever a man was concerned, especially if she were betrayed into feeling fond of him, she had to be extremely wary. She had a sudden flash of memory: a too big, too white, too insistent body that had not been Nick's, a chilly room in Kidd's Hotel where she had never wanted to be. Having to be on her guard against men, all the time, in case one of them did reach in and get her. But everything had been too dangerous and complicated for far too long. She passed Colombo the pipe again. The glass was empty now. Lucy breathed out smoke, and shut her eyes.

The important thing was that he should not touch her. Or was it important? Nicky had touched her in every possible way. She could remember now, as she had not done in all the years between, what that had been like. For the first time the feel of Nick's body against hers came back to her, not as a fact dug up like a fossil from an irrevocable past, but vividly present, a flesh-and-blood human being who'd felt and responded to her touch. She could feel the warmth of Colombo through his shirt. She wanted to touch him, feel his skin under her hands. She'd forgotten what it was like to want that. She tugged at his shirt, untucking it, and slid her hands up over his chest. She heard him take in his breath. Then he was kissing her, as no one had been allowed to do in thirteen years. He was stroking her, underneath her shirt. Her fingers were at his belt, undoing it, the same as she'd undone Nick's.

'Lucy. Come to bed. Please, come to bed.'

His bedroom was colder. On one of the plain white walls there was a photograph of a sea-green goblet merged with a glassy sea. 'That's Nicky's goblet.' It was like a dream to see it there, either a dream or something which had already happened. It was like a dream to undo the rest of his clothes and take them off him, to feel his hands moving over her bare skin. She hadn't even let herself realise before that she'd wanted to do this.

'No, that one's its twin. Lucy, I love you. You know that, don't you, *minha querida*? You believe me when I tell you that?'

'*Água mole em pedra dura, tanto dá até que fura.* Perhaps you'll tell me so many times that in the end I'll believe you.'

'Perhaps you believe me now.'

Lying against him, feeling his body entwined with hers, his mouth moving over her skin: that was like a dream too, of a lost younger time which had been real. In some far away part of herself she was crying, but it didn't matter. He licked the tears off her face. 'Lucy, it's all right. It's going to be all right.' She couldn't remember any more the reasons why she should not believe him, or Nicky either. Pray for us now and at the hour of our death. She had not prayed for him, or anyone, since the hour of his death. Perhaps it was not too late. To let Colombo do this now, to lie with her, to be alive and moving inside her, to take Nick's place as if there were no reason left in the world why he should not: perhaps even now it wasn't all too late. She was waking up, her dammed-up senses brimming over, everything inside her that she'd thought had to be dead and gone, was suddenly aware. She was alive even though he was dead; she was here, now, doing this with him, even though Nicky would never come back again.

Colombo was trying to file everything away before anyone came in and saw what he was doing, but the filing cabinet was stuffed full, and there were papers piling up everywhere, more and more of them. If he didn't get rid of them they'd be found, and meanwhile the front door bell was ringing and ringing, on and on right through his head. He groaned and rolled over. It didn't feel like morning, he was not alone in his bed, and the front door bell shrilled imperatively. The bell was not a dream. He was in bed with Lucy. That part wasn't a dream either. He made himself open his eyes. It wasn't quite light. The front door bell kept on ringing. He could hear her even breathing beside him. She didn't stir. There was a steady low-pitched knocking at the front door. The bell rang again.

He groped his way sleepily to the door, pulling on a black silk dressing-gown as he went. Outside the landing light burned dimly. He peered out.

'Jed! What on earth . . .'

'I'm sorry to wake you. They've let me out.'

'Now? What time is it?'

'Gone five. They let me out around one. A sort of final touch, I suppose, seven hours after the last bus. Not that I had any money for the fare. I'm sorry.'

Colombo tried to gather his wits. 'Don't be silly. Come in. They've let you out, then.' He touched Jared briefly on the shoulder, and made himself wake up a bit more. 'It's good to see you! Man, that's good! Come on in.' He led the way into the kitchen. Jared followed, bringing with him a powerful smell of disinfectant. 'Drink? Something to eat?'

'I wouldn't mind a cup of tea.'

'Sure.' Colombo reached for the kettle.

'Can I have it in a cup?'

'A cup?'

'Yes. A china cup, if you don't mind, with a handle. And a saucer.'

'Of course.' Colombo opened the cupboard. 'Anything to eat? You're sure? They let you out at *one* did you say?' He glanced at the kitchen clock. 'Where've you been all night, for God's sake?'

'Walking around. It's a warm night. It was nice to be outside.'

'You've been walking around for four hours?'

'Yes. It took a while to get back to the town. The Port road's a mess still, and there were no lights. By the time I got to the street lights I just felt like going on. Like I say, it's a nice night, and I needed some exercise. But I'd quite like to go to sleep now.'

'Of course.' Wide awake now, Colombo looked Jared over for the first time. He looked thinner, the bones in his face more sharply defined, and he was uncharacteristically pale. His freckles had almost gone. He had the remains of a black eye, a big purple bruise turning yellowish. The other eye looked bruised too, but that, Colombo thought, was just exhaustion. His beard had grown enough to make it look as if it was meant to be there. Colombo was aware of a gut reaction that was neither curiosity nor pity. He thought it must be liking. Aloud he said, 'You're OK, are you? Undamaged?'

Jared grinned. 'Yeah, I guess so. Undamaged.' He took the cup of tea. 'Thanks. So, it was a bit of a surprise. They came and woke me up. They didn't say what for. That shook me a bit. I didn't know what was going on. They said to have a shower. I was bloody glad of that, though I did just wonder if they might be purifying the sacrifice. I mean, why suddenly make a fellow have a shower in the middle of the night? They even gave me bug dope. Do I smell of it? I thought so. I can smell it myself. So I knew something was up. Then they let me have my things back. It's quite strange wearing proper clothes, you know, sort of tight and scratchy, but it does make you feel like you're a human being again. As soon as I'd put them on they just shoved me out the door. And that was that. Do you know why?'

'Yes.' Colombo's mind was working fast again. He gave Jared a lucid but succinct account of the whole story that would appear tomorrow morning in *The Hesperides Times*. He answered all Jared's questions fully. Luckily Jed was wholly taken up with the drugs angle. He didn't ask anything about Baskerville's particular interest, or the possibility of blackmail. When Colombo realised there was no reason at all why the other connection should even occur to him, he began to relax, and became much more animated. When he gave Jed a graphic, if third-hand, account of Sidony's capture of Olly West, Jared laughed out loud, and the shadow of the prison lifted suddenly. For a moment he looked his old self. Even as he laughed in response Colombo remembered something else. 'Ssh. Keep your voice down, Jed.' Jared looked surprised. 'I'm not on my own tonight. I mean, I've got someone sleeping here.'

'Oh?' Jared glanced towards the kitchen door. 'Well, I guess you won't have room for me as well. It's OK. It's nearly morning.'

'Don't be silly. You can have the sofa. The sitting room's empty.'

'Oh.' Jared took in the implications of this. 'Oh, look then, you're not going to want me here too. That's OK. I'll be fine. Could you lend me a jersey maybe?'

It shamed Colombo that he'd had the same thought himself. He said roughly, 'Quit being so damned self-effacing. You'll sleep here.' He stood up. 'What about tomorrow? What do you want to do?'

'Find Sidony,' said Jared promptly. 'And then go home and see if everything's all right. So I guess I'll go to Ravnscar first.'

'She's not at Ravnscar. After they came and got Olly, Ishmael took her back to Ferdy's Landing. Apparently she said she'd be OK at Ravnscar on her own, but Ishmael talked her into going back with him.'

'On her own? But where's Lucy?'

'Oh, God,' said Colombo. 'Well, it seems you're going to find out soon enough. Lucy's here.'

'Oh.' Jared glanced at the door again. 'You know what? I think it might be a good idea if I went. I don't want to be in anyone's way.'

'Oh, for God's sake! You come here straight out of prison and you want me to throw you into the street! Who do you think I am? Shut up, Jed. I'm going to get you some bedding.'

Lucy sat swirling black coffee round in a big Breton cup. On the table in front of her there were two hot croissants, fresh that morning from the Harbour Bakery. There was butter in a blue dish and a pot of blueberry jam from Finnegan's, but Lucy hadn't touched any of it. Colombo went on buttering his croissant, one mouthful at a time, and waited for her to finish what she had to say to him.

'You *knew* I was in a vulnerable state! You *saw* how upset I was. And what did you do? You bloody well *drugged* me. You took your chance on what had happened, and you *deliberately* got me stoned out of my mind. You pretty much *raped* me. That's what it amounts to. I'll never trust you again. Ever.'

'If you think I raped you I'm surprised you want to go on sitting there drinking my coffee. Anything else?'

'You can't deny you drugged me! You gave me everything you could think of that would get me out of my head. You got me drunk! You got me stoned! You gave me all that stuff, *on purpose!*'

'I gave you everything I could think of that would make you feel better.'

'If you think I feel better because you got me into that state and then *seduced* me . . .'

'Oh, so it's not rape any more. That's good.'

'And then you go off in the middle of the night and tell Jared everything! *Jared*! What do you think that makes me feel, you telling Jared all about how you've got me into bed at last! What do you think I felt like, having to face him this morning? Jesus, I'd have thought you'd have had more sensitivity than that!'

'I got the impression he was more interested in croissants than he was in you. What would you have had me do? Throw him out at five in the morning?'

'Yes! He could have gone somewhere else! Jed's got loads of friends! You could have said it wasn't a good time to come here!'

'Not a good time to be let out of prison, eh? You wanted me to tell Jed that? Suggest he chose a more convenient time?'

'It couldn't have been a *worse* time! He'll tell Sidony. He'll tell *everyone*!'

'I doubt it. Would it matter if he did?'

'I don't want anyone to know, *ever*! As far as I'm concerned it didn't even *happen*! I wasn't in my right mind, and you know it. I'll forgive you, I suppose, but only if we forget it. It was a terrible mistake. That's the only way I can ever even *see* you again. If we forget it ever even *happened*.'

'It did happen. I can't possibly forget any of it. And it wasn't a mistake. We both knew what we were doing.'

'I *didn't*! I wasn't even able to *think*! You didn't *let* me! How could you? *You* didn't think about *me*! You didn't care! Supposing I'm pregnant! You didn't think about that either, did you? You wouldn't even care if you'd done that to me!'

'Yes, I would. I'd care very much.'

'But you didn't do anything to prevent it!'

'No. I'm afraid I didn't think of it. At least, when I did it was too late. I'm sorry.' He met her eyes for a fleeting moment. 'How likely do you think it is?'

'*Now* you ask me! *Now*! I don't know how you *dare*! How should *I* know? Why ever should I . . .'

As soon as the phone started ringing he jumped up and answered it, as if he'd rather be doing anything, Lucy thought resentfully, than talking to her.

'Ishmael . . . yes, yes . . . No, I haven't . . . No, I'm still having breakfast . . . I know, but I didn't get much sleep . . . What? . . . *What*? . . . Where, where? . . . Not Dorrado? . . . Not towards Dorrado? . . . Oh my God . . . You mean this is it? . . . It is? . . . No, no, nothing . . .' Colombo glanced out of the window behind him. 'Not a thing . . . Nothing . . . Easterly, I suppose . . . Jesus, I don't believe it . . . I'll go right over there . . . You are? Now? . . . Jesus Christ, I never thought . . .'

There was a long pause. Colombo was listening, and Lucy, her attention arrested, stared at Colombo as if she could read his face. Suddenly she jumped up and stood beside him, putting her ear to the phone as well. She could just hear Ishmael's voice '. . . not coming fast. But it's on the move, there's no doubt about that. There's nothing to see here. But we can smell it. I spoke to the President. He agreed to let Allardyce open up the Pele Centre. Allardyce was up there by six. I sent Peterkin up to give him a hand. Allardyce was going on down to Dorrado. I'm meeting him there. I don't think there's any danger in the town. But I want to see for myself.'

'I'll come right over. But wait . . . Ishmael, Jed's here. He's out. He got here at five this morning.'

'Thank the Lord for that. They left it a bit late didn't they? Is he OK?'

'He's fine. They released him at one but he decided to take a stroll around the town. He fetched up here at five.'

'Can I speak to him?'

'He's not here. He went to the swimming pool.'

'The *swimming pool*?'

'Yes, he said he'd been having fantasies all the time he was in there about lying in the hot springs. So that's what he's gone to do. I gave him breakfast, and then he borrowed some soap and shampoo and a towel and a tube of arnica, and off he went. That must have been . . .' Colombo glanced at the clock, 'over an hour ago.'

'To lie in a hot spring? When there's everything to do today? He has to see Utterson and give his deposition; there's the apology from Government House – it was like pulling teeth to get that out of them – he needs to pick that up before some bureaucrat thinks better of it; the police in Ogg's Cove want him as a witness; I've got a letter sitting here for him from the *National Geographic* about his Spanish treasure which'll probably make him his fortune; there's his girl here eating her heart out for him and refusing to budge out of earshot of the telephone; Mount Brasil's spewing out boiling lava; and Jared just decides he'll go and lie in a hot spring all morning. Is the man crazy? What on earth's he thinking of?'

'He's thinking about how he's feeling, I expect,' said Colombo.

'Well, get him out of there and bring him to Dorrado. Tell him the mountain's on fire and see if that moves him.'

'OK. I'll bring Lucy too.'

'Yes, do that. She's wanted at Ogg's Cove police station too.'

'That'll have to wait. We're coming to Dorrado.'

TWENTY-SIX

Sidony Redruth. Ile de l'Espoir. August 3rd.
Notes for *Undiscovered Islands* (working title).

RED-HOT LAVA is like spouting blood. I've never seen a serious injury, thank God. I know bodies are fragile, and in the end they'll disappear back to where they came from, but I've never had to confront that yet. The earth has always been cool and solid under my feet. I see the marks of the glaciers on our worn-down hills at home, but I've never had fully to comprehend that the land won't endure for ever. But standing on the slopes of Mount Brasil, a mile up from Dorrado, for the first time in my life, I saw.

This place that I've grown to love: it's not for ever. It's on the move all the time, either growing or dying, or fluctuating unpredictably between the two. It came out of the sea five million years ago, which isn't long by the earth's standards, and one day it will sink back, and be gone. Tomorrow, or five million years from now. No one can be sure.

This was just a job; I didn't mean to fall in love with the place. I didn't mean to set my heart on anything that might not last. I've let this country, which wasn't even mine, entangle me. I'm beguiled. And now I find it promises nothing back, not even that it'll be here tomorrow.

I wrote down in my notebook yesterday, as nearly as I could, what the eruption was like:

Half a mile from where I sit, a curtain of red-hot lava shoots into the air. Fountains of fire rise and fall along the fissure where the earth has cracked open like an over-ripe apricot, its insides bursting out in what seems to me, used as I am now to a soft landscape of blues and greens and greys, like something that should only be on celluloid. The inside of the planet is red and visceral. I suppose I knew that. The line of fire stretches from the Dorrado foothills to the rocks just below the summit of Mount Brasil. The horizon shimmers through the gases that rise from the melted rock. I can feel the heat from here; it's like facing an autumn bonfire. The place is full of a noise which is neither fire nor river, but something between the two. I inhale sulphur. Oddly enough, I like the smell. It's acrid but almost sweet, not at all how I imagine the fires of hell. The forecast says this light easterly wind won't change, but what if it did? There's a red-black plume coming out of the top of the mountain. It billows up for a thousand feet or more, and then the tail of it drifts west over the sea and dissipates, like the smoke from a gigantic steamer that's gone over the horizon along with the age it came from. If the wind changes and the plume curls back inland, it will rain brimstone and ashes. Just now the sky over our heads is the fragile blue of blackbirds' eggs.

The lava is spilling over from the fountains and trickling slowly down the hill like boiling jam overflowing the pan. It's rock, it's liquid, and it's fire: three incompatible things made one. There's a foolish part of me that watches it move slowly across the green hillside and the grey basalt outcrops, over the pastures where the small flowers grow – chickweed, milkwort, eyebright and the pink patches of the fading thrift – and just thinks what a terrible mess it's making. It's remorseless, like a tank ploughing its way through someone's garden. It's an outrage. But nobody is responsible for this.

Unless I am. I can't rid myself of the insane notion that somehow this is all my fault. It would be appalling if this lovely land should all be gone, but the worst thing of all, the thing that would make it impossible to bear, would be if I were responsible. Of course I'm not. But I knew I was doing wrong to go up to the top of the volcano by myself. I felt guilty all the time. *Forgive us our trespasses*. There is nothing I could have possibly caused to happen just by being there yesterday. I didn't trigger anything; the volcano was going to erupt anyway. Think of all those earthquakes we've had ever since I arrived. I'm being crazy, but I wish someone would tell me that the eruption of Mount Brasil was nothing to do with me. They can't, of course, because I won't tell anybody now that I was there. *As we forgive them that trespass against us*. I'm being silly; no one here would blame me in the least even if they knew.

I wrote all that, read it over, and realised it would never do for a guidebook. It was all about me. I crossed out the final paragraph, stood up, and walked a little further so I could see down into the next fold of the foothills.

A river of rock, half-a-mile across, was moving slowly down the southern slopes of Mount Brasil. In the middle it was silvery-grey, like mercury, but round the edges it was the colour of red-hot coals. Last time I looked there was a green strip between the lava and the coast; you could still have walked along the path where Jared had taken me. But just in the past hour the strip had vanished, and now the rock was cascading in slow motion over the fifty-foot cliffs along the shore. The sea foamed into clouds of hissing steam that rose like geysers, then melted like flurries of snow falling into a lake. I saw red rock hit the water and go grey, as if the sea were an alchemist's elixir going backwards, turning fire to stone. Behind the clouds of steam the pall of dust and ashes was still spreading seawards, like the fall-out from Genesis Day Three.

I turned and faced the other way, south towards Dorrado. The sky was blue, the land clean and ordinary. I couldn't see the town from here, but the derelict whaling station was visible at the mouth of the Dorrado river. There were people scattered across the hills like tourists out for a picnic in a London park, except that they were all looking one way, towards the plume of murky smoke and the inconceivable red flow behind me. I surveyed the crowd to see if I could find Anna and the children. She'd said they might start walking back to Dorrado, and she'd expect me when she saw me.

I saw Jared. He was walking up the hill, just past where we'd parked the van the day we'd come out here together. He was wearing the same jeans and checked shirt he'd put on the morning we were on Despair, the last time I'd seen him. I jumped up on to the nearest rock and called his name.

The second time I shouted he heard me. I jumped off the rock, ran downhill, and met him halfway. Then he was in my arms and hugging me and saying things and kissing me in a most un-British fashion, in front of a whole crowd of people. But I didn't care; I wasn't even embarrassed any more. I suppose it wouldn't necessarily be a *moral* dereliction if a person failed to finish writing a guidebook and just went native instead.

Probably I should have tried to meet Anna and tell her where I'd gone, even though she'd said not to bother. I should have found Lucy and made sure she was all right. Jared said she was with Colombo, but when I saw Colombo he was busy scrambling over the rocks taking photographs. I should have told someone where I was, a thing which my mother taught me always to do. With an erupting volcano behind me, in a situation where no one had any idea at all what might happen next, it was my duty to make sure no one was worried about me and everyone was happy. But I didn't. I went back to the Red Herring with Jared. I had just enough money for us to have supper. Jared only had the change from two pounds he'd borrowed from Colombo to get into the swimming pool that morning. The problem about money in Hy Brasil is that it weighs such a lot. I'm always leaving piles of pennies in my bedroom and then wishing I had them with me.

We walked back to Dorrado along the track we'd driven

when Jared first brought me to the back of the mountain. The boggy patches were churned to mud by hoofprints, and when we came down the sunken track through the terraces we had to tread carefully between prolific cow-pats. All the animals had been herded off the hill, so when we reached the water meadows they were crowded. I never heard such a Babel of mooing and baaing, tinkling goat-bells and deep-toned cattle bells. 'It sounds like the Day of Judgment,' I said to Jared. He said he thought it was more like Exodus. 'And that had the advantage of being real,' he added. 'The flocks and herds part, anyway.'

It was eerie walking through the town. There were people standing in the square in little groups, talking and watching. I think I was the only stranger. They'd put a police barrier on the Dorrado road, and were only letting through the people who belonged. Jared said they'd recognised Colombo's car coming from St Brandons and waved them through. They'd let the Pereiras and myself through as well because Anna's parents live in Dorrado. I think Ishmael would have persuaded them anyway if there'd been any difficulty. Later Ishmael had gone off with Allardyce, a taciturn man who looks as if he's spent his entire adult life being toasted in a desert. He seems to be running the Pele Centre now.

The bar of the Red Herring was packed with locals. We sat in the garden instead and watched the clouds of steam rising from where the lava met the sea. They must be nearly a hundred feet high, Jared said, to be visible over the curve of the land between. We were still totting up what we could afford to eat when Ernest came out to speak to us. He shook Jared by the hand hard and lengthily, and Jared said, 'Colombo told me what you did. Thank you.'

'We won't mention that here,' said Ernest.

'You'll be full tonight?'

'The devil's in it that I'm not. I was expecting a bus-load of foreign journalists, but they're not letting anyone into the country. All flights to Hy Brasil cancelled except for natives wanting to get home. I thought this morning we'd have a full house, but it's no go.'

'Good. I mean, that's tough on you; what a shame. Ernest, I don't have any money on me, but I can pay later. You could have us instead of the journalists. How about that?'

I wondered whether to protest that I hadn't been consulted, but with Ernest offering us lobster, on the house, which he'd bought in for the expected journalists, I felt it would be churlish to make a fuss. Also, it was an incredible scoop for the book. I'd be the only foreigner in Dorrado tonight. Ernest said they were still on red alert for possible evacuation. The eruption seemed to have settled since the morning into the contained flow we'd been looking at. But once the fountains stopped jetting, we could expect an increased stream of lava. The fluidity of the lava was reassuring in one way, as it reduced the possibility of gas exploding inside the mountain, but in another way it meant that the flow could move fast and spread far. The talk from the bar was a steady hum, like telegraph wires, not loud at all, but low and anxious. Around the fountain in the square, there were still those tight knots of people standing about in a curious tense idleness, even though it was six o'clock and everyone should be indoors having tea. Even the children weren't playing. They were circling restively around the adults, their eyes fixed on the sooty plume rising from the hidden summit of Mount Brasil. It felt like the beginning of a war. Even the clouds of steam along the coast looked like the billows of gunfire in the picture of Waterloo that hangs over the mantelpiece in my grandfather's study in Clifton.

It gave me the unsettling feeling in my stomach that comes just before an exam. It wasn't just the volcano; it was my feelings too. I was sad, even though I'd found Jared again, because it was different from how I'd thought it would be. The time we'd missed when he was taken away from Despair had gone, and would never happen now. He hadn't been away for very long.

When I think of my grandfather, who was a prisoner-of-war for five years, what happened to Jared was nothing. There are things in history that I can't justly imagine. All I know from my own experience is that unexpected things had changed. While he was gone I'd thought I'd known him better than I really had, and now he was back I was shocked by how strange he was to me. It was only now that I remembered how little time we'd actually spent together. All that evening we were beginning again, quite tentatively. The only thing I was sure about was that I did want to begin again. Begin whatever it was: I didn't have an answer to that.

As I struggled with my lobster I also thought about Knossos, and Pompeii, and Herculaneum, and Stong, and St Pierre, and all the unsuspecting communities that had been swept out of history, each in one single unimaginable moment. Several people today had reassured me yet again that this wasn't a Pelean sort of eruption, but perhaps I'm naturally more nervous than I like to think. I was glad when a bottle of white wine appeared; I had no recollection of ordering it but it made me feel better. I began to feel light-headed and rather decadent, more like a sightseer from Nero's palace watching Rome burn than a victim of Vesuvius. Jared, engaged with his lobster, had no spare attention for conversation. If this were Imperial Rome, I thought, he'd have to be a barbarian from Gaul; I couldn't fit him in any other way. I could see Colombo, for example, in a toga, and Lucy would be quite at home in many ways. Even Jared wouldn't have to be an *uncivilised* barbarian. I thought about the Roman poets, and tried to remember where they came from. *Atque in perpetuum, frater, ave atque vale.*

I was disorientated by the strange mixture of delight and instability, comfort and uncertainty. The bathroom at the Red Herring is palatial. It has a black-and-white mosaic floor with a huge cast-iron tub in the middle of it with claw feet and big brass taps. When I turned on the hot tap, boiling water and a cloud of steam came out and I jumped back for fear of being scalded in the face. The water was stained red and smelled of sulphur. Jared said all the hot water in Dorrado comes directly from a cistern on the mountain. 'It must be going berserk up there,' he said. But that didn't stop us from having a deep and most luxurious bath. 'You don't think it'll suddenly blow up?' I asked him. 'Ignited by Pears soap?' he replied. 'I doubt it.'

We took the main bedroom that faces west across the bay. I never saw such a sunset before in all my life. The sky was aflame, and the sea reflected back the red and gold as bright as glass. The sun, swollen to twice the size it should be, was blood-red behind streaks of smoke like scribbled charcoal. It slid down the horizon as if it were dropping into a sea of fire and we'd come to the end of the world. As dusk fell we began to see a red glow in the sky to the right, like the neon lights of a phantom city. I knew what it reminded me of, and when I told Jared he was able to say it by heart: 'he took not away the pillar of cloud by day, nor the pillar of fire by night, from before the people'.

'I never read it as a threat before,' I said.

'Didn't you?' said Jared. 'Not even with all those commandments right next to it? I think I always saw it as an imposition.'

Imposed or not, it was magnificent, somehow orchestral: I had to remind myself that it was in reality quite silent. A cool salt-laden breeze drifted in from the sea through the open window, and mingled with the stench of sulphur. I sniffed it and was terrified. 'The wind's changing, Jared!' He said no, it was only because it was evening, and that was how it was meant to be.

We drew the curtains right back and opened the windows wide so we could watch. There were at least eight pillows on the bed. I remembered from last time the inimitable smell of the clean laundry at the Red Herring. The sulphur hadn't been able to drown it. We heaped the pillows up and curled ourselves up in the hollow of them, while we watched the colours intensify, and the red sun sink towards the sea. The light that came in through the window was red too. It touched us where we lay and flushed my skin pink. It turned Jared honey-coloured, and all the hairs on his body shone as if he'd been dipped in gold.

We had so much to talk about. We didn't try to say it all at once, but now and then one of us would think of something, and we'd say what it was out loud, and then we'd go on from there for a bit until we drifted away into other things. I was happy that it really mattered to him that yesterday – was it only yesterday? – I'd climbed the volcano. He seemed to think that was even cleverer than capturing Olly West, though that pleased him too. He said he was glad I'd seen the volcano the way he'd known it, because it would never be like that again. I was right: that spur of lava was the place he'd climbed down. He explained that being frightened had been part of the point, which didn't make much sense to me, but he said he never felt like that now. Gradually I began to understand better what had changed in him since we were on Despair. It wasn't just that he was thinner, or paler, or that he'd let his beard grow. It wasn't just that he'd been hit and mauled about and there were still bruises all over his body. It was more, I realised, that he'd faced the possibility that the life he'd known was over, maybe for ever. When he said that, I was aware of what I still had to say to him, and I knew, without feeling nervous about it any longer, that by morning I would have told him. But before morning there was all the time in the world, and it wasn't the moment yet.

The sun touched the sea at last. Yellow flames licked across the horizon. A red road shot across the water, straight from the drowning sun to the bay below the window. At first the sea seemed to dip away from the sun as if it were scorched, but a moment later it was the sun that was vanishing, and the sea was swallowing it voraciously. As the sun disappeared the night came in. Only the glow from the mountain on our right kept on growing, but it didn't shine in to where we lay, so we could only feel each other in the darkness. In the world I come from it seems that reality always has to be disappointing in the end. But I reckon the moments that can't last are also real.

We fell asleep without covering ourselves up, so when I woke up again it was still night, and I was cold. The red glow in the sky had spread itself right to the horizon while no one was looking. It no longer seemed gorgeous, but dull and sinister. I sat up and groped for the covers. Jared didn't stir. I found the duvet and tucked it round both of us. It felt cold. I huddled up against Jared. He was warm and relaxed as a baby, apparently dead to the world. I shifted him so I was comfortable, and his breathing never even altered.

Before it was morning he woke me. It was just getting light. After a while we were talking again, not wanting to go back to sleep, and that was when he mentioned how when he was in prison he'd thought a good deal about his father. I realised that the time had come.

'Jared.' I was lying half on top of him, looking down into his face. 'I have to tell you about that. I know what happened to your father.'

At first he just looked puzzled. 'You know? But how could you? You're a stranger here. You couldn't possibly.' I shook my head. He was beginning to believe me, I think, because he looked suddenly wary, half-frightened even. 'What do you mean, you know?'

I told him. I explained how Ishmael had guessed that the violent reaction to Jared's raid on the Pele Centre was not only about smuggling, but also connected with Jared's discovery of Nicky's treasures. I skipped over everything to do with the drugs, because Colombo had told him all of that already. I said how Ishmael was looking for something else, that would explain both Baskerville's concern with Nicky's goblet, and why this had to do with Jared. I told him what Anna had told me: that Ishmael had an idea what he was looking for, but he hadn't realised until he found it exactly what it would be.

I described to Jared, as precisely as I could remember, the three letters I had read, who wrote them, and what they said.

He turned over without a word, and lay on his front with his face hidden. I began to be scared of what I'd done. Perhaps he was angry with me. I didn't suppose that I could offer him any comfort. What could I have said? I was, as he'd pointed out, a stranger. I hoped he was glad that I was there. He didn't make a sound. But after a bit I knew that he was crying because I could feel it through my hand on his back. Cautiously I stroked his hair. I was getting used to the feel of it now: very straight and thick, but surprisingly soft as well. He didn't react, so I went on doing it, hoping that he didn't mind. I waited, and looked out of the window. It was light, but the mist was down. Only the smell of sulphur told me the mountain was still on fire.

He turned over at last, and sat up. I watched him gaze out at the mist, not asking for anything. There was a blinded look about him, though, that it wrenched my heart to see. In the end what he did say wasn't what I'd been expecting. 'And Colombo *knew*?'

'Colombo?' I couldn't think what the connection was. 'Yes, Colombo knew. He was there when Ishmael found the letters.'

'Colombo knew when I talked to him last night.' It was a statement this time. He didn't look at me. 'Ishmael knew, when he came to the prison. And Nicky knew. Nicky knew all the time he was at Ferdy's Landing. And Lemuel knew, long before that, when he used to come and see my mother.'

I got it then. 'No,' I said quickly. 'Ishmael didn't know until after he saw you in the prison. But yes, Colombo knows. And Nicky Hawkins knew.'

'Oh.' He didn't say anything else for a long time, but just stared out of the window with that stunned look which made me remember how the coastguard hit him in the face after they'd handcuffed him, back on Despair. The mist was slowly lifting. I could see the jagged outline of Tegid Voel like an etching on a slate. 'Who told you to tell me?' He sounded like a weary stranger.

'Nobody.' I was indignant, which instantly drove away my uncertainty. 'I didn't need to be told! I knew myself because

Anna let me read the photocopies. But she never told me what I should do! I could decide that for myself!' I wondered whether to go on, and decided it was better to get the whole thing out and done with. 'Ishmael doesn't know that Anna showed me the copies. She didn't tell him.'

He just went on looking into the mist. It was growing lighter. I had almost opened my mouth to speak again, when he said, 'What made you decide to tell me?'

'What?' It seemed such a ridiculous question. 'How could I *not* tell you? It wasn't a case of "decide"! I didn't know I'd be the one, not till I saw you yesterday. You didn't say anything, and after a bit I realised you still didn't know. So I knew it was going to have to be me that told you. Maybe that's fair enough. I didn't get you out of prison. I didn't know how to save you. Your friends did that. I wouldn't have had any idea what to do. So maybe it's fair I say what they couldn't.'

He brushed his hand across his eyes. 'I would have told them if I were in their position.'

'I know,' I said. 'You couldn't not. But people vary.'

I don't know what I did right, but in the end he did start talking to me. What he said didn't fill in the gaps in the story I'd heard so much as change it altogether. It was his mother, not his father, that he told me about. It dawned on me that this had been the unsaid thing: by now quite a lot of people had told me stories about Jack Honeyman. Every one of Jared's friends seemed to be concerned in some way with what had happened to Jared's father. I'd thought, just a few minutes ago, that Jared was crying because of his father, and it's true: in part he was. But it was only when he gave me his version that I appreciated that Josie Honeyman had been anyone more than a name, and that it had been unjust of me to have no image of her in my mind at all. It was only now I finally took on board the simple fact that Jared and his mother had been together, just themselves, for ten years. She brought him up. I began to understand that whoever had done anything to make things worse for her, it would be very hard for him to forgive.

He made me wish for the first time that she wasn't dead. I'd never previously thought of her as being anything else; in my mind I'd made her insubstantial in some way, already doomed from the beginning. Maybe it's as unfair to have to die of cancer at fifty-one as to be shot for a traitor at forty-eight. It's a less newsworthy way to lose out, that's all. She was tough. I hadn't realised that. She wasn't anybody's victim. She was soft-spoken, he said, and people who didn't listen to her thought she was quiet, and didn't hear the irony, but, said Jared, it was no joke getting the sharp end of her tongue; he'd never been able to argue with her, but if it wasn't coming at you, it had to be funny. The worse things got, the more caustic the wit she'd come back with. When he was small she could make him giggle himself into hiccups, however angry he'd been, and even when he was older, and people who knew nothing about them were always accusing his mother of not being able to control him, she could always turn his point of view around on him and make him laugh. That was how she dealt with what life threw at her. You couldn't take yourself too seriously. Cynical, maybe, but never defeated, never dull. I think she must have been pretty formidable.

There was one thing that gave her away. She'd never go out in the morning until the postman had come. Every day her anxiety was palpable, hoping, dreading and permanently waiting for the letter that never came. When she couldn't get up to fetch the letters out of the box any more she'd always want to know at once what had come, every day, right up until the day she died. It was the last thing she ever asked him, had he checked the post? He'd caught the habit off her, and even now he says he can't collect his mail in Lyonsness without that same twinge of apprehension, the unlaid ghost of a hope that was once real. That's why he hates waiting for letters. He said when he saw the envelope that came this spring from the Mayda Trust, about the *Cortes*, he felt sick, and it was a couple of hours before he could bring himself to open it. I suppose there's no one in the world who's what you'd call completely normal, once you start to know about them.

I've almost never stayed in bed all morning. My mother won't have that sort of thing. When we were in our teens she'd give us till about half past nine, and then she'd knock on our doors every five minutes and keep saying what a lovely day it was outside, or didn't we have any homework? A more successful tactic was to start cooking bacon and let the smell waft up the stairs. I felt embarrassed about appearing downstairs at the Red Herring just before they closed the bar lunches, but in fact there was no one about except a spotty youth I hadn't seen before, who turned out to be Colombo's eldest nephew. The wind hadn't changed, he said, but in the night the fountains had died down, and now a great sea of lava was spreading southwards. It had reached the first of the terraced orchards. Jared told me the Dorrado terraces are thought to be the oldest in Hy Brasil. It was here that the prized Dorrado apple variety was first bred. It's small and red and sweet, with slightly pinkish flesh, a bit like Beauty of Bath. It was horrible to think of those delicate, perfectly pruned trees being consumed by fire and sulphur.

But Penelope said that it was true. We met her at the wicket gate which led from the water meadows on to a small path that took us by a short cut to the cattle track. Already we could smell the burning vegetation, as if someone were having a huge autumn bonfire. Penny was coming back down. 'My dears,' she said when she saw us, and held out a hand to each of us. 'So you're free again, my poor boy. I kept telling Jim I was sure you'd never done anything dishonourable, and now he has to admit I was right. That dreadful Olly West – and then trying to lay the blame on Lucy too – so ungentlemanly. I always told Jim it was a mistake to have anything to do with him. But it never does any good to interfere.'

Jared looked at his feet and mumbled something inaudible, so I asked Penelope about the lava. She said she'd seen enough, and she was going home. 'You see, sweetheart, I've lived here all my life. People go away more and more, flitting about all over the place. I haven't done that. I've seen what's happening, and now I know that nothing will ever be the same again. I don't need to stand and watch it happen.'

She said she had to go and attend to her horses, who'd been agitated ever since the eruption started. 'They always know,' she said. She didn't repeat her invitation to come and look over the stables, though I think she might have done if I'd been alone.

Before we'd reached the end of the sunken cattle track we could hear the fire as well as smell it. The trees that covered the southern flank of the mountain were all in flames up above us, less than a mile away. Thick black smoke billowed into the clean air, and the trees cracked and spat as the flames consumed them. When we came out of the orchards we could see dark figures up there on the hillside, beating out the flames that crept forward over the grass. To the east the fire was almost at the top terrace of apple trees, though where we stood the orchards were still protected by a long spur of rock that divided the farmlands from the open hill. We climbed up on to it, and saw a crowd of people already standing there. There were no children today, and the crowd wasn't scattered over the hill, but gathered in a tight line on the basalt ridge that snaked west among the terraces almost to the bay.

There was a new lava river right at our feet, just a step away, about ten feet below the rock on which we stood. It was silver in the centre, with flashes of ruby in its folds, and a border of blood-red. It creaked and sighed as it moved. I could feel the heat from it. It must have been a hundred yards wide at least. Untouched grass lay beyond, where we'd walked yesterday, but there was no way of reaching the open hillside now. A mile to the west the head of the flow was moving towards the coast, in a direct line to the abandoned slipway of the whaling station. It was uncanny, like watching the deliberate advance of an unhuman army, or a huge headless beast that grew and widened as it went. In front of it was the green land, and then it came, and the land was gone, thousands of years of shaping and growing, just gone for ever. It seemed horrible enough to me, and it wasn't mine. I looked at the faces round me. Silent, intent, serious faces, not saying anything at all. There was nothing anyone could say. This was their land, but there was nothing that anyone could do.

Part of me refused to let it be real, as if we could wake up tomorrow and everything would be back where it belonged. Because I seemed to be in a dream, I recognised figures in the crowd without surprise, almost without reaction. There was Colombo, about thirty yards uphill from us, his hands in his pockets and his camera with the lens still open slung around his neck. There was Baskerville standing next to him, glooming over the flowing furnace at their feet. There were Ishmael and dried-up Allardyce, both on a high outcrop that overlooked what had been yesterday a bright river flowing through a mossy gorge. Between us and them I saw the President, standing with arms folded, his eyes fixed on the distant plume of black ashes that rose from the mountain and spread across the western sky. Right next to him I saw Nesta Kirwan, her hair tucked up in a black beret, kneeling on the rock with her camera at her feet. She must be changing the film. A little way behind them, half hidden among the apple trees on the untouched side of the ridge, I saw Ernest with Maeve and the harbour master. They weren't speaking, they were looking up at the President where he stood outlined on the little ridge.

I turned to Jared to tell him Colombo was here. But Jared was standing rigid, his eyes on Hook, tense as a cat about to spring. I'm such a fool, such a single-minded fool: it was only at that moment, I swear it, that I realised the implications of what I'd done. I'd been thinking about the past, and what he felt. I'd never considered the future, or what he'd do. My body seemed to stop; I turned cold inside. I'd set this going, and now it was happening, right in front of my eyes. I couldn't stop it. It would wipe out everything: this moment just unfolding could never be unmade, and I'd done it.

I unfroze just as he did. I think he'd have gone straight for the President, fifteen yards up from us with the red river just behind. He'd have thrown himself on Hook, and might have hurled both of them over the edge, only I clutched his arm in both hands and hung on with all the strength I had. 'No, Jared! No!' Faces turned. I didn't even know I'd screamed. There was a small crack like a balloon bursting. I heard another scream, not mine. Someone was screaming, fifteen yards away. I was fighting Jared. He forced my hands off his arm with his left hand. I grabbed back on. He wrenched my arm round behind my back and I cried out. Then suddenly he stopped.

Everything went slow. I raised my head. I saw them all, a circle of statues, transfixed around the place where the President was not.

The screaming hadn't stopped. I saw where it came from. Nesta Kirwan. She still knelt, alone on the rock, her hands pressed against her cheeks. Suddenly she jumped up, facing them all. 'You shot him! You shot him! You've shot him!' Her beret had fallen off. She covered her face with her hands, and fell to her knees again, sobbing wildly.

Someone jumped from the outcrop above, ran down the rock, and scooped her into his arms. It was Colombo. Her face was hidden against his shoulder. Her white hands gripped his sleeve. She was still screaming.

There were people moving over the rock. Men giving orders, making the crowd move back. They weren't in uniform, but there was nothing hidden about their function now that it was too late. The crowd lapped at the edge of the rock. They gazed aghast at the glistening surface of that fiery river. Opaque, viscous, beyond consciousness, it told nothing. No one spoke. There was nothing to say. I saw Ishmael turn his back on the flowing lava, and look searchingly over the crowd. His gaze rested on us for a moment. Jared was standing rooted to the spot, with my two hands still gripping his right arm. Ishmael met his eyes, held them for a moment, and passed on.

Jared took one deep, shuddering breath, and looked down at me. 'Did I hurt you?' He looked dazed, as if he wasn't quite sure what he was saying.

'Me? I'm all right.' As soon as I'd said it I found I wasn't. My legs were shaking. I loosed my hold on his arm. I could feel my lips trembling. I made myself stop. I wasn't the one who should cry. It wasn't my country; I had no right to make a fuss. Maybe that was a foolish thing to think, but all the same I thought it.

Then Nesta's voice rang out, high-pitched and shrill. 'He was shot! He was! I saw it! I saw him shot! I *know*! I *saw*!'

She was facing them again, Colombo at her back. Ishmael was up there next to her. So was Baskerville. And there was Ernest, and all the others, down on the grass below.

Ishmael said, not shouting but so that everyone could hear. 'There was no shot. He fell. God help him, he fell.'

'He was shot! He was shot! I saw him shot!'

She was screaming again. I couldn't bear it. I turned my back, and made my way blindly back into the shelter of the apple trees. I just wanted to get away, out of earshot, away from the terrible lava and the screams. I was crying, so I could hardly see as I stumbled through the orchards. Unripe windfalls crunched under my feet, the little red apples of Dorrado. There was a terrace and a six-foot drop. I sat on the wall to jump down, but found I couldn't go on. Instead I sat there shivering. I didn't hear Jared follow me, but he came, and sat on the wall beside me. We didn't move or say anything for a long time. At last he said, 'I think I'd better take you home.'

'Home?' I must have been in shock, or I'd have been more rational. 'How can I go home? It's thousands of miles away, and there aren't even any aeroplanes!' The very thought set me weeping again.

He was patient, which is more than I might have been. 'Then will I take you to Despair?'

I might have gone on being pathetic, only it flashed in upon me that he was as shocked as I was. The one thing he wanted to do now was to get back to his island. The longing I'd picked up on wasn't mine but his. I felt it clearly, and for that second I saw Despair through his eyes, as a place where one might be content, not a way out of the world so much as the right place to be in it. Not for ever, because nothing is, but for now sufficient. It made sense to me.

'Yes,' I said. 'Yes. We'll go back to Despair.'

TWENTY-SEVEN

THE COUNTRY WAS in turmoil, and nowhere had the agitation been greater than in the editor's office at *The Hesperides Times*. An erupting volcano was a simple matter by comparison, especially now that the crater had ceased to spew black clouds of ash, and the lava flow had slowed down and started to solidify barely a mile north of Dorrado. The *Times* had vociferously demanded a twenty-four-hour watch from the Pele Centre, and it seemed that the government had fallen over backwards to comply. Fifteen students and five professors from the University were putting in regular shifts under the aegis of the new director, George Allardyce. The *Times* had chosen to present this as a major victory won by media pressure, and since no one was in a position to contradict them the story stood unchallenged. Tidesman had graphically represented the dangers of corruption in an essential national monitoring service, and in the same issue two full-time jobs for qualified geophysicists appeared in the Situations Vacant column. There had already been enquiries from more than half-a-dozen countries, and the *Times* had been quick to claim the credit, even though most of the letters were responding to the advertisement in *Science*, not the column in *The Hesperides Times*.

With politics the editorial board was on much more uncertain ground. Without any official communiqués from Government House they were at a loss; or rather, since official communiqués arrived, with different signatures on them, every half hour or so, they were at a loss which ones to choose. Who knew what the new line to take would be? Colombo had said acidly at yesterday's meeting that this might be the moment to create one. Newspapers, he had said, can make governments; they don't necessarily have to wait on them. 'The choice is ours,' he'd insisted, which made them all look anxiously over their shoulders, as if hoping that he was addressing somebody else. 'We owe it to ourselves and to the country to take it. Isn't that what we're here for? If it isn't, I suggest we all go quietly home and wait for the coastguards to come in the night and get us.'

His contribution had been less than popular. Saturday's paper, it seemed, was to be a black-bordered edition devoted to non-controversial eulogies of the late President. If Tidesman ventured to suggest anything awkward at this stage, Colombo was told, Tidesman might be the first casualty of the new order, whatever that might be. Colombo, in a state of impotent fury, had stormed out of the office to keep his appointment for coffee with Ishmael at Caliban's Fast Food Diner. He'd returned in a much more amenable mood, and this morning he was perfectly willing to devote Tidesman's energies to the production of a seemly epitaph.

The screen was blue and blank under its heading, 'Document 1'. What could one possibly say? Colombo clicked back to the main directory. 'TIDESMAN'. The last file on the alphabetical list had been keyed in six days ago: 'volcano'. An attenuated version of it had gone into *The Hesperides Times*: Saturday August 2nd, 1997 under STOP PRESS. He'd finished it by 2 a.m. on the Friday night, and it had made the second edition. It was the third occasion in the two-hundred-year history of *The Hesperides Times* that there'd even been a second edition. By the time he'd got back from Dorrado on Friday it had been too late to change *Tidesman*, which had been printed just as he'd left it on that memorable Thursday evening, before going home, as he'd thought, to a relaxing evening with a pipe and his brother-in-law's best homegrown. He'd been pleased with that piece. There was the file heading in the directory now: OllyW.

He clicked on 'volcano'. It was a pity the complete version would never be printed. He skimmed through it. In retrospect the best passage was the quotation. Fair enough; one didn't expect to compete with one of the most observant witnesses who ever lived. That was why he'd looked up Pliny in the first place, and very apposite he'd found it. Colombo had been in a foul mood when he wrote the piece, but sometimes it seemed that this was a prerequisite for doing his best work. It was unfortunate: he didn't want to have to believe that he only wrote well when life was more than usually angst-filled. Naturally he'd been relieved that the worst eruption of Mount Brasil for two hundred and four years was probably going to spare his town and his family. But after that first day at Dorrado he'd driven back, furious and alone, at a speed which could well have been death to anything coming the other way. Luckily, with Dorrado facing a night that might be its apocalypse, nothing had.

He'd gone to Dorrado to work, of course, but he hadn't bargained for Lucy going off with Penelope Hook almost as soon as they'd arrived, and he certainly hadn't expected, when he'd turned up there in the evening to take her home, to be told that she'd accepted a lift back to St Brandons three hours earlier, that she'd drive herself home from there, and that she'd left a message saying she knew he'd be busy for a while, so there was no need for him to contact her. He'd been aware of her mounting frustration on the drive over, because with Jared in the back of the car she hadn't been able to go on telling him what she thought of him. It had been vaguely soothing to have Jed around, after Lucy had abandoned him, but then Colombo had climbed up the rocks to take a photo, and the next thing he knew he'd looked down and there was Jed being passionately embraced by Sidony Redruth with half of Dorrado looking on. This uninhibited behaviour from a girl who'd amused him from the day he met her by epitomising all the absurdities of British reserve, had left him wondering, a little resentfully, what it was that Jed had known how to do to bring it about. It wasn't that Colombo had ever wished that Sidony would treat him the same way; it would perhaps be pleasant if somebody did.

And now it was Thursday, and Tidesman had to come up with an appropriate obituary for a dead President. It would be a lot easier if Tidesman were not emotionally involved. In one way it was just as well Lucy had retreated to her fastness, because Colombo had been needed, as he had never in his life expected to be, elsewhere. But it made writing about Jim extraordinarily hard. He couldn't see the logic of that, but there it was. He clicked back to 'Document 1'. Nothing. There was the screen, like his mind, blue and blank. In desperation he picked up his Pliny, which was still sitting on the desk, and opened it at the marker.

'*Petis, ut tibi avunculi mei exitum scribam* . . . Your request that I would send you an account of my uncle's end, so that you may transmit a more exact relation of it to posterity . . .' There was the clue, perhaps: the answer was to be Roman about it . . . 'For notwithstanding he perished . . . in the destruction of a most beautiful region, and by a misfortune memorable enough to promise him a kind of immortality . . .' Which is why Jim's death had stayed in the world's headlines for the last five days, thought Colombo; it fits everybody's myth too damn well. It's also why this assignment is so impossible if you happened to know the fellow '. . . notwithstanding he has himself composed many and lasting works . . .' The base thought crossed Colombo's mind that he could just paraphrase the lot. After all, who read Pliny? '. . . Happy I esteem those whom Providence has gifted with the ability either to do things worthy of being written, or to write in a manner worthy of being read . . .' Baskerville did. Baskerville would smell the faintest whiff of plagiarism from forty miles away. He wouldn't let Tidesman get away with that. Damn him.

Colombo put the book down, and pulled the telephone

towards him. For the sixth time that morning he dialled the same number. He listened to the ringing tone for a full half-minute, and imagined the phone in the kitchen at Ravnscar echoing on and on under the barrel vaulting. For all he knew someone might be standing there, waiting for it to stop. He slammed down the receiver. Immediately it started ringing.

'Colombo? Per Pedersen here. I'm sorry to disturb you while you're at your work. It must be a busy week for you.'

'It's no bother.'

'It's good of you to say so. Well now, I was wondering if you had any idea where Mr Baskerville might be?'

'Baskerville? I've not seen him since – since Saturday. Do you want him?'

'I do not. But I'm a little worried about it, because Jared's been here. He's just borrowed my bike and he's gone along to Ferdy's Landing. I'm hoping Ishmael will have a talk with him. Colombo, did you know what was in those letters that Ishmael took away from the Pele Centre?'

Colombo hesitated for a moment, then he said. 'Yes, I knew. Did Ishmael tell you?'

'No, he did not. Jared told me just now. When he saw that this was news to me, he was, I would say, very much affected. I did say I wasn't surprised, because I've always been sure that if Jack had been alive he'd have written to Josie. He wasn't the kind of man who could have left her in such doubt. So, as I told Jed, I wasn't surprised, but there were other aspects to the matter that did surprise me.'

'So Jed knows.' Colombo stared at the screen, and in its blue depths a monstrous shape began to formulate, the ghost of a possibility he didn't want to see. He looked away. '*When* did he know?'

'I think that's neither here nor there. He asked me just now if I'd heard anything at all about Mr Baskerville. If he were back in St Brandons? I asked him what he was thinking of. He said not to worry because conscience makes cowards of us all. I would think the opposite myself, which I told him, only he sounded quite bitter about it, and that bothered me. He told me a piece of poetry – you know how he does – something about having a pale cast of thought, and the tide turning before the action, not that anyone can do anything about that, naturally, only he has bad dreams. I don't know if he meant the dreams were his own, or whether they were just part of the poem, but I didn't find it reassuring. Colombo, I understand that you knew all about these letters?'

'I knew after the raid, when Ishmael and I read them. I knew nothing before that.'

'No,' said Per. 'Well, I suppose we all do what seems best to us. It might be a good idea if you were to talk to Jed, perhaps, and make it right with him.'

'Make what right?' It was a foolish question, because Colombo knew quite well, and he didn't want to hear Per's answer to it. He hurried on, 'It's true, I've not seen Baskerville since Saturday, and that's odd. I tell you what, Per, will Jed be on the mainland all day?'

'He and Sidony will be here again at tea time. She's gone to Ravnscar with Miss Lucy to collect her things. And he went to get some money from the bank so they could do some shopping later. I did say to him that he should not borrow from Sidony, and it seems he took that on board. Our Jed can be led sometimes but not driven. But this is neither here nor there. What do you want me to say to him?'

Colombo looked at his watch, and at the empty screen, and back again. 'Say I've gone to find Baskerville and talk to him. When I've done that I'll come to Lyonsness. Tell him to wait.'

'Will you want your tea? I was thinking to give them kippers. There would be enough for all.'

Baskerville lived in Artillery Mansions, a grimy block of serviced flats close to the library. The porter greeted Colombo with relief. 'He came in Saturday evening and that's the last I saw of him. Last time before that was late on Wednesday. That's normal; sometimes he stops on at that Museum till God knows what hour. But he was back all right, 'cos he had his meals sent in Thursday and Friday, but I don't think he went out nohow. None of us saw him – I spoke to Starkey as does the late shift – and we thought maybe the gentleman was ill. But he didn't ask for no one. Then Saturday he rings to get his paper sent in, and an hour later out he comes – first he knows about the volcano, I reckon, 'cos he don't have TV and I guess he's not been listening to the radio – and I bring round his jeep for him and he's off to Dorrado. Then back he comes around tea time and he must of known about the President then but he didn't say nothing to me. I heard about it on the news at six just ten minutes after. And a couple of hours later out comes Mr Baskerville and off he goes again – not a word about the President, not a word to any of us about nothing. And we ain't seen him since, and he's not answering his phone neither. Starkey hasn't neither, 'cos I called him again after I come on this morning. And that's five days ago, with God knows what all happening out there in the country. He don't never go away, not Mr Baskerville. Where to *would* he go? That's what I said to Starkey. Unless he came back one night between two and six in the morning, and let himself in with his own key, but he can't of done that, because he's not had no meals sent in nor nothing. I said to Starkey maybe we should have a look, and he says, give it another day, he says, because going into the apartments without we're ordered, see, that could be trouble.'

'You've got a key though? I can go in.'

The heavy green curtains were still drawn in Baskerville's sitting room. The room was empty, and smelled of damp, old woodsmoke, and unaired clothes. Colombo trod quietly across to the window as if he were afraid of waking someone, and drew the curtains back. There were grains of corn and spattered droppings on the windowsill. Feeding the pigeons and sparrows of the town was one of Baskerville's smaller eccentricities.

Colombo had never been alone in this room before. He looked round at the framed prints of the tall ships, at the little display case on the wall with Baskerville's six medals in it, beginning with the white-and-purple one with the silver cross, at the glass-fronted bookcases crammed with pre-war hardbacks, at the matching prints of Woolwich College on one side of the fireplace and Trinity College Cambridge on the other, at the eighteenth-century ship in a bottle on the mantelpiece next to the Ormulu clock, and the Turner seascape above it. On the round mahogany dining table in the window there was a jigsaw puzzle depicting the Grand Canal, with less than fifty pieces still unplaced. Incredibly, there were no open books or papers anywhere. Not only was the leather-topped kneehole desk quite clear, except for a brass inkstand and pen tray and a smudged blotter, but there were no scattered papers on the table, the chairs, the ottoman, or on the low reading table under the anglepoise lamp by Baskerville's leather armchair. On one of the pair of Victorian pie-crust tables there was a copy of last week's *Times*, open at the Tidesman article that gave the public account of the raid on the Pele Centre. Colombo bit his lip. His gaze moved on, to the charred ashes of many papers in the grate, and his heart sank.

He crossed the dim hall again, and looked into the other rooms. Even in August the bathroom retained its sepulchral chill, which the antique cast iron and mahogany did little to dispel. The kitchen, which seemed much taller than it was broad, looked and smelt as if nothing had been touched since 1914. Only the service lift, which brought the trays up from the restaurant on the ground floor, looked polished by much handling. There seemed to be nothing to eat or drink but an ancient tin of Abernethy biscuits and an opened packet of Darjeeling tea. Colombo opened the yellowed fridge. There was a half-empty bottle of milk in the door. He took it out and sniffed it gingerly. It certainly hadn't been bought this week.

The boxroom contained nothing but a painted sea-chest and

a newspaper-covered table holding a partially constructed model of Sir Richard Grenville's *Revenge*, sunk off Terceira in 1591. The sails were marked on a piece of thin white canvas, but had not yet been cut out, and the black cotton rigging was still far from complete. Lastly, with lagging steps, Colombo approached the bedroom.

It was empty. The high wooden bed had not been slept in. The counterpane had been turned down to reveal greyed cotton sheets and a pair of blue striped pyjamas folded on the pillow. Colombo had never looked in here before. The floor was bare oak boards with a single threadbare rug beside the bed. There was an immense blackened clothes press against one wall. The single picture was a Victorian romanticised representation of Charles I on his way to execution. The huge sash windows badly needed cleaning. There were four books on the bedside table. Colombo went over to look: *The Concise Dictionary of National Biography*, *A Voyage to Virginia in 1609*, Gilbert White's *The Natural History of Selbourne* and *The Tiger in the Smoke* by Marjory Allingham. The last one had a red leather marker in it.

Colombo turned the green-and-white paperback over, and put it back on the pile. He considered the clothes press. There must be papers somewhere: in the drawers of the desk, in the cupboards, in the sea-chest even. He would have had little compunction about searching, only it was too soon. He was aware of a certain pathos: oddly enough, it was the innocence of the life revealed to him that struck him most forcibly. He was sure, without having to look, that if, or when, alien hands turned over every item that belonged in Baskerville's very private existence, they'd find nothing, out of a whole lifetime, that anyone might wish to leave unrevealed. The little pile of ashes next door, Colombo knew, would have contained everything. *Requiescat in pacem*. There was no body here. Even so, he crossed himself, and stood quite still for a minute or two, before he went away, closing the front door behind him.

* * *

'Jed,' said Ishmael, 'Try to understand. The only way I could get you freed was by giving my word that I'd not tell you. I had to promise Hook that I'd say nothing while he and Baskerville were still living. If I'd not given my word, you wouldn't have come out of prison alive. That's the bottom line of it. What would you have done?'

Jared dropped the brown envelope on Ishmael's desk, and sank his head in his hands. 'I don't know. I don't know any more. I just don't know.'

'Jed, do you want to read them? Do you want me to leave you alone?'

'No, no! I mean, yes, I will. Soon. Soon I will.' Jared swung round on the office chair so he had his back to Ishmael, and hid his face in his arms, leaning on Ishmael's desk.

'Shall I go?' No answer. 'Do you want me to stay?' No answer. 'Those copies are yours, if you want to take them away.'

'When I realised that you didn't mean to tell me,' said Jared's muffled voice, 'I felt like I never wanted to speak to you again.'

'I'm sorry about that.' Ishmael paused, and getting no reply, he went on, 'I'm sorry about it all, Jed. I'm sorry any of it ever had to happen. But supposing I had broken my word? What then? If Hook were alive, what would you have done about it? I know you well enough to be quite sure you couldn't have lived with the facts and done nothing. Exile or death, Jed. That would have been the choice. What would you have done?'

Jared shook his head, still hiding his face. Ishmael watched him for a moment, then he came over and put his hand on Jared's shoulder. 'Jed, it's done. You don't have to find an answer any more. Things have moved on. Let it go. We've got to make a future, and we've got to do it now. I've been in St Brandons all week; Per just caught me when he phoned, so I waited for you. The country's in turmoil. Do you want to know what's happening?'

'Not really.' Jared raised his head, and stared down at his

clenched hands. 'Sidony says we have to have a radio,' he said inconsequently. 'She's going to buy one today in Lyonsness.'

'You should thank heaven for her common sense. Jed, this is Thursday. Tomorrow the interim government, such as it is, will announce a date for a Presidential election. Do you want to come to St Brandons with me?'

'No.'

'You're not interested in what's happening to your country?'

'No.'

Ishmael sat down on the other chair. 'Jed, what is it? You can't hide on Despair for ever. It's not just that I didn't tell you about Jack, is it? Come on, man, what is it? Let's have it.'

Jared lifted his head. He looked quite distraught, but his voice sounded merely sullen. 'You were wrong, Ishmael. There was a shot.'

'Who says that?'

'Nesta Kirwan said it, loud and clear, when it happened. And she was right. I saw.'

'You saw what?' asked Ishmael quickly.

'I was looking right at him. I hadn't thought – I hadn't decided – I didn't know he'd be there. Penelope didn't say, maybe she didn't like to because of – of the other thing, the prison and everything – I didn't expect to see him, and I guess I'd have gone for him, only Sidony had me by the arm. I could have thrown her off, but I didn't want to hurt her. I was still watching Hook. Ishmael, I never took my eyes off him. And I saw – he was sideways on to me, leaning a bit forward, looking down at the lava. He had his back to the people.

He didn't fall. He wasn't moving. He was hit. He flung his arms up and pitched forward. Just like that. No one ever fell like that. I tell you, I *saw*.'

'Jed, I was watching him too. He fell. He tripped on the rock and fell.'

'No!' It was a cry of desperation. 'Ishmael, I *saw*. He threw his arms wide and pitched forward. I heard the shot, and so did Nesta!'

'Very well,' said Ishmael unemotionally. 'So he was shot. Whom do you accuse?'

'Me? I'm not accusing anybody! I'm telling you what I saw!'

'If he was shot, then someone shot him. You know who was there. Who are you saying that it was?'

'I'm not accusing anybody!' cried Jared in anguish. 'How could I?'

'If it was no one, then he must have fallen.' Ishmael leaned back in his chair. 'Jed, there's no point getting in this state. Hook's dead. You have to admit it makes life easier for you – no, don't speak – of course you didn't shoot him. You hadn't a gun, and you had Sidony hanging on to your arm. She was shouting, and quite a few people saw you both. I didn't shoot him either, as it happens. Nobody did, but I saw him fall. So he's dead. Now we have to move on. Within the next week we'll have a government again. How do you want it to begin? With a witch hunt? A murder trial? Executions? Reprisals? Civil war? Or don't you care, since you'll be doing your ostrich act on Despair? All right, so you don't care. But I do. I care as much as I care about anything in this world. I care that Hy Brasil should be a country in which no one is afraid of their government, and no one is punished or killed unjustly. Ever. I intend to do everything in my power to give my country the leadership it deserves. And I say that Hook fell. What's more, anyone who contradicts that simple fact will be discredited by all the means I can muster.'

Jared was shaking his head. He looked at Ishmael as if hoping he might suddenly say something quite different. 'I don't know what to do,' he repeated dully.

'Have you talked to anyone else about it?'

'Only Sidony.'

'And she said?'

'To talk to you.'

'Well, you've done that now.' Ishmael stood up. 'Jed, I wouldn't ask you to involve yourself in politics. Well, I'd be mad if I did. I just ask you to go on with your life without making things impossible for yourself. You're going to be all right. You've done nothing wrong, and you've not connived at anything wrong either. You're lucky that your role is that simple. I have some good news for you, if you're ready to hear it.'

'Good news?' Jared looked round in a dazed sort of way, as if he expected to be handed a present. 'What sort of news?'

'Remember those letters we sent out the day after we found the goblet, and how Brendan Hook's colleague offered to sponsor your application? Well, he did speak for it at the committee of the *National Geographic*.' Ishmael picked a letter out of his in-tray. 'Read that.'

Jared took the single sheet of thick writing paper. His hand shook a little. He glanced at the embossed letterhead, and read:

> Dear Sir,
>
> *Cortes, Hy Brasil*
>
> The committee has read with interest Mr Honeyman's proposal for the archeological survey and salvage of the Spanish galleon *Cortes*, which foundered on October 31st, 1611, on Ile de l'Espoir, Hy Brasil. We are glad to be able to inform you that the committee unanimously agreed that this is a project that the *National Geographic* will be pleased to sponsor, subject to the following conditions . . .

'Oh!' Jared read on to the end. 'He says they're willing to fund it. It does say that, doesn't it?'

'You can read, can't you? I spoke to Brendan yesterday. He's with his mother in Dorrado of course, but he said after the Memorial Service he'd be happy to fill you in. It was presented to the Committee by a colleague of his in Marine Archeology. Brendan said he fancied visiting you on Despair; apparently it's twenty years or more since he was last there.'

'Oh,' said Jared again. 'We can salvage the *Cortes*. Ishmael, we can have a proper archeological survey and salvage operation. We can salvage the *Cortes*.'

'You can, Jed. You can get your friend over from Key West. He's an archeologist. I'm not.'

'You mean you don't want to be on the team?'

'Man, I'd like to be, but I'm going to be too busy. It wouldn't be fair to you. I can still be useful to you.'

'Oh,' said Jared. Then he said, 'Brendan Hook.'

'That's right. Brendan's the one you owe for this. Now then, I've something else.' He took a shoebox off the top of the filing cabinet, and handed it to Jared.

Jared recognised it at once. He opened it gently, and took out the goblet. There was a shell-head from Gallipoli in the box too, and an ebony snuffbox.

'I guess they're yours, Jed. No one else has any claim on them.'

Jared laid the three treasures on Ishmael's desk, next to the computer, and considered them. 'I'd give the goblet to the museum,' he said. 'But there's Baskerville.' He picked up the two smaller items. 'I'll take these home. I can't take the glass just now. I'm on Per's bike and I haven't got my rucksack. Put it on the kitchen mantelpiece; it's used to being there. I'll collect it some day.' He folded the letter carefully, and put it in his jacket pocket with the treasures. He picked up the unopened brown envelope. Then he got up and held out his hand to Ishmael. 'I seem to owe you everything,' he said, 'but somehow I feel like I don't really know you any more. I guess it'll pass.'

Ishmael shook his hand. 'I hope so, for my sake as well as yours. I hope you'll very soon find that it does.'

The car and the motorbike passed each other about half a mile east of the Ravnscar turning. They both ground to a halt a moment later. Colombo reversed down the hill, and Jared turned the bike on the narrow road, and waited for him to come alongside. Colombo wound down the window.

There you are. I was hoping I'd find you up here. Did Per tell you?'

'What?' Jared unstrapped his helmet. 'Say that again.'

'I said, I came to find you. I'm having tea with you at Per's. Jed, are you all right? Has something else happened?'

'I'm fine. That's nice you're coming to tea. So's Lucy.'

'Ah.' Colombo looked inscrutable. 'She's not at Ravnscar just now?'

'Were you going to look for her? They'll have gone back to Lyonsness by now. Her and Sidony, that is.'

Colombo drummed his fingers on the steering wheel, and frowned at the road ahead. 'Jed, I'm going up to Ravnscar. Will you come with me?'

'Now? There's nobody in, I tell you.'

'Good. Follow me up. We need to talk.'

The Land Rover had gone, but the conservatory was open. Colombo took the back door key from under the mat and unlocked the door within the door. Jared followed him into the kitchen. Ginger and Simpkin appeared, and wound themselves around their legs, miaowing pathetically. 'All right,' said Jared, picking up Simpkin. 'She'll be back tonight.'

He sat down opposite Colombo at the round table in the window, absentmindedly stroking the cat. Doves cooed softly outside the open window.

'Three things,' said Colombo. 'First of all, Per told me you know about those letters – I mean – about Jack Honeyman – you know now what happened to your father.'

'Yes,' said Jared stonily. 'What about it?'

'I'm very sorry.'

'Oh.' Jared's hand was still, and Simpkin butted it with his head. 'Well, that's nice of you.'

'I'm very sorry that it happened. A lot more sorry than I know how to say. I'm sorry I agreed not to tell you about it,' pursued Colombo doggedly. 'Perhaps I did wrong. I'm glad you know. If you're angry, I can understand why.'

Jared stroked the cat and looked out of the window. Colombo watched him, and waited. Presently Jared met his eyes. 'All right. I'm not angry now.'

'Thank you. Second thing.' It was Colombo's turn to pause. 'This is difficult, but I need to ask you. What were you doing when Hook fell from the rock?'

This time Jared held his gaze. 'All right.' He sighed. 'I'd just caught sight of him. I didn't know he'd be there. I hadn't thought what I'd do. I mean, I'm not living in a revenge tragedy, but I guess I was feeling pretty churned up. I'd only known for a few hours. I might have gone for him. I'd never have reached him. The peelers would have stopped me. The place was crawling with them, I knew that, but I wasn't thinking, not right then. But Sidony grabbed my arm and I was trying to push her off. But I was still looking at him, all the time.' Jared spread his hands open on the table, and the affronted cat leapt off his knee. 'Colombo, I saw him fall.'

'So did I.' Colombo looked out of the window. 'Thanks. I'm glad you told me that.'

'Colombo . . .'

'Leave it there.' Colombo met Jared's questioning gaze, and held it. 'Leave it. Third thing. Have you any idea what's happened to Baskerville?'

'Happened to him? Why, don't you know where he is?'

Colombo described how he'd spent the morning. 'And then I went to Ogg's Cove and drove up to the Pele Centre. This is what I found: Baskerville's jeep is parked at the turning place where the tarmac ends.'

He watched Jared register the significance of that. It only took a moment. 'He's gone down the hidden road!'

'So you do know? I thought you would. If only you'd been there, you could have shown me the way, I suppose.'

'I know where the door is. I never found out a way to open it.'

'But you did grow up in Ogg's Cove. Jed, how much do you know about the Pirate Kings?'

'Not a lot. We always knew when they were in the caverns, because they used to park their cars in the old quarry where the Pele Centre is now. I know where the secret entrance is, because Pat and I once followed them, but we never got in because it's barred and locked. I was scared too. Nicky told me they put curses on you with dead men's bones. And I can remember Pappa saying that secret societies were not only bloody daft but downright dangerous as well. Even when I was a kid I found it all pretty distasteful.'

'You know the other way in though, through the cellars here?'

'I know the way down to the door, if I can still remember it. I only went in once. I didn't like it at all. That was – what? – fifteen years ago.'

'Will you come down now?'

Jared stared at him. 'Now? You think he'll still be down there? It must have taken you all of two hours to drive round from Ogg's Cove, unless you came by the back track. You'd have been quicker to walk. Christ, man, what are you saying?'

'I haven't got a four-by-four, and I needed the car in case I had to hunt you down in Lyonsness. I came round the mountain, and I left Ogg's Cove just before two. What I'm saying is I came here to have a look. I'm saying I'd like it a lot better if you came with me.'

After the flight of steps down from the wine cellar neither of them remembered the way exactly. Twice they had to retrace their steps, rewinding the string as they went. They both recognised the big cavern. Jared pointed out the small passage opposite. 'Down there. But we're nearly at the end of the string.' He picked up a stone that might well have been placed there for the purpose, and held the loose end down with it. 'It's OK. I'm fairly sure the path doesn't fork again.'

Colombo said nothing, but kept close at Jared's heels. The passage was high, but very narrow. 'Do you think there's a weight restriction on membership?' asked Jared, as he squeezed past a projecting corner of rock.

Colombo didn't smile. Pale and silent, he followed Jared, who was holding the torch, as closely as he could. It wasn't far before the way was barred by a solid, iron-studded door. There was a wider space just in front of it. Jared squeezed back against the wall, so they could stand side by side. Even so, they were almost touching. In the torchlight the spidery writing, though faded, was quite legible. Jared shone the torch.

Look thou not on beauty's charming –
Sit thou still when kings are arming –
Taste not when the wine-cup glistens –
Speak not when the people listens –
Stop thine ear against the singer –
From the red gold keep thy finger –
Vacant heart and hand and eye –
Easy live and quiet die.

'I hate that!' said Jared violently. 'No wonder I hated the place. I'd forgotten it was here.'

'Well, you can't deny there's a certain truth to it. But perhaps this is hardly the moment for literary criticism.' Colombo's voice belied the insouciance of his words. He cleared his throat.

'All right?' Jared shone the torch on him for a moment. 'I'm going to open the door.'

Colombo nodded, and stood back.

Jared turned the handle, and pushed. He tried the other way. He pushed harder, and shook the door. It was wedged solid, and didn't even rattle. He handed Colombo the torch and used both hands to turn the handle back again. Then he shoved with all his weight. The door didn't move. He let go, and looked at the door. 'There's no lock.'

'No.' Colombo cleared his throat again. 'There are bolts,' he said hoarsely. 'I remember seeing them when I came before.'

'Bolts?' Jared looked at the blank face of the door. 'You mean . . .'

'On the inside. Yes.'

'Jesus.' Jared shook the door again. 'And there's no other way in?'

'No.'

'And he's definitely been gone since Saturday?'

'Yes.'

'Jesus fucking Christ.' Jared took the torch out of Colombo's hand, and shone it round the door frame. There was no gap at all. Door and frame fitted as tightly as if they were all one piece of wood. 'Oh my God. You'd need dynamite to break that down.'

'Not here,' said Colombo shakily. 'You couldn't use explosives here. We're right under Ravnscar, and the whole hill's hollow.'

'Jesus,' said Jared again, and tried the handle once more. 'You try.'

He stood back. Colombo grimly turned the handle, shook and pushed, turned the handle again, threw his shoulder against the door. Jared added his weight as well, then he stood back.

'It's no good, Colombo. Leave it. It's no good.'

Colombo glared at the door, out of breath and panting. Suddenly he hurled himself against it, hammering on it with his bare fists, oblivious of the iron studs. 'Baskerville! Mr Baskerville!' His shouts echoed and multiplied between the narrow walls.

'Stop it! Man, stop that!' Jared wrenched him away. 'You'll mash yourself to pieces. Come on, let's get out of here.'

Colombo shook his head, and leaned back against the scribbled writing, trembling. 'I should have known. I should have thought on Saturday. God have mercy, I should have known.'

'No.' Jared held out his hand. 'Come away. You can't do more. Come away.'

'You go. I'll follow.'

'No, I'll wait.'

'There's something I want to do.'

'I know.' Jared smiled wryly. '"And my ending is Despair Unless I be reliev'd by prayer." Far be it from me to mock at you. But I'm not leaving you down here in the dark, man. It's the diving, you see, we're trained not to. I won't get in your way.'

He put down the torch so that it lay shining on the door, turned his back politely, and gazed into the dark. He couldn't help catching the words that were whispered against the locked door behind him, even though they were not quite what he had expected: 'No man may deliver his brother, nor make agreement unto God for him; but God hath delivered his soul from the place of hell, and he shall receive him. Be thou not afraid . . .'

The rest was inaudible.

TWENTY-EIGHT

Sidony Redruth: Ile de l'Espoir. August 14th,
Notes for *Undiscovered Islands* (working title).

IT WAS YEARS since I'd had rock. Sweet, sticky, and cellophane-wrapped, it reminded me of summer holidays when I was young. This particular sample was greenish-blue on the outside, with greenish-blue letters going right through: *Hy Brasil 12.8.97*. It tasted fairly disgusting, but it was all part of the festivities, besides which Lucy had bought it for me, so I sucked away without being pernickity about it.

We sat at the top of the fifteen-foot-high stone wall above the harbour, which had once been part of the Portuguese defences. The old fort had long gone, and instead there was a small flat park containing a couple of Victorian cannon and some grave-shaped beds planted with begonias, salvias and alyssum in lurid geometric arrangements. We had a prime view of Water Street as it skirted the harbour front. It was lucky Lucy had insisted we get here early. The crowd behind us was already five or six deep, even though this was a less popular viewpoint than the courtyard outside Government House, the roof of the Cathedral, the steps of the lawcourts, the High Street pavement or the public park. Here we'd only catch the procession at the end of its route, before it wound back up the hill to St Brendan's Cathedral, where it dominates the skyline to the south.

We couldn't see anything yet, but we'd been hearing the

music from different parts of town ever since we'd got here. The town band had started at the market cross, processed up to Government House, and, to judge by the sound, had tagged on to the end of the main procession coming down Cathedral Street and into High Street where it joins Fraternity Street. The pipe band had begun somewhere in the vicinity of St Martin's, woven an in-and-out course through the top part of the town, and emerged from round the back of the lawcourts, where it became absorbed into the general medley. The massed choirs had started from the Cathedral, and as far as we could hear they'd taken the broad straight path down Cathedral Street, left into Water Street and along the seafront to the harbour. It was hard to get it all clear, because there was a small orchestra playing Purcell's 'Tune and Air for trumpet and orchestra', under a wooden cupola in the park just behind us. A few elderly people were sitting around in striped deckchairs, eating picnics out of paper bags, just as if there were nothing else going on at all.

By a miracle the whole procession, when it did finally heave into sight at the far end of Water Street, was marching to the same rhythm. The tunes were all different, but there was an underlying beat that all seemed to share: a steady thump thump thump, beating a time which every pedestrian in town couldn't help but mark, however independent-minded they might wish to appear.

And now we could see them coming. St Brendan came first. He stood stiffly in his wooden shrine like a guard in a sentry box. That was my first thought, when I saw the rigid little figure swaying along above the heads of the crowd. When he came a bit closer he was more like a cuckoo in a clock: not in shape, obviously, but in his unexpected air of benign domesticity. He wore a blue sea-cloak, and his right hand was raised in bene-diction. He was touchingly disproportionate: his white hand was at least as large as his chest, and under the blue cloak there was hardly room for any legs to speak of. It was his smile I liked. It reminded me of the archaic smile on the oldest Greek statues, in the way that his painted lips turned up very slightly at the corners. Or maybe he was more like the smiling Buddha, whose face I first saw behind a glass case in the British Museum when I was ten. I thought even then that this was a kinder image than that of the tortured god I'd grown up with. The Dalai Lama's smile impressed me for the same reason, when I saw it on television a year or two back. It seemed to me to be a more considered response than despair or indignation.

I hadn't expected St Brendan to have such an effect on me. He wasn't a great work of art; I knew that. When I went round the Cathedral, the first week I was in Hy Brasil, the verger said no one was sure of his history, but he'd always been here. When I'd seen him up there in his usual place behind the High Altar, he'd struck me as being more like the figurehead on a sailing ship than an artifice of eternity from the golden smithies of the Emperor, a bit too crude for a Diocesan See in fact.

The Bishop with a posse of less-exalted clergy walked directly behind the saint, and after them came the Episcopalian archdeacon and a flock of non-conformist dignitaries got up like crows. Next came a bevy of choirboys in red cassocks and frilled surplices. They were singing Beethoven's 'Ode to Joy'. The trebles swept past like a flock of nightingales, and on came the altos, the tenors and the basses. The wall I was sitting on seemed to vibrate to their resounding notes. Then came the Mayor of St Brandons with the Corporation at his heels, heralded by a bald and sweating official carrying a mace. They were followed by the band, playing Sousa's 'Stars and Stripes For Ever'. They'd just got to the part with the piccolo when they came past us. After the band came the University of the Hesperides, represented by a bunch of embarrassed-looking academics in gowns and hoods who were doing their best not to keep time with the band, and failing. The students who followed them were in a state of frank hilarity, shooting off ticker tape and fountains of fizzy cider into the crowd. After them came the schools: St Brandons Academy, the City High School, St Martin's Elementary, Back Lane Elementary. Each school had a band of its own. I liked Back Lane band best. They had six drums, a whole load of cymbals, tambourines and castanets, and some straggling kindergarteners with triangles. Not one of them seemed in the least inhibited by what the rest of the band was doing.

After the schools came the Chamber of Commerce, who were on the whole more portly than the Mayor and Corporation, succeeded by a phalanx of lean and hungry coastguards in green uniforms. Then came a motley collection of banners: the Fishermen's Guild, the Hesperides Cider Factory, the Farmers of Hy Brasil, Hy Brasil Telecommunications, St Brandons' Civic Society, the Hy Brasil Rural Women's Institutes, the St Brandons First Scout and Guide Troops, and finally a float bearing St Martin's Nursery School disguised as pirates on a schooner.

Next came the 227 bus. It was full of people, but, peering in as well as we could through the steamed-up windows, we could see no cohering factor. They were just a bunch of stray people of both genders, and of varying age, colour, taste in clothing and political allegiance. We could be sure of the latter, because they were all waving different coloured flags from the open ventilators. The bus was covered with streamers, and a bunch of gas balloons dipped and bobbed from the driver's window. It was closely followed by the pipe band, which was playing 'Flower of Scotland'.

The last organised element in the procession was the Pirate Kings. They had a red banner with a skull and crossed bones embroidered on it, and the legend, *Vince aut Submerge*. I looked at them with interest, but apart from the lack of women, they were as nondescript a bunch of characters as you'd expect to see if you got into a country bus on market day. I was startled to see both Peterkin and the landlord of the Red Herring among the motley crew.

After that the procession turned into a crowd. But such a crowd! They had music of their own: guitars, pipes, fiddles, drums, tin whistles. For the first time in my life I saw what was meant by dancing in the street. At home it just doesn't happen. They danced, and they marched, and in among them cars crawled through, hooting, decorated with ticker tape and balloons and slogans.

Lucy and I counted the blue-and-green banners, as against the orange and the pink. There were more blue-and-green than either of the others, but not more than both the pink and orange put together. Names were shouted, and met by whistles, cheers or cat-calls. One name, and I don't think this was our imagination, seemed to dominate.

'Pereira!' 'Pereira!' 'Ishmael Pereira!'

But it wasn't a clear-cut thing, not by any means. Sometimes a whole section of the passing crowd would be orange, or pink, and then any stray blue-and-green banners were met with jeers and rotten apples. Some of the cars that came through were decked in pink on one side, and in blue-and-green on the other.

I nudged Lucy. 'What the hell does *that* signify?'

She looked. 'Simple. One car in the family, and at least two voters. Some people can agree to differ.'

The crowd beneath us wasn't moving any more. The procession had turned into a party. A tumbling act started up in the middle of Water Street, with accompanying jugglers, and people gathered round to watch. In the distance we could still hear the pipe band, but it was so far away that the orchestra behind us had become audible again. Now they were playing Elgar's 'Pomp and Circumstance No. 1'.

'I just can't believe it,' I said to Lucy. 'I've voted in two elections in my life. We just strolled down to the village school in the afternoon and dropped our papers in the box. Last May was the first time I even bothered to stay up through the night and watch the results coming in. Even then I wasn't sure until nearly halfway through if there was much point. But this – this isn't an *election*. This is *wild*.'

'It's our kind of election,' said Lucy, 'and I don't think much of yours, by the sound of it.' She wiped her sticky hands on her handkerchief. 'Well, that's that. How about something to eat?'

Caliban's was packed out. We had to sit on the pavement, and there was nothing left to eat but hot dogs, which I abominate, and green-and-blue, orange or pink ice cream. But I was starving, so we sat leaning against the wall, with people stepping over our legs as they surged by, their faces far above us. Lucy squeezed tomato sauce on her hot dog, and passed the rest of the sticky envelope over to me.

'What are you laughing at?' I asked her.

'Nothing. I mean, just everything. I don't know. Life's a mess. My life's a mess anyway. But look at us! Look at all of this. Do you realise,' – she nudged me so I squeezed ketchup all over the knee of my pale blue trousers – 'do you realise nothing like this has ever happened before? I've never voted before in my life.' She laughed again. 'Maybe it's silly. A tin-pot republic, is that what you're thinking? Toyland? I don't care if you do. I think it's *splendid*.'

'I wasn't thinking anything like that,' I licked my fingers. 'You know, when we went into Lyonsness Junior High this morning, and you cast your vote, I was wishing I had one too. I was thinking I'm the only person over eighteen in Hy Brasil who hasn't got one. I felt left out.'

'Well, you needn't. The place is heaving with foreign journalists. I never saw so many strangers in my life. Butting in. What business is this of theirs?'

'It'll be the whole world's business on the news tomorrow.'

'For five minutes. Then it's back to where we came from. Into the shadows. Do you know what the punishment used to be for giving away the bearings of Hy Brasil? If you sold a foreigner our latitude and longitude we'd cut off your tongue and your right hand, and a whole day later we'd keelhaul you, and then hang you from the yard arm. Charming, eh? But necessary.'

'I like the legend better: the island that isn't always there.'

The crowd in front of us thinned suddenly. Two policemen on motorbikes drove by, both armed with sub-machine guns.

'Tough,' said Lucy. 'If you're here, the island *is* always there. There's no getting away from that.' She wiped her hands. 'Are you done? Shall we walk around a bit?'

We wandered through the crowds, eating blue-and-green ice-cream in cones. It was like being at a fair. Only perhaps it was a fair in a dream, because at every street corner there were police in green uniforms, with guns. No one seemed to be taking any notice of them, except me. They seemed like extras who'd strayed into the wrong film. Or maybe it was the crowds and the music and the colour that were out of sync, and the green men with the guns were what was real. 'I don't like seeing them,' I said to Lucy.

'Then shut your eyes,' she said impatiently.

'It's not that simple.' We were in one of the back lanes behind the library, between high walls with fuchsia hedges atop of them. The flagstones at our feet were sticky with pink and red petals. Something I'd been wanting to say to her, but hadn't quite dared, suddenly surfaced, and I heard myself speaking out loud almost before I'd decided I'd do it. 'I keep thinking about that man's sentence,' I told her. 'I mean, it's my doing in a way. Imagine being shut up for *life*. I'm not sure anything as dreadful as that should happen to anybody, and if it wasn't for me he might have escaped. Got clear out of the country.'

'And done it all again somewhere else?' said Lucy. 'For God's sake, can't you draw a line around what you're responsible for, and be done with it? You didn't sentence him. And a life sentence never is life anyway, not nowadays. Can't you see that having the trial right now, in the middle of all this, is just a tactic? Like, the manifesto is, "Some trades are out. Look what good guys we are. Merciful too. Don't you realise we could so much more easily have had him shot?" It's all politics. Get real, Sidony.'

'If the new government has Olly West shot, I shall feel as if it's all my fault.'

'I think that's pretty self-indulgent. But they won't. You'll see, ten years from now he'll be skipping about in a state of nature on Ogg's Cove sands again, and we'll have to go back to swimming from Hogg's Beach.' She took my arm and gave me a little shake. 'Come on, m'dear. It'll all end happily.'

When we were tired of walking round the town, we had tea and doughnuts at Finnegan's. They'd had a crowd through, but things were growing quieter. We talked for a long time, mostly about men. It made me realise I'd been missing my friends at home. Certainly I'd never felt so close to Lucy before. I realised that for her my way of dealing with life is completely foreign. My friends and I cope with relationships and stuff like that by telling each other all about it for hours and hours. That was partly why I broke up with my Fiction 1700–1900 tutor, or so I think in retrospect. It seemed at the time as if he'd dumped me, but in fact it was driving me demented having to be so discreet all the time, and the thing that made him really nervous was that I didn't always succeed. I told Lucy all about that too. She said I'd be hard put to it to find anyone more open about what he was up to than Jared. We talked about her situation too. I'm amazed how calmly she deals with this latest development, about which she swore me to secrecy, but advice is utterly wasted on her. She listens to my opinion, and I think she's learning to like the way I talk about things, but I know all the time she's not going to act on anything I suggest. But at least now we don't have to pretend that nothing's happening.

She admitted that the events of the last week had shaken her. The police, guided by the landlord of the Red Herring, had used the hidden road for what they had to do. No one had come to Ravnscar, except a soft-spoken inspector, who had gently explained to her what Jared and Colombo had told us already, and warned her that she might hear sounds and odd noises from below, but nothing to hurt. 'But then Cally Simpson came over from Ogg's Cove with coley for the cats,' she said, 'And he was full of it. Two police cars and a mortuary van parked by the Pele Centre, he said, and guys in yellow helmets going in with blow torches and God knows what. By the evening they were gone, so I guess they did what they had to do. Colombo says the memorial service will be announced in the *Times*. Funeral private. No flowers.'

'I liked Mr Baskerville, I think,' I said. 'God, it's all so complicated.' She looked an enquiry. 'I mean, I read the letter he wrote to Lemuel. I care about Jared. But even so I can't hate Baskerville.'

'Hate is a very tiring emotion,' said Lucy. 'You should thank heaven you're spared it.' She took a large jammy bite of doughnut, and a moment later said with her mouth full, 'Is Jed OK? About the letters, I mean? He's not said a word to me, and I'm not likely to ask him. Is he very upset?'

I took a moment to think about what Jared would consider private. 'He has nightmares,' I told her.

'About that?'

In fact, I realised, it was a relief to talk to somebody, and if there's one thing I know Lucy can do, it's keep a secret. 'The copies that Ishmael gave him – he keeps them on the fish crate by the bed. I know he reads them, over and over, though never in front of me. Already the paper's getting quite worn and dog-eared. I guess he knows those letters off by heart. In the daytime he doesn't mention it much. But, like I say, he has bad dreams.'

'Does he tell you what about?'

'Yes.'

When she realised I wasn't going to elaborate, she said, 'Do you think it's a good idea keeping them on the bedside table? It seems a bit morbid to me.'

'They won't be there for ever,' I said. 'He'll read them as many times as he has to, and then I reckon he won't read them any more.' I poured out the rest of the coffee, dividing it equally between our two mugs. 'You see, in the daytime he doesn't worry about the past. He's got a life; the present is what he thinks about when he's awake. But the other is there too; one can't pretend it isn't. I don't mind being woken in the night, anyway. It's not as if either of us has to get up early for anything just at present.'

It was already evening when we came out into the street again. It was almost time, and we joined the bands of people who were climbing up the narrow streets and gathering in the courtyard outside Government House. The crowd was quiet now. We could hear the sound of many footsteps like the pattering of hailstones, and voices coming together in one long subdued muttering. We reached the vantage point at the top of the steps up from the High Street, and there was the view I now knew so well, over the ranks of red-tiled roofs to the harbour. I stood with my back to the statue of the Trojan horse and the four underdressed warriors, and looked out on the seething town.

I saw it all so differently now, in the late summer twilight. Opposite us, directly up the hill from the harbour, rose St Brendan's Cathedral. That roof just below it was the library, with the weathercock on its gable. That was the museum next door. The building with a grey slate roof could only be that grimy block of flats, Artillery Mansions. The line of roofs between it and where we stood was the High Street. The tallest one, with the fluted chimney pots, must be Kidd's Hotel, and so that would be the Tourist Board diagonally opposite; so coming down from there: that must be Finnegan's, that the Bank; then that would be Gunn and Selkirk, and that the house above Kirwan's photography shop. Then coming north from the High Street; there was the block of flats where Colombo lived, and I'd visited with Ishmael when they were plotting to get Jared out of prison. And two streets across from there, five minutes from where we stood in front of Government House, was that lovely Queen Anne brick terrace, where Colombo once told me that Nesta Kirwan lived.

I looked across the harbour. There was a grey haze over the industrial area between the town and Port o' Frisland, but I could see the outline of the cider factory, and the concrete rectangle of the abandoned jail. On the tip of Port o' Frisland was the hexagonal outline of the British fort. Jared says that's the first thing you see when you come into the harbour on the ferry from Southampton. Then you turn the corner, into the harbour entrance, and there's the whole town suddenly laid out before you.

The town was still full of noises. I could make out 'Men of Harlech' and the distant echo of the Marseilleise. All of a sudden the bells of St Brendan's pealed out, striking the hour. The deep tones of the clock followed: ONE TWO THREE FOUR FIVE SIX SEVEN EIGHT. There was a sudden hush, as if the whole town were holding its breath. And then the bells rang out: St Brendan's, St Martin's, St Mary's, St Bride's, St Anthony's, St Columba's, St John's, all in one marvellous cacophony of sound. Every ship in the harbour hooted its horn at the same time, some piercing, some deep and low. The brass band broke into the wild swirling melody of the Hy Brasil National Anthem down at the Market Cross. The pipe band picked up the same tune and skirled it along the High Street. A deep chord went up from the town like a long-drawn clap of thunder, as if the red roofs themselves were crying out with one great voice. The polls were closed.

We drove over the mountain, in the scarlet light of yet another volcanic sunset, back to Lyonsness, and started watching it all again, this time on Per's television. Lucy and I were curled up on the sofa. Jared lay on the floor at my feet with Per's cat purring loudly on his stomach. Per sat in his usual chair and smoked his pipe. I looked round the room in the flickering light from the screen. It was strange to think that a month ago I'd never been inside this house at all. I seemed now to know it very well. I looked at the empty grate piled with pine cones, at the brass coal scuttle and fire tongs glinting in the changing light. I looked at the framed photograph of Cape Horn over the mantelpiece, taken from the deck of a Royal Navy destroyer, and its companion piece, of Table Mountain, above us over the sofa. There on the mantelpiece were the china dogs and the imitation carriage clock, and next to it the photo of a young couple on the steps of St Ninian's Presbyterian church in Lyonsness, she in her white dress with the veil pushed back, he in the uniform of a Royal Navy petty officer. He was instantly recognisable: Per had outwardly changed remarkably little in forty-five years.

He insisted on making us fish and chips as we hadn't really had supper. I think Per feeds us too often, considering he never visits us, except that one time when he came to go over the gannet records with Jared, when he did stay to have some mutton stew. Jared says Per likes to cook for people, and I should stop doing all these addition sums in my head, because that isn't what it's about.

We'd just started to eat when the results began coming through. Somehow I'd got it fixed in my head, because I'm used to being one of millions, that it would take all night, and when the camera shifted to Ogg's Cove just after ten it gave me quite a shock. But there it was: the infant classroom at Ogg's Cove Elementary. In the background you could see the children's paintings of erupting volcanoes on the walls: lots of red and black paint. In the foreground I could see Ishmael and Anna, and various vaguely familiar faces. The returning officer came to the microphone.

Jared sat up. Lucy put down her plate and leaned forward. Per sat motionless, his fork halfway to his mouth. I looked round at them. I was the only one in the room who hadn't voted.

The officer read the names of the other two candidates first. Their tally was pitiful. We knew then what was coming. He read the last name, and we could hear the shout go up, from the classroom at Ogg's Cove and from the crowd outside, who suddenly appeared on the screen in front of us.

MARGARET ELPHINSTONE

'Ishmael Pereira! Ishmael Pereira!'

It was all one babble of voices, in Per's sitting room and on the screen, all mingling in with one another. And then another hush. Lyonsness. We were in the Assembly Hall at Lyonsness Junior High, just down the road from where we sat.

'We should be out there!' Lucy burst out.

'Hush!'

Again there were faces there that I knew. The owner of Trink's Garage. Mr Allardyce. Peterkin's aunt.

Again, the returning officer read the others first. They'd done better than the opposition in Ogg's Cove; between the two of them they'd at least pulled in the majority. Jared gripped my knee. 'He's done it! He's done it!'

There was the crowd again. Only the setting looked different. I could see the harbour. For one unreal moment I could see *Cerberus* moored at the end of the jetty where we'd left her this morning. Then we panned back to a sea of faces, cheering in unison:

'Pereira! Pereira! Ishmael Pereira!'

We cut suddenly to a shot of a blue-and-white fishing boat coming neatly into a jetty. 'There's the Mayda ferry!' said Lucy and Jared together. I realised then that there was no fishing gear on that spick-and-span wooden deck. A rope was cast ashore. The camera zoomed in on the captain at the wheel, and I recognised Colombo's eldest brother-in-law. Then, before they'd finished tying up, another man jumped ashore clasping a couple of wooden boxes that looked for all the world like the collection box in our church at home.

The Community Hall, Dorrado. The last time I'd seen it, in real life, it had been full of coastguards and voluntary services preparing for possible evacuation. I tried to peer behind the commentator. I could see the same trestle tables, but this time they were being used by a team of polling officers, all still counting. In the foreground all the focus was on those little boxes from Tuly and Mayda.

On Tuly, the recording officer told us, there were thirty-two inhabitants over the age of eighteen.

First candidate: no votes. Second candidate: one vote. Third candidate, Ishmael Pereira: thirty-one votes.

'Must be a story behind that one,' remarked Per. 'But I don't suppose we'll ever hear it.'

On Mayda, they told us, there were nine inhabitants over the age of eighteen.

First candidate: no votes. Second candidate: no votes. Third candidate: one vote.

'They always did keep themselves to themselves on Mayda,' said Per.

The commentator announced that they were doing a recount at Dorrado. There was a pause for a while, with panoramic views of St Brandons interspersed with a desultory argument between the Bishop of St Brendan's, the Professor of Political Science from the University and the editor of *The Hesperides Times*. Jared turned down the sound, while Per poured out cider for us all from a big earthenware jug. The editor mentioned Tidesman, and I pricked up my ears, but I couldn't hear what they were saying, because Lucy and Per and Jared were all speaking at once. The picture changed. 'We're back in Dorrado!' I squealed. They shut up at once, and Jared turned up the volume. I could feel the tension through the room.

The returning officer was the landlord of the Red Herring. He read from his paper like Moses just back from Sinai. We held our breath.

First candidate: two-thousand-one-hundred-and-seven votes. Second candidate: two-thousand-nine-hundred-and-twenty-seven votes. It was going to be a very close thing. Third candidate: Ishmael Pereira, two-thousand-nine-hundred-and-thirty-eight votes.

Jared jumped about a foot into the air, and the rest of my cider went flying. I carefully mopped up Per's chintz sofa and the carpet, which luckily is brown, while the television went mad in the corner.

'He's done it! He's done it!'

'Not yet,' said Lucy. 'St Brandons is more than half the country. Twenty-three thousand. And the President has to have a majority vote from the country as a whole. That's what it says in the paper.'

An hour went by. We ate cheese and apples. The clock struck midnight. It was echoed, a millisecond later, by the peal of St Brendan's Cathedral. And there on the screen was the familiar skyline. Lucy and I leaned forward. I could feel Jared's back tense against my knees.

Government House. There was Ishmael again. The Grand Cherokee must have been driven at some speed. Lucy squealed beside me, 'There's Colombo.' And then she blushed. It was the first time I ever saw her do it, and maybe it'll be the last. The other two didn't even look round.

First candidate: four-thousand-seven-hundred-and-nine votes. Second candidate: five-thousand-nine-hundred-and-fourteen votes. Third candidate: twelve-thousand-seven-hundred-and-sixty-eight votes.

There was Ishmael, on the screen. There was the crowd, yelling in the dark, with the Trojan Horse floodlit behind. Jared and Per and Lucy were on their feet. I hung back. I'm still a little overwhelmed by the way these people fall into each other's arms when the spirit moves them. At home we don't. But Jared dragged me to my feet. At least I'm used to his embraces, and the other two were also friends.

Presently we sat down again, and listened to Ishmael. I found it most peculiar. I kept saying to myself, 'but I *know* this guy'. That was foolish, because what I realised now was that I didn't. It occurred to me that Ishmael was not in fact secretive. He'd probably talked to a great many people. But some of us – Jared, Lucy, me – had had our minds on other things. I thought, as I listened, that Colombo was probably the least surprised of any of my friends.

Ishmael made a very good speech. Everyone says so. I'd put

it down here, only unfortunately I don't remember a single word of it. Jared says it will all be in the *Times* next Saturday, so I can copy bits from there.

Before Ishmael was done we started to hear the fireworks. Then he finished, and they were exploding right across the screen in front of us. And not just there. Jared drew back the curtains, and the fireworks had leapt from the screen to the sky. They blazed like comets over Lyonsness, illuminating the whole town in rainbow colours, then falling and fading, vanishing into the darkness of the sea.

'Let's go down!'

We walked four-abreast along the harbour road. The sea sighed on our left, and as our eyes got used to the darkness we could make out the faint far-off outline of Despair. Then more fireworks shot into the sky ahead, and everything dissolved into a Babel of colour. Jared began to run.

We caught up with him in Market Street just outside The Admiral Inn. Then we were swept on, and in, into the crowd and the shouting and the fireworks, into the wild and sleepless night. I forgot I didn't have a vote. I forgot I was a stranger. I forgot it wasn't anything to do with me. I'd find it easier to write history if I wasn't expected to live it at the same time. I said that to Jared when finally we were cruising cautiously across the sound, our boat feeling its way through the dark to its home mooring. He laughed at me, and said I should worry about writing tomorrow.

As we climbed up the hill to the lighthouse I could see the first pale streaks of light away to the east. Jared switched off the torch, and we could see the island dimly taking shape around us. I looked at it, and I thought, yes, I will, I'll write it all, tomorrow or some day. That's one part I can play, even if I haven't any other. But then Jared said, as if he'd heard me, 'To hell with history. At least we can leave it over the water.' He took my hand and pulled me up the steep bit. He was laughing. 'I'll share my island with you, Sidony,' he said. 'If you want it I'll share the whole damn lot. But from here on in it's private. You can write down all the history you like. Only not here. Not now. This bit is for living, just for its own sake, and you don't get to write it down.'

'All right,' I said, laughing back at him. 'I'll do my book. Lots and lots of books, maybe. But I don't mind drawing the line somewhere.' I drew an imaginary line across the turf with my foot. 'Maybe here,' I said, and stepped over it.

TWENTY-NINE

COLOMBO DROVE OUT of Dorrado, and took the winding uphill road in second, much too fast. The engine snarled and groaned, and on each hairpin the back tyres sent up a shower of gravel from the outside curve. Colombo kept one hand on the wheel, and the other on the horn, which he sounded hard and long on each blind corner. His mouth was set in a hard line, and his brown eyes looked black and thunderous. He knew he was driving recklessly. He didn't care. He was suddenly, gloriously, angry. They'd all used him: fate had used him; women had used him; Ishmael had used him; the government had used him. He had thought he could use Tidesman; Tidesman too had used him. He had given all he had to this wretched country that might vanish into the sea at any moment, and what had it ever given him? He was the only man on Hy Brasil who hadn't got a life. Tidesman was famous, Tidesman was an institution, and Tidesman had swallowed up Colombo MacAdam and now Tidesman was spitting out the pips.

The road levelled out, and forked. The left hand road wound around the foothills of Mount Brasil to Lyonsness and Ravnscar. It had been recently tarred, and a battered notice saying:

ROAD CLOSED: DIVERSION
ESTRADA IMPEDIDA: DESVIO

lay in the ditch with a couple of sandbags chucked on top of it. The right-hand road dipped down into a lush valley full of freshly harvested apple orchards, heading back to St Brandons. Colombo shot off the road just before the junction, and jerked to a stop in the parking place just below the wayside shrine, amid a cloud of dust and a smell of hot rubber. From the shelter of her shrine the Madonna in her blue robe gazed impassively down on him, nursing her fat white cuckoo of a child. Someone had laid fresh roses at her feet.

Colombo had helped to make a revolution. Fifteen miles away Mount Brasil simmered ominously, turning the very idea of history into a cruel conceit. The lingering smell of sulphur seemed far too apposite. All Colombo had succeeded in doing, he thought savagely, was to be nice to everybody. That made him angry, but a small part of him still believed passionately that this had been the only thing worth doing.

Was there anything left? Pereira had established a proper democracy. Following further elections the second Parliament of Hy Brasil was already six weeks into its first session. The legend was over, and justice was about to begin. Two people had died, and a few others thought they were happier than they'd been before. Colombo MacAdam could write articles about it if he liked. Colombo MacAdam could go to hell.

Colombo MacAdam loved two women, or thought he did. Each was in love with a dead man. If he lay with either of them, he'd be aware of the shadow of the dead hovering there with him, and know that she was embracing a dream, a ghost, closing her eyes so that she would not see that really it was him, Colombo. Possibly in the future he might be useful to either, temporarily salving the pain by holding her in his living arms, and telling her what just for the moment she might want to hear. But she wouldn't be listening for him.

He thought of Nesta alone in her apartment which Hook had given her, looking out over St Brandons and the harbour while the sun moved away from her window, and the afternoon shadows crept in. If he went to Nesta she'd make love to him savagely, perhaps, the way she sometimes did, as if that would wipe out the past and Jim, her own Jim, would walk back in tomorrow. That was the only reason she'd ever wanted Colombo, he realised now. It was the piquancy of him not being Jim, because Jim would always be back next day. But at least Nesta would touch him, at least they'd make love, as often as he could want, because that's what she wanted too.

Or at least they could do that until she grew old. She was old. She was thirteen years older than he was. She'd never had a child. She used to say she'd never wanted one. That seemed unnatural in a beautiful woman. If she'd been ugly it would have been easier to accept. Even if she wasn't too old – or was she? He'd never heard of a woman of forty-nine having a child, but for all he knew it could happen – even if she wasn't too old, she'd refuse. The thought surprised him, as until that moment it had never crossed his mind that anyone would dream of asking her.

He had adored Lucy for far too long. Sometimes she'd phone and want to see him urgently; sometimes she wouldn't let him come anywhere near her at all. She'd use him when she was desperate to stave off the nightmares that she insisted on retaining, but she'd give him nothing, and she'd leave him frustrated as hell.

In mid-April there would be an heir to Ravnscar. Its mother was already totally, passionately committed to its future well-being, which was, Colombo reckoned, worth a good deal more than its other inheritance: a castle filled with treasures beyond price. Apparently the one gift that would be denied it, the curse at its christening, you could say, was the possession of a father. Lucy wouldn't even confirm that she was going to put his name on its birth certificate. She said she'd think about it.

Whether it was a girl or a boy – he hoped it might be a girl, for some reason – he guessed it would be beautiful. It would be – must already be, come to think of it – dark-haired, olive-skinned, brown-eyed. Both he and Lucy had Portuguese mothers. Her mother had been a De Rosas, the oldest family in Hy Brasil. His mother had first come here as an immigrant from Madeira, who got a job as chambermaid at the Red

Herring, back in the days when Ewan MacAdam first had the ferryboat that ran from Dorrado to Mayda and Tuly.

Colombo glared at the fork in the road. One fork led to Nesta, who might grieve for ever but who would be only momentarily cast down. Perhaps she was already thinking about her work again. Perhaps right now she was developing the photos she'd taken in Dorrado on August 3rd, 1997. She would face that film some time, he knew, because that was her way. She would face it and then grow old, because she was older than he was, and of all the men she'd known so very well, the only one that had really mattered was Jim.

The other road led to Lucy, immured at Ravnscar. It was a perfect October day; she was probably in the garden, harvesting vegetables, or maybe she'd be sitting on the courtyard parapet writing her endless journal in the yellow folder entitled *Chemistry Notes*. Or maybe she was hunting through old chests and closets, looking out the last hundred years' worth of infant clothing and children's toys. Toys that belonged in the nursery at Ravnscar, where Lucy, an only daughter, had once played almost daily with a neighbour's child, Nicky Hawkins.

It was a golden afternoon. The autumn trees blazed in the sunshine, brown and gold. The sky was a hard crystalline blue. There were sea eagles circling over Ailbe. He realised for the first time that the colours were free of smoke. The summit of Brasil was out of sight. Today, one could believe it was an ordinary autumn day. One could almost believe that nothing irrevocable had happened.

Colombo put his head down on the steering wheel and sobbed once. But weeping was too difficult. He shoved the car into first, and shot into the road. The decision was made before he knew it. The tyres ground against the verge as he swept into the turn, and in a sputter of gravel and flying grass he was gone. The ancient engine roared and faded, gradually dying away into the distance. Then the silent afternoon settled down in the place where the three roads met, as if no one had ever passed that way at all.